Penguin Books
The Group

Mary McCarthy, well-known novelist and
critic, was born at Seattle, Washington, of
mixed Catholic, Protestant, and Jewish
descent. She and her three younger brothers
were orphaned as young children. Since
graduating at Vassar College, New York, she
has been an editorial assistant in a publishing
house, an editor and theatre critic, and an
instructor in English at Bard College and
Sarah Lawrence College. Her second husband
was Edmund Wilson, the famous American
critic. Mary McCarthy, who is now married to
James West and has a son, lives in Paris. Among the
books she has published are *The Company She
Keeps*, *The Oasis*, which won the *Horizon* prize,
The Groves of Academe, *A Charmed Life*,
Venice Observed, *Memories of a Catholic Girlhood*,
Sights and Spectacles 1937-1958, *The Stones of
Florence*, *On the Contrary*, *Vietnam*, *Hanoi*, *The
Writing on the Wall*, *Medina*, *The Seventeenth Degree*,
The Mask of State: a gallery of Watergate portraits,
and *Cannibals and Missionaries*. She has also edited
The Life of the Mind (two volumes) by Hannah
Arendt.

Mary McCarthy

The Group

Penguin Books

Penguin Books Ltd, Harmondsworth, Middlesex, England
Penguin Books, 625 Madison Avenue, New York, New York 10022, U.S.A.
Penguin Books Australia Ltd, Ringwood, Victoria, Australia
Penguin Books Canada Ltd, 2801 John Street, Markham, Ontario, Canada L3R 1B4
Penguin Books (N.Z.) Ltd, 182–190 Wairau Road, Auckland 10, New Zealand

First published in the U.S.A. 1963
Published in Great Britain by Weidenfeld & Nicolson 1963
Published in Penguin Books for sale outside the United Kingdom 1964
Reprinted 1965
This edition published 1966
Reprinted 1966 (twice,) 1967, 1968, 1970, 1971, 1975, 1977, 1981

Set, printed and bound in Great Britain by
Cox & Wyman Ltd, Reading
Set in Monotype Fournier

Some of the material in this book appeared originally in
somewhat different form, in the *New Yorker*, *Partisan Review*,
and in *Avon Book of Modern Writing, No. 5*

Chapter 1

It was June 1933, one week after Commencement, when Kay Leiland Strong, Vassar '33, the first of her class to run around the table at the Class Day dinner, was married to Harald Petersen, Reed '27, in the chapel of St George's Church, P.E., Karl F. Reiland, Rector. Outside, in Stuyvesant Square, the trees were in full leaf, and the wedding guests arriving by twos and threes in taxis heard the voices of children playing round the statue of Peter Stuyvesant in the park. Paying the driver, smoothing out their gloves, the pairs and trios of young women, Kay's class-mates, stared about them curiously, as though they were in a foreign city. They were in the throes of discovering New York, imagine it, when some of them had actually lived here all their lives, in tiresome Georgian houses full of waste space in the Eighties or Park Avenue apartment buildings, and they delighted in such out-of-the-way corners as this, with its greenery and Quaker meeting-house in red brick, polished brass, and white trim next to the wine-purple Episcopal church – on Sundays, they walked with their beaux across Brooklyn Bridge and poked into the sleepy Heights section of Brooklyn; they explored residential Murray Hill and quaint Macdougal Alley and Patchin Place and Washington Mews with all the artists' studios; they loved the Plaza Hotel and the fountain there and the green mansarding of the Savoy Plaza and the row of horse-drawn hacks and elderly coachmen, waiting, as in a French *place*, to tempt them to a twilight ride through Central Park.

The sense of an adventure was strong on them this morning, as they seated themselves softly in the still, near-empty chapel; they had never been to a wedding quite like this one before, to which invitations had been issued orally by the bride herself, without the intervention of a relation or any older person, friend of the family. There was to be no honeymoon, they had heard, because Harald

5

(that was the way he spelled it – the old Scandinavian way) was working as an assistant stage manager for a theatrical production and had to be at the theatre as usual this evening to call 'half-hour' for the actors. This seemed to them very exciting and of course it justified the oddities of the wedding: Kay and Harald were too busy and dynamic to let convention cramp their style. In September, Kay was going to start at Macy's, to be trained, along with other picked college graduates, in merchandising techniques, but instead of sitting around all summer, waiting for the job to begin, she had already registered for a typing course in business school, which Harald said would give her a tool that the other trainees wouldn't have. And, according to Helena Davison, Kay's room-mate junior year, the two of them had moved right into a summer sublet, in a nice block in the East Fifties, without a single piece of linen or silver of their own, and had spent the last week, ever since graduation (Helena had just been there and seen it), on the regular tenant's sublet sheets!

How like Kay, they concluded fondly, as the tale passed along the pews. She had been amazingly altered, they felt, by a course in Animal Behaviour she had taken with old Miss Washburn (who had left her brain in her will to Science) during their junior year. This and her work with Hallie Flanagan in Dramatic Production had changed her from a shy, pretty, somewhat heavy Western girl with black lustrous curly hair and a wild-rose complexion, active in hockey, in the choir, given to large tight brassieres and copious menstruations, into a thin, hard-driving, authoritative young woman, dressed in dungarees, sweat shirt, and sneakers, with smears of paint in her unwashed hair, tobacco stains on her fingers, talking airily of 'Hallie' and 'Lester', Hallie's assistant, of flats and stippling, of oestrum and nymphomania, calling her friends by their last names loudly – 'Eastlake', 'Renfrew', 'MacAusland' – counselling premarital experiment and the scientific choice of a mate. Love, she said, was an illusion.

To her fellow group members, all seven of whom were now present in the chapel, this development in Kay, which they gently labelled a 'phase', had been, nevertheless, disquieting. Her bark was worse than her bite, they used to reiterate to each other, late at night in their common sitting-room in the South Tower of Main Hall, when Kay was still out, painting flats or working on the electricity with Lester in the theatre. But they were afraid that some man, who did not know the old dear as they did, would take her at her word. They had pondered about Harald; Kay had met him last summer when she was working as an apprentice at a summer theatre in Stamford and both sexes had lived in a dormitory together. She said he wanted to marry her, but that was not the way his letters sounded to the group. They were not love letters at all, so far as the group could see, but accounts of personal successes among theatrical celebrities, what Edna Ferber had said to George Kaufman in his hearing, how Gilbert Miller had sent for him and a woman star had begged him to read his play to her in bed. 'Consider yourself kissed,' they ended, curtly, or just 'CYK' – not another word. In a young man of their own background, as the girls vaguely phrased it, such letters would have been offensive, but their education had impressed on them the unwisdom of making large judgements from one's own narrow little segment of experience. Still, they could tell that Kay was not as sure of him as she pretended she was; sometimes he did not write for weeks, while poor Kay went on whistling in the dark. Polly Andrews, who shared a mailbox with her, knew this for a fact. Up to the Class Day dinner, ten days ago, the girls had had the feeling that Kay's touted 'engagement' was pretty much of a myth. They had almost thought of turning to some wiser person for guidance, a member of the faculty or the college psychiatrist – somebody Kay could talk it out to, frankly. Then, that night, when Kay had run around the long table, which meant you were announcing your engagement to the whole class, and produced from her winded bosom a funny Mexican silver ring to prove it, their alarm had dissolved into a docile amusement; they clapped, dimpling and twinkling, with an air of prior knowledge. More gravely, in low posh tones, they assured their parents, up for the Commencement ceremonies, that the engagement was of long standing, that Harald was 'terribly nice' and 'terribly in love' with Kay. Now, in the chapel, they rearranged their fur pieces and smiled at each other, noddingly, like mature little martens and sables: they had been right, the hardness was only a phase; it was certainly a point for *their* side that the iconoclast and scoffer was the first of the little band to get married.

'Who would have thunk it?' irrepressibly remarked 'Pokey' (Mary) Prothero, a fat cheerful New York society girl with big red cheeks and yellow hair, who talked like a jolly beau of the McKinley period, in imitation of her yachtsman father. She was the problem child of the group, very rich and lazy, having to be coached in her subjects, cribbing in examinations, sneaking week-ends, stealing library books, without morals or subtleties, interested only in animals and hunt dances; her ambition, recorded in the yearbook, was to become a vet; she had come to Kay's wedding good-naturedly because her friends had dragged her there, as they had dragged her to college assemblies, throwing stones up at her window to rouse her and then thrusting her into her cap and rumpled gown. Having now got her safely to the church, later in the day they would propel her into Tiffany's, to make sure that Kay got one good, thumping wedding present, a thing Pokey, by herself, would not understand the necessity of, since to her mind wedding presents were a part of the burden of privilege, associated with detectives, bridesmaids, fleets of limousines, reception at Sherry's or the Colony Club. If one was not in society, what was the point of the folderol? She herself, she proclaimed, hated being fitted for dresses, hated her coming-out party, would hate her wedding, when she had it, which, as she said, was bound to happen since, thanks to Daddy's money, she had her pick of beaux. All these objections she had raised in the taxicab on the way down, in her grating society caw, till the taxi-driver turned round at a stop light to look at her, fat and fair, in a blue faille suit with sables and a *lorgnon* of diamonds, which she raised to her weak sapphire eyes to peer at him and at his picture, concluding, in a loud firm whisper, to her room-mates, 'It's *not* the same man.'

'What perfect pets they look!' murmured Dottie Renfrew, of Boston, to quiet her, as Harald and Kay came in from the vestry and took their places before the surpliced curate, accompanied by little Helena Davison, Kay's ex-room-mate from Cleveland, and by a shallow blond young man with a moustache. Pokey made use of her *lorgnon*, squinting up her pale-lashed eyes like an old woman; this was her first appraisal of Harald, for she had been away hunting for the week-end the one time he had come to college. 'Not too bad,' she pronounced. 'Except for the shoes.' The groom was a thin, tense young man with black straight hair and a very good, supple figure, like a fencer's; he was wearing a blue suit, white shirt, brown suède shoes, and dark-red tie. Her scrutiny veered to

Kay, who was wearing a pale-brown thin silk dress with a big white *mousseline de soie* collar and a wide black taffeta hat wreathed with white daisies; around one tan wrist was a gold bracelet that had belonged to her grandmother; she carried a bouquet of field daisies mixed with lilies of the valley. With her glowing cheeks, vivid black curly hair, and tawny hazel eyes, she looked like a country lass on some old tinted postcard; the seams of her stockings were crooked, and the backs of her black suède shoes had worn spots, where she had rubbed them against each other. Pokey scowled. 'Doesn't she know,' she lamented, 'that black's bad luck for weddings?' '*Shut up,*' came a furious growl from her other side. Pokey, hurt, peered around, to find Elinor Eastlake, of Lake Forest, the taciturn brunette beauty of the group, staring at her with murder in her long, green eyes. 'But Lakey!' Pokey cried, protesting. The Chicago girl, intellectual, impeccable, disdainful, and nearly as rich as herself, was the only one of the group she stood in awe of. Behind her blinking good nature, Pokey was a logical snob. She assumed that it was taken for granted that of the other seven room-mates, only Lakey could expect to be in *her* wedding, and vice versa, of course; the others would come to the reception. '*Fool,*' spat out the Madonna from Lake Forest, between gritted pearly teeth. Pokey rolled her eyes. 'Temperamental,' she observed to Dottie Renfrew. Both girls stole amused glances at Elinor's haughty profile; the fine white Renaissance nostril was dinted with a mark of pain.

To Elinor, this wedding was torture. Everything was so jaggedly ill-at-ease: Kay's costume, Harald's shoes and necktie, the bare altar, the sparsity of guests on the groom's side (a couple and a solitary man), the absence of any family connexion. Intelligent and morbidly sensitive, she was inwardly screaming with pity for the principals and vicarious mortification. Hypocrisy was the sole explanation she could find for the antiphonal bird twitter of 'Terribly nice', and 'Isn't this exciting?' that had risen to greet the couple in lieu of a wedding march. Elinor was always firmly convinced of other people's hypocrisy since she could not believe that they noticed less than she did. She supposed now that the girls all around her *must* see what she saw, *must* suffer for Kay and Harald a supreme humiliation.

Facing the congregation, the curate coughed. 'Step forward!'

he sharply admonished the young couple, sounding, as Lakey observed afterwards, more like a bus conductor than a minister. The back of the groom's neck reddened; he had just had a hair-cut. All at once, the fact that Kay was a self-announced scientific atheist came home to her friends in the chapel; the same thought crossed every mind: what had happened in the interview in the rectory? Was Harald a communicant? It seemed very unlikely. How had they worked it, then, to get married in a rock-ribbed Episcopal church? Dottie Renfrew, a devout Episcopal communicant, drew her clasped furs closer around her susceptible throat; she shivered. It occurred to her that she might be compounding a sacrilege: to her certain knowledge, Kay, the proud daughter of an agnostic doctor and a Mormon mother, had not even been baptized. Kay, as the group knew too, was not a very truthful person; could she have lied to the minister? In that case, was the marriage invalid? A flush stole up from Dottie's collarbone, reddening the patch of skin at the V opening of her handmade crêpe de Chine blouse; her perturbed brown eyes canvassed her friends; her eczematous complexion spotted. She knew by heart what was coming. 'If any man can show just cause, why they may not be lawfully joined together, let him now speak, or else hereafter for ever hold his peace.' The curate's voice halted, on a questioning note; he glanced up and down the pews. Dottie shut her eyes and prayed, conscious of a dead hush in the chapel. Would God or Dr Leverett, her clergyman, really want her to speak up? She prayed that they would not. The opportunity passed, as she heard the curate's voice resume, loud and solemn, as if almost in reprobation of the couple, to which he now turned. 'I require and charge you both, as ye will answer at the dreadful day of judgement, when the secrets of all hearts shall be disclosed, that if either of you know any impediment, why ye may not be lawfully joined together in Matrimony, ye do now confess it. For be ye well assured, that if any persons are joined together otherwise than as God's Word doth allow, their marriage is not lawful.'

You could have heard a pin drop, as the girls agreed later. Every girl was holding her breath. Dottie's religious scruples had given way to a new anxiety, which was common to the whole group. The knowledge, shared by them all, of Kay's having 'lived with' Harald filled them with a sudden sense of the unsanctioned. They glanced stealthily around the chapel and noted for the *n*th time the absence of parents or *any older person*; and this departure from convention, which had been 'such fun' before the service began, struck them now as queer and ominous. Even Elinor Eastlake, who knew scornfully well that fornication was not the type of impediment alluded to in the service, half-expected an unknown presence to rise and stop the ceremony. To her mind, there was a spiritual obstacle to the marriage; she considered Kay a *cruel, ruthless, stupid* person who was marrying Harald from ambition.

Everyone in the chapel had now noticed something a little odd, or so it seemed, in the curate's pauses and stresses; they had never heard 'their marriage is not lawful' delivered with such emphasis. On the groom's side, a handsome, auburn-haired, dissipated-looking young man clenched his fist suddenly and muttered something under his breath. He smelled terribly of alcohol and appeared extremely nervous; all through the ceremony he had been clasping and unclasping his well-shaped, strong-looking hands and biting his chiselled lips. 'He's a painter; he's just been divorced,' whispered fair-haired Polly Andrews, who was the quiet type but who knew everything, on Elinor Eastlake's right. Elinor, like a young queen, leaned forward and deliberately caught his eye; here was someone, she felt, who was as disgusted and uncomfortable as she was. He responded with a stare of bitter, encompassing irony, followed by a wink directed, unmistakably, at the altar. Having moved into the main part of the service, the curate had now picked up speed, as though he had suddenly discovered another appointment and was running off this couple as rapidly as possible: this was only a $10 wedding, his manner seemed to imply. Behind her large hat, Kay appeared to be oblivious of all slights, but Harald's ears and neck had turned a darker red, and, in his responses, he began, with a certain theatrical flourish, to slow down and correct the minister's intonations.

This made the couple on the groom's side smile, as if at a familiar weakness or fault, but the girls, in *their* pews, were scandalized by the curate's rudeness and applauded what they called Harald's victory over him, which they firmly intended to make the centre of their congratulations after the ceremony. There were some who, then and there, resolved to speak to Mother and get her to speak to Dr Reiland, the rector, about it; a capacity for outrage, their social birthright, had been redirected, as it were, by education. The fact that Kay and Harald were going to be poor as church mice was no excuse, they thought staunchly, for such conduct on the part of a priest, in these times especially, when everybody was having to retrench. Even among their own number, one girl had had to accept a scholarship to finish college, and nobody thought the worse of her for it: Polly Andrews remained one of their *very* dearest friends. They were a different breed, they could assure the curate, from the languid buds of the previous decade: there was not one of them who did not propose to work this coming fall, at a volunteer job if need be. Libby MacAusland had a promise from a publisher; Helena Davison, whose parents, out in Cincinnati, no, Cleveland, lived on the income of their income, was going into teaching — she already had a job sewed up at a private nursery school; Polly Andrews, more power to her, was to work as a technician in the new Medical Centre; Dottie Renfrew was slated for social work in a Boston settlement house; Lakey was off to Paris to study art history, working towards an advanced degree; Pokey Prothero, who had been given a plane for a graduation present, was getting her pilot's licence so as to be able to commute three days a week to Cornell Agricultural School, and, last but not least, yesterday little Priss Hartshorn, the group grind, had simultaneously announced her engagement to a young doctor and landed a job with the NRA. Not bad, they conceded, for a group that had gone through college with the stigma of being high-hat. And elsewhere in the class, in the wider circle of Kay's friends, they could point out girls of perfectly good background who were going into business, anthropology, medicine, not because they had to, but because they knew they had something to contribute to our emergent America. The group was not afraid of being radical either; they could see the good Roosevelt was doing, despite what Mother and Dad said; they were not taken in by party labels and thought the Democrats should be given a chance to show what they had up their sleeve. Experience was just a question of learning through trial and error; the most conservative of them, pushed to the wall, admitted that an honest socialist was entitled to a hearing.

The worst fate, they utterly agreed, would be to become like Mother and Dad, stuffy and frightened. Not one of them, if she could help it, was going to marry a broker or a banker or a cold-fish corporation lawyer, like so many of Mother's generation. They would rather be wildly poor and live on salmon wiggle than be forced to marry one of those dull purplish young men of their own set, with a seat on the Exchange and bloodshot eyes, interested only in squash and cockfighting and drinking at the Racquet Club with his cronies, Yale or Princeton '29. It would be better, yes, they were not afraid to say it, though Mother gently laughed, to marry a Jew if you loved him – some of them were awfully interesting and cultivated, though terribly ambitious and inclined to stick together, as you saw very well at Vassar: if you knew them you had to know their friends. There was one thing, though, truthfully, that made the group feel a little anxious for Kay. It was a pity in a way that a person as gifted as Harald and with a good education had had to pick the stage, rather than medicine or architecture or museum work, where the going was not so rough. To hear Kay talk, the theatre was pretty red in tooth and claw, though of course there were some nice people in it, like Katherine Cornell and Walter Hampden (he had a niece in the Class of '32) and John Mason Brown, the thingummy, who talked to Mother's club every year. Harald had done graduate work at the Yale Drama School, under Professor Baker, but then the depression had started, and he had had to come to New York to be a stage manager instead of just writing plays. That was like starting from the bottom in a factory, of course, which lots of nice boys were doing, and there was probably no difference between backstage in a theatre, where a lot of men in their undershirts sat in front of a mirror putting on make-up, and a blast furnace or a coal mine, where the men were in their undershirts too. Helena Davison said that when Harald's show came to Cleveland this spring, he spent all his time playing poker with the stagehands and the electricians, who were the nicest people in the show, and Helena's father said he agreed with him, especially after seeing the play – Mr Davison was a bit of a card and more democratic than most fathers, being from the West and more or less self-made. Still, nobody could afford to be stand-offish nowadays. Connie Storey's fiancé, who was going into journalism, was working as an office boy at *Fortune*, and her family, instead of having conniptions, was taking it very calmly and sending her to cooking school. And lots of graduate architects, instead of joining a firm and building rich men's houses, had gone right into the factories to study industrial design. Look at Russel Wright, whom everybody thought quite the thing now; he was using industrial materials, like the wonderful new spun aluminium, to make all sorts of useful objects like cheese trays and water carafes. Kay's first wedding present, which she had picked out herself, was a Russel Wright cocktail shaker in the shape of a skyscraper and made out of oak ply and aluminium with a tray and twelve little round cups to match – light as a feather and non-tarnishable, of course. The main point was, Harald was a natural gentleman – though inclined to show off in his letters, which was probably to impress Kay, who was inclined to drop names herself and talk about people's butlers and Fly and A D and Porcellian and introduce poor Harald as a Yale man when he had only gone to graduate school at New Haven. . . . That was a side of Kay that the group did its best to deprecate and that drove Lakey wild. A lack of fastidiousness and consideration for the other person; she did not seem to realize the little social nuances. She was always coming into people's rooms, for instance, and making herself at home and fiddling with things on their bureaux and telling them about their inhibitions if they objected; it was she who insisted on playing Truth and on getting everybody in the group to make lists of their friends in the order of preference and then compare the lists. What she did not stop to think about was that somebody had to be on the bottom of every list, and when that somebody cried and refused to be consoled, Kay was always honestly surprised; *she* would not mind, she said, hearing the truth about herself. Actually, she never did hear it because the others were too tactful to put her at the bottom, even if they wanted to, because Kay was a little bit of an outsider and nobody wanted her to feel that. So instead they would put Libby MacAusland or Polly Andrews – someone they had known all their lives or gone to school with or something. Kay did get a bit of a shock, though, to find that she was not at the top of Lakey's list. She was crazy about Lakey, whom she always described as her best friend. Kay did not know it, but the group had had a pitched battle with Lakey over Easter vacation, when they had drawn straws to see who was to invite Kay home for the holidays and Lakey had got the shortest straw and then refused to play. The group had simply borne down on Lakey in a body and accused her of being a poor sport, which was true. After all, as they had swiftly pointed out to her, it was she who had invited Kay to group with them in the first place; when they saw that they could get the South Tower for themselves if they had eight in the group instead of six, it was Lakey's idea that they should invite Kay and Helena Davison to join forces with them and take the two small single rooms.

If you were going to use a person, then you had to make the best of her. And it was not 'using', anyway; they all liked Kay and Helena, including Lakey herself, who had discovered Kay as a sophomore, when they were both on the Daisy Chain. She had taken Kay up for all she was worth, because Kay, as she said, was 'malleable' and 'capable of learning'. Now she claimed to have detected that Kay had feet of clay, which was rather a contradiction, since wasn't clay malleable? But Lakey was very contradictory; that was her charm. Sometimes she was a frightful snob and sometimes just the opposite. She was looking so furious this morning, for instance, because Kay, according to her, should have got married quietly in City Hall instead of making Harald, who was not to the manor born, try to carry off a wedding in J. P. Morgan's church. Now was this snobbish of Lakey or wasn't it? Naturally, she had not said any of this to Kay; she had expected Kay to feel it for herself, which was just what Kay couldn't do and remain the blunt, natural, unconscious Kay they all loved, in spite of her faults. Lakey had the weirdest ideas about people. She had got the bee in her bonnet, last fall, that Kay had worked her way into the group out of a desire for social prestige; this was not at all the way it had happened, and it was a peculiar thing, really, to think about a girl who was so unconventional that she had not even bothered to have her own parents to her wedding, though her father was very prominent in Salt Lake City affairs.

It was true, Kay had rather angled to get Pokey Prothero's town house for the reception, but she had taken it with good grace when Pokey had loudly lamented that the house was in dust covers for the summer, with only a caretaking couple to look after Father on the nights he spent in town. Poor Kay – some of the girls thought that Pokey might have been a little more generous and offered her a card to the Colony. In fact, on this score, nearly all the group felt a little bit conscience-stricken. Each one of them, as the others knew, had a house or a big apartment or a club membership, if it was only the Cosmopolitan, or a cousin's digs or a brother's that might possibly have been put at Kay's disposal. But that would have meant punch, champagne, a cake from Sherry's or Henri's extra help – before one knew it one would have found oneself giving the wedding and supplying a father or a brother to take Kay down the aisle. In these times, in sheer self-protection, one had to think twice, as Mother said, fatigued; there were so many demands. Fortunately, Kay had decided that she and Harald should give the wedding breakfast themselves, at the old Hotel Brevoort down on Eighth Street: so much nicer, so much more appropriate.

Dottie Renfrew and Elinor Eastlake made their way out of the chapel together, on to the sunny pavement. The service had seemed awfully short. There had been no blessing of the ring and 'Who giveth this Woman' had had to be left out, obviously. Dottie frowned and cleared her throat. 'Wouldn't you have thought,' she dared to suggest, in her deep military rumble, 'that she would have had *someone*? Isn't there a cousin in Montclair?' Elinor Eastlake shrugged. 'The plan miscarried,' she said. Libby MacAusland, an English major from Pittsfield, thrust her head into the tête-à-tête. 'What's this, what's this?' she said jovially. 'Break it up, girls.' She was a tall, pretty blonde with perpetually dilating brown eyes, a long, arching, inquisitive neck, and a manner of anxious conviviality; she had been president of the class sophomore year and had just missed being elected president of Students. Dottie laid a cautionary hand on Lakey's silken elbow; Libby, as everyone knew, was an unrestrained gossip and gabbler. Lakey lightly shook off Dottie's fingers; she detested being touched. 'Dottie was asking,' she said distinctly, 'whether there wasn't a cousin in Montclair.' There was a faint smile in the depths of her green eyes, which had a queer dark-blue rim around the iris, a sign of her Indian blood; she was searching the distance for a taxi. Libby became exaggeratedly thoughtful. She laid a finger to the centre of her forehead. 'I believe there is,' she discovered, nodding three times. 'Do you really think – ?' she began eagerly. Lakey raised a hand for a taxi. 'Kay kept her cousin in the background, hoping that one of us would supply her with something better.' 'Lakey!' murmured Dottie, shaking her head in reproach. 'Really, Lakey,' said Libby, giggling. 'Nobody but you would ever think of such a thing.' She hesitated. 'If Kay wanted somebody to give her away, she had only to ask, after all. Father or Brother would have been glad, any of us would have been glad . . .' Her voice broke off, and she precipitated her thin form into the taxi, where she took the jump seat, turning around, in half a minute, to survey her friends with cupped chin and brooding eyes: all her movements were quick and restive – she had an image of herself as a high-bred, tempestuous creature, a sort of Arab steed in an English sporting primitive. 'Do you really think?' she repeated, covetously, biting her upper lip. But Lakey said no more; she never enlarged on a suggestion, and for this had been named the Mona Lisa of the Smoking Room. Dottie Renfrew was distressed; her gloved hand twisted the pearls that had been given her for her twenty-first birthday. Her conscience was troubling her, and she resorted, from habit, to the slow, soft cough, like a perpetual scruple, that caused her family such anxiety and made them send her to Florida twice a year, at Christmas and Easter. 'Lakey,' she said gravely, ignoring Libby, 'one of us, don't you think, should have done it for her?' Libby MacAusland caracoled about on the jump seat, a hungry look in her eyes. Both girls stared into Elinor's impassive oval face. Elinor's eyes narrowed; she fingered the coil of Indian-black hair at the nape of her neck and readjusted a hairpin. 'No,' she said, with contempt. 'It would have been a confession of weakness.'

Libby's eyes protruded. 'How hard you are,' she said admiringly. 'And yet Kay adores you,' pondered Dottie. 'You used to like her best, Lakey. I think you still do, in your heart of hearts.' Lakey smiled at the cliché. 'Perhaps,' she said and lit a cigarette. She was fond, at present, of girls like Dottie who ran true to type, like paintings well within a style or a tradition. The girls she chose to collect were mystified, usually, by what she saw in them; they humbly perceived that they were very different from her. In private, they often discussed her, like toys discussing their owner, and concluded that she was awfully inhuman. But this increased their respect for her. She was also very changeable, which made them suspect great depths. Now, as the cab turned towards Fifth Avenue on Ninth Street, she made one of her abrupt decisions. 'Let me out here,' she commanded in her small, distinct, sweet voice. The driver instantly stopped and turned to watch her step out of the cab, rather stately, despite her fragility, in a high-necked black taffeta suit with a white silk muffler, small black hat, like a bowler, and black, very high-heeled shoes. 'Go *ahead*,' she called back impatiently, as the cab lingered.

The two girls in the taxi interrogated each other. Libby Mac-Ausland craned her gold head in a flowered hat out the window. 'Aren't you coming?' she cried. There was no answer. They could see her straight little back proceeding south, in the sun, on University Place. 'Follow her!' said Libby to the driver. 'I'll have to go round the block, lady.' The cab turned into Fifth Avenue and passed the Brevoort Hotel, where the rest of the wedding party was arriving; it went on into Eighth Street and back up University Place. But there was no sign of Lakey anywhere. She had disappeared. 'Wouldn't that jar you?' said Libby. 'Was it something I said, do you think?' 'Go round the block again, driver,' interposed Dottie quietly. In front of the Brevoort, Kay and Harald were climbing out of a taxi; they did not see the two frightened girls. 'Did she just up and decide not to go to the reception?' continued Libby, as the cab made the second circuit, without any result. 'She seemed terribly off Kay, I *must* say.' The cab paused before the hotel. 'What are we going to *do*?' demanded Libby. Dottie opened her pocketbook and gave a bill to the driver. 'Lakey is her own law,' she said firmly to Libby as they dismounted. 'We must simply tell everyone that she felt faint in the church.' A disappointed expression came into Libby's sharp-boned, pretty face; she had been looking forward to the scandal.

In a private dining-room of the hotel, Kay and Harald stood on a faded flowered carpet, receiving their friends' congratulations. A punch was being served, over which the guests were exclaiming: 'What *is* it?', 'Perfectly *delicious*', 'How did you ever think of it?' and so on. To each one, Kay gave the recipe. The base was one-third Jersey applejack, one third maple syrup, and one-third lemon juice, to which White Rock had been added. Harald had got the applejack from an actor friend who got it from a farmer near Flemington; the punch was adapted from a cocktail called Apple-jack Rabbit. The recipe was an ice-breaker – just as Kay had hoped, she explained aside to Helena Davison: everyone tasted it and agreed that it was the maple syrup that made all the difference. A tall shaggy man who was in radio told several funny stories about Jersey Lightning; he warned the handsome young man in the knitted green necktie that this stuff packed an awful wallop. There was a discussion about applejack and how it made people quarrelsome, to which the girls listened with fascination; none of them had ever tasted applejack before. They were very much interested, just at this time, in receipts for drinks; they all adored brandy Alexanders and White Ladies and wanted to hear about a cocktail called the Clover Club that was one-third gin, one-third lemon juice, one-third grenadine, and the white of an egg. Harald told about a drugstore he and Kay knew on West Fifty-ninth Street, where you could get prescription whisky without a prescription, and Polly Andrews borrowed a pencil from the waiter and noted down the address: she was going to be on her own this summer, keeping house for herself in her Aunt Julia's apartment with a terrace, and she needed all the tips she could get. Then Harald told them about a liqueur called anisette that an Italian in the theatre orchestra had taught him to make, from straight alcohol, water, and oil of anis, which gave it a milky colour, like Pernod. He explained the difference between Pernod, absinthe, arrack, and anisette; the girls spoke of green and yellow chartreuse, green and white crème de menthe, which Harald said varied only in the colour that was added, artificially, to suit a fancy market. Then he told them about an Armenian restaurant in the twenties, where you got rose-petal jelly for dessert, and explained the difference between Turkish and Armenian and Syrian cooking. 'Where did you get this *man*?' the girls cried, in unison.

In the pause that followed, the young man in the knitted tie drank a glass of punch and came over to Dottie Renfrew. 'Where's the dark beauty?' he asked in a confidential voice. Dottie lowered her voice also and glanced uneasily towards the far corner of the dining-room, where Libby MacAusland was whispering to two of the group. 'She felt faint in the chapel,' she murmured. 'I've just explained to Kay and Harald. We've packed her off to her hotel to lie down.' The young man raised an eyebrow. 'How perfectly *frightful*,' he said. Kay turned her head quickly to listen; the mockery in the young man's voice was evident. Dottie flushed. She cast about bravely for a new subject. 'Are you in the theatre too?' The young man leaned back against the wall, tilting his head upward. 'No,' he said, 'though your question is natural. In point of fact, I'm in welfare work.' Dottie eyed him gravely; she remembered now that Polly had said he was a painter, and she saw she was being teased.

He looked very much the artist – handsome as a piece of Roman statuary but somewhat battered and worn; the muscles of the cheeks were loosening, and there were sombre creases on either side of the flawless, straight, strong nose. She waited. 'I do posters for the Women's International League for Peace,' he said. Dottie laughed. 'That's not welfare work,' she retorted. 'In a manner of speaking,' he said. He glanced down at her, carefully. 'Vincent Club, Junior League, work with unwed mothers,' he enumerated. '*My* name is Brown. I come from Marblehead. I'm a collateral descendant of Nathaniel Hawthorne. My father keeps a general store. I didn't go to college. I'm not in your class, young lady.' Dottie remained silent, merely watching him sympathetically; she now thought him very attractive. 'I am an ex-expatriate,' he continued. 'Since the fall of the dollar I occupy a furnished room on Perry Street, next to the bridegroom's, and do peace posters for the ladies, as well as a little commercial work. The john, as you girls call it, is down the hall, and in the closet there's an electric grill. Hence you must excuse me if I smell like a ham-and-egg sandwich.' Dottie's beaver-brown eyes twinkled reproachfully; from the theatrical way he spoke she could see that he was proud and bitter, and she knew he was a gentleman from his well-cut features and his good, if old, tweed suit. 'Harald is moving on to higher things,' said Mr Brown. 'An apartment on the fashionable East Side – above a cordial shop and a cut-rate cleaner's, I'm told. We met like two passing elevators, to modernize the figure, one on the way up, one on the way down. Yesterday,' he went on, frowning, 'I was divorced downtown in Foley Square by a beautiful young creature named Betty from Morristown, New Jersey.' He leaned forward slightly. 'We spent last night in my room to celebrate. Are any of you people named Betty?' Dottie reflected. 'There's Libby,' she said. 'No Libbys, Beths, or Betsys,' he cautioned. 'I don't like the names you girls have nowadays. But what of the dark beauty? How is she called?'

At this moment, the door opened and Elinor Eastlake was shown in by a waiter, to whom she handed two brown-paper parcels she was carrying in her black kid-gloved hand; she appeared perfectly composed. 'Her name is Elinor,' whispered Dottie. 'We call her Lakey because her last name is Eastlake and she comes from Lake Forest, outside of Chicago.' 'Thank you,' said Mr Brown, but he made no move to leave Dottie's side and continued to talk to her in an undertone, out of the corner of his mouth, offering wry comments on the wedding party. Harald had hold of Lakey's hand, which he swung back and forth, as he stood back to admire her suit, a Patou model. His quick, lithe movements went oddly with his solemn long head and face, almost as if his head, a thinking machine, did not belong to him and had been clapped on his body in a masquerade. He was an intensely self-absorbed young man, as the girls knew from his letters, and when he spoke of her career, as he was doing now to Lakey, he had a detached impersonal eagerness, as though he were discussing disarmament or deficit spending. Yet he was attractive to women, as the girls knew from his letters too; the group admitted that he had SA, the way some homely men teachers and clergymen had, and there was something about him, a dynamic verve, that made Dottie wonder, even now, as she and her companion watched him, how Kay had brought him to the point. The idea that Kay might be enceinte had stolen more than once into her quiet thoughts, though Kay, according to herself, knew all about taking precautions and kept a douche in Harald's closet.

'Have you known Kay long?' asked Dottie curiously, remembering in spite of herself the toilet he had mentioned in the hall of Harald's rooming-house. 'Long enough,' replied Mr Brown. This was so crudely outright that Dottie flinched, just as though it had been said of *her*, at her own wedding reception. 'I don't like girls with big legs,' he said, with a reassuring smile. Dottie's legs and slim, well-shod feet were her best points. Disloyally, Dottie looked with him at Kay's legs, which were indeed rather beefy. 'A sign of peasant forebears,' he said, waving a finger. 'The centre of gravity's too low — mark of obstinacy and obtuseness.' He studied Kay's figure, which was outlined by the thin dress; as usual, she was not wearing a girdle. 'A touch of steatopygia.' 'What?' whispered Dottie. 'Excessive development of the rump. Let me get you a drink.' Dottie was thrilled and horrified; she had never had such a risqué conversation. 'You and your social friends,' he continued, 'have a finer functional adaptation. Full, low-slung breasts' — he stared about the room — 'fashioned to carry pearls and *bouclé* sweaters and faggoting and tucked crêpe de Chine blouses. Narrow waists. Tapering legs. As a man of the last decade, I prefer the boyish figure myself: a girl in a bathing-cap poised to jackknife on a diving-board. Marblehead summer memories; Betty is a marvellous swimmer. Thin women are more sensual; scientific fact – the nerve-ends are closer to the surface.' His grey eyes narrowed, heavy-lidded, as though he were drifting off to sleep. 'I like the fat one, though,' he said abruptly, singling out Pokey Prothero. 'She has a thermal look. Nacreous skin, plumped with oysters. Yum, yum, yum; money, money, money. My sexual problems are economic. I loathe under-privileged women, but my own outlook is bohemian. Impossible combination.'

To Dottie's relief, the waiters came in with the breakfast – eggs Benedict – and Kay shooed everyone to the table. She put the best man, a very silent person who worked on the *Wall Street Journal* (advertising department), on her own right, and Helena Davison on Harald's right, but after that all was confusion. Dottie was left stranded at the end of the table between Libby, her *bête noire*, and the radio man's wife, who was a stylist at Russek's (and who, of course, should have been seated on Harald's left). It was a hard table to seat, with so many girls; still, a more tactful hostess could have arranged it so that the duller ones were not all put together. But the radio man's wife, a vivacious beanpole of a woman, dressed in plumes and jet accessories like a film vamp, seemed perfectly content with her company; she was a graduate of the University of Idaho, Class of '28, who loved, she said, a good hen fest. She had known Harald from a boy, she announced, and his old folks too, though long time nô see. Anders, Harald's father, had been the principal of the high school in Boise she and Harald had gone to, way back when. 'Isn't Kay a honey?' she at once demanded of Dottie. 'Awfully nice,' said Dottie, warmly. Her neighbour was the sort that used to be called 'peppy'; on the whole, Dottie agreed with the English teacher who said that it was wiser not to use slang because it dated you so quickly. 'How come her parents didn't show?' the woman continued, lowering her voice. '"Show"?' repeated Dottie, at a loss – could she mean show dogs or cats? 'Turn up for the wedding.' 'Oh,' said Dottie, coughing. 'I believe they sent Kay and Harald a cheque,' she murmured. 'Rather than make the trip, you know.' The woman nodded. 'That's what Dave said – my husband. He figured they must have sent a cheque.' 'So much more useful,' said Dottie. 'Don't you agree?' 'Oh, sure,' said the woman. 'I'm kind of an old softy, myself. I was married in a veil. . . . You know, I told Harald I'd have liked to give the wedding at my place. We could have scrounged up a minister and Dave could have taken some pictures, to send to the folks back home. But Kay had made all the arrangements, it seemed, by the time I got my bid in.' She stopped on a rising note and looked inquiringly at Dottie, who felt herself in deep waters. Kay's plans, she said tactfully, turning it into a joke, were 'as the laws of the Medes and the Persians'; nobody could change her. 'Who was it said,' she added, twinkling, 'that his wife had a whim of iron? My father always quotes that when he has to give in to Mother.' 'Cute,' said her neighbour. 'Harald's a swell gent,' she went on, in a different voice, more thoughtful and serious. 'Kind of a vulnerable gent, too. Though you might not think so.' She looked hard at Dottie and her plumes nodded belligerently as she downed a glass of punch.

Across the table, farther down, on Kay's left, the auburn-haired descendant of Hawthorne, who was talking to Priss Hartshorn, caught Dottie's troubled eye and winked. Not knowing what else to do, Dottie gamely winked back. She had not imagined she was the type men winked at. The oldest of the group, nearly twenty-three now, thanks to the poor health that had kept her out of school as a child, she knew she was a bit of an old maid; the group teased her for her decorum and staid habits and mufflers and medicines and the long mink coat she wore on campus to keep off the cold, but she had a good sense of humour and quietly joined in the laugh. Her beaux had always treated her with respect; she was the sort of girl·that people's brothers took out and she had a whole string of pale young men who were studying archaeology or musicology or architecture in the Harvard Graduate School; she read out bits of their letters to the group – descriptions of concerts or of digs in the Southwest – and, playing Truth, admitted to having had two proposals. She had fine eyes, everyone told her, and a nice flashing set of white teeth and a pretty, if thin, cap of hair; her nose was rather long, in the pointed New England way, and her brows were black and a little heavy; she resembled the Copley portrait of an ancestress that hung in the family hall. In a modest way, she was fun-loving and even, she suspected, rather sensuous; she loved dancing and harmonizing and was always crooning to herself snatches of popular songs. Yet nobody had ever tried to take a liberty with her; some of the girls found it hard to believe this, but it was true. And the strange thing was, she would not have been shocked. The girls found the fact funny, but D. H. Lawrence was one of her favourite authors: he had such a true feeling for animals and for the natural side of life.

She and Mother had talked it over and agreed that if you were in love and engaged to a nice young man you perhaps ought to have relations once to make sure of a happy adjustment. Mother, who was very youthful and modern, knew of some very sad cases within her own circle of friends where the man and the woman just didn't fit down there and ought never to have been married. Not believing in divorce, Dottie thought it very important to arrange that side of marriage properly; defloration, which the girls were always joking about in the smoking-room, frightened her. Kay had had an awful time with Harald; five times, she insisted, before she was penetrated, and this in spite of basketball and a great deal of riding out West. Mother said you could have the hymen removed surgically, if you wanted, as royal families abroad were said to do; but perhaps a very gentle lover could manage to make it painless; hence it might be better to marry an older man, with experience.

The best man was proposing a toast; looking up, Dottie found Dick Brown's (that was his name) bright grey eyes on her again. He raised his glass and drank to her, ceremoniously. Dottie drank in return. 'Isn't this fun?' cried Libby MacAusland, arching her long neck·and weaving her head about and laughing in her exhausted style. 'So much nicer,' purred the voices. 'No receiving line, no formality, no older people.' 'It's just what I want for myself,' announced Libby. 'A young people's wedding!' She uttered a blissful scream as a Baked Alaska came in, the meringue faintly smoking. 'Baked Alaska!' she cried and fell back, as if in a heap, on her chair. 'Girls!' she said solemnly, pointing to the big ice-cream cake with slightly scorched peaks of meringue that was being lowered into position before Kay. 'Look at it. Childhood dreams come true! It's every children's party in the whole blessed United States. It's patent-leather slippers and organdie and a shy little boy in an Eton collar asking you to dance. I don't know when I've been so excited. I haven't seen one since I was twelve years old. It's Mount Whitney; it's Fujiyama.' The girls smiled forbearingly at each other; Libby 'wrote'. But in fact they had shared her delight until she began talking about it, and a sigh of anticipation went up as they watched the hot meringue slump under Kay's knife. Standing against the wall, the two waiters watched rather dourly. The dessert was not all that good. The meringue had browned unevenly; it was white in some places and burned black in others, which gave it a disagreeable taste. Underneath the slab of ice-cream, the sponge cake was stale and damp. But fealty to Kay sent plates back for seconds. The Baked Alaska was the *kind* of thing that in Kay's place the group hoped *they* would have thought of – terribly original for a wedding and yet just right when you considered it. They were all tremendously interested in cooking and quite out of patience with the unimaginative roasts and chops followed by moulds from the caterer that Mother served; they were going to try new combinations and foreign recipes and puffy omelettes and soufflés and interesting aspics and just one hot dish in a Pyrex, no soup, and a fresh green salad.

'It's a hotel trick,' explained the radio man's wife, speaking across the table to Priss Hartshorn, who was going to be married herself in September. 'They have the ice-cream frozen hard as a rock and then, whoosh, into the oven. That way they take no chances, but between you and me it's not what Mamma used to make.' Priss nodded worriedly; she was a solemn, ashy-haired little girl who looked like a gopher and who felt it her duty to absorb every bit of word-of-mouth information that pertained to consumer problems. Economics had been her major, and she was going to work in the consumer division of N R A. 'Working conditions,' she declared, with her slight nervous stammer, 'in some of our best hotel kitchens are way substandard, you know.' She had begun to feel her liquor; the punch *was* rather treacherous, even though applejack, being a natural product, was one of the purest things you could drink these days. In her haze, she saw the radio man stand up. 'To the Class of Thirty-three,' he toasted. The others drank to the Vassar girls. 'Bottoms up!' cried the man's wife. From the silent best man came a cackling laugh. Tiddly as she was, Priss could tell that she and her friends, through no fault of their own, had awakened economic antagonism. Vassar girls, in general, were not liked, she knew, by the world at large; they had come to be a sort of symbol of superiority. She would have to see a good deal less of some of them after she was married if she wanted Sloan to keep in with his colleagues on the staff of the hospital. She stared sadly at Pokey Prothero, her best friend, who was sitting sprawled out, across the table, putting ashes into her plate of melting ice-cream and soggy cake with the very bad table manners that only the very rich could afford. There was a long spill down the front of her beautiful Lanvin suit. Mentally, Priss applied Energine; her neat little soul scrubbed away. She did not know how Pokey would ever get along in life without a personal maid to take care of her. Ever since Chapin, she herself had been picking up after Pokey, making her use an ashtray in the smoking-room, collecting her laundry and mailing it home for her, creeping into the common bathroom to wash the ring off the tub so that the others would not complain again. Poor Pokey, when she was married, would be doomed to a conventional establishment and a retinue of servants and governesses; she would miss all the fun and the alarums, as Mother called them, of starting on your own from scratch, with just a tweeny to help with the dish-washing and the heavy work.

Great wealth was a frightful handicap; it insulated you from living. The depression, whatever else you could say about it, had been a truly wonderful thing for the propertied classes; it had wakened a lot of them up to the things that really counted. There wasn't a family Priss knew that wasn't happier and saner for having to scale down its expenditures; sacrifices had drawn the members together. Look at Polly Andrews' family: Mr Andrews had been in Riggs Clinic when the depression hit and all his investments went blotto, whereupon, instead of sinking deeper into melancholia and being put into a state mental hospital (grim thought!), he had come home and made himself useful as the family cook. He did every bit of the cooking and the marketing and served the most scrumptious meals, having learned about *haute cuisine* when they had their château in France; Mrs Andrews did the scullery work and the vacuuming; everybody made his own bed; and the children, when they were home, washed up. They were the *gayest* family to visit, on the little farm they had managed to save near Stockbridge; Lakey went there last Thanksgiving and never had a better time – she only wished, she said, that *her* father would lose his money, like Mr Andrews. She meant it quite seriously. Of course, it made a difference that the Andrews had always been rather highbrow; they had inner resources to fall back on.

Priss herself was a dyed-in-the-wool liberal; it ran in the blood. Her mother was a Vassar trustee, and her grandmother had been reform mayor of New York. Last year, when she had had to be a bridesmaid in a big social wedding at St James', with the carpet and and awning and so on, she had not been able to get over the sight of the unemployed crowding round the church entrance, with the police holding them back. It was not that Priss felt she had to change the world single-handed, as her brother, who went to Yale, was always jeering, and she did not blame the class she was born into for wanting to hold on to its privileges – that was part of their conditioning. She was not in the least bit a socialist or a rebel, though even Sloan liked to tease her about being one. To be a socialist, she thought, was a sort of luxury, when the world itself was changing so fast and there was so much that had to be done here and now. You could not sit down and wait for the millennium, any more than you could turn the clock back. The group used to play the game of when in history you would like to have lived if you could choose, and Priss was the only one who stuck up for the present; Kay picked the year 2000 (A.D., of course) and Lakey was for the *quattrocento* – which showed, incidentally, what a varied group they were. But seriously Priss could not imagine a more exciting time to come of age in than right now in America, and she felt awfully sorry for a person like Dick Brown, on her right, with his restless, bitter face and white unsteady hands; having talked with him quite a while (probably boring him stiff!), she could see that he was typical of that earlier generation of expatriates and bohemian rebels they had been studying about in Miss Lockwood's course who were coming back now to try to find their roots again.

The gabble of voices slowly died down. The girls, confused by alcohol, cast inquiring looks at each other. What was to happen now? At an ordinary wedding, Kay and Harald would slip off to change to travelling costume, and Kay would throw her bouquet. But there was to be no honeymoon, they recalled. Kay and Harald, evidently, had nowhere to go but back to the sublet apartment they had just left this morning. Probably, if the group knew Kay, the bed was not even made. The funny, uneasy feeling that had come over them all in the chapel affected them again. They looked at their watches; it was only one-fifteen. How many hours till it was time for Harald to go to work? Doubtless, lots of couples got married and just went home again, but somehow it did not seem right to let that happen. 'Should I ask them to Aunt Julia's for coffee?'

whispered Polly Andrews to Dottie, across the table. 'It makes rather a lot,' murmured Dottie. 'I don't know what Ross would say.' Ross was Aunt Julia's maid and quite a character. 'Bother Ross!' said Polly. The two girls' eyes went up and down the table, counting, and then met, grave and startled. There were thirteen — eight of the group and five outsiders. How like Kay! Or was it an accident? Had someone dropped out at the last minute? Meanwhile, the radio man's wife had been exchanging signals with her husband; she turned to Dottie and spoke *sotto voce*. 'How would some of you gals like to drop around to my place for some Java? I'll give Kay and Harald the high sign.' Dottie hesitated; perhaps this would really be more suitable, but she did not like to decide for Kay, who might prefer Aunt Julia's. A sense that everything was getting too involved, wheels within wheels, depressed her.

Pokey Prothero's voice, like a querulous grackle, intervened. 'You two are supposed to go away,' she suddenly complained, crushing out her cigarette and looking through her *lorgnon* with an air of surprised injury from the bride to the groom. Trust Pokey, thought the girls, with a joint sigh. 'Where should we go, Pokey?' answered Kay, smiling. 'Yes, Pokey, where should we go?' agreed the bridegroom. Pokey considered. 'Go to Coney Island,' she said. Her tone of irrefutable, self-evident logic, like that of an old man or a child, took everyone aback for a second. 'What a splendid idea!' cried Kay. 'On the subway?' 'Brighton Express, via Flatbush Avenue,' intoned Harald. 'Change at Fulton Street.' 'Pokey, you're a genius,' said everyone, in voices of immense relief. Harald paid the bill and launched into a discussion of roller coasters, comparing the relative merits of the Cyclone and the Thunderbolt. Compacts came out; fur pieces were clipped together; daily remembrancers of dark-blue English leather were consulted. The room was full of movement and laughter. 'How did Pokey ever think of it?', 'The perfect end to a perfect wedding', 'Just right', the voices reiterated, as gloves were pulled on.

The party moved out to the street; the radio man, who had left his camera in the check room, took pictures on the sidewalk, in the bright June sunlight. Then they all walked along Eighth Street to the subway at Astor Place, while passers-by turned to stare at them, and right down to the turnstiles. 'Kay must throw her bouquet!' shrieked Libby MacAusland, stretching on her long legs, like a basketball centre, as a crowd of people massed to watch them. 'My girl's from Vassar; none can surpass 'er,' the radio man struck up. Harold produced two nickels and the newly-weds passed through the turnstile; Kay, who, all agreed, had never looked prettier, turned and threw her bouquet, high in the air, back over the turnstiles to the waiting girls. Libby jumped and caught it, though it had really been aimed at Priss just behind her. And at that moment Lakey gave them all a surprise; the brown-paper parcels she had checked in the hotel proved to contain rice. '*That* was what you stopped for!' exclaimed Dottie, full of wonder, as the wedding party seized handfuls and pelted them after the bride and the groom; the platform was showered with white grains when the local train finally came in. 'That's banal! That's not like you, Eastlake!' Kay turned and shouted as the train doors were closing, and everyone, dispersing, agreed that it was not like Lakey at all, but that, banal or not, it was just the little touch that had been needed to round off an unforgettable occasion.

Chapter 2

Just at first, in the dark hallway, it had given Dottie rather a funny
feeling to be tiptoeing up the stairs only two nights after Kay's
wedding to a room right across from Harald's old room, where the
same thing had happened to Kay. An awesome feeling, really, like
when the group all got the curse at the same time; it filled you with
strange ideas about being a woman, with the moon compelling you
like the tides. All sorts of weird, irrelevant ideas floated through
Dottie's head as the key turned in the lock and she found herself,
for the first time, alone with a man in his flat. Tonight was midsummer's night, the summer solstice, when maids had given up
their treasure to fructify the crops; she had that in background
reading for *A Midsummer Night's Dream*. Her Shakespeare teacher
had been awfully keen on anthropology and had had them study in
Frazer about the ancient fertility rites and how the peasants in
Europe, till quite recent times, had lit big bonfires in honour of the
Corn Maiden and then lain together in the fields. College, reflected
Dottie as the lamp clicked on, had been almost *too* rich an experience. She felt stuffed with interesting thoughts that she could only
confide in Mother, not in a man, certainly, who would probably
suppose you were barmy if you started telling him about the Corn
Maiden when you were just about to lose your virginity. Even the
group would laugh if Dottie confessed that she was exactly in the
mood for a long, comfy discussion with Dick, who was so frightfully attractive and unhappy and had so much to give.

But the group would never believe, never in a million years, that
Dottie Renfrew would come here, to this attic room that smelled of
cooking-fat, with a man she hardly knew, who made no secret of his
intentions, who had been drinking heavily, and who was evidently
not in love with her. When she put it that way, crudely, she could
scarcely believe it herself, and the side of her that wanted to talk was

still hoping, probably, to gain a little time, the way, she had noticed, she always started a discussion of current events with the dentist to keep him from turning on the drill. Dottie's dimple twinkled. What an odd comparison! If the group could hear that!

And yet when It happened, it was not at all what the group or even Mother would have imagined, not a bit sordid or messy, in spite of Dick's being tight. He had been most considerate, undressing her slowly, in a matter-of-fact way, as if he were helping her off with her outdoor things. He took her hat and furs and put them in the closet and then unfastened her dress, bending over the snaps with a funny, concentrated scowl, rather like Daddy's when he was hooking Mother up for a party. Lifting the dress carefully off her, he had glanced at the label and then back at Dottie, as though to match the two, before he carried it, walking very steadily to the closet and arranged it on a wooden hanger. After that, he folded each garment as he removed it and set it ceremoniously on the armchair, looking each time at the label with a frown between his brows. When her dress was gone, she felt rather faint for a minute, but he left her in her slip, just as they did in the doctor's office, while he took off her shoes and stockings and undid her brassière and girdle and step-ins, so that finally, when he drew her slip over her head, with great pains so as not to muss her hairdo, she was hardly trembling when she stood there in front of him with nothing on but her pearls. Perhaps it was going to the doctor so much or perhaps it was Dick himself, so detached and impersonal, the way they were supposed to be in art class with the model, that made Dottie brave. He had not touched her once, all the time he was undressing her, except by accident, grazing her skin. Then he pinched each of her full breasts lightly and told her to relax, in just the tone Dr Perry used when he was going to give her a treatment for her sciatica.

He handed her a book of drawings to look at, while he went into the closet, and Dottie sat there in the armchair, trying not to listen. With the book on her lap, she studied the room conscientiously, in order to know Dick better. Rooms told a lot about a person. It had a skylight and a big north window and was surprisingly neat for a man; there was a drawing-board with some work on it which she longed to peek at, a long plain table, like an ironing-table, monk's-cloth curtains, and a monk's-cloth spread on the single bed. On the chest of drawers was a framed photograph of a blonde woman, very striking, with a short, severe haircut; that must be 'Betty', the wife. Tacked up on the wall there was a snapshot that looked like her in a bathing-suit and a number of sketches from the nude, and Dottie had the sinking feeling that they might be of Betty too. She had been doing her very best not to let herself think about love or let her emotions get entangled, for she knew that Dick would not like it. It was just a physical attraction, she had been telling herself over and over, while trying to remain cool and collected despite the pounding of her blood, but now, suddenly, when it was too late to retreat, she had lost her sang-froid and was jealous. Worse than that, even, the idea came to her that Dick was, well, *peculiar*. She opened the book of drawings on her lap and found more nudes, signed by some modern artist she had never heard of! She did not know, a second later, just what she had been expecting, but Dick's return was, by contrast, less bad.

He came in wearing a pair of white shorts and carrying a towel, with a hotel's name on it, which he stretched out on the bed, having turned back the covers. He took the book away from her and put it on a table. Then he made Dottie lie down on the towel, telling her to relax again, in a friendly, instructive voice; while he stood for a minute, looking down at her and smiling, with his hands on his hips, she tried to breathe naturally, reminding herself that she had a good figure, and forced a wan, answering smile to her lips. *'Nothing will happen unless you want it, baby.'* The words, lightly stressed, told her how scared and mistrustful she must be looking. 'I know, Dick,' she answered, in a small, weak, grateful voice, making herself use his name aloud for the first time. 'Would you like a cigarette?' Dottie shook her head and let it drop back on the pillow. 'All right, then?' 'All right.' As he moved to turn out the light, she felt a sudden harsh thump of excitement, right in *there*, like what had happened to her in the Italian restaurant when he said 'Do you want to come home with me?' and fastened his deep, shadowed eyes on her. Now he turned and looked at her steadily again, his hand on the bridge lamp; her own eyes, widening with amazement at the funny feeling she noticed, as if she were on fire, in the place her thighs were shielding, stared at him, seeking confirmation; she swallowed. In reply, he switched off the lamp and came towards her in the dark, unbuttoning his shorts.

32

This shift gave her an instant in which to be afraid. She had never seen *that* part of a man, except in statuary and once, at the age of six, when she had interrupted Daddy in his bath, but she had a suspicion that it would be something ugly and darkly inflamed, surrounded by coarse hair. Hence, she had been very grateful for being spared the sight of it, which she did not think she could have borne, and she held her breath as the strange body climbed on hers, shrinking. 'Open your legs,' he commanded, and her legs obediently fell apart. His hand squeezed her down there, rubbing and stroking; her legs fell farther apart, and she started to make weak, moaning noises, almost as if she wanted him to stop. He took his hand away, thank heaven, and fumbled for a second; then she felt it, the thing she feared, being guided into her as she braced herself and stiffened. 'Relax,' he whispered. 'You're ready.' It was surprisingly warm and smooth, but it hurt terribly, pushing and stabbing. 'Damn it,' he said. 'Relax. You're making it harder.' Just then, Dottie screamed faintly; it had gone all the way in. He put his hand over her mouth and then settled her legs around him and commenced to move it back and forth inside her. At first, it hurt so that she flinched at each stroke and tried to pull back, but this only seemed to make him more determined. Then, while she was still praying for it to be over, surprise of surprises, she started to like it a little. She got the idea, and her body began to move too in answer, as he pressed *that* home in her slowly, over and over, and slowly drew it back, as if repeating a question. Her breath came quicker. Each lingering stroke, like a violin bow, made her palpitate for the next. Then, all of a sudden, she seemed to explode in a series of long, uncontrollable contractions that embarrassed her, like the hiccups, the moment they were over, for it was as if she had forgotten Dick as a person; and he, as if he sensed this, pulled quickly away from her and thrust that part of himself onto her stomach, where it pushed and pounded at her flesh. Then he too jerked and moaned, and Dottie felt something damp and sticky running down the hill of her belly.

Minutes passed; the room was absolutely still; through the skylight Dottie could see the moon. She lay there, with Dick's weight still on her, suspecting that something had gone wrong – probably her fault. His face was turned sideward so that she could not look into it, and his chest was squashing her breasts so that she could hardly breathe. Both their bodies were wet, and the cold perspiration from him ran down her face and matted her side hair and made a little rivulet between her breasts; on her lips it had a salty sting that reminded her forlornly of tears. She was ashamed of the happiness she had felt. Evidently, he had not found her satisfactory as a partner or else he would say something. Perhaps the woman was not supposed to move? 'Damn it,' he had said to her, when he was hurting her, in such a testy voice, like a man saying 'Damn it, why can't we have dinner on time?' or something unromantic like that. Was it her screaming out that had spoiled everything? Or had she made a *faux pas* at the end, somehow? She wished that books were a little more explicit; Krafft-Ebing, which Kay and Helena had found at a secondhand bookstore and kept reading aloud from, as if it were very funny, mostly described nasty things like men making love to hens, and even then did not explain how it was done. The thought of the blonde on the bureau filled her with hopeless envy; probably Dick at this moment was making bitter comparisons. She could feel his breathing and smell the stale alcohol that came from him in gusts. In the bed, there was a peculiar pungent odour, and she feared that it might come from her.

The horrible idea occurred to her that he had fallen asleep, and she made a few gentle movements to try to extricate herself from under him. Their damp skins, stuck together, made a little sucking noise when she pulled away, but she could not roll his weight off her. Then she knew that he was asleep. Probably he was tired, she said to herself forgivingly; he had those dark rings under his eyes. But down in her heart she knew that he ought not to have gone to sleep like a ton of bricks on top of her; it was the final proof, if she still needed one, that she meant nothing to him. When he woke up tomorrow morning and found her gone, he would probably be glad. Or perhaps he would not even remember who had been there with him; she could not guess how much he had had to drink before he met her for dinner. What had happened, she feared, was that he had simply passed out. She saw that her only hope of saving her own dignity was to dress in the dark and steal away. But she would have to find the bathroom somewhere outside in that unlit hall. Dick began to snore. The sticky liquid had dried and was crusting on her stomach; she felt she could not go back to the Vassar Club without washing it off. Then the worst thought, almost, of all struck her.

Supposing he had started to have an emission while he was still inside her? Or if he used one of the rubber things and it had broken when she had jerked like that and that was why he had pulled so sharply away? She had heard of the rubber things breaking or leaking and how a woman could get pregnant from just a single drop. Full of determination, Dottie heaved and squirmed to free herself, until Dick raised his head in the moonlight and stared at her, without recognition. It was all true then, Dottie thought miserably; he had just gone to sleep and forgotten her. She tried to slide out of the bed.

Dick sat up and rubbed his eyes. 'Oh, it's you, Boston,' he muttered, putting an arm around her waist. 'Forgive me for dropping off.' He got up and turned on the bridge lamp. Dottie hurriedly covered herself with the sheet and averted her face; she was still timorous of seeing him in the altogether. 'I must go home, Dick,' she said soberly, stealing a sideward look at her clothes folded on the armchair. '*Must* you?' he inquired in a mocking tone; she could imagine his reddish eyebrows shooting up. 'You needn't trouble to dress and see me downstairs,' she went on quickly and firmly, her eyes fixed on the rug where his bare handsome feet were planted. He stooped and picked up his shorts; she watched his feet clamber into them. Then her eyes slowly rose and met his searching gaze. 'What's the matter, Boston?' he said kindly. 'Girls don't run home, you know, on their first night. Did it hurt you much?' Dottie shook her head. 'Are you bleeding?' he demanded. 'Come on, let me look.' He lifted her up and moved her down on the bed, the sheet trailing along with her; there was a small bloodstain on the towel. 'The very bluest,' he said, 'but only a minute quantity. Betty bled like a pig.' Dottie said nothing. 'Out with it, Boston,' he said brusquely, jerking a thumb towards the framed photograph. 'Does *she* put your nose out of joint?' Dottie made a brave negative sign. There was one thing she had to say. 'Dick,' and she shut her eyes in shame, 'do you think I should take a douche?' 'A douche?' he repeated in a mystified tone. 'Why? What for?' 'Well, in case ... *you* know ... birth control,' murmured Dottie. Dick stared at her and suddenly burst out laughing; he dropped on to a straight chair and threw his handsome head back. 'My dear girl,' he said, 'we just employed the most ancient form of birth control. *Coitus interruptus*, the old Romans called it, and a horrid nuisance it is.' 'I thought perhaps . . .?' said Dottie. 'Don't think. What did you think? I promise you, there isn't a single sperm swimming up to fertilize your irreproachable ovum. Like the man in the Bible, I spilled my seed on the ground, or, rather, on your very fine belly.' With a swift motion, he pulled the sheet back before she could stop him. 'Now,' he said, 'lay bare your thoughts.' Dottie shook her head and blushed. Wild horses could not make her, for the words embarrassed her frightfully; she had nearly choked on 'douche' and 'birth control,' as it was. 'We must get you cleaned up,' he decreed after a moment's silence. He put on a robe and slippers and disappeared to the bathroom. It seemed a long time before he came back, bringing a dampened towel, with which he swabbed off her stomach. Then he dried her, rubbing hard with the dry end of it, sitting down beside her on the bed. He himself appeared much fresher, as though he had washed, and he smelled of mouthwash and tooth powder. He lit two cigarettes and gave her one and settled an ashtray between them.

'You *came*, Boston,' he remarked, with the air of a satisfied instructor. Dottie glanced uncertainly at him; could he mean that thing she had done that she did not like to think about? 'I beg your pardon,' she murmured. 'I mean you had an orgasm.' Dottie made a vague, still-inquiring noise in her throat; she was pretty sure, now, she understood, but the new word discombobulated her. 'A climax,' he added, more sharply. 'Do they teach that word at Vassar?' 'Oh,' said Dottie, almost disappointed that that was all there was to it. 'Was that . . . ?' She could not finish the question. 'That was it,' he nodded. 'That is, if I am a judge.' 'It's normal then?' she wanted to know, beginning to feel better. Dick shrugged. 'Not for girls of your upbringing. Not the first time, usually. Appearances to the contrary, you're probably highly sexed.'

Dottie turned even redder. According to Kay, a climax was something very unusual, something the husband brought about by carefully studying his wife's desires and by patient manual stimulation. The terms made Dottie shudder, even in memory; there was a horrid bit, all in Latin, in Krafft-Ebing, about the Empress Maria Theresa and what the court doctor told her consort to do that Dottie had glanced at quickly and then tried to forget. Yet even Mother hinted that satisfaction was something that came after a good deal of time and experience and that love made a big difference. But when Mother talked about satisfaction, it was not clear exactly what she meant, and Kay was not clear either, except when she quoted from books. Polly Andrews once asked her whether it was the same as feeling passionate when you were necking (that was when Polly was engaged), and Kay said yes, pretty much, but Dottie now thought that Kay had been mistaken or else trying to hide the truth from Polly for some reason. Dottie had felt passionate, quite a few times, when she was dancing with someone terribly attractive, but that was quite different from the thing Dick meant. You would almost think that Kay did not know what she was talking about. Or else that Kay and Mother meant something else altogether and this thing with Dick *was* abnormal. And yet he seemed so pleased, sitting there, blowing out smoke rings; probably, having lived abroad, he knew more than Mother and Kay.

'What are you frowning over now, Boston?' Dottie gave a start. 'To be highly sexed,' he said gently, 'is an excellent thing in a woman. You mustn't be ashamed.' He took her cigarette and put it out and laid his hands on her shoulders. 'Buck up,' he said. 'What you're feeling is natural. "*Post coitum, omne animal triste est*," as the Roman poet said.' He slipped his hand down the slope of her shoulder and lightly touched her nipple. 'Your body surprised you tonight. You must learn to know it.' Dottie nodded. 'Soft,' he murmured, pressing the nipple between his thumb and forefinger. 'Detumescence, that's what you're experiencing.' Dottie drew a quick breath, fascinated; her doubts slid away. As he continued to squeeze it, her nipple stood up. 'Erectile tissue,' he said informatively and touched the other breast. 'See,' he said, and they both looked downward. The two nipples were hard and full, with a pink aureole of goose pimples around them; on her breasts were a few dark hairs. Dottie waited tensely. A great relief had surged through her; these were the very terms Kay cited from the marriage handbooks. Down there, she felt a quick new tremor. Her lips parted. Dick smiled. 'You feel something?' he said. Dottie nodded. 'You'd like it again?' he said, assaying her with his hand. Dottie stiffened; she pressed her thighs together. She was ashamed of the violent sensation his exploring fingers had discovered. But he held his hand there, between her clasped thighs, and grasped her right hand in his other, guiding it downward to the opening of his robe and pressed it over that part of himself, which was soft and limp, rather sweet,

37

really, all curled up on itself like a fat worm. Sitting beside her, he looked into her face as he stroked her down there and tightened her hand on him. 'There's a little ridge there,' he whispered. 'Run your fingers up and down it.' Dottie obeyed, wonderingly; she felt his organ stiffen a little, which gave her a strange sense of power. She struggled against the excitement his tickling thumb was producing in her own external part; but as she felt him watching her, her eyes closed and her thighs spread open. He disengaged her hand, and she fell back on the bed, gasping. His thumb continued its play and she let herself yield to what it was doing, her whole attention concentrated on a tense pinpoint of sensation, which suddenly discharged itself in a nervous, fluttering spasm; her body arched and heaved and then lay still. When his hand returned to touch her, she struck it feebly away. 'Don't,' she moaned, rolling over on her stomach. This second climax, which she now recognized from the first one, though it was different, left her jumpy and disconcerted; it was something less thrilling and more like being tickled relentlessly or having to go to the bathroom. 'Didn't you like that?' he demanded, turning her head over on the pillow, so that she could not hide herself from him. She hated to think of his having watched her eyes while he brought *that* about. Slowly, Dottie opened her eyes and resolved to tell the truth. 'Not quite so much as the other, Dick.' Dick laughed. 'A nice normal girl. Some of your sex prefer that.' Dottie shivered; she could not deny that it had been exciting but it seemed to her almost perverted. He appeared to read her thoughts. 'Have you ever done it with a girl, Boston?' He tilted her face so he could scan it. Dottie reddened. 'Heavens, no.' 'You come like a house afire. How do you account for that?' Dottie said nothing. 'Have you ever done it with yourself?' Dottie shook her head violently; the suggestion wounded her. 'In your dreams?' Dottie reluctantly nodded. 'A little. Not the whole thing.' 'Rich erotic fantasies of a Chestnut Street virgin,' remarked Dick, stretching. He got up and went to the chest of drawers and took out two pairs of pyjamas and tossed one of them to Dottie. 'Put them on now and go to the bathroom. Tonight's lesson is concluded.'

Having locked herself into the hall bathroom, Dottie began to take stock. 'Who would have thunk it?' she quoted Pokey Prothero, as she stared, thunderstruck, into the mirror. Her ruddy, heavy-browed face, with its long straight nose and dark-brown eyes, was just as Bostonian as ever. Somebody in the group had said that she looked as if she had been born in a mortarboard. There was something magistral about her appearance, she could see it herself, in the white men's pyjamas with her sharp New England jaw protruding over the collar, like an old judge or a blackbird sitting on a fence – Daddy sometimes joked that she ought to have been a lawyer. And yet there was that fun-loving dimple lurking in her cheek and the way she loved to dance and sing harmony – she feared she might be a dual personality, a regular Jekyll and Hyde. Thoughtfully, Dottie rinsed her mouth out with Dick's mouth-wash and threw back her head to gargle. She wiped off her lipstick with a bit of toilet tissue and peered anxiously at the soap in Dick's soap dish, thinking of her sensitive skin. She had to be awfully careful, but the bathroom, she noted with gratitude, was *scrupulously* clean and placarded with notices from the landlady: 'Please leave this room as you would expect to find it. Thank you for your cooperation'; 'Please use mat when taking shower. Thank you.' The landlady, Dottie reflected, must be very broad-minded, if she did not object to women's coming to visit. After all, Kay had spent whole week-ends here with Harald.

She did not like to think of what women guests Dick had had, besides Betty, whom he had already mentioned. What if he had brought Lakey here the other night, after they took Dottie home? Breathing hard, she steadied herself on the washbasin and nervously scratched her jaw. Lakey, she argued, would not have let him do what he had done with *her*; with Lakey, he would not have dared. This line of thought, however, was too unsettling to be pursued. How had he known that *she* would let him? There was one queer thing that her mind had been running away from: he had not really kissed her, not once. Of course, there could be explanations; perhaps he did not want her to smell the liquor on his breath or perhaps she had hali herself . . . ? *No*, said Dottie firmly; she would have to stop thinking this way. One thing was clear; anyone could see it. Dick had been hurt, very much hurt, she repeated, nodding, by a woman or women. That made him a law unto himself, as far as she was concerned. If he did not feel like kissing her, that was *his* business. Her lustrous contralto rose humming as she combed out her hair with her pocket comb: 'He's the kind of a man needs the kind of a woman like me-e.' She did a gay dance step, stumbling

39

a little in the long pyjamas, to the door. Her fingers snapped as she pulled out the overhead light.

Once she was settled in the narrow bed, with Dick sleeping heavily beside her, Dottie's bird thoughts flew affectionately to Mother, Class of 1908. Urge herself as she would to get her beauty sleep after a *very* tiring day, she felt a craving to talk and share the night's experiences with the person whom she designated as the nicest person in the world, who never condemned or censured, and who was always so tremendously interested in young people's doings. Tracing back the steps of her initiation, she longed to set the scene for Mother: this bare room way west in Greenwich Village, the moon's ray falling on the monk's-cloth bedspread, the drawing-table, the single wing chair with the neat slip cover, some sort of awning material, and Dick himself, of course, such an individual, with his restless chiselled face and incredible vocabulary. There were so many details of the last three days that would appeal to Mother: the wedding and going with him and Lakey that afternoon to the Whitney Museum and the three of them having dinner afterwards in a dinky Italian restaurant with a billiard table in front and wine in white cups and listening to him and Lakey argue about art and then going to the Modern Museum the next day, again the three of them, and to an exhibition of modernistic sculpture, and how Dottie had never suspected that he was even thinking of *her* because she could see that he was fascinated by Lakey (who wouldn't be?) and how she was still sure of that when he turned up at the boat this morning to see Lakey off, pretending that he wanted to give her some names of painters in Paris for her to meet. Even when he had asked *her*, at the dock, when the boat had sailed and there was a sort of a letdown, to have dinner with him tonight at that same restaurant (what a time she had finding it in a taxi, from the New Weston!), she had told herself that it was because she was Lakey's friend. She had been scared stiff at being alone with him because she was afraid he would be bored. And he *had* been rather silent and preoccupied until he looked straight into her eyes and popped that question. '*Do you want to come home with me?*' Would she ever, ever forget the casual tone of his voice when he said it?

What *would* startle Mother, undoubtedly, was the fact that there had been no thought of love on either side. She could hear her own low voice explaining to her pretty, bright-eyed parent that she and Dick had 'lived together' on quite a different basis. Dick, poor chap, her voice announced coolly, was still in love with his divorced wife, and, what was more (here Dottie took a deep breath and braced herself), deeply attracted to Lakey, her *very* best friend this year. In Dottie's imagination, her mother's blue eyes widened and her gold curls trembled with the little palsied shake of her head, as Dottie leaned forward, impressively, and reiterated, 'Yes, Mother, I could still swear it. Deeply attracted to Lakey. I faced the fact that night.' This scene, which her fancy was rehearsing, was taking place in her mother's little morning-room on Chestnut Street, though her mother, in actuality, had already left for the cottage at Gloucester, where Dottie was expected tomorrow or the day after: tiny Mrs Renfrew was dressed in her tailored powder-blue Irish linen dress, with bare, tanned arms, from golfing; Dottie herself was wearing her white shark-skin sports dress and brown-and-white spectator pumps. She finished her piece, stared at her toes, and fingered the box pleats of her dress, waiting calmly for her mother to speak. 'Yes, Dottie, I see. I *think* I can understand.' Both of them went on talking in low, even, musical voices, her mother a little more staccato and Dottie rumbling slightly. The atmosphere was grave and thoughtful. 'You are sure, dear, the hymen was punctured?' Dottie nodded, emphatically. Mrs Renfrew, a medical missionary's daughter, had been an invalid too in her youth, which gave her a certain anxiety about the physical aspect of things.

Dottie turned restlessly in the bed. 'You'll adore Mother,' she said to Dick in imagination. 'She's a terrifically vital person and much more attractive than I am: tiny, with a marvellous figure, and blue eyes and yellow hair that's just beginning to go grey. She cured herself of being an invalid, by sheer will power, when she met Daddy, her senior year at college, just when the doctors said she'd have to drop out of her class. She decided that it was wrong for a sick person to marry and so she got well. She's a great believer in love; we all are.' Here Dottie flushed and inked out the last few words. She must *not* let Dick think she was going to spoil their affair by falling in love with him; a remark like that one would be fatal. To let him see that there was no danger, it would be best, she decided, to frame a statement of some sort, clarifying her position. 'I'm very religious too, Dick,' she essayed with an apologetic smile. 'But I think I'm more pantheistic than most communicants of the Church. I love the Church for its ritual, but I believe God is everywhere. My generation is a little different from Mother's. *I* feel – all of us feel – that love and sex can be two separate things. They don't have to be, but they can be. You mustn't force sex to do the work of love or love to do the work of sex – that's quite a thought, isn't it?' she appended hurriedly, with a little nervous laugh, as her sources began to fail her. 'One of the older teachers told Lakey that you have to live without love, learn not to need it, in order to live *with* it. Lakey was terrifically impressed. Do you agree?' Dottie's fancied voice had been growing more and more timid as she proffered her philosophy to the sleeping man by her side.

Her imagination had dared to mention Lakey's name to him in connexion with love because she wanted to show that she was not jealous of the dark beauty, as he always called her; he did not like 'Lakey' for a nickname. One thing Dottie had noticed was the way he absently straightened his tie whenever Lakey turned to look at him, like a man catching sight of himself in a subway mirror. And the way he was always serious with her, not mocking and saturnine, even when they disagreed about art. Yet when Dottie had murmured, several times, 'Isn't she striking?' as they stood waving at her from the pier, in an effort to gain his confidence and share Lakey between them, he had merely shrugged his shoulders, as though Dottie were annoying him. 'She has a mind,' he retorted, the last time Dottie mentioned it.

Now that Lakey was on the high seas and *she* was in bed with Dick warm beside her, Dottie ventured to try out a new theory. Could it be, she asked herself, that Dick was attracted to Lakey platonically and that with herself it was more a physical thing? Lakey was awfully intelligent and knew a lot, but she was cold, most people thought. Maybe Dick only admired her beauty as an artist and liked Dottie better the other way. The idea was not very convincing, in spite of what he had said about her body surprising her and all that. Kay said that sophisticated men cared more about the woman's pleasure than they did about their own, but Dick (Dottie coughed gently) had not seemed to be carried away by passion, even when he was exciting her terribly. A wanness crept over her as she thought of Kay. Kay would tell her bluntly that she did not have Lakey's 'candle power', and that Dick obviously was using her as a substitute for Lakey, because Lakey was too much of a challenge, *too* beautiful and rich and fascinating for him to cope with in this bleak furnished room. 'Dick wouldn't want a girl who would involve his feelings' – she could hear Kay saying it in her loud, opinionated, Western voice – 'as Lakey would be bound to do, Renfrew. You're just an outlet for him, a one-night safety valve.' The assured words crushed Dottie like a steamroller, for she felt they were true. Kay would probably say also that Dottie had wanted to be 'relieved' of her virginity and was using Dick simply as an instrument.

Was that true too – awful thought? Was that how Dick had seen her? Kay meant well, explaining things so clearly, and the terrible part was, she was usually right. Or at least she always *sounded* right, being so absolutely disinterested and unconscious of hurting your feelings. The moment Dottie let herself listen to Kay, even in imagination, she lost her own authority and became the person Kay decreed her to be: a Boston old maid with a 'silver-cord' tie to her mother. It was the same with all the weaker members of the group. Kay used to take their love affairs, as Lakey once said, away from them and return them shrunk and labelled, like the laundry. That was what had happened to Polly Andrews' engagement. The boy she was supposed to marry had insanity in his family, and Kay had shown Polly so many charts about heredity that Polly had broken off with him and collapsed and had to go to the infirmary. And of course Kay was right; anybody would agree that Mr Andrews was enough of a liability without marrying into another family with melancholia in the background. Kay's advice was for Polly to live with him, since she loved him, and marry someone else later, when she wanted to have children. But Polly did not have the courage, although she wanted to terribly. The whole group, except Lakey, had thought what Kay did, at least about not marrying, but none of them had had the heart to say it, straight out, to Polly. That was usually the case: Kay came right out and said to the person what the others whispered among themselves.

Dottie sighed. She wished that Kay would not have to find out about her and Dick. But it was probably pretty inevitable, Dick being Harald's friend. Not that Dick would tell, being a gentleman and considerate; more likely, Dottie would tell herself, for Kay was very good at getting things out of you. In the end, you told Kay, wanting to hear her opinion more than you did *not* want to hear it. You were afraid of being afraid of the truth. Besides, Dottie saw, she could not really tell Mother or not for a long time, for Mother, being a different generation, would never see it as Dottie did, no matter how hard she tried, and the difference would just make her worried and unhappy. She would want to meet Dick, and then Daddy would meet him too and start wondering about marriage, which was utterly out of the question. Dottie sighed again. She knew she would have to tell someone – not the most intimate details, of course, but just the amazing fact that she had lost her virginity – and that someone was bound to be Kay.

Then Kay would discuss her with Dick. This was the thing Dottie shrank from most; she could not bear the idea of Kay dissecting and analysing her and explaining her medical history and Mother's clubs and Daddy's business connexions and their exact social position in Boston, which Kay greatly overestimated – they were not 'Brahmins', horrid word, at all. A gleam of amusement appeared in Dottie's eye; Kay was such an innocent, for all her know-it-all airs about clubs and society. Someone ought to tell her that only tiresome people or, to be frank, outsiders were concerned about such things nowadays. Poor honest Kay: five times, Dottie recalled drowsily, before she was penetrated and so much blood and pain. Didn't Lakey say she had a hide like a buffalo? Sex, Dottie opined, was just a matter of following the man, as in dancing – Kay was a frightful dancer and always tried to lead. Mother was quite right, she said to herself comfily, as she drifted off to sleep: it was a *great* mistake to let girls dance together as they did in so many of the boarding-schools of the second rank.

Chapter 3

'Get yourself a pessary.' Dick's muttered *envoi*, as he propelled her firmly to the door the next morning, fell on Dottie's ears with the effect of a stunning blow. Bewildered, she understood him to be saying 'Get yourself a peccary', and a vision of a coarse pig-like mammal they had studied in Zoology passed across her dazed consciousness, like a slide on a screen, followed by awful memories of Krafft-Ebing and the girl who had kept a goat at Vassar. Was this some variant she ought to know about, probably, of the old-maid joke? Tears dampened her eyes, though she tried to wink them back. Evidently, Dick hated her for what had taken place between them in the night; some men were like that, Kay said, after they had yielded to their passions: 'an expense of spirit in a waste of shame'. They had had the most dismal breakfast, which he had fixed, not letting her help him, on a grill in the clothes closet – scrambled eggs and coffee and the remains of a coffee ring from the bakery; no fruit or fruit juice. While they ate, he had hardly spoken; he had passed her the first section of the paper and then sat there, with his coffee, reading the sports news and the classified ads. When she had tried to give him the news section, he had impatiently pushed it back to her. Yet up to this very moment she had been telling herself that he might have got up 'on the wrong side of the bed', as Mother said; Daddy was cross too, sometimes, in the morning. Now she saw, though, that there was no use pretending any more; she had lost him. In his dressing-gown, with his hair disordered and his cruel biting smile and bitter taunts, he reminded her of someone. Hamlet – of course – putting Ophelia away from him. 'Get thee to a nunnery.' 'I loved you not.' But she could not say, like Ophelia, 'I was the more deceived' (which was the most pathetic moment in the whole play, the class had decided), because Dick had not deceived her; it was she who had been fooling herself. She stared at him, swallowing hard; a tear slid out of one eye. 'A female contraceptive, a plug,' Dick threw out impatiently. 'You get it from a lady doctor. Ask your friend Kay.'

Understanding dawned; her heart did a handspring. In a person like Dick, her feminine instinct carolled, this was surely the language of love. But it was a mistake to show a man that you had been unsure of him even for a second. 'Yes, Dick,' she whispered, her hand twisting the doorknob, while she let her eyes tell him softly what a deep, reverent moment this was, a sort of pledge between them. Luckily, he could never imagine the thing she had been thinking about the peccary! The happiness in her face caused him to raise an eyebrow and frown. 'I don't love you, you know, Boston,' he said warningly. 'Yes, Dick,' she replied. 'And you must promise me you won't fall in love with me.' 'Yes, Dick,' she repeated, more faintly. 'My wife says I'm a bastard, but she still likes me in the hay. You'll have to accept that. If you want that, you can have it.' 'I want it, Dick,' said Dottie in a feeble but staunch voice. Dick shrugged. 'I don't believe you, Boston. But we can give it a try.' A meditative smile appeared on his lips. 'Most women don't take me seriously when I state my terms. Then they get hurt. In the back of their heads, they have a plan to make me fall in love with them. I don't fall in love.' Dottie's warm eyes were teasing. 'What about Betty?' He cocked his head at the photograph. 'You think I love her?' Dottie nodded. He looked very serious. 'I'll tell you,' he said. 'I like Betty better than I've liked any woman. I've still got hot pants for her, if you want to call that love.' Dottie lowered her eyes and shook her head. 'But I won't change my life for her, and so Betty lit out. I don't blame her; I'd have done the same if I were made like Betty. Betty is all woman. She likes money, change, excitement, things, clothes, possessions.' He rubbed his strong jaw line with a thumb, as though he were studying a puzzle. 'I hate possessions. It's a funny thing, because you'd think I hated them because they meant stability, wouldn't you?' Dottie nodded. 'But I *like* stability; that's just the rub!' He had become quite tense and excited; his hands flexed nervously as he spoke. To Dottie's eyes he suddenly appeared boyish, like the worried young life-guards in their drifting boats at Cape Ann who sometimes dropped in at the cottage to discuss their futures with Mother. But of course that was what he must have been, once, growing up in Marblehead in the middle of the summer people; he was built like a swimmer, and she could picture him, brooding, in the lifesaving boat in one of those red jackets they wore – Mother said those boys were often marked for life by the experience of being betwixt and between, *with* the summer people but not *of* them.

'I like a man's life,' he said. 'A bar. The outdoors. Fishing and hunting. I like men's talk, that's never driving to get anywhere but just circles and circles. That's why I drink. Paris suited me – the crowd of painters and newspapermen and photographers. I'm a natural exile; if I have a few dollars or francs, I'm satisfied. I'll never pass third base as a painter, but I can draw and do nice clean work – an honest job. But I hate change, Boston, and I don't change myself. That's where I come a cropper with women. Women expect an affair to get better and better, and if it doesn't, they think it's getting worse. They think if I sleep with them longer I'm going to get fonder of them, and if I don't get fonder that I'm tiring of them. But for me it's all the same. If I like it the first time, I know I'm going to keep on liking it. I liked you last night and I'll keep on liking you as long as you want to come here. But don't harbour the idea that I'm going to like you more.' A truculent, threatening note had come into his voice with the last words; he stood, staring down at her harshly and teetering a little on his slippered feet. Dottie fingered the frayed tassel of his dressing-gown sash. 'All right, Dick,' she whispered.

'When you get yourself fixed up, you can bring your things here and I'll keep them for you. Just give me a call after you've been to the doctor.' A breath of last night's liquor wafted into her face; she fell back a step and averted her head. She had been hoping to know Dick better, but now, all at once, his strange philosophy of life gave her a sinking feeling. How would she fit him in this summer, for instance? He did not seem to realize that she would have to go up to Gloucester, the way she always did. If they were engaged, he could come up to visit, but of course they weren't and never could be; that was what he was telling her. To her horror, now that he had said he wanted her on *his* terms, Dottie found herself having second thoughts: what if she had lost her virginity with a man who scared her and who sounded, from his own description, like a pretty bad hat? For a moment, Dottie felt cornered, but her training had instilled the principle that it was a mark of low breeding

47

to consider that you might have been wrong in a person. 'I can't take you out,' he said more gently, as if he read her thoughts. 'I can only ask you to come here whenever you're in town. The welcome mat will be out. I've nothing but my bed to offer you. I don't go to theatres or night clubs and very seldom to restaurants.' Dottie opened her mouth, but Dick shook his head. 'I don't like ladies who want to pay my check. What I make with my posters and commissions takes care of my simple wants: my car fare, my bar bill, and a few frugal canned goods.' Dottie's clasped hands made a gesture of pity and remorse; she had been forgetting he was poor, which was why, of course, he was so short and gruff about seeing her – it was his pride that made him talk that way. 'Don't worry,' he reassured her. 'There's an aunt up in Marblehead who comes through with a cheque now and then. Some day, if I live long enough, I'll be her heir. But I hate possessions, Boston – forgive me if I think of you generically. I hate the itch to acquire. I don't care for this kinetic society.' Dottie felt the time had come to interpose a gentle remonstrance; she thought Dick's aunt would not altogether approve of his point of view. 'But Dick,' she said quietly, 'there are false possessions and true possessions. If everybody thought like you, the human race would never have got anywhere. We'd still be living in caves. Why, the wheel wouldn't even have been invented! People need an incentive, maybe not a money incentive . . .' Dick laughed. 'You must be the fiftieth woman who has said that to me. It's a credit to universal education that whenever a girl meets Dick Brown she begins to talk about the wheel and the lever. I've even had a French prostitute tell me about the fulcrum.' 'Good-bye, Dick,' Dottie said quickly. 'I mustn't keep you from your work.' 'Aren't you going to take the phone number?' he demanded, shaking his head in mock reproach. She handed him her little blue leather address book, and he wrote down his name and his landlady's telephone number in heavy drawing-pencil with a flourish; he had very striking handwriting. 'Good-bye, Boston.' He took her long chin beneath his thumb and forefinger and waggled it back and forth, absently. 'Remember: no monkey business; no falling in love. Honour bright.'

Notwithstanding this agreement, Dottie's heart was humming happily as she sat, three days later, beside Kay Petersen, in the woman doctor's office suite. Actions spoke louder than words, and whatever Dick might say, the fact remained that he had sent her here, to be wedded, as it were, by proxy, with the 'ring' or diaphragm pessary that the woman doctor dispensed. With her hair freshly waved and her complexion glowing from a facial, she wore a look of quiet assurance, the look of a contented matron, almost like Mother and her friends. Knowledge was responsible for her composure. Kay would hardly believe it, but Dottie, all by herself, had visited a birth-control bureau and received a doctor's name and a sheaf of pamphlets that described a myriad of devices – tampons, sponges, collar-button, wishbone, and butterfly pessaries, thimbles, silk rings, and coils – and the virtues and drawbacks of each. The new device recommended to Dottie by the bureau had the backing of the whole U.S. medical profession; it had been found by Margaret Sanger in Holland and was now for the first time being imported in quantity into the U.S.A., where our own manufacturers could copy it. It combined the maximum of protection with the minimum of inconvenience and could be used by any woman of average or better intelligence, following the instructions of a qualified physician.

This article, a rubber cap mounted on a coiled spring, came in a range of sizes and would be tried out in Dottie's vagina, for fit, wearing comfort, and so on, in the same way that various lenses were tried out for the eyes. The woman doctor would insert it, and having made sure of the proper size, she would teach Dottie how to put it in, how to smear it with contraceptive jelly and put a dab in the middle, how to crouch in a squatting position, fold the pessary between thumb and forefinger of the right hand, while parting the *labia majora* with the left hand, and edge the pessary in, so that it would snap into place, shielding the cervix, and finally how to follow it with the right middle finger, locate the cervix or soft neck of the uterus and make certain it was covered by the rubber. When this process had been rehearsed several times, to the watching doctor's satisfaction, Dottie would be taught how and when to douche, how much water to use, the proper height for the douche bag, and how to hold the labia firmly around the lubricated nozzle in order to get the best results. As she was leaving the office, the nurse would present her with a Manila envelope containing a tube of vaginal jelly and a small flat box with Dottie's personalized contraceptive in it. The nurse would instruct her how to care for the pessary: to wash it after each use, dry it carefully, and dust it with talcum before returning it to its box.

Kay and Harald had just about fainted when they heard what Dottie had been up to, behind their back. She came to see them in their apartment, bringing a Georgian silver creamer for a wedding present, just the sort of thing an old aunt would have inflicted on you, and a bunch of white peonies; Kay could not have been more disappointed when she thought that for the same money they could have had something plain and modern from Jensen's Danish shop. Then, when Harald went to the kitchen to start their supper (minced sea clams, the new canned kind, on toast), Dottie had quietly told Kay, who wanted to know what she had been doing, that she had taken Dick Brown for her lover. Coming from Dottie, that imperial phrase was simply perfect; Kay immediately saved it to tell Harald. It had happened only the night before, it seemed, in that studio room of Dick's, and already, today, Dottie had scurried around to the birth-control bureau and got all this literature, which she had with her in her pocketbook. Kay did not know what to say, but her face must have shown how appalled she was. She thought Dottie must be insane. Underneath that virile mask, which was what Harald called it, Dick Brown was a very warped personality, a dipsomaniac and a violent misogynist, with a terrible inferiority complex because of what had happened with his socialite wife. *His* motives were plain enough; he was using Dottie to pay back society for the wound it had inflicted on his ego – Kay could hardly wait till she could hear how Harald would analyse it, when they were alone. But in spite of her impatience, she asked Dottie to stay for supper with them, greatly to Harald's surprise, when he came in with the tray of drinks: after Harald had gone to the theatre, Dottie would be bound to tell more. 'I *had* to ask her,' she apologized to Harald, in a quick exchange in the kitchen. She put her lips to his ear. 'An awful thing has happened, and we're responsible! Dick Brown has seduced her.'

Yet every time she looked at Dottie, sitting in their living-room, so serene and conventional in her pearls and dressmaker suit, with white touches, and smart navy-blue sailor, sipping her Clover Club cocktail out of the Russel Wright cup and wiping a moustache of egg white from her long upper lip with a cocktail napkin, she just could not picture her in bed with a man. Afterwards, Harald said that she seemed quite an appetizing piece, in her chipmunk style, with her brown friendly eyes gleaming with quiet fun and her lashes aflutter whenever she looked at him. What he did not see was that a lot of it was clothes, for, thanks to a clever mother, Dottie dressed to perfection: she was the only one of the Boston contingent at Vassar who knew better than to wear tweeds and plaid mufflers, which made the poor things look like gaunt, elderly governesses out for a Sunday hike. But, according to Harald, her deep-bosomed figure, as revealed by her bias-cut blouses, gave promise of sensuality. Probably it meant something, Kay could not deny it, that it was Dick himself, on his own initiative, it seemed, who had told her to go and get fitted with a pessary!

'He said to consult *me*?' Kay repeated, wondering and somewhat flattered, after Harald had gone and they were washing the dishes. She had always thought Dick did not like her. The fact was that, though she knew about pessaries, she herself did not possess one. She had always used suppositories with Harald, and it embarrassed her a little now to have to confess this to Dottie, who seemed to have forged ahead of her so surprisingly and after only one night. ... She envied Dottie's enterprise in going to the birth-control bureau; until she was married, she herself would never have had the nerve. Dottie wanted to know whether Kay thought it was a good sign, Dick's saying that to her, and Kay had to admit that on the surface it was; it could only mean that Dick was expecting to sleep with her regularly, if you thought *that* was good. Examining her own emotions, Kay found she was piqued; it nettled her to guess that Dottie might have been better than *she* was in bed. Still, truth compelled her to tell Dottie that if it were only a half-hearted affair Dick would just use condoms (the way Harald had at first) or practise *coitus interruptus*. 'He must like you, Renfrew,' she declared, shaking out the dish mop. 'Or like you enough, anyway.'

That was Harald's verdict too. Riding on the top of a Fifth Avenue bus, on the way to the doctor's office, Kay repeated to Dottie what Harald had said of the etiquette of contraception, which, as he explained it, was like any other etiquette – the code of manners rising out of social realities. You had to look at it in terms of economics. No man of honour (which Dick, in Harald's opinion, was) would expect a girl to put up the doctor's fee, plus the price of the pessary and the jelly and the douche bag, unless he planned to sleep with her long enough for her to recover her investment. Of that, Dottie could rest assured. A man out for a casual affair found it simpler to buy Trojans by the dozen, even though it decreased his own pleasure; that way, he was not tied to the girl. The lower classes, for instance, almost never transferred the burden of contraception to the woman; this was a discovery of the middle class. A workingman was either indifferent to the danger of conception or he mistrusted the girl too much to leave the matter in her hands.

This mistrust, Harald said, which was deep in the male nature, made even middle-class and professional men wary of sending a girl for a pessary; too many shotgun weddings had resulted from a man's relying on a woman's assurance that the contraceptive was in. Then there was the problem of the apparatus. The unmarried girl who lived with her family required a place to keep her pessary and her douche bag where her mother was not likely to find them while doing out the bureau drawers. This meant that the man, unless *he* was married, had to keep them for her, in his bureau drawer or his bathroom. The custodianship of these articles (Harald was so entertaining in his slow-spoken, careful, dry way), assumed the character of a sacred trust. If their guardian were a man of any delicacy, they precluded the visits of other women to the apartment, who might open drawers or rummage in the medicine cabinet or even feel themselves entitled to use the douche bag hallowed to 'Her'.

With a married woman, if the affair was serious, the situation was the same: she bought a second pessary and a douche bag, which she kept in her lover's apartment, where they exercised a restraining influence if he felt tempted to betray her. A man entrusted with this important equipment was bonded, so to speak, Harald said, like a bank employee; when he did stray with another woman, he was likely to do it in her place or in a hotel room or even a taxi – some spot not consecrated by the sacral reminders. In the same way, a married woman pledged her devotion by committing her second pessary to her lover's care; only a married woman of very coarse fibre would use the same pessary for both husband and lover. So long as the lover had charge of the pessary, like a medieval knight with the key to his lady's chastity belt, he could feel that she was true to him. Though this could be a mistake. One adventurous wife Harald described was said to have pessaries all over town, like a sailor with a wife in every port, while her husband, a busy stage director, assured himself of her good behaviour by a daily inspection of the little box in her medicine cabinet, where the conjugal pessary lay in its dusting of talcum powder.

'Harald has made quite a study of it, hasn't he?' commented Dottie with a demure twinkle. 'I'm spoiling it,' replied Kay seriously. 'The way Harald tells it, you can see the whole thing in terms of property values. The fetishism of property. I told him he ought to write it up for *Esquire*; they publish some quite good things. Don't you think he should?' Dottie did not know what to answer; Harald's approach, she felt, was rather 'unpleasant', so cold and cerebral, though perhaps he knew what he was talking about. It was certainly a different angle from what you got in the birth-control pamphlets.

Furthermore, Kay quoted, the disposal of the pessary and the douche bag presented a problem when a love affair was breaking up. What was the man to do with these 'hygienic relics' after he or the woman tired? They could not be returned through the mail, like love letters or an engagement ring, though crude lads, Harald said, had been known to do this; on the other hand, they could not be put in the trash basket for the janitor or the landlady to find; they would not burn in the fireplace without giving off an awful smell, and to keep them for another woman, given our bourgeois prejudices, was unthinkable. A man could carry them, stuffed into a paper bag, to one of the city's wastebaskets late at night or dump them into the river, but friends of Harald's who had done this had actually been halted by the police. Probably because they acted so furtive. Trying to get rid of a woman's pessary and fountain syringe, the corpus delicti of a love affair, was exactly, as Harald put it, like trying to get rid of a body. '*I* said, you could do the way murderers do in detective stories: check them in the Grand Central parcel room and then throw away the check.' Kay gave her rollicking laugh, but Dottie shivered. She saw that it would not be funny if the problem came up for her and Dick; every time she thought of the future, of the terrible complications a secret affair got you into, she almost wanted to give up and go home. And all

Kay's conversation, though doubtless well meant, seemed calculated to dismay her with its offhand boldness and cynicism.

The upshot, continued Kay, was that no bachelor in his right mind would send a girl to the doctor to be fitted if he did not feel pretty serious about her. The difficulties only arose, of course, with respectable married women or nice girls who lived with their parents or with other girls. There were women of the looser sort, divorcées and unattached secretaries and office workers living in their own apartments, who equipped themselves independently and kept their douche bags hanging on the back of their bathroom door for anybody to see who wandered in to pee during a cocktail party. One friend of Harald's, a veteran stage manager, always made it a point to look over a girl's bathroom before starting anything; if the bag was on the door, it was nine to one he would make her on the first try.

They descended from the bus on lower Fifth Avenue; Dottie's complexion had come out in those blotches like hives or shingles – a sure sign that she was nervous. Kay was sympathetic. This was a big step for Dottie; she had been trying to give her an inkling of just how big a step it was, much more than losing your virginity. For a married woman, naturally, it was different; Harald had agreed immediately that it would be a good idea for her to make an appointment and go along with Dottie to be fitted too. She and Harald both loathed children and had no intention of having any; Kay had seen in her own family how offspring could take the joy out of marriage. Her tribe of brothers and sisters had kept her Dads' nose to the grindstone; if he had not had so many children, he might have been a famous specialist, instead of a hard-worked G.P., with only a wing in the hospital to commemorate the work he had done in orthopædics and on serums for meningitis. Poor Dads had quite a kick out of sending her east to Vassar; she was the oldest and the brightest, and she had the feeling that he wanted her to have the life he might have had himself, out in the big world, where he would have got the homage he deserved. He still had invitations to come and do research in the big eastern laboratories, but now he was too old to learn, he said; the cerebral arteries were hardening. He had just crashed through nobly with a cheque; she and Harald had been moved almost to tears by the size of it – far more than he and Mums would have spent on trains and hotels if they had come on for the wedding. It was a declaration of faith, said Harald. And she and Harald did not intend to betray that faith by breeding children, when Harald had his name to make in the theatre. The theatre – strange coincidence! – was one of Dads' big passions; he and Mums went to see all the touring companies in Salt Lake City and had tickets every night, nearly, when they came to New York for medical meetings. Not leg shows, either; Dads' favourite playwright, after Shakespeare, was Bernard Shaw. Harald thought it would be a nice idea for Kay to keep the programmes of the worthwhile plays he and she saw and send them on to Dads; that way, he would feel in touch.

Dads, like all modern doctors, believed in birth control and was for sterilizing criminals and the unfit. He would certainly approve of what Kay was doing. What he would think about Dottie was another question. Kay herself had been horrified to hear that Dottie had made the appointment in her real name: 'Dorothy Renfrew', not even 'Mrs'. As though she were living in Russia or Sweden, instead of the old U.S.A. A lot of people who would not be shocked at her for sleeping with Dick (that could happen to anybody) would look at her askance if they could see what she was up to this minute. The things you did in private were your own business, but this was practically public! Kay ran an apprehensive eye up and down Fifth Avenue; you could never tell who might be watching them from a passing bus or a taxi. She had begun to be nervous herself, on Dottie's behalf, and to be crosser and crosser with Dick. Harald would never have exposed *her* to an ordeal like this. After the first few times, he had gone to the drugstore himself and bought her suppositories and a bulb type of douche and Zonite, so that she would not have to face the druggist herself. Kay gripped Dottie's arm, to steady her as they crossed the street with the traffic light; she rued the day she had invited Dick to her wedding, knowing what he was. Why, the office might be raided and the doctor's records impounded and published in the papers, which would *kill* Dottie's family, who would probably turn around and blame Kay, as the pathfinder of the college group. She felt she was making quite a sacrifice in coming with Dottie today, to lend moral support, though Dottie insisted that birth control was perfectly legal and aboveboard, thanks to a court decision that allowed doctors to prescribe contraceptives for the prevention or cure of disease. As they rang the doctor's bell, Kay had to laugh, suddenly, at Dottie's expression: you could almost see Mrs Pankhurst in her resolute eye.

And indeed Dottie's zealotry was reflected in the furnishings of the woman doctor's office, which had a sort of militant plainness, like the headquarters of a missionary sect. There was a single upholstered couch, with two antimacassars aligned on its back; against the tan walls was a series of straight chairs. The magazine rack held copies of *Hygeia, Parents, Consumers' Research Bulletin*, a current issue of the *Nation*, and a back number of *Harper's*. On the walls were etchings showing overcrowded slums teeming with rickety children and a lithograph of an early hospital ward in which untended young women, with babies at their side, were dying – of puerperal fever, Dottie whispered. There was a pious hush in the atmosphere which was emphasized by the absence of any smoking equipment and by the solemn whirring of a fan. Kay and Dottie, who had automatically taken cigarettes out of their cases, replaced them after a survey of the room. There were two other patients waiting, reading *Hygeia* and *Consumers' Research Bulletin*. One, a sallow thin woman of about thirty, with a pair of cotton gloves on her lap, wore no wedding ring, a fact which Dottie silently called to Kay's attention. The second patient, in rimless glasses and worn Oxfords, was almost middle-aged. The sight of these two women, far from well-to-do, and of the prints on the walls had a sobering effect on the girls. Kay, made to reflect on 'how much good the doctor was doing', a thing often said of her father by the élite of Salt Lake City, felt ashamed of the brittle, smart way she had talked about birth control on the bus, though she had only been quoting Harald. 'Extend your antennae, girls,' was a favourite apothegm of the teachers she had respected most, and Kay, reminded of her father's non-paying patients, saw, to her discomfiture, that she and Dottie were just the frills on the doctor's practice.

What she could not remember, though Harald kept drilling it into her, was that she and her friends did not count any more, except as individuals, in the wider picture of American society, exemplified by these two women, right here in this office. Last night, after the theatre, when the three of them had gone to have a beer in a speak-easy, Harald had been explaining just that to Dottie. The transfer of financial power, he showed, from Threadneedle Street to Wall Street was an event in world history comparable to the defeat of the Spanish Armada, which had ushered in the era of capitalism. When Roosevelt, just now, had gone off the gold standard, it was a declaration of independence from Europe and an announcement of a new, flexible epoch. The NRA and the eagle were symbols of the arrival of a new class to power. Their class, the upper middle, he told the two girls, was finished politically and economically; its best elements would merge with the rising class of workers and farmers and technicians, of which he, as a stage technician, was one. Take the theatre as an example. In the days of Belasco, the director used to be king; today, the director was dependent, first of all on his backers, who might be a combine, and second, and even more important, on his master electrician, who could make or break a play by the way he handled the lighting – behind every name director, like Jed Harris, for instance, there was a genius electrician, just as there was a genius camera-man behind every name movie director. The same in radio; it was the engineers, the men in the control room, who really counted. A doctor today was dependent on his technicians, on the men in the lab and the X-ray room. 'They're the boys who can make or break a diagnosis.'

Last night, it had thrilled Kay to imagine the future he predicted, of mass abundance through the machine. She had enjoyed watching him impress Dottie, who had not suspected he was such a social thinker since he did not put that side of himself in his letters. 'As individuals,' he said, 'you girls have something to pass on to individuals in the rising class, just as old Europe still has something to pass on to America.' It relieved her to hear him say this, with his arm clasping her waist and Dottie looking on, wide-eyed, for Kay did not want to be left behind by history and at the same time she was not really strong for the idea of equality; she liked, she had to confess, to be superior. Harald, when he was in a good mood, as he was last night, seemed to think this would still be possible, though with a difference, in the new age.

Last night, he had explained technocracy to Dottie, to show her there was nothing to fear from the future, if it was managed with scientific intelligence. In an economy of plenty and leisure, which the machine had already made feasible, everybody would only have to work a few hours a day. It was through such an economy that his class, the class of artists and technicians, would come naturally to the top; the homage people paid to money today would be paid in the future to the engineers and contrivers of leisure-time activities. More leisure meant more time for art and culture. Dottie wanted to know what would happen to the capitalists (her father was in the import business), and Kay looked inquiringly at Harald. 'Capital will blend into government,' said Harald. 'After a brief struggle. That's what we're witnessing now. The administrator, who's just a big-scale technician, will replace the capitalist in industry. Individual ownership is becoming obsolete; the administrators are running the show.' 'Take Robert Moses,' put in Kay. 'He's transforming the whole face of New York with his wonderful new parkways and playgrounds.' And she urged Dottie to go to Jones Beach, which was an inspiring example, she really felt this herself, of planning on a large scale for leisure. 'Everybody from Oyster Bay,' she added, 'drives over there now to swim. It's quite the thing to do, instead of swimming at a club.' Private enterprise, suggested Harald, still had a part to play, if it had breadth of vision. Radio City, where he had worked for a while as a stage manager's assistant, was an example of civic planning, undertaken by enlightened capitalists, the Rockefellers. Kay brought in the Modern Museum, which had Rockefeller backing too. New York, she honestly thought, was experiencing a new Renaissance, with the new Medicis competing with public ownership to create a modern Florence. You could see it even in Macy's, agreed Harald, where enlightened merchant-Jews, the Strauses, were training a corps of upper-middle-class technicians, like Kay, to make the store into something more than a business, something closer to a civic centre or permanent fairgrounds, with educational exhibits, like the old Crystal Palace. Then Kay talked about the smart new renovated tenements in the Fifties and Eighties, along the East River, black with white trim and white Venetian blinds; they were still another example of intelligent planning by capital! Vincent Astor had done them. Of course, the rents were rather high, but look what you got: views of the river just as good as from Sutton Place mansions, sometimes a garden, the Venetian blinds, like the jalousies but modernized, and completely up-to-date kitchens. When you thought that they had just been eyesores, probably full of vermin and unsanitary hall toilets, till the Astor interests fixed them up!

And other landlords were following their example, turning old blocks of barracky tenements into compact apartment buildings four and five stories high, with central courts planted with grass and shrubs and two- and three-room apartments for young people – some with fireplaces and built-in bookcases and all with brand-new plumbing and stove and refrigerator. A lot of waste space was being eliminated in these buildings – no more foyers or dining-rooms, which were obsolete conventions. Harald, Kay explained, was a perfect fanatic about waste space. A house, he thought, should be a machine for living. When they found a permanent apartment, they were going to have everything built in: bookcases, bureaux, chests. The beds were going to be mattresses and springs, supported by four low pegs, and they were thinking about having a table to eat on that would fold up into the wall like a Murphy bed – a single leaf of wood shaped like an ironing-board but broader.

Kay had seldom been happier than she was just then, outlining these plans to Dottie, while Harald listened with one quizzically raised eyebrow, correcting her whenever she made a mistake. It was Dottie who slightly spoiled things by asking, in those gently rumbling tones, what happened to the poor people who had lived in those tenements before. Where did they go? This was a question Kay had never thought to ask herself, and Harald did not know the answer, which at once put him in a darker mood. '*Cui bono?*' he said. '"Who profits?" Eh?' And he signalled the waiter for another round of beer. This alarmed Kay, who knew he had an understudy rehearsal at ten in the morning. 'Your question is at once simple and profound,' he went on, to Dottie. '"What happens to the poor?"' He stared gloomily ahead of him, as if into empty space. 'Do they go to Mr Moses' big clean white antiseptic beach that Kay finds so inspiring and "civic-minded"? No; they don't, my girls; they lack the price of admission and the car to transport them. Instead, it becomes the perquisite of the Oyster Bay set – damnable profiteers and grabbers, with their pretty powdered noses sniffing at the public trough.' Kay saw that he was sinking into a Slough of Despond (they had coined this name for his sudden, Scandinavian fits of bitter depression), but she managed to steer the conversation into safer channels by getting him to talk to Dottie about recipes and cooking, one of his favourite themes, so that they were home and in bed by one-thirty. Harald was very paradoxical; he would whirl around and attack the very things he believed in most. As she sat in the doctor's waiting-room and covertly examined the other patients, she could easily imagine him saying that she and Dottie were 'profiteering' on the birth-control crusade, whose real aim was to limit the families of the poor. Mentally, she began to defend herself. Birth control, she argued, was for those who knew how to use it and value it – the educated classes. Just like those renovated tenements; if poor people were allowed to move into them, they would wreck them right away, through lack of education.

Dottie's thoughts too were running on the night before. She was fascinated by the way Kay and Harald had their whole life planned. When Kay started at Macy's in September, Harald would get their breakfast every morning and then sweep and clean and do the marketing, so that everything would be ready for Kay to get the dinner when she came home from work; over the week-end, they would map out the meals for the week. Right now, Harald was teaching her to cook. His specialties were Italian spaghetti, which any beginner could learn, and those minced sea clams – terribly good – they had the other night, and meat balls cooked in salt in a hot skillet (no fat), and a quick-and-easy meat loaf his mother had taught him: one part beef, one part pork, one part veal; add sliced onions, pour over it a can of Campbell's tomato soup and bake in the oven. Then there was his chile con carne, made with canned kidney beans and tomato soup again and onions and half a pound of hamburger; you served it over rice, and it stretched for six people. That was his mother's too. Kay, not to be outdone – she said, laughing – had written *her* mother for some of the family recipes, the cheaper ones: veal kidneys done with cooking sherry and mushrooms, and a marvellous jellied salad called Green Goddess, made with lime gelatin, shrimps, mayonnaise, and alligator pear, which could be fixed the night before in ramekins and then unmoulded on lettuce cups. Kay had found a new cookbook that had a whole section on casserole dishes and another on foreign recipes – so much more adventurous than Fannie Farmer and that old Boston Cooking School. On Sundays, they planned to entertain, either at a late breakfast of chipped beef or corned-beef hash or at a casserole supper. The trouble with American cooking, Harald said, was the dearth of imagination in it and the terrible fear of innards and garlic. He put garlic in everything and was accounted quite a cook. What made a dish, Kay said, was the seasoning. 'Listen to how Harald fixes chipped beef. He puts in mustard and Worcestershire sauce and grated cheese – is that right? – and green pepper and an egg; you'd never think it bore any relation to that old milky chipped beef we got at college.' Her happy laugh rang out in the speak-easy. If Dottie wanted to learn, she should study the recipes in the *Tribune*. 'I *love* the *Tribune*,' she said. 'Harald converted me from the *Times*.' 'The *Tribune*'s typography has it all over the *Times*'s,' observed Harald.

'How lucky you are, Kay,' Dottie said warmly, 'to have found a husband who's interested in cooking and who's not afraid of experiment. Most men, you know, have awfully set tastes. Like Daddy, who won't hear of "made" dishes, except the good old beans on Saturday.' There was a twinkle in her eye, but she really did mean it that Kay was awfully lucky. Kay leaned forward. 'You ought to get your cook to try the new way of fixing canned beans. You just add catsup and mustard and Worcestershire sauce and sprinkle them with plenty of brown sugar, cover them with bacon, and put them in the oven in a Pyrex dish.' 'It sounds terribly good,' said Dottie, 'but Daddy would die.' Harald nodded. He began to talk, very learnedly, about the prejudice that existed in conservative circles against canned goods; it went back, he said, to an old fear of poisoning that derived from home canning, where spoilage was common. Modern machinery and factory processes, of course, had eliminated all danger of bacteria, and yet the prejudice lingered, which was a pity, since many canned products, like vegetables picked at their peak and some of the Campbell soups, were better than anything the home cook could achieve. 'Have you tasted the new Corn Niblets?' asked Kay. Dottie shook her head. 'You ought to tell your mother about them. It's the whole-kernel corn. Delicious. Almost like corn on the cob. Harald discovered them.' She considered. 'Does your mother know about iceberg lettuce? It's a new variety, very crisp, with wonderful keeping powers. After you've tried it, you'll never want to see the old Boston lettuce again. Simpson lettuce, they call it.' Dottie sighed. Did Kay realize, she wondered, that she had just passed the death sentence on Boston lettuce, Boston baked beans, and the Boston School cookbook?

Nevertheless, Dottie did intend, when she got up to the cottage, to pass some of Kay's tips on to Mother. She had had Mother terribly on her conscience ever since she had got back to the Vassar Club that fatal morning (was it only two days ago?) and found a message that Gloucester had been calling the night before and again at 9.00 a.m. Telling her mother her first real lie – that she had spent the night with Polly in Polly's aunt's apartment – was one of the hardest things she had ever done. It still cut her heart to think that she could not tell Mother about her visit to the birth-control bureau and now to this doctor's office, all of which would have interested Mother so tremendously as a Vassar woman with Lucy Stoners and women's-rights fighters in her own college class. The cruel sense of withholding something had made Dottie more than usually alert to the small items of interest she could bring back to Gloucester in compensation – like Kay and Harald's menus and housekeeping arrangements, which would vastly amuse Mother. Perhaps she could even tell her that *Kay* had been to birth-control headquarters and been sent on here to get this new device?

'Miss Renfrew,' called the nurse softly, and Dottie started and got up. Her eyes met Kay's in a last desperate look, like a boarding-school girl summoned to the headmistress' office, and she advanced slowly into the doctor's consulting-room, her knees shaking and knocking so that they would hardly hold her. At the desk sat a white-coated, olive-skinned woman with a big bun of black hair. The doctor was very handsome, about forty years old; her large black brilliant eyes rested on Dottie briefly like electric rays, while one broad hand with tapering fingers motioned Dottie to a chair. She began to take the medical history, just as if it were an ordinary consultation; her pencil matter-of-factly wrote down Dottie's answers about measles and whooping cough, eczema and asthma. Yet Dottie became aware of a mesmeric, warm charm that emanated from her and that seemed to tell Dottie not to be afraid. It occurred to Dottie, almost with surprise, that they were both women. The doctor's femininity was a reassuring part of her professional aspect, like her white coat; on her hand shone a broad gold wedding ring, which seemed to Dottie serene and ample, like the doctor herself.

'Have you ever had intercourse, Dorothy?' The question appeared to flow so naturally from the sequence of operations and previous diseases that Dottie's answer was given before she had time to gulp. 'Good!' exclaimed the doctor, and when Dottie glanced up, wonderingly, the doctor gave an encouraging smile. 'That makes it easier for us to fit you,' she said, commending, as though Dottie had been a good child. Her skill astonished Dottie, who sat with wondering eyes, anaesthetized by the doctor's personality, while a series of questions, like a delicately manoeuvring forceps, extracted information that ought to have hurt but didn't. This painless interrogation revealed no more curiosity about the why and the who of Dottie's defloration than if Dick had been a surgical instrument: had Dottie been completely penetrated, had there been much bleeding, much pain? What method of contraception had been used, had the act been repeated? 'Withdrawal,' murmured the doctor, writing it down on a separate pad. 'We like to know,' she explained, with a quick, personal smile, 'what methods our patients have used before coming to us. When was this intercourse had?' 'Three nights ago,' said Dottie, colouring and feeling that now, at last, they were going to touch the biographical. 'And the date of your last period?' Dottie supplied it, and the doctor glanced at her desk calendar. 'Very good,' she said. 'Go into the bathroom, empty your bladder, and take off your girdle and step-ins; you may leave your slip on, but unfasten your brassière, please.'

Dottie did not mind the pelvic examination or the fitting. Her bad moment came when she was learning how to insert the pessary by herself. Though she was usually good with her hands and well co-ordinated, she felt suddenly unnerved by the scrutiny of the doctor and the nurse, so exploratory and impersonal, like the doctor's rubber glove. As she was trying to fold the pessary, the slippery thing, all covered with jelly, jumped out of her grasp and shot across the room and hit the sterilizer. Dottie could have died. But apparently this was nothing new to the doctor and the nurse. 'Try again, Dorothy,' said the doctor calmly, selecting another diaphragm of the correct size from the drawer. And, as though to provide a distraction, she went on to give a little lecture on the history of the pessary, while watching Dottie's struggles out of the corner of her eye: how a medicated plug had been known to the ancient Greeks and Jews and Egyptians, how Margaret Sanger had found the present diaphragm in Holland, how the long fight had been waged through the courts here. . . . Dottie had read all this, but she did not like to say so to this dark, stately woman, moving among her instruments like a priestess in the temple. As everybody knew from the newspapers, the doctor herself had been arrested only a few years before, in a raid on a birth-control clinic, and then been freed by the court. To hear her talk on the subject of her life-long mission was an honour, like touching the mantle of a prophet, and Dottie felt awed.

'Private practice must be rather a letdown,' she suggested sympathetically. To a dynamic person like the doctor, fitting girls like herself could not be much of a challenge. 'There's still a great work to be done,' sighed the doctor, removing the diaphragm with a short nod of approval. She motioned Dottie down from the table. 'So many of our clinic patients won't use the pessary when we've fitted them or won't use it regularly.' The nurse bobbed her white-capped head and made a clucking noise. 'And those are the ones, aren't they, doctor, who need to limit their families most? With our private patients, Miss Renfrew, we can be surer that our instructions are being followed.' She gave a little smirk. 'I won't need you now, Miss Brimmer,' said the doctor, washing her hands at the sink. The nurse went out, and Dottie started to follow her, feeling herself a rather foolish figure, with her stockings rolled down around her ankles and her brassière loose. 'Just a minute, Dorothy,' said the doctor, turning, and fixing her with her brilliant gaze. 'Are there any questions?' Dottie hesitated; she wanted awfully, now that the ice was broken, to tell the doctor about Dick. But to Dottie's sympathetic eye, the doctor's lightly lined face looked tired. Moreover, she had other patients; there was still Kay waiting outside. And supposing the doctor, when she heard, should tell her to go back to the Vassar Club and pack and take the six o'clock train home and never see Dick again? Then the pessary would be wasted, and all would have been for nothing.

'Medical instruction,' said the doctor kindly, with a thoughtful look at Dottie, 'can often help the patient to the fullest sexual enjoyment. The young women who come to me, Dorothy, have the right to expect the deepest satisfaction from the sexual act.' Dottie scratched her jaw; the skin on her upper chest mottled. What she especially wanted to ask was something a doctor might know, above all, a married doctor. She had of course not confided in Kay the thing that was still troubling her: what did it mean if a man made love to you and didn't kiss you once, not even at the most thrilling moment? This was something not mentioned in the sex books, so far as Dottie knew, and perhaps it was too ordinary an occurrence for scientists to catalogue or perhaps there was some natural explanation, as she had thought before, like hali or trench mouth. Or maybe he had taken a vow, like some people vowing never to shave or never to wash till a certain thing they wanted came about. But she could not get it out of her mind, and whenever she recalled it, not meaning to, she would flush all over, just as she was doing now. She was afraid, down in her heart, that Dick was probably what Daddy called a 'wrong un'. And here was her chance to find out. But she could not, in this gleaming surgery, choose the words to ask. How would you put it in technical language? 'If the man fails to osculate?' Her dimple ruefully flashed; not even Kay could say such a thing. 'Is there anything abnormal . . . ?' she began and then stared helplessly at the tall, impassible woman. 'If prior to the sexual act . . .' 'Yes?' encouraged the doctor. Dottie gave her throaty, scrupulous cough. 'It's terribly simple,' she apologized, 'but I can't seem to say it.' The doctor waited. 'Perhaps I can help you, Dorothy. Any techniques,' she began impressively, 'that give both partners pleasure are perfectly allowable and natural. There are no practices, oral or manual, that are wrong in love-making, as long as both partners enjoy them.' Goose flesh rose on Dottie; she knew, pretty well, what the doctor meant, and could not help wondering, with horror, if the doctor, as a married woman, practised what she preached. Her whole nature recoiled. 'Thank you, doctor,' she said quietly, cutting the topic off.

In her gloved hand, when she was dressed and powdered, she took the Manila envelope the nurse in the ante-room handed her and paid out new bills from her billfold. She did not wait for Kay. Across the streets was a drugstore, with hot-water bottles in the window. She went in and managed to choose a fountain syringe. Then she seated herself in the phone booth and rang Dick's number. After a long time, a voice answered. Dick was out. This possibility had never occurred to her. She had assumed without thinking that he would be there waiting for her, when she had carried out her mission. 'Just give me a call.' Now she walked slowly across Eighth Street and into Washington Square, where she sat down on a park bench, with her two parcels beside her. When she had sat there nearly an hour, watching the children play and listening to some young Jewish men argue, she went back to the drugstore and tried

Dick's number again. He was still out. She returned to her park bench, but someone had taken her place. She walked about a bit till she found another seat; this time, because the bench was crowded, she held the packages on her lap. The syringe in its box, was bulky, and kept slipping off her lap every time she moved or crossed her legs; then she would have to bend down to pick it up. Her underwear felt sticky from the lubricants the doctor had used, and this nasty soiled sensation made her fear she had got the curse. Soon the children began leaving the park; she heard the church bells ringing for evensong. She would have liked to go in to pray, which she often did at vesper time (and to take a hurried look, with no one watching, at the back of her skirt), but she could not, because of the packages, which would not be decent in a church. Nor could she face going back to the Vassar Club with them; she was sharing a room with Helena Davison, who might ask what she had been buying. It was getting late, long past six o'clock, but the park was still light, and everyone, she thought, now noticed her. The next time, she tried Dick from the phone in the Brevoort Hotel lobby, after going first to the ladies' room. She left a message: 'Miss Renfrew is waiting in Washington Square, on a bench.' She was afraid to wait in the hotel lobby, where someone she knew might come in. Going back to the square, she was sorry she had left the message, because, after that, she did not dare annoy the landlady by calling back again. It now seemed to her strange that Dick had not rung her up at the Vassar Club, just to say hello, in the two and a half days that had passed since she left him. She considered calling there, to ask if there were any messages for her, but she dreaded getting Helena. And anyway, she could not leave the square, in case Dick should come. The park was getting dark, and the benches were filling up with pairs of lovers. It was after nine o'clock when she resolved to leave because men had started to accost her and a policeman had stared at her curiously. She remembered Kay's remarks on the bus about the 'corpus delicti' of a love affair. How true!

It did not prove anything, she told herself, that Dick was not at home. There could be a thousand reasons; perhaps he had been called out of town. Yet it did prove something, and she knew it. It was a sign. In the dark, she began quietly to cry and decided to count to a hundred before going. She had reached a hundred for the fifth time when she recognized that it was no use; even if he got her message, he would never come tonight. There seemed to be only one thing left to do. Hoping that she was unobserved, she slipped the contraceptive equipment under the bench she was sitting on and began to walk as swiftly as she could, without attracting attention, to Fifth Avenue. A cruising taxi picked her up at the corner and drove her, quietly sobbing, to the Vassar Club. The next morning early, before the town was stirring, she took the train for Boston.

Chapter 4

One afternoon in September, Harald lost his new job. When he told
the director, softly, where to get off, the nance gave him notice. If
Kay could only write, she could have sold the story of it to the *New
Yorker*, she thought. She was just back from work that day and
tying on her apron when she heard his step on the stairs and wondered – they did not usually break for dinner till six-thirty or seven.
He had a pint of gin from the cordial shop with him, and there was
a glitter in his hollow, dark eyes. The minute she saw him, she
guessed what had happened. 'I'm aware,' he said to her stiffly,
'of the bitter irony behind this. You seem to have picked a lemon.'
'Why do you say that?' protested Kay, starting to cry because that
was not at all what she was thinking.

And yet it *was* ironical, you had to admit. 1 October, their summer sublet was up, and they were due to move into an apartment of
their own, in a new smart building made over from some old tenements, with a landscaped court and an inside doorman in a little
booth, like a concierge. They had signed the lease and paid the first
month's rent – $102.50, including gas and electricity. This was
more than Harald had ever *dreamed* of paying, but Kay had argued
that economists said you were supposed to count one-fourth of
your income for rent; she made $25 a week at Macy's, and he would
be making $75 when the show opened. This allowed them to pay
$100 (or would have till this afternoon!), and they would really be
paying less, when you subtracted the utilities. Manwise, Harald
had pointed out that you weren't *obliged* to pay a quarter of your
income – a mere factual observation, he insisted, when Kay wanted
to quote it to their friends to show how witty he could be. She loved
Harald's *risus sardonicus*, as Helena Davison's mother called it.

Yet now, strange to tell, as she followed him into the living-
room and watched him coolly fit a cigarette into his holder with

that enigmatic half-smile he had, she felt her furies rising. She was certain, just looking at him, that he was going to want to renege on the lease because of losing his job, and the evil thought flashed through her mind that he had lost it as a *pretext* for not moving into the apartment. 'Slow there, Strong!' she warned herself (after three months, she still could not get used to 'Petersen'). 'Put on the brakes.' Tonight, of all nights, Harald needed her sympathy, though his pride would not let him show it.

Poor Harald, he had been unemployed nearly all summer. The play he was with had folded when the hot weather came; the Saturday after their wedding, the closing notices went up. By that time, it was too late to get anything in one of the summer theatres, though in his place Kay thought she might have *tried*. Harald did not have her perseverance; that was a thing about him she had discovered. Getting married, instead of spurring him on, seemed, she sometimes feared, to have produced almost the contrary effect. But finally, out of the blue, he had been sent for about this new job, the best he had had yet, being in charge of the book of a satiric revue on the depression called 'Hail Columbia' which was going to open in October; officially, he was only the stage manager, but the producer told him he could have a crack at directing the sketches, since the over-all director, an old Shubert whore, was only used to doing girl shows. The producer, it turned out, had had his eye on Harald for quite a while and was giving him this chance to prove himself.

'Isn't it almost too good to be true?' Kay had exulted; she could see Harald's name on the programme with a credit as assistant director. But in the second week of rehearsals came the rift in the lute. The producer did not make clear the different spheres of authority; the way Harald analysed it, it was because of an inner conflict: he was undecided himself as to just what kind of show he wanted, a literate revue with some bright songs and really topical sketches or the usual stupid omnium-gatherum held together by a couple of stars. So he was using Harald as a sort of guinea-pig. Harald would rehearse a scene, and as soon as he had it set, the director would come and change it – introduce a line of show girls into an unemployment march or gag up a sketch about the milk strike with some farmerettes in straw hats. The authors were a hundred per cent on Harald's side, but the producer, when appealed to, would just vacillate, saying 'Try it this way for a while' or 'Wait!' Meanwhile, all through rehearsals, the director had been riding Harald every chance he got – if Harald was a few minutes late after the dinner break or missed a music cue – because Harald was loyal to the authors' conception, till finally, this afternoon, Harald, very quietly, in front of the whole company, had told him that he was incompetent to direct a book with a mind behind it. Kay would have given anything to have seen that. The director, unable, naturally, to match wits with Harald, had started screaming at him to get out of the theatre. So, before the show had even opened, there he was, out on the street. When he went upstairs to the office to protest (Kay could have told him that it was a mistake to delude himself that he still had the producer's ear), the producer, too ashamed to see him, sent word that at this stage he could not go over the director's head; the treasurer paid him two weeks' salary and offered him a drink, and that was that.

What Kay smelled was the prescription Scotch the treasurer had given him, to buck him up; for one awful moment, when she first opened the door for him and saw him standing there with the bottle of gin and alcohol on his breath, she was afraid that he might have been fired for drinking on the job. Once she had heard the story, she could see how unfair that was. Not only the treasurer, but the whole company had showed their sympathy for Harald. Most of the principals had made a point of stopping him, as he was leaving, to say they were sorry. The authors (one of them wrote regularly for *Vanity Fair*) had rushed up from their seats to argue with the director; one of the show girls had cried. . . .

Kay sat, nodding, in the cute red apron with white appliqués her mother had sent her, while Harald paced the living-room, recreating the scene in the theatre. Every now and then, she interrupted to ask a searching question, which she tried to make sound casual. Before she wrote her parents, she wanted to be sure that he was telling her the whole truth and not just his own partial view of it. That was the big thing they taught you at Vassar: keep your mind open and always ask for the evidence, even from your own side.

Though she believed Harald's version, because all the evidence she had supported it, she could see that an outside person, like her Dads, might think that Harald might have been wiser to tend to his knitting – see to the cues and the props and the prompt book and not give the director any excuse for picking on him. Like being late. But who was to blame for that? The producer or whoever was responsible for the awful hours they rehearsed. 'Take an hour for dinner!' How did they expect Harald to get home, with those slow crosstown buses, eat, and go back again, all in sixty minutes? Most of the company, according to Harald, caught a bite in a drugstore or a speak-easy, next door to the theatre. But Harald was newly married, though nobody seemed to care or take that into consideration. Yet they knew he was married, because he had let her come once to a rehearsal and the star had caught sight of her in the house and made a rumpus, stopping right in the middle of a song and pointing to Kay and demanding to know what she was doing there; when she found it was Harald's bride, she said, 'I'm so sorry, darling,' and asked them both to her apartment for a drink. But the director had told Harald never to bring her again; it upset the principals, he said, to have strangers watching them rehearse, as Harald ought to know. It was the first time she had seen Harald eat humble pie, and it had given her the most dismal feeling, as if she were a sort of encumbrance; when they went to the star's apartment (a penthouse on Central Park South), she was conscious of her heavy legs and the hairs scattered on them and it was no consolation to remember that she had directed a Hall Play and been on the Daisy Chain at Vassar.

She thought that Actors Equity ought to *do* something about rehearsal hours, which Priss Hartshorn agreed were absolutely medieval and would not be tolerated in a substandard factory. She and Harald had hardly had intercourse since he got this job – how could they? The company did not break at night till one or two in the morning, and by that time *she* was asleep; when she left for work the next morning, *Harald* was still snoozing. One night, he did not get home till four, after a conference in the producer's office, yet he had to be back for rehearsal the next day at ten, even though it was a Sunday and the two of them might have had a leisurely breakfast together for once. And after rehearsals the show was going out of town to open, so that she would be alone for two weeks while Harald kept company with the dancers and the show girls – one of them was quite intelligent (Harald had found her backstage reading Katherine Mansfield) and had a house in Connecticut. So, naturally, Kay was glad when Harald tooled home (that was one of his favourite expressions) for dinner, instead of eating with the others in that speakeasy. Once he had brought one of the authors, and Kay had made salmon loaf with cream pickle sauce. That would have to be the night they broke for dinner early, and there was quite a wait ('Bake 1 hour', the recipe went, and Kay usually added fifteen minutes to what the cookbook said), which they had to gloss over with cocktails. Harald did not realize what a rush it was for her, every day now, coming home from work at Mr Macy's and having to stop at Gristede's for the groceries; Harald never had time any more to do the marketing in the morning. And, strange to say, ever since *she* had started doing it, it had been a bone of contention between them. He liked the A. & P. because it was cheaper, and she liked Gristede's because they delivered and had fancy vegetables – the Sutton Place trade, Harald called it. Then Harald liked to cook the same old stand-bys (like his spaghetti with dried mushrooms and tomato paste), and she liked to read the cookbook and the food columns and always be trying something new. He said she had no imagination, following recipes with her glasses on and measuring the seasonings and timing everything: cooking was a lively art and she made it academic and lifeless. It was funny, the little differences that had developed between them, in the course of three months; at first, she had just been Harald's echo. But now if he said why not be sensible and open a can (this was another night when dinner was not ready), she would scream that she could not do that, it might be all right for him, but she could not live that way, week in, week out, eating like an animal, just to keep alive. Afterwards, when he had left, she was sorry and made a resolution to be a better planner and budget her preparation time, the way the food columns said. But when she did manage to have dinner waiting in the oven, having fixed a casserole the night before, he would get irritated if she tried to hurry him to the table by reminding him what time it was. 'Less wifely concern, please,' he would say, waving his forefinger at her in the owly way he had, and deliberately shake up another cocktail before he would consent to eat.

This made her feel a bit guilty; he had never had the cocktail habit until he knew her. 'Your class rite,' he called it, and she was not sure whether he meant Class of '33 or social class; back in Salt Lake City, her parents never dreamed of having liquor even when they entertained, despite the fact that Dads could get prescription whisky. But in the East, it was the social thing to do, for older people too, as she knew from staying with Pokey Prothero and Priss and Polly. In Cleveland, as Harald had seen himself, Helena Davison's family had sherry. So, to please Kay, they had started having cocktails every night in the aluminium cocktail shaker. The difference between them was that what she liked was the little formality and what Harald liked was the liquor. One or two cocktails, of course, could never hurt anybody; still, during rehearsals, they should probably have done without, for Harald's sake. Yet it would have seemed such a comedown to just put the food on and sit down and eat, like her parents.

Harald had gone to the kitchen and fixed himself a gin and bitters; this was a bad sign – he knew Kay hated the taste of straight liquor and did not like to see him drink it. Now he put tobacco in his pipe, lit it, and poured a second. 'What can I fix you?' he said. 'A silver fizz?' Kay frowned; she was wounded by the mocking courtesy of his manner. 'I don't think I'll have anything,' she replied thoughtfully. Harald's dark, wiry eyebrows shot up. 'Why this departure?' he said. Kay had suddenly determined to turn over a new leaf, but she felt this was not quite the right moment to announce it; you never knew how Harald would take things when he had been drinking. 'I just don't feel like it,' she said. 'I'm going to start dinner.' She rose from her chair. Harald stared at her, with his hands on his hips and pursed lips. 'My God!' he said. 'You are the most tactless, blundering fool that ever lived.' 'But what have I said?' cried Kay, too astonished, even, to be hurt. '"I don't think I'll have anything,"' he quoted, imitating her voice and adding a smug note that she could swear had not been there when she spoke. If he only knew, she was dying for a silver fizz and was doing without because she blamed herself, more than a little, for the trouble during rehearsals. What would happen if she went to work at Macy's after having had two cocktails before breakfast? It was the same thing, no? You could learn a lot, she always found, if you transferred your behaviour to a different context and looked at it there, objectively. Had *she* just been fired, for instance, she would want to sit right down and trace the contributory causes, no matter how small. But maybe Harald was doing that and not letting on? '"I just don't feel like it,"' he went on. 'Don't take that tone.

73

It doesn't suit you. You're a terrible actress, you know.' 'Oh, can it!' Kay said abruptly and walked out to the kitchen. Then she listened to hear if Harald would go out, slamming the door, as he had the other night when she brought home from the store the Continental String Bean Slicer that did not work. But he was still there.

She opened a can of beans and dumped them into a baking-dish; on top she put strips of bacon. On the way home on the El she had decided to make Welsh rabbit with beer, to surprise Harald, but now she was afraid to, in case it should curdle and give Harald a chance to lecture her. She pulled apart a head of lettuce and started her salad dressing. All at once, thinking of the Welsh rabbit that they were not going to have tonight just because Harald had lost his job, she gave a loud sob. Everything now was going to be changed, she knew it. By this, she really meant the Apartment; she was *living* for the moment they could move. Their present place belonged to the widow of an etcher who was now in Cornish, New Hampshire, and it was full of antiques and reproductions – Spanish chests and Oriental rugs and piecrust tables and Hepplewhite-style chairs and brass and copper that had to be polished. Kay could hardly wait to get out of this museum and move in with their own things. Harald knew this, yet so far he had not said a word about the Apartment, which he must have guessed was the thing uppermost in her mind from the moment she opened the door and saw him: what were they going to *do*? Hadn't this thought occurred to him too?

In her pocketbook on the lowboy in the living-room were samples of upholstery material she had brought home to show him; she had spent her whole lunch hour in Macy's Forward House choosing a modern couch and two side chairs in muslin. And she had priced draperies just for fun, to show Harald how much they were saving thanks to the fact that the management gave you Venetian blinds free, the way they did in most of the smart new buildings. With the Venetian blinds you would not need draperies. To have had them made, she had found out today, even at Mr Macy's with the discount, would have run to $100 or $120, so you could treat that amount as a reduction of the first year's rent. And that was unlined; lined would be even more.

She glanced at her beans in the oven – not yet brown. In the living-room, she opened the drop-leaf table and set two places, meanwhile stealing a look at Harald, who was reading the *New Yorker*. He raised his eyes. 'How would you like,' he said, 'to ask the Blakes in for bridge after dinner?' His negligent tone did not fool her; this, from Harald, was an apology. He was trying to make it up to her for nearly ruining their evening. 'I'd love it!' Kay was delighted; it was a long time since they had had a foursome of bridge. 'Shall I call them or will you?' 'I will,' he said, and, pulling Kay down to him, he kissed her hard. She released herself and hurried to the kitchen. 'I've got three bottles of beer in the icebox!' she called out. 'Tell them that!'

But in the kitchen her face fell. It struck her, all at once, that there was method in Harald's madness. Why the Blakes, of all people? Norine Blake, her classmate, was very left wing; at college she was always leading Socialist rallies and demonstrations, and her husband, Putnam, was a registered Socialist. And both of them had a complex about economy and living within a budget, though Putnam had a private income and came from a very good family. Kay could foresee what was coming. The Blakes, when they heard about Harald losing his job, would immediately start worrying the subject of the Apartment. Kay was already sick of hearing that Norine and Put had found a nice basement with a real garden for only $40 a month – why couldn't she and Harald? She wouldn't live in a basement; it was unhealthy. She glanced at her beans again and slammed the oven door. Put would argue (she could hear him!) that Harald was perfectly justified in going back on his legal obligation, which was what a lease was, because a lease was a form of exploitation and rent was unearned increment – something like that. And Norine would talk about car-fares. She was hipped on the subject. The last time the four of them had played bridge, she had cross-questioned Kay about how she got to work. 'You take the crosstown bus?' she asked, looking at her husband as if the cross-town bus were the most unheard-of luxury. '*And* the Sixth Avenue El?' Then she looked at her husband again, nodding. 'That makes two fares,' she relentlessly concluded. Norine's *idée fixe* was that all young couples should live near a subway stop. And she thought that Harald, because he worked in the Times Square area, should live on the West Side, not more than two blocks from an express stop. Kay and Harald had laughed at Norine's transportation obsession, but just the same it had put a bee in Harald's bonnet. And that very night, when Kay had served coffee and toasted cheese sandwiches after bridge, Norine had cried out, 'What, real *cream*?' Apparently anybody but a millionaire was expected to live on evaporated. All these months Kay had been telling Harald that everybody she knew bought cream as a matter of course (he wanted to use the top of the bottle), and she had turned red as a beet with confusion, as though Norine had exposed her in a lie. Yet Harald, strange to relate, instead of taking this amiss, had only teased Kay about it. 'What, real *cream*!' he had murmured, afterwards, squeezing her breasts.

Harald was always saying that she was transparent. Sometimes, like tonight, he meant it as a criticism, but sometimes he seemed to love her for being easy to see through, though what he saw or thought he saw she could not exactly make out. This reminded her of the funny letter she had found, night before last, when she was straightening up his papers to get ready for their move. It was a letter from Harald to his father and must have been written, she had figured out, the Saturday before she and Harald were married. She could not resist reading it when she saw her own name in the middle of the first page.

'Kay is not afraid of life, Anders' – that was what he called his father. 'You and Mother and I are, all of us, a little. We know that life can hurt us. Kay has never found that out. That, I think, is why I've decided finally to marry her, though the cynics advise me to wait for a rich girl, who could buy me a piece of a show. Don't think I haven't thought of it. Between ourselves – this isn't for Mother's eyes – I've known a few such, in the Biblical sense. I've made love to them in their roadsters and raided their fathers' liquor cabinets and let them pay for me at the speak-easies where they have charge accounts. So I speak from experience. They're afraid of life too, have the death urge of their class in them; they want to annihilate experience in a wild moment of pleasure. They're like the Maenads who destroyed Orpheus – do you remember the old Greek myth? In the last analysis, they're afraid of the future, just like the Petersen family. You and Mother worry about your losing your job again or reaching retirement age; ever since the crash, the gilded girls worry that Papa might lose his money or have a revolution take it away from him. Kay is different; she comes from the secure class you never quite made, the upper professional class.

Her father is a big orthopaedist in Salt Lake City; look him up in *Who's Who* (if you haven't done so already!). That class still believes in its future and in its ability to survive and govern, and quite rightly too, as we see from the Soviet Union, where the services of doctors and scientists, no matter what their "bourgeois" background, are at a premium, like the services of film directors and literary men. I see that belief, that pioneer confidence, in Kay, though she's unconscious of it herself; it's written all over her, the "outward and visible sign of an inward and spiritual grace", as the Episcopal prayer book says. Not that she is graceful, except in outdoor sports, riding and swimming and hockey too, she tells me. Speaking of the prayer book (read it some time for its style), Kay wants us to be married in J. P. Morgan's church; I'm agreeing, in a spirit of irony, and consoling myself with the thought that Senator Cutting (Bronson Cutting of New Mexico, one of my minor heroes – have I mentioned this? – a fighting gentleman progressive) worships there too when he's in town. (His sister has something to do with the Social Register.)

'I don't know how you feel out in Boise, but there's a big change here in the East since Roosevelt came in. Probably, as an old Townley man, you distrust him; frankly, I don't. You've read about the influx of professors into government; that is the key to the change, which may mean a bloodless revolution in our own time, with brain replacing finance capital in the management of our untapped resources. The Marxist boys here in New York make a mistake when they expect a final struggle between capital and labour; both capital and labour in their present morphology can be expected to dissolve. The fact that Roosevelt is a patrician is significant, and Kay tells me, by the way, proudly, that he was a trustee of Vassar. I'm wandering a little from the point, but I guess you see the bearing: I feel that my marriage to Kay is a pledge to the future. That sounds rather mystical, but I do have a mystical feeling about her, a sense of "rightness" or destiny, call it what you will. Don't ask whether I love her; love, apart from chemical attraction, is still an unknown quantity to me. Which you may have divined. She's a very strong young woman with a radiant, still-undisciplined vitality. You and Mother may not like her at first, but that vitality of hers is necessary to me, it wants form and direction, which I think I can give her.

'By the way, would Mother mind asking Kay to call her Judith when she writes? Like all modern girls, she has a horror of calling a mother-in-law "Mother", and "Mrs Petersen" sounds so formal. Make Mother understand. Kay already thinks of you as Anders and is moved by the quality of our relationship – yours and mine, I mean. I've been trying to put the story of your life into a play, but Kay, who has studied theatre at Vassar under a funny, electric little woman, says I have no knack yet for dramatic construction; she may be right, I fear. Oh, Anders . . .'

Here the letter broke off; it had never been finished, and Kay wondered what he had said in the letter he finally wrote. There were other unfinished letters too in his rickety suitcase, some to her at Vassar, and several beginnings of a short story or novel, so old that the paper was turning yellow, and the first two acts of his play. The letter, Kay thought, was awfully well written, like everything Harald did, yet reading it had left her with the queerest, stricken feeling. There was nothing in it that she did not already know in a sense, but to know in a sense, apparently, was not the same as knowing. Harald, she had had to admit, had never concealed from her that he had had relations with other women and had even toyed with the idea of marrying them or being married by them. And she had heard all that about her social class (though, when he talked to her, he usually said it was finished) and Roosevelt and his not feeling sure that he loved her and 'in a spirit of irony'. Maybe it was just that that made reading the letter so disappointing. It was finding that Harald was just the same all through, which in a funny way made him different. Curiosity was a terrible thing; she had started reading the letter, knowing she shouldn't, with the thought that she might learn more about him and about herself too. But instead of telling her more about him, the letter was almost a revelation of the limitations of Harald. Or was it only that she did not like to see him 'baring his soul' to his father?

Yet the letter *had* told her something, she reflected now as she listened to Harald on the telephone (the Blakes evidently were coming) and methodically tossed her salad. The letter explained, in so many words, what her attraction was – something she had never been clear about. When she had first met him in the summer theatre he had treated her like one of the *hoi polloi*, ordering her around, criticizing the way she hammered flats, sending her on errands to the hardware store. 'You've got paint in your hair,' he told her one night when the company was having a party and he had asked her to dance; he had just had a fight with the leading lady, a married woman, with whom he was sleeping – her husband was a lawyer in New York. Another time, when they were all having beer in a roadhouse, he had strolled over to her table, where she was sitting with some of the other apprentices, to say – guess what – that her shoulder straps showed. Kay could hardly believe it when he promised to write to her after she went back to Vassar, but he had – a short, casual note – and she had answered, and he had come up for a week-end to see the Hall Play she directed, and now here they were, married. Yet she had never felt sure of him; up to the last minute, she had feared he might be using her as a pawn in a game he was playing with some other woman. Even in bed, he kept his sang-froid; he did the multiplication tables to postpone ejaculating – an old Arab recipe he had learned from an Englishman. Kay dished up her beans. She was 'not afraid of life', she repeated to herself; she had 'a radiant vitality'. Their marriage was 'a pledge to the future'. Instead of feeling chagrined and wishing he had said something more romantic, she should realize that this was her strong suit and play it; never mind those Blakes – a lease was a pledge to the future. No matter what people said, she would *not* give up the Apartment. She did not know why it meant so much to her – whether it was the Venetian blinds or the concierge or the darling little dressing-room or what. She felt she would die if they lost it. And what would they do instead – go back to that sordid Village room across the hall from Dick Brown till Harald's plans were more 'settled'? No! Kay set her jaw. 'There are other apartments, dear,' she could hear her mother say. She did not want another apartment; she wanted this one. It was the same as when she had wanted Harald and feared she was going to lose him every time she did not get a letter. She had not given up and said 'There are other men', the way a lot of girls would; she had held on. And it was not only her; for Harald it would be an awful disaster psychologically to relinquish his Life plan and go backward after a single defeat – not to mention losing the deposit, a whole month's rent.

They sat down to the meal. The Blakes were coming at 8.30. Kay kept glancing at the lowboy, just behind Harald, where her

pocketbook was lying stuffed with upholstery samples. She wondered whether she should not get it over with and show them to
Harald before Norine and Putnam came. After bridge, it would be
late, and Harald, she suspected, would be wanting to have intercourse; on a night like this she could hardly say no, even though it
meant that after her douche it would be one o'clock before she
closed her eyes (thanks to those multiplication tables) and tomorrow morning before going to work would be no time to show him
the samples; he would be snappish if she woke him up for that. Yet
they would have to decide soon; two weeks on upholstery was the
rule at Macy's. The beds and pots and pans and lamps and a table
and all that would have to be ordered too, but at least they were
there in the warehouse and you only needed two days for delivery.
She thought they should have hair mattresses, which were more
expensive but healthier; Consumers' Research admitted that. Her
confidence fled as she passed the butter to Harald; only the other
night, they had had quite a debate, ending in tears on her part, about
margarine vs. butter – margarine, Harald maintained, was just as
tasty and nourishing, but the butter interests had conspired to keep
the margarine people from colouring their product; he was right,
yet she could not bear to have that oily white stuff on her table,
even if her reaction to the whiteness was a conditioned reflex based
on class prejudice. Now he speared a piece of butter with a bitter
smile, which Kay tried not to notice. Maybe she was not afraid of
life, but she was certainly afraid of Harald.

She decided to edge in to the topic of the samples by a little
light chatter about her day in the store; she was worried that if she
did not talk Harald might sink into one of his Scandinavian
glooms. 'You know what?' she said gaily. 'I think I was "shopped"
today.' That was like having a sprung test in college: a professional
Macy shopper, pretending to be a customer, was assigned to eval-
uate every trainee at one time during his or her six months' training.
The bosses did not tell you this would happen, but of course the
word leaked out. 'I'm in "Better Suits" this week, did I tell you?'
Harald knew that Kay would be shifted around so that she would
learn every aspect of merchandising, besides listening to lectures
from the executives of the different departments. 'Well, this afternoon I had this customer who insisted on trying on every suit on
the floor and was dissatisfied with just about everything. It got to

be almost closing time, and she couldn't make up her mind between a black wool with caracul trim and a blue severe tweed, fitted, with a dark-blue velvet collar. So she wanted me to send for the fitter, to get her opinion, and the fitter said she should take both and winked at me, to give me a tip, I guess. They grade you on politeness, good humour, general personality, but the main point is whether you can sell. You flunk if the shopper goes away without buying anything. And, what do you think, thanks to the fitter, this woman in the end bought both suits. Not really "bought" of course; instead of going down to the workrooms, the suits are returned to stock if the customer is a Macy shopper. That way you can tell. But on the other hand if a real customer buys something and returns it, that counts as a mark against you; it means you oversold. . . .'

Harald sat chewing in silence; finally, he laid down his fork. In the face of this coldness, Kay could not continue. 'Go on, my dear,' he said, as her voice flagged and halted. 'This is highly interesting. From what you say, I expect you'll be valedictorian of your Macy class. You may even find me a job in the rug department or selling refrigerators – isn't that considered a man's sphere?' 'Yes.' replied Kay, mechanically responding to a request for information. 'Only they never start a man in those departments; you have to have other experience in selling first.' Then she dropped her fork and buried her curly head in her hands. 'Oh, Harald! Why do you hate me?'

'Because you ask tedious questions like that,' he retorted. Kay's face flamed; she did not want to cry, because the Blakes were coming. Harald must have thought of the same thing, for when he spoke again it was in a different tone. 'I don't blame you, dear Kay,' he said gravely, 'for comparing yourself to me as a bread-winner. God knows you have a right to.' 'But I *wasn't* comparing myself to you!' Kay raised her head in outrage. 'I was just making conversation.' Harald smiled sadly. 'I was not blaming you,' he repeated. 'Harald! Please believe me!' She seized his hand. 'The thought of a comparison never entered my mind! It couldn't. I know that you're a genius and that I'm just a B-average person. That's why I can coast along in life and you can't. And I haven't helped you enough; I know it. I shouldn't have let you come home to dinner while you were rehearsing; I shouldn't have made us

have cocktails. I should have thought of the strain you were under
. . .' She felt his hand go flaccid in hers and realized she was blundering again; at least she had avoided naming his lateness at the
theatre, which was the real thought that kept preying on her
conscience.

He flung her hand aside. 'Kay,' he said. 'How many times have
I pointed out to you that you're an unconscionable egotist? Observe how you've shifted the centre of the drama to yourself. It
was I who was fired today, not you. You had nothing to do with
it. Being late' – he smiled cruelly – 'had nothing to do with it,
despite what you've been insinuating in your clumsy way for the
last two weeks. You've developed a time-clock mentality. Nobody
takes that "hour for dinner" seriously in the theatre – except you.
You saw the night you were there; nothing started for half an hour
after we pulled in. Everybody sits around playing pinochle. . . .'
Kay nodded. 'All right, Harald. Forgive me.' But he was still
angry. 'I'll thank you,' he said, 'for keeping your petty-bourgeois
conscience out of my affairs. It's your way of cutting me down to
size. You pretend to accuse yourself, but it's me you're accusing.'
Kay shook her head. 'No, no,' she said. 'Never.' Harald raised a
sceptical eyebrow. 'You protest too much,' he remarked, in a
lighter tone; she could see that his mood was changing again. 'In
any case,' he continued, 'all that had nothing to do with it. You are
on the wrong track, my girl. The nance hates me; that's all.' 'Because you're superior,' murmured Kay.

'That, yes,' said Harald. 'Doubtless, there was that.' '"Doubtless"?' cried Kay, affronted by the judicious, qualifying note in
his voice. 'Why, of course that was it.' It would be just like Harald
to start hairsplitting now, when they were both agreed that the
basic motivations were as clear as noonday. 'What do you mean,
"doubtless"?' He shook his head and smiled. 'Oh, Harald, please
tell me!' Harald lit his pipe. 'Do you know the story of Hippolytus?' he said finally. 'Why, naturally,' protested Kay. 'Don't you
remember, we did it at college in Greek, with Prexy playing
Theseus? I wrote you, I built the scenery – the big statues of Ar-
temis and Aphrodite. Golly, that was fun. And Prexy forgot his
lines and ad-libbed "To be or not to be" in Greek, and only old
Miss MacCurdy, the head of the Greek department, knew the
difference. She's deaf but she spotted it even with her ear trumpet.'

Harald waited, drumming his fingers. 'Well?' said Kay. 'Well,' 'if you change the sex of Phaedra . . .' 'I don't understand. What would happen if you changed the sex of Phaedra?' 'You would have the inside story of my getting the axe. Now, make us the coffee.' Kay stared, nonplussed. She could not see the connexion.

'Buggery,' said Harald. 'I, though not a virgin, am the chaste Hippolytus of the farce, which the play, incidentally, is. A male defending his virtue is always a farcical figure.' Kay's jaw dropped. 'You mean somebody wanted to bugger you? Who? The director?' she gasped. 'The other way round, I believe. He assured me that he had a luscious ass.' 'When? This afternoon?' Kay was torn between horror and curiosity. 'Flits have always been attracted to me' – he had told her that last summer (there had been two who were like that in the company), and then it had made her excited and sort of envious. 'No, no, some weeks ago,' said Harald. 'The first time, that is.' 'Why didn't you *tell* me?' The thought that he had kept such a thing from her cut her to the heart. 'There was no reason for you to know.' 'But how did it happen? What did he say to you? Where were you?' 'In Shubert Alley,' he said. 'I was a little liquored up that evening, and in my mood of geniality, I may have given him what he took for signs of encouragement. He suggested that we repair to his apartment later.' 'Oh, God!' cried Kay. 'Oh, Harald, you didn't—?' 'No, no,' he replied soothingly. 'It was an uninviting prospect. The old fruit must be forty.' For a second, Kay was relieved and, at the same time (wasn't that queer?), almost let down; then a fresh suspicion attacked her. 'Harald! Do you mean you would have *done* it with someone younger? A chorus boy?' She felt sick thinking of the nights he had worked late, and yet there was this funny itch to know. 'I can't answer hypothetical questions,' Harald said, rather impatiently. 'The problem hasn't come up.' 'Oh,' said Kay, dissatisfied. 'But the director – did *he* try again?' Harald admitted that he had. One night late, he had reached for Harald's crotch. 'And what happened?' Harald shrugged. 'Erection is fairly automatic in the normal male, you know.' Kay turned pale. 'Oh, Harald! You encouraged him!' All at once, she was frenzied with jealousy; it took Harald some time to calm her. In her heart was the horrible certainty that erection would not have been so automatic if she had not always been asleep when Harald tiptoed into their bedroom. And how did she know he tiptoed? Because (did he ever suspect this?) she was not always really asleep. Tonight, she decided, they would have intercourse no matter how tired she was when the Blakes left.

Kay yawned and slipped off Harald's lap, where he had taken her to comfort her ('I like your freckles,' he had whispered. 'And your wild black gipsy hair)'. 'I'll make the coffee,' she said. As she turned to go, he reached out and patted her behind, which made her think, distrustfully, of the director. What had got into her, recently, that prompted her to distrust Harald and to always think there was something more than he was telling her behind every little incident he related? To tell the truth, she had wondered sometimes if there could not be some other explanation of the director's persecution, and now that she knew what it was ('Hell hath no fury like a woman scorned'), she still wondered whether there was not more to *that* than Harald said. How far had he let the 'nance' go? She could not help remembering a story he had told her, while she was still in college, about undressing an older actress in her apartment and then just leaving her up in the air on her blue percale sheets with scalloped borders.

Kay believed in Harald completely; she had no doubt he was bound to be famous, sooner or later, in whatever field he chose. But believing in him was different from believing him. In fact, the more impressed she was by him intellectually (his IQ must be in the genius percentile), the more she noticed his little lapses. And why was it that, with all his talent, he was still a stage manager when other people of his own age, people not nearly as bright, had forged ahead of him? Was there something wrong with him that was evident to producers and directors and not to her? She wished he would let her give him the Binet and some of the personality tests she had tried on the group at Vassar.

Once, during exam week (and nobody knew this but her), he had tried to commit suicide by driving somebody's car off a cliff. The car had rolled over without hurting him, and he had climbed out and walked back to the place where he was staying. The next day the couple he was visiting had sent for a tow truck to pull the car up and the only damage was that acid from the battery had dripped over the upholstery, making holes in it, and ruined Harald's English hat, which had fallen off his head when the car turned over. This suicide attempt had impressed her terrifically, and she treasured the letter in which he described it; she could not imagine having the coolness to do such a thing herself and certainly not in someone else's car. He had done it, he said, on a sudden impulse, because he saw his future laid out for him and he did not want to be a tame husband, not even hers. When the attempt failed so miraculously, he had taken it as a sign, he wrote her, that Heaven had decreed their union. Now, however, that she knew Harald better, she wondered whether he had not driven off the cliff by accident; admittedly, he had been drinking applejack at the time. She hated having these suspicions of Harald and she did not know which was worse: to be scared that your husband might kill himself if the slightest little thing went wrong or to be guessing that it was all a cover-up for something commonplace like driving-under-the-influence.

Harald was histrionic; Lakey had found the right word for him. Yet that was why, with his intellect and learning, he would make such a marvellous director. Kay had been giving a lot of thought to Harald's problems during her lonely evenings while he was at the theatre, and she had decided that the main thing that acted as a drag on him was his strong identification with his father. He was still fighting his father's battles, any psychologist could see that. No wonder, then, that Kay felt impatient with that relation. 'Anders' and 'Judith'! – she had come to loathe the very names of the old pair, if Harald only knew it. She would almost rather commit suicide herself than make Judith's 'quick-and-easy meat loaf'. The sight of her mother-in-law's laboured pencil recipes, enclosed in letters from 'Anders', made her cold and hard as nails. Ever since she had seen 'Judith's' handwriting, she could not abide Harald's chile con carne, though it was still a big success with company, who did not know the source and thought it was something glamorous he had learned in the theatre. She had no doubt that 'Judith' used oleomargarine; she could see a white slab of it on their humble oilcloth with a cheap plated-silver butter knife (the kind you sent in coupons for) lying by its moist side!

Turning off the coffee (Maxwell House), Kay made a face. She had a ruthless hatred of poor people, which not even Harald suspected and which sometimes scared her by its violence, as when she was waiting on some indigent in the store. Objectively, of course, she ought to pity old Anders, a poor Norwegian immigrant who had taught manual training in the Idaho public-school system and then had studied nights to become an algebra teacher and finally risen to be principal of a high school in Boise, where he made an enemy of the vice-principal, who brought about his dismissal. Harald's play told the story of that. In the play, he had made his father a college president and put him at odds with the state legislature. To her mind, that was very unconvincing and accounted for the weakness of the play. If Harald wanted to write about his father, why glorify him? Why not simply tell the truth?

According to Harald, his father, in real life, had been framed and railroaded out of his position because (shades of Ibsen!) he had discovered some funny business about the high-school bookkeeping. But if he had really been as innocent as Harald claimed, it was peculiar that all through Harald's adolescence he could not get reinstated in the school system and had to support the family doing odd jobs of carpentry, non-union, while Harald went to work as a newsboy. Harald said it was all part of a conspiracy in which some crooked city officials had been involved too, and that they had to crucify his father to keep the real facts from being known. But then a reform party got elected (Harald's father was a sort of populist radical whose god was some man called Townley), and he was taken on again, as a substitute teacher; meanwhile, in high school Harald had made a big name for himself, being quarterback of the football team and star of the dramatic society and editor of the school paper. A group of Boise ladies had raised a scholarship fund to send him to Reed College, in Oregon, and then to Yale Drama School, and he could still have a job, any time he wanted, running their Little Theatre for them – you should see the silver water pitcher they had sent from Gump's in San Francisco for a wedding present. But Harald would not go back to Boise till his father's name had been vindicated. He meant till his play had been produced; he expected all of Boise to read about it in the papers and recognize poor old Anders, who was now a regular teacher again (half-time algebra and half-time manual training), in the wronged president of a big state university. The play was called *Sheepskin*, and Harald had merged in it the story of his father's life with some of the story of Alexander Meiklejohn at Wisconsin, not admitting to himself that his father and Meiklejohn were horses of a different colour.

What worried Kay most, though, was that Harald was identifying with failure. One of her first thoughts, when she heard the news this afternoon, was that Harald might be repeating his father's pattern. She wondered how many people who knew Harald, besides herself, would think of this. This made it important to get the true facts into circulation, for it would hurt Harald's career if he got the name of a troublemaker, of a person who went around *wanting* to be fired, *needing* to fail. She did not think Harald should be soft about telling what the director had tried to do to him; knowing the director's proclivities, everyone would realize how he had been subtly provoking Harald to finally give him a piece of his mind; if it had not happened today, he would have goaded him till it did.

The doorbell rang just as they were finishing their coffee. Listening to the Blakes on the stairs (Norine had a heavy walk), Kay thought fast. Whatever was said about the Apartment, she was going to keep mum; let the others talk. And tomorrow morning, first thing, she would slip up to Forward House and order the upholstery job. She could always pretend that she had done it today, before she heard the news, and had not mentioned it on purpose, seeing how upset Harald was. She could even make up a story of trying desperately to cancel the order (that would be tomorrow morning) and being told it was too late – the material had already been cut. And it could have happened that way; it was just chance that she had decided to take the samples home to show Harald, instead of settling on the one she wanted – the Fireman Red – herself. If she had, it *would* be too late.

Kay opened the door. 'Hi!' she said. 'Greetings!' She spoke in a low, muffled voice, to prepare them, as though Harald, just behind her, lighting his pipe again, were sick or a spectre or something – how were you supposed to act when your husband had joined the ranks of the unemployed right in the middle of the depression? For a moment, thinking of it that way, she felt a wild surge of fear, like what she had felt that first instant when she heard Harald's key scratching at the lock and *knew* what he was going to tell her. But something inside her hardened immediately and she had a new idea: now Harald would be able to work on his play and get that out of his system; the dinette would be perfect for a study for him, and he could build in shelves for his papers below the china cabinet.

There was no reason, now, that he could not do all the carpentry and build in the bed too, the way they had once planned, and make a bookcase for the living-room. Behind her, Harald spoke. '*Morituri te salutamus*. I've got the sack,' he said. 'Oh, Harald,' said Kay eagerly. 'Wait till they've got their things off. And tell it the way you told me. Start from the beginning and don't leave anything out.'

Chapter 5

Harald and Kay were giving a party to celebrate Harald's having sold an option on his play to a producer. It was Washington's Birthday, and Kay had the day off from the store. The group had made a point of coming, in their nicest winter dresses and hats. Harald, poor fellow, had been out of work for months, it seemed, ever since September when, according to Polly Andrews, a director had molested him. They had not paid the rent for months either; the real-estate people were 'carrying' them. When they got the cheque for the option ($500), the telephone was about to be shut off. It was a mystery what they had been living on, even with Kay's salary. On faith, hope, and charity, Kay said, laughing: Harald's *faith* in himself gave his creditors *hope*, which made them extend *charity*. And she told how Harald had proposed that they invite a select group of their creditors to the party: the man from the real-estate office, the man from the telephone company, Mr Finn from the Internal Revenue, and their dentist, Dr Mosenthal – wouldn't that have been a howl?

Kay had been showing the apartment to everyone who hadn't seen it. Two rooms, plus dinette and kitchen, plus a foyer, plus Kay's pride and joy, a darling little dressing-room, so compact, with closets and cupboards and bureau drawers built in. Pure white walls and woodwork and casement windows, a whole row of them, looking out on a sunny court with young trees and shrubs. The latest models of stove, sink, and icebox; built-in cupboards for dishes, broom closet, linen closet. Every stick of furniture was the latest thing: blond Swedish chairs and folding table (made of birch with natural finish) in the dinette, which was separated from the kitchen by a slatted folding door; in the living-room, a bright-red modern couch and armchairs to match, a love seat covered in striped grey-and-white mattress ticking, steel standing lamps, a coffee table that was just a sheet of glass that Harald had had cut at the glazier's and mounted on steel legs, built-in bookcases that Harald had painted canary yellow. There were no rugs yet and, instead of curtains, only white Venetian blinds at the windows. Instead of flowers, they had ivy growing in white pots. In the bedroom, instead of a bed, they had a big innerspring mattress with another mattress on top of it; Harald had nailed red pegs to the bottom one to keep it off the floor.

Instead of a dress, Kay was wearing a cherry-red velvet sleeveless hostess gown (Harald's Christmas present) from Bendel's; they had an old coloured maid from Harlem passing canapés in a modern sectioned hors-d'oeuvre tray. Instead of cocktails, they had had Fish House Punch, made from One Dagger Rum, in a punch bowl with twenty-four matching glass cups they had borrowed from Priss Hartshorn Crockett, who had got it for a wedding present when she was married in Oyster Bay in September.

On *that* occasion, only four of the group had been able to make it. Today, *mirabile dictu*, the only one missing was Lakey, who was now in Spain. Pokey Prothero had flown down from Cornell Agricultural in a helmet and goggles; Helena Davison, who had spent the summer and fall in Europe, was in town from Cleveland. Dottie Renfrew had come back from Arizona, where her family had sent her for her health, with a marvellous tan and an engagement ring – a diamond almost as big as her eyes; she was going to marry a mining man who owned half the state.

This was quite a change from Dottie's modest plans for working in a settlement house and living at home in Boston. 'You'll miss the concerts and the theatre,' Helena had remarked dryly. But Dottie said that Arizona had a great deal to offer too. There were lots of interesting people who had gone there because of TB and fallen in love with the country – musicians and painters and architects, and there was the riding and the incredible wild flowers of the desert, not to mention the Indians and some fascinating archaeological digs that attracted scientists from Harvard.

The party was almost over; only one mink coat was left in the bedroom. At the high point, there had been five – Harald had counted them. Kay's supervisor's, Harald's producer's wife's, Connie Storey's, Dottie's, and a mink-lined greatcoat belonging to Connie's fiancé, that apple-cheeked boy who worked on *Fortune*.

Now Dottie's lay in solitary state, next to Helena's ocelot and a peculiar garment made of old grey wolf that belonged to Norine Schmittlapp Blake, another member of the Vassar contingent. Harald's producer had left after half an hour, with his wife (who had the money) and a star who had replaced Judith Anderson in *As You Desire Me*, but the Class of '33 had practically held a reunion, there was so much news to keep up with: Libby MacAusland had sold a poem to *Harper's*; Priss was pregnant; Helena had seen Lakey in Munich and met Miss Sandison in the British Museum; Norine Schmittlapp, who was there with her husband (the one in the black shirt), had been to the Scottsboro trial; Prexy (bless his heart!) had had lunch on a tray with Roosevelt in the White House. . . .

Helena, who was Class Correspondent, took a few terse mental notes. 'At Kay Strong Petersen's,' she foresaw herself inditing for the next issue of the *Alumnae Magazine*, 'I saw Dottie Renfrew, who is going to marry Brook Latham and live in Arizona. "The Woman Who Rode Away" – how about it, Dottie? Brook is a widower – see the Class Prophecy. Kay's husband, Harald, has sold his play, *Sheepskin*, to the producer, Paul Bergler – watch out, Harald. The play is slated for fall production; Walter Huston is reading the script. Norine Schmittlapp's husband, Putnam Blake (Williams '30), has started an independent fund-raising organization for labour and left-wing causes. Volunteer workers take note. His partner is Bill Nickum (Yale '29). Charles Dickens take note. Polly Andrews reports that Sis Farnworth and Lely Baker have started a business called "Dog Walk". It keeps them outdoors, Polly says, and they're swamped with applications from people who don't have butlers any more to take their canines walking in the Park. . . .'

Helena puckered her little forehead. Had she mastered (mistressed?) the idiom of the *Alumnae Magazine* Class Notes? She and Dottie were in the living-room, waiting tactfully to get their coats to leave. Harald and Kay were in the bedroom with the door closed, having 'words', she supposed. The party, to quote the host, had laid an egg. The main body of guests had decamped just as the old coloured maid had appeared, all smiles, with a Washington's Birthday cake she had brought for a present. Harald, reddening, had shooed her back to the kitchen, so as not to let people see, presumably, that they had been expected to stay longer. But Kay, who had always been a blurter, had let the cat out of the bag. 'But Harald was going to read his play!' she cried sadly after the departing guests. The whole party had been planned around that, she confided. Now the maid had gone home with her satchel, and the only guests remaining, besides Helena herself and Dottie, were a radio actor, who was helping himself copiously at the punch bowl, the two Blakes, and a naval officer Harald had met in a bar, whose sister was married to a famous architect who used ramps instead of stairs. The actor, who had wavy hair in a pompadour, was arguing with Norine about Harald's play. 'The trouble is, Norine, the line of the play is sheer toboggan. I told Harald that when he read it to me. "It's very interesting, the way you've done it, but I wonder: is it a *play*?"' He gestured, and some punch from his cup fell on his suit. 'If the audience identifies with a character, they want to feel he has a chance to win. But Harald's view of life is too blackly logical to give them that sop.' Across the room, Putnam Blake, a thin, white-faced young man with a close collegiate haircut, an unsmiling expression, and a low, tense voice, was explaining what he called his 'Principle of Accumulated Guilt' to the naval officer.

'Mr Blake,' said Dottie with a twinkle, 'has a system for finding rich people to give money to Labour. He was telling about it earlier. It sounds terribly interesting,' she added warmly. Glancing at their watches, at Norine and the actor, and at the closed bedroom door, the two girls drew near to listen. Putnam ignored them, dividing his attention between his pipe and the naval officer. Using Gustavus Myers' *Great American Fortunes*, Poor's *Register of Directors*, and Mendel's Law, he was able to predict, he said, when a wealthy family was 'due'. As a rule, this occurred in the third generation. 'What I've done,' he said, 'is take the element of chance out of fund-raising and put it on a scientific basis. I'm simplifying, of course, but roughly speaking the money guilt has a tendency to skip a generation. Or if it crops out in the second generation, as with the Lamont family, you will find it in a younger son rather than in the first-born. And it may be transmitted to the females while remaining dormant in the males. This means that the guilt tends to separate from the chief property holdings, which are usually transmitted from first-born male to first-born male. Thus the guilt, being a recessive character, like blue eyes, may be bred out of a family without any profit to the Left.' A ghostly quiver, the phantom of a smile, passed across his lips; he appeared eager to take the naval officer into his confidence, like some crazy inventor, thought Helena, with a patent, and it was as if some bashful ectoplasmic joke hovered in the neighbourhood of his Principle. 'I'm working now,' he continued, 'on the relation between mental deficiency and money guilt in rich families. Your ideal contributor (the Communists have found this), scion of a fortune, has a mental age of twelve.' Without altering his expression, he gave a quick parenthetic little laugh.

Helena quirked her sandy eyebrows, thinking of the Rich Young Man in the Bible and idly imagining a series of camels with humps of accumulated guilt lining up to pass through the eye of a needle. The conversation at this party struck her as passing strange. 'Read the *Communist Manifesto* – for its style,' she had heard Harald telling Kay's supervisor (Wellesley '28). She grinned .'Take *her*,' said Putnam suddenly to the naval officer, indicating Helena with a jab of his pipe. 'Her people live on the income of their income. Father is first vice-president of Oneida Steel. Self-made man – first generation. Bright girl, the daughter – only child. Does not respond to fund-raising appeals for labour victims. Charities confined, probably, to Red Cross and tuberculosis stamps. But if she has four children, you can expect that at least one of them will evince guilt characteristics. . . .'

Impressed despite herself, Helena lit a cigarette. She had met Mr Blake for the first time this afternoon and for a moment she felt he must have clairvoyance, like a mind reader in a movie house or, more accurately, a *fortune* teller. His confederate, of course, was Kay, drat her. She rued the day she had told her, as a curious fact, that her parents lived 'on the income of their income' – i.e. plainly. But Kay had had to turn it into a boast. Already this afternoon Helena had heard her telling Harald's producer that 'Helena's parents have never *felt* the depression.' 'What was the name?' inquired the producer, turning to examine Helena, as they always did. Kay supplied the name of Helena's father. 'Never heard of him,' said the producer. 'Neither have most people,' said Kay. 'But they know him down in Wall Street. And he's crazy about the theatre. Ask Harald. He saw a lot of the Davisons when his show was playing Cleveland last year. Her mother is president of one of the women's clubs there, quite a remarkable woman, always organizing classes and lectures for working-class girls; she scorns groups like the Junior League that don't mean business. . . .'

Helena blew smoke rings – an art she had perfected as an aid against self-consciousness; all her life, she had submitted to being talked *about*, first and foremost by her mother. She was a short, sandy-haired girl with an appealing snub nose and an air of being sturdy though she was really thin and slight. She very much resembled her father, a short, sandy Scot who had made a pile of money in steel through knowing about alloys; he had been born in a little town called Iron Mountain, Michigan. Helena was regarded as the droll member of the group, having a puckish sense of humour, a slow, drawling way of talking, and a habit of walking around nude that had startled the others at first. Her figure was almost undeveloped, and when you saw her from a distance, hiking down a corridor to the shower with a towel around her neck, you might have thought she was a freckled little boy on his way to a swimming-hole in the woods somewhere; her legs were slightly bowed, and her little patch of hair down there was a bright pinky red. She and Kay, when they first knew each other freshman year, used to climb trees together on Sunset Hill, back of the lake, and perform strange experiments in the Chem Lab, nearly blowing each other up. Yet Helena was intelligent, the group discovered, and in some ways very mature for her age. She had read a tremendous lot, particularly in modern literature, and listened to modern music, which was way over most of the group's heads; she collected limited editions of verse and rare phonograph records of pre-polyphonic church music. The group considered her quite an asset, almost a little mascot, in her neat Shetland sweater and skirt, riding across the campus on her bicycle or chasing butterflies with a net in the Shakespeare Garden.

The worst, from Helena's point of view, was that she *knew* all this, knew, that is, about the mascot and the swimming-hole and how she looked with the butterfly net; she had been watched and described too carefully by too many experts – all indulgent and smiling, like the group. She had been registered for Vassar at birth; her mother had had her tutored in every conceivable subject all through her childhood. Helena (as her mother said) could play the violin, the piano, the flute, and the trumpet; she had sung alto in the choir. She had been a camp counsellor and had a senior lifesaving badge. She played a good game of tennis, golfed, skied, and figure-skated; she rode, though she had never jumped or hunted. She had a real chemistry set, a little printing press, a set for tooling leather, a pottery wheel, a library of wild-flower, fern, and bird books, a butterfly collection mounted on pins in glass cases, collections of sea shells, agates, quartz, and cornelians; these educational souvenirs were still kept in cupboards in her little sitting-room in Cleveland, which had formerly been the nursery – her doll's house and toys had been given away. She could write a severe little essay, imitate birdcalls, ring chimes, and play lacrosse as well as chess, checkers, mah-jongg, parcheesi, anagrams, dominoes, slapjack, pounce, rummy, whist, bridge, and cribbage. She knew most of the hymns in the Episcopal and Presbyterian hymnbooks by heart. She had had dancing lessons, ballroom, classical, and tap. She had done field walks in Geology and visited the State Asylum for the Insane, bunked in the Outing Cabin, and looked over the printing presses of the *Duchess County Sentinel* in Poughkeepsie. She had swum in the waterfall near Washington's Crossing and attended the annual Greek play at the Bennett School in Millbrook. She and Kay, in Freshman Hygiene, were just about the only members of the class who actually inspected the dairies where the college cows were kept; one of the workmen had shown Helena how to milk. She knew china and had a small collection of snuffboxes at home that her mother had started for her; she knew Greek and Latin and could translate the worst passages of Krafft-Ebing without a shadow of embarrassment. She knew medieval French and the lays of the *trouvères*, though her accent was poor because her mother dis-approved of French governesses, having heard of cases where these women drugged children or put their heads in the gas oven to make them go to sleep. At camp, Helena had learned to sail and sing old catches and sea chanties, some of them rather off-colour; she improvised on the mouth-organ and was studying the recorder. She had had art lessons since she was six and showed quite a gift for drawing. When Kay, senior year, had the group making those lists of who liked whom best, Helena cannily said she couldn't decide and instead drew a big coloured cartoon which she called 'The Judgement of Paris', showing them all in the nude, like goddesses, and herself very small in a jerkin with a dunce's cap on her head and a wormy apple in her hand. Tickled, they hung it in their common sitting-room, and there was quite a controversy about whether they should take it down at Prom time when they had some of their beaux in to tea; the modest members of the group, like Dottie and Polly Andrews, were afraid of being considered fast because the likenesses were so realistic that somebody might have thought they had posed.

Having been Kay's room-mate (before they all grouped together) and had her to stay in Cleveland, Helena accepted her mother's dictum, that Kay was her 'best friend', though they were no longer as close as they had been before sex entered Kay's life. Helena had known about sex from a very early age but treated it as a joke, like what she called your plumbing. She was dry and distant towards the fond passion, as she called it, and was amused by Kay's ardours for Harald, whom she coolly dubbed 'Harald Handfast', an allusion to the Old English custom of bedding before wedding. To her, men in general were a curious species, like the unicorn; for Harald in particular her feelings were circumspect and consisted chiefly of a mental protest against the way he spelled his name. Her parents, however, liked him and approved of Kay's choice. When his play was in Cleveland last winter, Mr Davison had offered him a card to his club, which he did not use much himself, he said, 'being a plain fellow'.

Kay herself was a favourite with Helena's mother, and, whenever she came to stay, Mrs Davison, who was a great talker, liked to discuss Helena with her at breakfast, over her second cup of coffee in the handsome panelled breakfast room, while Helena herself was still sleeping and only the toby jugs and Mr Davison's collection of English china stirrup cups made in the form of foxes' heads were able (commented Helena) to listen. Knowing the two participants, Helena, in her sleep, could have told how the conversation would go. 'She has had *every opportunity*,' emphasized Mrs Davison, with an impressive look at Kay, who was respectfully drinking her orange juice, which was served in cracked ice. '*Every opportunity*.' This way of stressing and repeating her words would lead Kay to think that Mrs Davison was implying, for Kay's ears alone, that Helena had been a grave disappointment to her mother. But this was an error, as other chums of Helena's had found. Accustomed to public speaking, Mrs Davison always paused and intensified to let her words slowly sink in, even with an audience of one. Her real belief was that Helena was turning out extremely well, though she greatly wondered, she said to Kay, that Helena had not 'seen fit' to go on with her art at college. 'Davy Davison and I,' she explained, 'would have had no objection at all to Helena's becoming a painter. *After* she had finished her college work. Her teacher here considered that she had unusual promise, a *decided bent*, and so did Mr Smart at the museum. We had talked of giving her a year or two at the Art Students League in New York and of letting her have a studio in Greenwich Village. But her interests have widened at Vassar, dontcha know.' Kay agreed. Mrs Davison also wondered that Helena had failed to make Phi Beta Kappa. 'I said' (Kay reported to Helena) 'that only grinds made Phi Beta junior year.' 'Just as I told Davy Davison!' exclaimed Mrs Davison. 'Girls who had been coached and *crammed*.' Mrs Davison often spoke with detestation of 'crammers'.

'I am not a college woman myself,' Mrs Davison continued, 'and it's a thing I've bitterly regretted. I shall blame Davy Davison for it till they put pennies on my eyes.' This remark remained partly cryptic, like many of Mrs Davison's utterances, in which learned allusions – like this one to Roman burial customs – mingled with obscure personal reminiscence. Kay took her to mean that Mr Davison had married her (in Mrs Davison's own parlance) 'untimely', which she found hard to imagine because, much as she liked her, she could not imagine Mrs Davison young. Helena's mother was a tall fat woman with piles of grey hair done in unfashionable puffs on either side of her ears and large, pensive, lustrous dark eyes that seemed misplaced in her big, doughy, plain countenance, which was white and shapeless, like bread punched down and set to rise again in a crock. She was a Canadian, from the province of Saskatchewan, and spoke in somewhat breathy tones.

In point of fact, she had been a country school teacher and well along in life, rising thirty, when Mr Davison had met her, at the home of a metallurgist. If she could not write 'B.A.' after her name, it had been by her own choice: in the *annus mirabilis* (1901) when the university had opened at Saskatoon – a story she was fond of telling – she had gone to inspect the professors and found she knew more than they did. 'Like the Child Jesus in the temple, *toute proportion gardée*,' she avowed. Nevertheless, she harboured a mysterious grievance against Mr Davison for not having been permitted to finish, as she put it, her education. 'We'll have to buy Mother an honorary degree for her golden wedding anniversary,' Helena's father sometimes remarked.

Both Mr and Mrs Davison had an emphatic distaste for show. Mrs Davison wore no jewellery, except for her wedding and engagement rings and occasional Victorian brooches set with garnets, her birthstone, fastened to the bosom of her coin-print or polka-dot dresses. Helena had a set of moonstones, a cat's-eye brooch, an amethyst pin, and an Add-a-Pearl necklace that had been completed on her eighteenth birthday, when she was presented to society (that is, to the family's old friends) at a small tea given by her mother in their house, which was called 'The Cottage' and had a walled garden and English wallflowers.

The Davison house – Kay had told the group – was almost magical, like a house found in a fairy tale, though it was right in the heart of Cleveland, only two blocks from a street-car stop but hidden by tall privet hedges and the garden wall. It was small, compact, and silent, with chintz-cushioned window seats and rocking-chairs and cupboards and shelves and 'dressers' full of fragile, precious things that were used for everyday, like instructive toys you could play with – milk glass, Sandwich glass, Wedgwood, Staffordshire, Lowestoft, Crown Derby. A table seemed almost always to be set, for breakfast, lunch, tea, or dinner, with toast-racks, muffin warmers, a Lazy Susan (Kay had never heard the name before, even), muffineers full of powdered sugar, finger bowls in which flowers floated. Yet there were no butlers or footmen darting around to make you nervous for fear of using the wrong utensils. When Helena, who was always the last down, had finished her breakfast, the coloured maid would bring in a big china basin with pretty pink roses on it and a pitcher full of hot water, and Mrs Davison would wash the breakfast cups and saucers at the table (an old pioneer custom, she said) and dry them on an embroidered tea towel. At dinner, after the main course, the maid would bring in a salad bowl of Chinese porcelain, red and green, and an old cruet stand with olive oil, a mustard pot, and vials of different kinds of vinegar, and Mr Davison, standing up, would make the salad dressing himself and mix the salad, which was always sprinkled with fresh herbs. They did not entertain very often; most of the family friends, Kay said, were rather old, bachelors or widows, and neither Mr Davison (whose real name was Edward) nor Mrs Davison was enthusiastic about what they humorously called 'followers', though Helena, being an only child, had been given *every opportunity* at her progressive day school to meet boys and girls of her own age. Not to mention dancing school and Sunday school; neither Mr Davison nor Mrs Davison was a regular churchgoer (although Mrs Davison was a sharp judge of a sermon), but they felt it only right that Helena should know the Bible and the beliefs of the principal Christian creeds, so that she could make up her own mind.

After day school, she had gone to a sound boarding-school in New England with a well-rounded curriculum but no frills. In the summers, they had taken cottages at Watch Hill, Rhode Island, at Yarmouth in Nova Scotia, and at Biddeford Pool in Maine, and Helena had always had her friends come to visit her there and, after she was eighteen and had had driving lessons, the use of a small Ford runabout, as Mrs Davison described it, which Mr Davison had bought for a second car.

For the summer of 1930, after freshman year, they had planned a trip through the Lake District (Mrs Davison was a great admirer of *Dorothy* Wordsworth), but with business conditions what they were, they had concluded that it was best to stay home, where Mr Davison could keep an eye on developments. None of the other girls from Vassar was going, as Mrs Davison had ascertained.

This last June, it was Mr Davison who had suddenly declared that Helena needed a change. At Commencement, he had thought she looked peaked and had told her mother so. She had better go to Europe and look around for a few months by herself, before going to work at that nursery school, which was dang-fool nonsense anyway. With all Helena's education, she had elected to play the piano and teach Dalcroze and finger painting at an experimental school in Cleveland – to a darned lot of kikes' children, from what Mr Davison had heard. Where was the sense in that, he had asked Kay angrily at lunch after Commencement, while Mrs Davison said 'Now, Daddy!' and Kay and Helena exchanged looks. 'All right, Mother.' Mr Davison had subsided momentarily. Kay suspected that he was angry because Helena had failed to get *magna cum laude*, when a lot of the Jewish girls had. Mrs Davison evidently had the same thought, because she now cleared her throat and remarked that the simple *cum laude*, Helena's meed, was the sign of a real student as opposed to what, in *her* day, had been called 'a greasy grind'. 'I *watched* those *magnas* go up for their diplomas,' she announced, 'and I didn't like the look of them at all; they smell of the lamp, as I told Davy Davison. The midnight oil, dontcha know.' 'Oh, Mother!' said Helena and raised her eyebrows in distress. Mr Davison would not be diverted. 'Why should Helena take a job away from some girl who really needs it? Can you tell me that?' he demanded, pushing his fried chicken away. His small round cheeks had turned red. Kay started to answer, but Mrs Davison intervened. 'Now, Daddy,' she said placidly, 'do you mean to assert that a girl in Helena's position doesn't have the same rights as other girls?'

'I mean exactly that,' Mr Davison retorted. 'You've hit the nail smack on the head. We pay a price for having money. People in my position' – he turned to Kay – 'have "privilege". That's what I read in the *Nation* and the *New Republic*.' Mrs Davison nodded. 'Good,' said Mr Davison. 'Now listen. The fellow who's got privilege gives up some rights or ought to.' 'I'm not sure I understand,' said Kay. 'Sure you do,' said Mr Davison. 'So do Mother and Helena.' 'Let's choose another example,' said Mrs Davison thoughtfully. 'If Helena, say, were to paint a picture. Would she not have the right to sell it because other artists are impecunious?' 'A painting isn't a service, Mother,' said Mr Davison. 'Helena's offering a service that a hundred other girls in Cleveland could do as well.' At this point, the discussion broke off; the waiter presented the check, which Mr Davison paid. Helena herself had hardly said a word.

Afterwards, Kay declared that Mr Davison's ideas were surprisingly unfair and that the trip to Europe was a bribe that would corrupt Helena's integrity. She was amazed (and she repeated it today, right to Helena's face) that Helena had gone meekly off to Europe with her tail between her legs and stayed till just before Christmas. And now that she was back she was making no effort to get a job but talking of studying dry point in Cleveland and taking a course in acrobatic dancing at the Y.W.C.A., of all places. Nor was it a question of just marking time till she got married, like some other girls; Helena, Kay said, would never get married – she was a neuter, like a little mule. Therefore it was up to her to realize her potentialities. She and Kay were just the opposite of each other Kay had been telling Mr Bergler this afternoon.

'Really?' said Mr Bergler. 'How?' 'In college I wanted to be a director,' Kay replied. 'Come here, Helena,' she called loudly. 'We're talking about you.' Unwillingly, Helena approached; she was wearing a skullcap hat and a black velvet dress, with buttons straight down the front and a little old-lace collar with her cat's-eye brooch. 'I was saying I always wanted to be a director,' Kay continued. 'Well!' said the producer, an unassuming grey-haired Jewish man with white soft skin and flat grey fish eyes. 'So that's what you and Hal have in common.' Kay nodded. 'I directed one of the Hall Plays at college. That's different from D P – Dramatic Production, which Hallie teaches – Hallie Flanagan, have you heard of her? Anyway, the Hall Plays are part of Philaletheis, which is just a student thing. It sounds like stamp collecting. But it means something different – loving the theatre. In D P, Hallie would never let me direct. I worked on the lighting with Lester – Lester Lang, her assistant; you probably haven't heard of him. And I built scenery.' 'And now?' 'I gave it up,' said Kay with a sigh. 'Now I work at Mr Macy's, in the training squad. I have the drive but not the talent. That's what Harald said when he saw the Hall Play I directed. It was *The Winter's Tale* – in the Outdoor Theatre. Helena played Autolycus.'

The producer turned his eyes to Helena. 'That's what I started to say,' Kay went on, remembering. 'I lost the thread for a minute. I have the drive but not the talent, and Helena has the talents but not the drive.' 'You're interested in a stage career?' inquired the producer curiously, bending down to Helena. 'Oh no,' Kay answered for Helena. 'Helena's a mime but not an actress. That's what Harald thinks. No. But Helena has so many other talents that she can't choose between them – canalize. She writes and sings and paints and dances and plays I don't know how many instruments. The compleat girl. I was telling Mr Bergler about your parents, Helena. She has the most remarkable parents. How many magazines does your mother "take in"? Her mother is a Canadian,' she added, while Helena stood pondering with a fresh cup of punch in her hand. She was being called upon, she recognized, to perform for Mr Bergler, and she was going to do it, just as she used to recite or play under her mother's eye, feeling like a conscientious wind-up toy. She had a 'searching' anxious little gaze, which she now directed upward at Mr Bergler from under the reddish eaves of her brows.

'Well,' she began, grimacing and drawling her words, 'there's the *National Geographic*, *Christian Century*, the *Churchman*, *Theatre Arts Monthly*, the *Stage*, the *Nation*, the *New Republic*, *Scribner's*, *Harper's*, the *Bookman*, the *Forum*, the London *Times Literary Supplement*, the *Economist*, the *Spectator*, *Blackwood's Life and Letters Today*, the *Nineteenth Century and After*, *Punch*, *L'Illustration*, *Connaissance des Arts*, *Antiques*, *Country Life*, *Isis*, the *PMLA*, the *Lancet*, the *American Scholar*, the annual report of the College Boards, *Vanity Fair*, the *American Mercury*, the *New Yorker*, and *Fortune* (those four are for Daddy, but Mother "glances them over").'

'You're forgetting some,' said Kay. Mr Bergler smiled; he was supposed to be rather a Communist. 'The *Atlantic Monthly*, surely,' he suggested. Helena shook her head. 'No. Mother is having a "feud" with the *Atlantic Monthly*. She disapproved of something in the Jalna series and cancelled her subscription. Mother dearly loves cancelling her subscriptions – as a painful duty. Her feud with the *Saturday Review of Literature* has been very hard on her, because of the "Double-Crostic". She's thought of resubscribing in our maid's name, but she fears they might recognize the address.' 'She sounds a most awesome lady,' said Mr Bergler, responding to Helena's faint grin. 'Tell me, what does she find objectionable in the *Saturday Review of Literature*? Has sex reared its head there?' 'Oh,' said Helena. 'You misjudge my mother. She's impervious to sex.' A publisher's reader who lived in the apartment downstairs had come up to listen; he gave Libby MacAusland's arm a little squeeze. 'I love that, don't you?' he said. 'Mother's shock area,' continued Helena imperturbably, 'is confined to the higher brain centres; the "bump" of grammar and usage is highly developed. She's morally offended by impure English.' 'Like what?' encouraged Kay. 'Dangling modifiers. Improper prepositions. "Agravating" to mean "annoying", "demean" to mean "lower", "sinister".' '"Sinister"?' echoed the publisher's reader. 'Mother says it only means left-handed or done with the left hand. If you tell her a person is sinister, all she will infer, she says, is that he's left-handed. A deed, she allows, may be sinister, if it's done sidewise or "under the robe" or "on the wrong side of the blanket".' 'I never heard *that*!' cried Pokey, as if indignant. The group around Helena had grown larger and was forming into a circle. '"Infer", "imply",' prompted Libby, eager to be heard. 'Ummhum,' said Helena. 'But that's too commonplace to be under Mother's special protection. "Meticulous", which is not a synonym for "neat". She sets great store by Latin roots, you notice, but she frowns on the ablative absolute as a construction in English.' 'Yow!' said Harald's friend, Mr Sisson, the one who had taken pictures at the wedding. 'Oh, and "I cannot help but feel".' 'What's wrong with that?' asked several voices. '"I cannot help feeling" or "I cannot but feel".' 'More!' said the publisher's reader. Helena demurred. 'I cannot help feeling,' she said, 'that that is enough of Mother's "pet peeves".'

Her mother's habit of stressing and underlining her words had undergone an odd mutation in being transmitted to Helena. Where Mrs Davison stressed and emphasized, Helena inserted *her* words carefully between inverted commas, so that clauses, phrases, and even proper names, inflected by her light voice, had the sound of being ironical quotations. While everything Mrs Davison said seemed to carry with it a guarantee of authority, everything Helena said seemed subject to the profoundest doubt. 'I saw "Miss Sandison",' she had been telling Kay and Dottie, 'in the "British Museum",' signifying by the lifting of her brows and the rolling about of the names on her slow, dry tongue that "Miss Sandison" was an alias of some wondrous sort and the "British Museum" a front or imposture. This wry changing of pitch had become mechanical with her, like a slide inserted in a trombone. In fact, she had a great respect for her former Shakespeare teacher and for the British Museum. She had had a library card virtually from the time she could walk and was as much at home with the various systems of cataloguing as she was with the Furness *Variorum*. At college she had excelled at the 'note topic' – a favourite with Miss Sandison too – and had many wooden boxes full of neatly classified cards on her desk beside the portable typewriter she had got for Christmas junior year – Mrs Davison had not wished her to take up typing till her handwriting was formed; for a period in Cleveland she had had a calligraphy lesson every other day between her music lesson and her riding lesson and she had learned to cut her own quills from feathers. Nothing, moreover, was more natural than that she should find her teacher, an Elizabethan specialist, in the British Museum, yet Helena had gone on to explain methodically, as though it required accounting for, the circumstances that had brought this about: how Miss Sandison was doing a paper, in her sabbatical leave, on a little-known Elizabethan, 'Arthur Gorges', and Helena was looking up an early publication of 'Dorothy Richardson' and had stopped to see the 'Elgin Marbles'. In relating such 'true particulars', Helena lowered her voice and gravely puckered her forehead, with a confidential air like her mother's, as though giving privileged news from a sick room in which lay a common friend.

'A cute kid, that,' the producer told Harald, when he was leaving. 'Reminds me of the young Hepburn – before they glamorized her. Clubwoman mother there too.' Helena found nothing to object to in the last part of this 'tribute'. 'Mother *is* a clubwoman,' she pointed out mildly to Kay, who felt that Mrs Davison had been disparaged. 'And I don't like Katharine Hepburn.' She wished people would stop making this comparison. Mrs Davison had been the first to notice a resemblance. 'She was a Bryn Mawr girl, Helena. Class of '29. Davy Davison and I saw her with Jane Cowl. She wore her hair short like yours.'

Wearily, Helena eyed the bedroom door. She wanted to go home or, rather, to go have dinner with Dottie at the Forty-ninth Street Longchamps, across from the Vassar Club. She knew that when she got back to Cleveland, she would be bound to report to her mother how she had 'found' Kay and Harald, what their new apartment was like, and how Harald was making out in his career. 'I have always been partial to Kay,' Mrs Davison would state, satisfied, when Helena had finished her narration. It was one of Mrs Davison's peculiarities, well known to Helena, that, like royalty, she insisted that all news be favourable and reflect a steady advance of human affairs.

It was wonderful news, of course, that Harald's play was going to be produced, yet neither Kay nor Harald seemed very happy. Possibly, as Dottie suggested, success had been too slow in coming. Dottie had heard a painful story: that Harald had been helping a puppeteer who gave shows at vulgar rich people's parties; someone had seen him behind the scenes working the lights in the little portable puppet theatre – he was not allowed to mingle with the guests. Kay had never mentioned this to a soul. Today, she looked strained and tired, and Harald was drinking too much. He was right; the party had not 'jelled'. The producer and his wife had seemed mystified by so much Vassar; Helena feared Harald's stock had gone down. Kay craved the limelight for the group, but the limelight did not become them. As Harald said, they did not know how to 'project'. Of all the girls here this afternoon, only Kay, in his and Helena's opinion – they had agreed on this, by the punch bowl – was a genuine beauty. Yet she was losing her vivid colouring, which would distress Mrs Davison, who admired the 'roses' in Kay's cheeks.

The bedroom door opened. The love-birds had made it up. Kay was smiling dewily, and Harald's cigarette holder was cocked at a jaunty angle. He had a big bowl of chile con carne, Kay announced, that he had fixed this morning, and everyone was to stay and eat. Afterwards, if the guests were agreeable, he was going to read aloud an act from his play. There was no help for it, Helena and Dottie were bound to stay; Kay was counting on them. Harald went out to the kitchen, refilling his punch glass en route; he would not let Kay help him – she was tired, and this was her holiday. 'Isn't that touching?' murmured Dottie. Helena was not touched. Harald, she presumed, knew Kay as well as she did, and if there was anything Kay hated, it was being left out; she was a glutton for making herself useful. They heard Harald moving about in the kitchen, the rattle of plates, the creak of drawers opening. Kay could not contain herself. 'Can't I make the coffee?' she called out. 'No!' Harald's voice retorted. 'Entertain your guests.' Kay looked around the circle with a defeated, anxious smile. '*I'll* help him,' volunteered Dottie as the rattle of crockery continued. 'No,' said Norine. 'I'll do it. I know the kitchen.' With a purposeful stride, she went out; the shuttered door trembled as she pulled it shut. 'She'll make the coffee too weak,' Kay said sadly to Helena. 'And she'll want to use paper napkins.' 'Forget about it,' advised Helena.

The radio actor turned to Kay. He was more than a little drunk; the cigarette in his hand wavered. 'Give me a light, will you?' Kay looked around; there were no matches; all the little booklets were empty. Putnam silently proffered his burning pipe. As the actor stabbed his cigarette into the bowl, some coals fell on the newly waxed floor. 'Oh, dear!' cried Kay, stamping them out. 'I'll get some matches from the kitchen.' 'I'll do it,' said Helena.

In the small kitchen, behind the slatted door, she found Norine and Harald locked in an embrace. Her classmate's tall, rangy figure, like that of a big lynx or bobcat, was bent back as Harald kissed her, pressing forward in a sort of feral lunge. The scene reminded Helena, for some reason, of German silent films. Norine's tawny eyes were closed, and an Oriental turban she wore – her own millinery achievement – had come partly unwound. A dish towel was lying on the floor. Their wet mouths drew apart as Helena entered, and their heads turned to look at her. Then they heard Kay call. 'Did you find them? Harald, give her the kitchen matches, will you?' Helena saw the box of matches on the stove. Norine and Harald backed away from each other, and she hurriedly dodged between them. 'Gangway,' she said. She picked up the towel and tossed it to Harald. Then she seized the matches and made for the living-room. Her small hand shook with borrowed guilt as she struck the big sulphur match and held it for the actor to take a light from. It went out. She lit another. The room, she noted, was full of the smell of brimstone.

In a few minutes Norine strode in with a tray of plates and a box of paper napkins, and Harald followed with his chile. Everyone ate. The radio actor resumed his critique of *Sheepskin*. 'The fall of a just man is precipitous,' replied Harald, with a side glance at Helena. He set his plate down with a slight lurch. 'Excuse me while I go to the toilet.' 'The fall of a just man,' repeated the actor. 'How well Harald puts it. The college president starts at the top, politicians put the skids under him, and he shoots right down to the bottom. It's a bold conception, no doubt, but not an *actor*'s conception.' 'Wasn't Shakespeare an actor?' suddenly spoke up the naval officer. 'What's that got to do with my point?' said the actor. 'Well, I mean, *King Lear*,' said the officer. 'Doesn't he start at the top?' '*King Lear*,' remarked Helena, 'was hardly a just man.' They heard the closet flush. 'And there's relief in *Lear*,' said the actor. 'Cordelia. Kent. The fool. In Harald's play there's no relief. Harald claims that would be fakery.'

'Clara's cake!' cried Kay, as coffee was being served. 'Harald! We've got to serve Clara's cake. I promised her. I'm afraid her feelings were hurt when we wouldn't let her pass it with the punch.'

'When *I* wouldn't let her pass it,' corrected Harald with a melancholy air. 'Why don't you say what you mean, Kay?' Kay turned to the others. 'Wait till you see it. She made it for our party and brought it down from Harlem on a paper lace doily. Clara's a wonderful character. She runs a high-class funeral parlour. Tiger Flowers was buried from it. You ought to hear her description of him "laying in state". And I love it when she talks about her competitors. "Those fly-by-night undertakers are takin' our business away."' 'Get the cake,' said Harald. 'Your darky imitation is terrible.' '*You* imitate her, Harald!' 'Get the cake,' he repeated. They waited for Kay to come back. They could hear her washing up. The cat seemed to have got Norine's tongue, and 'Putnam Blake' was no conversationalist. Dottie passed the coffee again. When it was his turn to be served he nudged Helena. 'Look, real cream!' he said, his peculiar eyes aglow. Helena could see that this excited him more than anything that had happened at the party.

Kay came in with fresh plates and a cake on a doily on a pink glass platter. The frosting was decorated with a maraschino cherry tree and a chocolate hatchet. 'Oh, bless her heart!' said Dottie. 'Her old black heart,' said Harald, eyeing the cake askance. 'Straight from a Harlem bakery,' he pronounced. Kay put a hand to her cheek. 'Oh, no!' she said. 'Clara wouldn't tell me a lie.' Harald smiled darkly. 'A most villainous cake. "Let them eat bread." Don't you agree, my friend?' He turned to the naval officer. 'Look at the frosting,' said the actor. 'It's pure Lavoris.'

Tears appeared in Kay's eyes. Defiantly, she began to cut the cake. 'Kay loves to be a gull,' said Harald. 'In the simplicity of her heart, she imagines that old coon happily baking for "Miss Kay" and "Mister Man".' '*I* think it's touching,' said Dottie quickly. 'And I'll bet it tastes delicious.' She accepted a piece and began to eat it. The others followed suit, except for Harald, who shook his head when the platter was passed to him. 'Down the incinerator with it!' he declared with a flourish of his coffee spoon. There was a laugh and a silence. It appeared that Harald had been right. 'It's like eating frosted absorbent cotton,' murmured the actor to Helena. Helena set her plate aside. In Kay's place, she would not have served the cake – from a purely practical motive: so that the maid would not be encouraged to waste her money again. But she did not find Harald's 'antic hay' very amusing, all things considered.

He had put on the motley, she felt, for her special benefit to tell her that he was a Man of Sorrows. Was he afraid she would give him away, poor devil? Helena would have been glad to reassure him. 'I shall listen to no tales, Helena,' her mother had always admonished her if she came to report on a playmate. Helena did not 'care for' what she had seen, but she assumed the bottle was responsible and felt a certain sympathy for Harald's present discomfort. He was being bad to Kay, she supposed, because if he were amiable, Helena would consider him a whited sepulchre.

Across the room Kay was talking – rather boisterously, Helena felt – about wedding presents. Helena's pity for her had taken the form of acute embarrassment. Kay was on a stage without knowing it. Three ironic spectators, counting Helena, were watching her and listening. The *strangest* objects, she was saying, were still arriving by parcel post – right in a class with Clara's cake. 'Look at these, for instance.' She brought out an ugly red glass decanter and six little cordial glasses that had come (she could hardly believe it) from one of her childhood friends in Salt Lake City. 'What can we do with them? Send them to the Salvation Army?' 'Give them to Clara,' said the actor. Nearly everyone laughed. 'Down the incinerator with them!' said Harald suddenly.

They were examining the decanter, holding it up to the light, arguing about workmanship and mass production, when they heard the front door close. The pink glass platter with the remains of the cake on it was gone. Harald was gone too. 'Where did he disappear to?' said the naval officer. '*I* thought he was in the kitchen,' said Norine. Then the doorbell rang. Harald had locked himself out. 'Where have you been?' they demanded. 'Giving the cake a Viking's funeral. A *beau geste*, was it not?' He saluted the group. 'Oh, Harald,' said Kay sadly. 'That was Clara's cake plate.' The actor giggled. With an air of decision, Harald began to collect the little red cordial glasses. 'You take the decanter, my friend,' he said to the actor. The actor obeyed and followed him, humming the 'Dead March' from *Saul*. 'Are they spiffed?' whispered Dottie. Helena nodded. This time Harald left the door open, and the group in the living-room could hear a distant crash of glass breaking as the set went down the incinerator in the hall. 'Next?' said Harald, returning. 'What next, my dear?' Kay tried to laugh. 'I'd better stop him,' she said to the others, 'or he'll make a general holocaust of all our goods and chattels.' 'Yes, stop him,' urged Putnam. 'This is serious.' 'Don't be a wet blanket,' said the actor. 'Let's make a game of it. Everybody choose his candidate for the incinerator.' Kay jumped up. 'Harald,' she said, coaxing. 'Why don't you read us your play instead? You promised.' 'Ah yes,' said Harald. 'And it's getting late. And you have to work tomorrow. But you give me an idea.' He went into the dinette and took a manuscript in a grey folder from a cupboard.

'Down the incinerator with it!' His tall, lean, sinewy figure paused a moment by the bookcase, then began to skirt the furniture: Norine's voice was heard ordering someone to stop him, and Putnam and the naval officer moved to block his way to the door. The actor leaped for the manuscript, and there was a sound of tearing paper as Harald wrenched it away. Holding it tight to his chest, with his free hand he pushed off his pursuers, like somebody racing for a touchdown. At the door, there was a scuffle, but Harald managed to open it, and it slammed behind him. He did not return. 'Oh, well,' said Kay. 'Could he have thrown *himself* down the incinerator?' whispered Dottie. 'No,' said the actor. 'I thought of that. It's too small for a man's body.' For a moment no one spoke.

'But where has he gone, Kay?' said Norine. 'He hasn't got an overcoat.' 'Downstairs probably,' replied Kay matter-of-factly. 'To have a drink with Russell.' This was the publisher's reader. 'I guess you'd better go home,' Kay continued. 'He won't come back till you're all gone. I always used to be scared when he disappeared like that. I thought he was going to throw himself in the river. Then I found out that he went to Russell's. Or over to Norine and Put's.' Putnam nodded. 'But he can't be there,' he said simply. 'Because we're here.' They were all putting on their coats. 'And his manuscript, Kay?' said Dottie, venturing a discreet reminder. 'Oh,' said Kay. 'Don't worry. Bergler has a copy. And Walter Huston has one. And there're three on file with Harald's agent.' Kay, reflected Helena for the second time, had always been a 'blurter'.

In the taxi, Helena and Dottie held a post-mortem. 'Were you scared or did you guess?' asked Dottie. 'I was scared,' said Helena. 'Everyone in that room was gulled good and proper.' She grinned. 'Except Kay,' said Dottie. 'That's funny,' she added after a moment. 'Harald must have known Kay knew. That he had other copies, I mean.' Helena nodded. 'Did he count on her silence?' Dottie wondered, in a voice that still sounded impressed. 'And she betrayed him!' 'She's not a gangster's moll,' said Helena shortly. 'Would you have exposed him like that, in her place?' persisted Dottie. 'Yes,' said Helena.

She was dourly composing a new version of the Class Notes. 'Washington's Birthday Report. Yestreen I saw Kay Strong Petersen's new husband in Norine Schmittlapp Blake's arms. Both were looking well, and Kay is expecting a promotion at Macy's. Later in the evening the guests were treated to a ceremonial manuscript-burning. Kay served Fish House Punch, from an old colonial recipe. Kay and Harald have an elegant apartment in the East Fifties, convenient to the river, where Harald will be able to throw himself when his marriage goes "on the rocks". Re this, Anthropology major Dottie Renfrew opines that the little things, like lying, become so important in marriage. If she married a man who was a born liar, she would conform to his tribal custom. How about this, '33? Write me your ideas and let's have a really stimulating discussion.'

Chapter 6

The morning after Kay's party, Helena was planning to breakfast with her father, who had arrived on the sleeper from Cleveland; they were going to do the silversmiths together for her mother's anniversary present. She was to meet him at the Savoy Plaza, where he kept a bedroom and sitting-room for the times when he was in New York on business; they gave him a special rate. Helena herself usually stayed at the Vassar Club in the Hotel New Weston, where her mother sometimes joined her, finding the atmosphere 'suitable'. Mrs Davison had the heart of an alumna, and it was a cross to her not to be eligible for the Women's University Club in Cleveland, in which so many of her acquaintances were active and where she often figured as a guest. 'I am not a university woman myself,' she would begin when invited by the Chair to comment on a lecture that trenched on one of her fields of interest. 'I am not a college woman myself,' Helena would overhear her telling the Vassar Club secretary or some Class of '10 alumna in the lounge at teatime, laying aside the current issue of the *Vassar Alumnae Magazine* with the confidence of a born speaker. Simply by clearing her throat, her mother could command an audience, of which only Helena was an unwilling constituent. 'We are taking out a five-year membership for Helena at the Vassar Club here,' Mrs Davison's measured tones continued, 'so that she can always have a place to go, a *pied-à-terre*, like her father's in New York. "A Room of One's Own", dontcha know.' Her mother's 'decisions', especially those pertaining to Helena, were not simply announced, but promulgated. For this very reason, Helena was uncomfortable at the Vassar Club, which had come to seem to her like one of her mother's purlieus, yet she continued to stay there, whenever she was in New York, because, as Mrs Davison said, it was central, convenient, economical, and she could meet her friends in the lounge.

This morning the phone rang while she was still in the shower. It was not her father; it was Norine, calling from a pay station in a drugstore and declaring that she had to see Helena right away, as soon as Putnam had gone out. He was in the bathroom now, shaving. All Norine wanted from her, plainly, was the assurance that she was not going to tell anybody, but since Norine did not say this on the telephone, Helena could not say, either, that Norine did not have to worry. Instead, she found herself agreeing philosophically to come to Norine's place and cancelling her date with her father, who was quite put out; he could not see what was so urgent that it could not wait till afternoon. Helena did not specify; she never lied to her parents. She was unable to see, herself, to come down to brass tacks, why Norine couldn't have met her for tea or a cocktail or lunch tomorrow. But when Helena had proposed this in her driest tones, there had been a silence on the other end of the wire, and then Norine's clipped voice had said dully, 'Never mind; forget it. I should have guessed you wouldn't want to see me,' which had made Helena deny this and promise to come at once.

She did not look forward to the interview. Her light, mildly aseptic irony was wasted on Norine, who was unaware of irony and humorous vocal shadings; she listened only to the overt content of what was said and drew her own blunt inferences, as she had just now on the telephone. Under normal circumstances, Helena would have been interested to see Norine's apartment, which Kay had described as a 'sketch', but right now she would have preferred to meet Norine in more impersonal surroundings – the Vassar Club lounge, for instance. She had no curiosity to hear whatever explanation or extenuation Norine, she supposed, was going to offer her, and it struck her as unjust that she should be haled to Norine's place just because, through no fault of her own, she had witnessed something that was plainly none of her business. It was like the time her father had been hauled into court because he had innocently witnessed a traffic accident; when those darned lawyers got through with him, he declared he had no character left.

Norine, at any rate, did not live in some remote part of Greenwich Village, as might have been expected. Her apartment was quite near the New Weston Hotel, on a pretty street a block east of the Lexington Avenue subway stop that had trees and private houses with window boxes, a block just as good as Kay's block, if not somewhat better. This surprised Helena. She found Norine, dressed in an old pair of ski pants, a sweat skirt, and a man's leather jacket, sitting on the front stoop of a yellow stucco house and anxiously scanning the street; her hand shaded her eyes. 'Sister Ann, Sister Ann,' Helena, who knew most of the fairy tales in Grimm and Perrault by heart, muttered to herself, 'do you see anyone coming?' Putnam's bluish beard, a razored shadow on his white face, had caught her notice the night before. Sighting Helena, in her ocelot coat and bobbing Robin Hood cap with a feather, Norine waved and beckoned. 'Put has just gone,' she reported. 'You can come in.' She led Helena through an arched doorway into the ground floor of the house and past the open door of what appeared to be an office. The house, she explained, interrupting herself to call a greeting to someone unseen in the office, belonged to a firm of modern decorators, husband and wife, who had been hit by the depression; they lived on two floors upstairs and rented the garden apartment, which had formerly been a showroom, to Norine and Put; the top floor was rented to a secretary who worked for a law firm in Wall Street and doubled as a paid correspondent in divorce cases – 'the Woman Taken in Adultery,' Norine appended with a terse laugh.

Norine had a husky, throaty, cigarette voice and talked continuously, emitting a jerky flow of information, like an outboard motor. She had been regarded as 'nervous' by the medical staff senior year at college, and her abrupt, elliptical way of speaking, as if through a permanent cloud of cigarette smoke, had been developed at that time. When not leading a parade or working on the college newspaper or the literary magazine, she could be found off campus drinking Coca-Cola or coffee and baying out college songs at a table at Cary's with her cronies, all of whom had deep hoarse voices too. 'Here's to Nellie, she's true blue; she's a rounder through and through; she's a drunkard, so they say; wants to go to Heav'n, but she's going the other way.' Helena's musically trained ear, unfortunately, could still hear those choruses and the thump of glasses that accompanied them after 3.2 beer was made legal; and she could remember seeing Kay, now and then, sitting with those gruff Huskies and adding her true voice, harmonizing, to their ensemble, putting ashes into her coffee, as they did, to see if it would give them a 'lift' and playing a game they had invented of who could think of the worst thing to order: two cold fried eggs with chocolate sauce. Norine's chief interest at college had been journalism; her favourite course had been Miss Lockwood's Contemporary Press; her favourite book had been *The Autobiography of Lincoln Steffens*; her favourite art had been photography, and her favourite painter, Georgia O'Keeffe. Up until senior year, she had been one of the over-weight girls, given to Vassar 'Devils', a black fudgy mixture that Helena had never so much as tasted, and to trips to the Cider Mill, where doughnuts were served with cider; Helena and *her* friends bicycled to the Silver Swan, because the name reminded them of madrigals, or dined with a faculty member at the Vassar Inn, where they always ordered the same thing: artichokes and mushrooms under glass. But now Norine, like Kay, had grown thin and tense. Her eyes, which were a light golden brown, were habitually narrowed, and her handsome, blowsy face had a plethoric look, as though darkened by clots of thought. She rarely showed her emotions, which appeared to have been burned out by the continual short-circuiting of her attention. All her statements, cursory and abbreviated, had a topical resonance, even when she touched on the intimate; today she made Helena think of the old riddle of the newspaper – black and white and red all over. She spoke absently and with an air of preoccupation, as though conducting a briefing session from memorized notes.

'Your loyalties lie with her; I know it,' she threw out over her shoulder as they came into the apartment. The barking of a dog in the garden rerouted the train of her ideas. 'There's a bitch in heat upstairs,' she said with a jerk of her head, 'and we keep Nietzsche chained to prevent miscegenation.' Her short, monosyllabic laugh came out like a bark. This laugh, of the type called 'mirthless', was only a sort of punctuation mark, Helena decided – an asterisk indicating that Norine's attention had been flagged by one of her own remarks. Norine went on now, like some gruff veterinarian, to narrate the mating history of the dog upstairs, shunting off, via a parenthesis, to the mating history of its owners. Norine's language had roughened since she had been married; it was not clear to Helena whether the poodle or the wife of the landlord was the 'bitch upstairs' who was going to have an operation on her Fallopian tubes. 'Both,' said Norine shortly. 'Margaret's tubes are obstructed. That's why she can't conceive. She's going to have them blown out. Insufflation. *Liza*'s tubes are going to be tied up. They do it now instead of spaying. That way, she can still enjoy sex. Have some coffee.'

Helena looked around the apartment. It was painted black, so as not to show the dirt, she would have presumed if Norine had been practical. But doubtless the colour was a banner or slogan of some kind, as in Putnam's shirt, though a puzzling one to Helena, since black, she had always understood, was the colour of reaction, of clerical parties and fascists. The kitchen was part of the living-room, and the sink was full of unwashed dishes. Above it was a long shelf with cottage-cheese glasses, jelly glasses, plates, and cans of food, chiefly soups and evaporated milk. French doors tacked with orange theatrical gauze led to the garden. Along one wall, on either side of a white brick fireplace, were bookcases made of orange crates lined with folded black oilcloth and containing pamphlets, small magazines, and thin volumes of poetry. There were few full-size books, except for Marx's *Capital*, Pareto, Spengler, *Ten Days That Shook the World*, *Axel's Castle*, and Lincoln Steffens. Across the room, a big lumpy studio bed was covered with a black velveteen spread and piled with orange oilcloth cushions rudely stitched on a sewing-machine and coming apart at the corners. On the black-and-white linoleum floor was a very dirty polar-bear rug. Below the sink stood a dog's dish with some half-eaten food. On the walls were framed reproductions of Georgia O'Keeffe's vulval flowers and of details from murals by Diego Rivera and Orozco and framed Stieglitz photographs of New York City slum scenes. There were two steel lamps with improvised shades made of typewriter paper, a card table, and four collapsible bridge chairs. On the card table were a toaster, a jar of peanut butter, an electric curling-iron, and a hand mirror; Norine had evidently begun to curl her fine blonde hair and stopped midway through, for the hair on one side of her head was frizzed in a sort of pompadour and on the other hung loose. This sense of an operation begun and suspended midway was the keynote, Helena decided, of the apartment. Someone, probably Norine's husband, had tried to introduce method and order into their housekeeping: beside the icebox, on a screen, was an old-fashioned store calendar with the days crossed off in red pencil; next to the calendar was a pencilled chart or graph, with figures, which, Norine explained, was their weekly budget. On a spike driven into the wall by the stove were their grocery slips and other receipts; on the drainboard, a milk bottle was half-full of pennies, which Norine said were for postage.

'Put makes us keep a record of every two-cent stamp we buy. He got me a little pocket notebook, like his, for my birthday, to write down items like subway fares so I can transfer them at night to the budget. We do the accounts every night, before we go to bed. That way, we know where we are every day, and if we spend too much one day, we can economize on the next. All I have to do is look at the graph. Put's very visual. Tonight I'll be short a nickel, the one I used to call you. He'll take me back, step by step, over my day and say, "Visualize what you did next", till he can locate that nickel. He's nuts about accuracy.' A brief sigh followed this eulogy, which had caused Helena's eyebrows to rise in disapproval; she had been given her own bank account at the age of ten and taught to keep her own cheque stubs. 'Let me supply the nickel,' she said, opening her pocket-book. 'Why don't you make him give you an allowance?' Norine ignored the question. 'Thanks. I'll take a dime if you don't mind. I forgot. I called Harald first to find out where you were staying.' The click of the dime on the card table underscored the silence that fell. The two girls looked each other in the eyes. They listened to the dog bark.

'You never liked me at college,' Norine said, pouring coffee and offering sugar and evaporated milk. 'None of your crowd did.' She sank into a bridge chair opposite Helena and inhaled deeply from her cigarette. Knowing Norine and feeling this to be a lead sentence, Helena did not contradict. In reality, she did not 'mind' Norine, even now; ever since she had heard about the book-keeping, she felt a kind of sympathy for the big frowsty girl, who reminded her of a tired lioness caged in this den of an apartment, with that other animal chained in the garden and the flattened polar bear on the linoleum. And at college she and Norine had worked together quite amicably on the literary magazine. 'You people were the aesthetes. We were the politicals,' Norine continued. 'We eyed each other from across the barricades.' This description appeared to Helena fantastic; the scholar in her could not allow it to pass. 'Isn't that a rather "sweeping statement", Norine?' she suggested with a 'considering' little frown shirring and ruching her forehead in the style of the Vassar faculty. 'Would you call Pokey an aesthete? Or

Dottie? Or Priss?' She would have added 'Kay' but for an unwillingness to name her casually this morning or to seem to discuss her with Norine. 'They didn't count,' replied Norine. 'The ones who counted were you and Lakey and Libby and Kay.' Norine had always been an expert on who 'counted' and who did not. 'You were Sandison. We were Lockwood,' pursued Norine sombrely. 'You were Morgan. We were Marx.' 'Oh, pooh!' cried Helena, almost angry. 'Who was "Morgan"?' In her cool character the only passion yet awakened was the passion for truth. 'The whole group was for Roosevelt in the college poll! Except Pokey, who forgot to vote.' 'One less for Hoover, then,' remarked Norine, *Wrong!*' said Helena, grinning. 'She was for Norman Thomas. Because he breeds dogs.' Norine nodded. 'Cocker spaniels,' she said. 'What a classy reason!' Helena agreed that this was so. 'All right,' Norine conceded after a thoughtful pause. 'Kay was Flanagan, if you want. Priss was Newcomer. Laker was Rindge. I may have been oversimplifying. Libby was M. A. P. Smith, would you say?' 'I guess so,' said Helena, yawning slightly and glancing at her watch; this kind of analysis, which had been popular at Vassar, bored her.

'Anyway,' Norine said, 'your crowd was sterile. Lockwood taught me that. But, God, I used to envy you!' This confession embarrassed Helena. 'Dear me, why?' she inquired. 'Poise. Social savvy. Looks. Success with men. Proms. Football games. Junior Assemblies. We called you the Ivory Tower group. Aloof from the battle.' Helena opened her mouth and closed it; this view of the group was so far from the facts that she could not begin to correct it; she herself, for instance, had no particular looks and had never been to a college football game (Mrs Davison despised 'spectator' sports) or a prom, except at Vassar, where she had had to make do with Priss Hartshorn's brother for a 'man'. But she was not going to be drawn by Norine into a counter-confession; she supposed, moreover, that if you rolled the whole group into one girl, she would be what Norine said – a rich, assured, beautiful bluestocking. 'You mean Lakey,' she said seriously. 'She summed up the group. Or what Miss Lockwood would call its "stereotype". But nobody was really like her. We were her satellites. Old Miss Fiske used to say that we "shone in her reflected light".' 'Lakey had no warmth,' asserted Norine. 'She was inhuman, like the moon. Do you remember the apples?'

Helena felt herself colour, remembering very well the quarrel with Norine over Cézanne's still-lifes of apples in the new Museum of Modern Art. 'The smoking-room of Cushing,' she admitted with a grimace. 'When was that? Freshman year?' 'Sophomore,' said Norine. 'You and Kay had come to dinner with somebody. And Lakey was there. You two were playing bridge. And Lakey was playing solitaire, as usual, and smoking ivory-tipped cigarettes. It was the first time she ever spoke to me.' 'Us too,' said Helena. 'And it was the first time I remember seeing *you*, Norine.' 'I was a mess,' said Norine. 'I weighed a hundred and sixty, stripped. All soft blubber. And you stuck your harpoons into me, the three of you.' Helena raised her candid eyes from her coffee cup. 'The "spirit of the apples",' she quoted, 'versus "significant form".' She could not remember, exactly, what mushy thoughts Norine, sprawled on a sofa, had been expressing about the Cézannes to the smoking-room at large, but she could see Lakey now, on whom she and Kay had had a distant crush, look up suddenly from her solitaire as she said coldly and distinctly that the point of the Cézannes was the formal arrangement of shapes. Norine had begun repeating that it was 'the *spirit* of the apples' that counted; whereupon Kay, laying down her bridge hand and glancing towards Lakey for approval, had charged in with 'significant form', which she had learned about in Freshman English with Miss Kitchel, who had them read Clive Bell and Croce and Tolstoy's *What is Art?* 'You're denying the spirit of the apples.' Norine had insisted, and Helena, laying down *her* bridge hand, had mildly cited T. S. Eliot: 'The spirit killeth, and the letter giveth life.' With everybody watching, Norine had started to cry, and Lakey, who had no pity for weakness, had called her a 'bovine sentimentalist'. Norine, yielding the field, had lumbered out of the smoking-room, sobbing, and Lakey, uttering the single word 'oaf', had gone back to her solitaire. The bridge game had broken up. On the way home to their own dormitory, Helena had said that she thought that three against one had been a bit hard on poor Miss Schmittlapp, but Kay said that Schmittlapp was usually in the majority. 'Do you think she'll remember that we came to her rescue?' she demanded, meaning Lakey. 'I doubt it,' said Helena, having sat next to Miss Eastlake (Davison being just ahead of her in the alphabet) for a full half-term in an art-history course without evoking a sign of notice. But Lakey had remembered Kay, when they were on the Daisy Chain together that spring, and talked to her about Clive Bell and Roger Fry, so that you might say, Helena reflected, that the argument with Norine had pointed the way that had led, in the end, to their grouping with Lakey and the others in the South Tower. Helena, who was as immune to social snobbery as she was to the 'fond passion', had not felt the charm of the South Tower group to the same extent as Kay, but she had raised no objections to the alliance, even though her teachers and her parents had worried a little, thinking that an 'exclusive élite' was a dangerous set to play in, for a girl who had real stuff in her. Mrs Davison's comment, on first meeting the group, was that she hoped Helena was not going to become a 'clothes rack'.

'I reacted against Lakey's empty formalism,' Norine was saying. 'I went up to my room that night and spewed out the window. That was Armageddon for me, though I didn't see it yet. I didn't discover socialism till junior year. All I knew that night was that I believed in something and couldn't express it, while your team believed in nothing but knew how to say it – in other men's words. Of course, I envied you that too. Let me show you something.' She rose from her chair, motioning Helena to follow and flung open a door, disclosing the bedroom. Over the bed, which was made, hung a reproduction of a Cézanne still-life of apples. 'Well, well, the apples of discord!' remarked Helena in the doorway, striving for a sprightly note; she had stumbled over a dog's bone in the matted fur of the polar bear; her ankle hurt; and she could not imagine what the apples were expected to prove 'Put had them in his college room,' Norine said. 'He'd made them the basis for his credo too. For him, they stood for a radical simplification.' 'Ummm,' said Helena, glancing about the room, which was clearly Putnam's sphere. It contained steel filing cabinets, a Williams College pennant, an African mask, and a typewriter on a card table. It struck her that Norine's apartment was all too populous with 'significant form'. Every item in it seemed to be saying something, asserting something, pontificating; Norine and Put were surrounded by articles of belief, down to the last can of evaporated milk and the single, monastic pillow on the double bed. It was different from Kay's apartment, where the furniture was only asking to be admired or talked *about*. But here, in this dogmatic lair, nothing had been admitted that did not make a 'relevant statement', though what the polar bear was saying Helena could not make out.

The two girls returned to their seats. Norine lit a fresh cigarette. She stared meditatively at Helena. 'Put is impotent,' she said. 'Oh,' said Helena, slowly. 'Oh, Norine, I'm sorry.' 'It's not your fault,' said Norine hoarsely. Helena did not know what to say next. She could still smell Put's tobacco and see his pipe in an unemptied ashtray. Despite the fact that she had had no sexual experience, she had a very clear idea of the male member, and she could not help forming a picture of Put's as pale and lifeless, in the coffin of his trousers, a veritable *nature morte*. She was sorry that Norine, to excuse herself for last night, had felt it necessary to make her this confidence; she did not want to be privy to the poor man's private parts. 'We got married in June.' Norine enlarged. 'A couple of weeks after Commencement. I was a raw virgin. I never had a date till I knew Put. So when we went to this hotel, in the Pennsylvania coal fields, I didn't catch on right away. Especially since my mother, who hates sex like all her generation, told me that a gentleman never penetrated his bride on the first night. I thought that for once Mother must be right. We'd neck till we were both pretty excited, and then everything would stop, and he'd turn over and go to sleep. 'What were you doing in the coal fields?' inquired Helena, in hopes of a change of subject. 'Put had a case he was working on – an organizer who's been beaten up and jailed. In the daytime, I interviewed the women, the miners' wives. Background stuff. Put said it was very useful. That way, he could write off our whole honeymoon on office expenses. And at night we were both pretty bushed. But when we came back to New York, it was the same thing. We'd neck in our pyjamas and then go to sleep.' 'What possessed him to want to get married?' 'He didn't know,' said Norine.

'Finally,' she continued hoarsely, 'I faced the truth. I went to the Public Library. They've got a Viennese woman there in Information – very *gemütlich*. She drew me up a reading list on impotence, a lot of it in German; quite a bibliography. There are different types: organic and functional. Put's is functional. He's got a mother-tie; his mother's a widow. Some men are incapable of erection altogether, and some are incapable except in certain circumstances. Put's capable of full erection, but only with whores and fallen women.' She gave her short laugh. 'But you didn't find all that out in the library,' objected Helena; she had heard her mother declare that it was possible to get a 'university education in our great public-library system', but there was a limit to everything. 'No,' said Norine. 'Only the over-all picture. After I'd read up on the subject, Put and I were able to talk. He'd had all his early sex experience with whores and factory girls in Pittsfield, it turned out. They'd pull up their skirts, in an alley or a doorway, and he'd ejaculate, sometimes at the first contact, before he got his penis all the way in. He'd never made love to a good woman and never seen a woman naked. I'm a good woman; that's why he can't make it with me. He feels he's fornicating with his mother. That's what the Freudians think; the Behaviourists would claim that it was a conditioned reflex. But of course he couldn't know any of that ahead of time. It's been an awful blow to him. I excite him but I can't satisfy him. His penis just wilts at the approach to intercourse. Lately, I've been bunking in the living-room' – a jerk of her head indicated the couch – 'because he has a horror of contact with a good woman's crotch in his sleep. Though we both wore pyjamas, he had insomnia. Now at least I can sleep raw.' She stretched.

'Have you tried a doctor?' Norine laughed darkly. 'Two. Put wouldn't go, so I went. The first one asked me whether I wanted to have children. He was an old-fashioned neurologist that my mother knew about. When I said no, I didn't, he practically booted me out of the office. He told me I should consider myself lucky that my husband *didn't* want intercourse. Sex wasn't necessary for a woman, he said.' 'Good heavens!' said Helena. 'Yes!' nodded Norine. 'The second one was a G.P. with a few more modern ideas. Put's partner, Bill Nickum, sent me to him. He was pretty much of a Behaviourist. When I explained Put's sexual history, he advised me to buy some black chiffon underwear and long black silk stockings and some cheap perfume. So that Put would associate me with a whore. And to try to get him to take me that way, with all my clothes on, in the afternoon, when he got home from work.' 'Mercy!' said Helena. 'What happened?' 'It was almost a success. I went to Bloomingdale's and got the underwear and the stockings.' She pulled up her sweat shirt, and Helena had a glimpse of a black chiffon 'shimmy' with lace inserts. 'Then I thought of that polar-bear rug. My mother had it in storage; it used to belong to my grandmother Schmittlapp, who was a rich old aristocrat. "Venus in Furs" – Sacher-Masoch. I arranged so that Put would find me on the rug when he got home from the office.' Helena smiled and made a noise like a whistle. 'Put ejaculated prematurely,' said Norine sombrely. 'Then we had a fight about how much I'd spent at Bloomingdale's. Put's an ascetic about money. That's why he won't consider psychoanalysis, though Bill Nickum thinks he should.' Helena's eyebrows arched; she decided not to ask how 'Bill Nickum' came to know of Put's 'trouble'. Instead, she put another question. 'Are you *very* broke, Norine?' Norine shook her head. 'Put has a trust fund, and my father gives me an allowance. But we put that into household expenses. Put and Bill sink most of their own dough in Common Causes.' '"Common causes"?' repeated Helena, mystified. 'That's the name of their outfit. Of course, they draw salaries, and the rest of the staff is volunteer. But their mailing and printing costs are pretty staggering. And then we have to entertain labour people and celebrities and rich do-gooders and some of the working press. We use this place as sort of a cross between a salon and a café.' Helena looked around her and said nothing.

'Bill says it would take the strain off our marriage if Put could go to a brothel. Or find a taxi-dance girl. Though they're likely to be infected. But he could learn to use a prophylactic kit. Have you ever seen one? It's as simple as brushing your teeth. Put's offered me a divorce, but I don't want that. That's what the older generation would have done. The generation that ran away from everything. My mother and father are divorced. If Put were a drunkard or beat me up, that would be different. But sex isn't the only thing in marriage. Take the average couple. They have intercourse once a week, on Saturday night. Let's say that's five minutes a week, not counting the preliminaries. Five minutes out of 10,080. I figured it out in percentages – less than .05 of one per cent. Supposing Put were to spend five minutes a week with a whore – the time it takes him to shave? Why should I mind? Especially when I knew it didn't mean anything to him emotionally?' A dismayed expression had come over Helena's face as Norine jerked out these figures; she was fighting off the certainty that she had to go to the toilet. She had travelled all over Europe scoffing at a fear of germs, drinking the water, making use of a Spanish peasant's outhouse or of the simple drain in the floor provided as a urinal by an Italian *osteria*, but she shrank from the thought of Norine's bathroom. The need to relieve her bladder heightened the sense of unreality produced by Norine's statistical calculations and by the steady barking of the dog outside and the drip-drip of water in the sink; she felt she had slipped into eternity. Yet when she finally did ask for the john, it was a long time before she could urinate, though she put paper down on the toilet seat, which Put had left flipped up, like a morbid reminder of himself; in the end, she had to run the water in the basin to prime the pump.

When she returned to the living-room, Norine suddenly came to the point. 'I guess Harald had become a sort of male potency symbol for me,' she said in her uninflected voice, blowing smoke with a careless air, but behind the ˜smoke-screen her narrowed topaz eyes were watching Helena as if to measure her reaction. As Norine went on talking, in her rapid-fire, memo-pad style, Helena lit a cigarette herself and settled down to listen critically, taking mental notes and arranging them under headings, just as though she were at a lecture or a meeting.

The reasons, she noted, for Harald's becoming 'a male potency symbol' to the deprived Norine were as follows (A) The Group. Norine had always envied them their 'sexual superiority'. (B) Kay's role as a neutral, 'passing between both camps'. I.e., Norine had sat next to Kay senior year in Miss Washburn's Abnormal Psychology and found her 'a good scout'. (C) Envy of Kay for 'having the best of both worlds'. I.e. she had lost her virginity and stayed at Harald's place week-ends without becoming '*déclassée*'. Norine's situation was the obverse. (D) Proximity. Norine had met Kay on the street the day she and Put came back from their honeymoon. They found they were neighbours and the two couples had started playing bridge together in the evenings. (E) Harald was a better bridge player than Put. *Ergo*, Harald had come to figure in Norine's mind as an 'erect phallus' just out of her reach, like the Tower group. Which was why Helena had found the two of them kissing in the kitchen and why it did not 'mean anything'.

Helena wrinkled her forehead. It seemed to her on the contrary that, if you accepted Norine's chain of reasoning, it meant a great deal. If Harald was to be treated as a phallic symbol, instead of as Kay's husband, it made their kisses 'meaningful' in just the sense that would appeal to Norine. She had been yielding to the Force of Logic, which poor Kay herself had set in motion.

'If it didn't mean anything, why dwell on it?' said Helena. 'To make you understand,' replied Norine. 'We both know you're intelligent and we don't want you to feel you have to tell Kay.' Something in Helena sat up at the sound of those 'we's', but she puffed at her cigarette nonchalantly. What made them think she would tell Kay? That embrace, in her books, did not amount to a row of pins, so long as things stopped there; Harald, after all, had been drinking, as Norine ought to know for herself.

'I wouldn't want to wreck her marriage,' mused Norine. 'Then don't,' said Helena, in a voice that sounded like her father's. 'Forget about Harald. There're other fish in the sea. Don't feel you have to finish something just because you've started it.' She grinned candidly at her hostess, believing she had read her psychology.

Norine hesitated. Idly, she picked up the curling-iron. 'It's not that simple,' she threw out. 'Harald and I have been lovers quite a while.' Helena bit her lip; this was what, underneath, she had been afraid of hearing. She made a grimace. The simple word 'lovers' had a terrible and unexpected effect on her.

Put was out all day, Norine went on to explain, and Kay was out all day too. 'It undercuts Harald that she works to support him. He has to assert his masculinity. You saw what happened last night – when he burned his play. That was a sort of immolation rite, to propitiate her; he was making a burnt offering of his seed, the offspring of his mind and balls. . . .' At these words Helena's normal droll self assumed command again. 'Oh, Norine!' she protested. 'Do come down to brass tacks.' '"The Brass Tack,"' Norine said, frowning. 'Wasn't that your name for a literary magazine at college?' Helena agreed that it was. Norine flicked on the curling-iron. 'What is it,' she wondered, eyeing Helena, 'that makes you want to puke at the imponderables? Do you mind if I curl my hair?' As the curling-iron heated, she continued with her narrative. Harald, it seemed, left alone all day, had started dropping in, afternoons, for a cup of tea or a bottle of beer at Norine's place. Sometimes, he brought a book and read aloud to her; his favourite poet was Robinson Jeffers. 'Roan Stallion,' supplied Helena. Norine nodded. 'How did you know?' 'I guessed,' said Helena. She well remembered the fatal week-end that Harald had read Roan Stallion to Kay. 'One day,' Norine said, 'I told him about Put. . . .' 'Enough said,' dryly remarked Helena. Norine flushed. 'My first *affaire* – before Harald – started the same way,' she admitted. 'It was a man I met in the Public Library, a progressive-school teacher with a wife and six children.' She gave an unwilling laugh. 'He was curious about the stuff I was reading. We used to sit in Bryant Park, and I told him about Put. He took me to a hotel and deflowered me. But he was afraid his wife would find out.' 'And Harald?' asked Helena. 'Underneath his bravado, I guess he's afraid too. Married men are funny; they all draw a line between the wife and the concubine.' She commenced to curl her hair. Soon the smell of singed hair was added to the smell of cigarette smoke, of dog, pipe tobacco, and of a soured dishcloth in the sink. Watching her, Helena granted Norine a certain animal vitality, an 'earthiness' that was underscored, as if deliberately, by the dirt and squalor of the apartment. Bedding with her, Helena imagined, must be like rolling in a rich mouldy compost of autumn leaves, crackling on the surface, like her voice, and underneath warm and sultry from the chemical processes of decay. It came back to her that Norine had written a famous rubbishy paper for Miss Beckwith's Folk Lore, on Ge, the Earth Mother, and the steamy chthonian cults, that had been turned down by the *Journal of Undergraduate Studies*, on the ground of 'fuzzy thinking', a favourite faculty phrase. Helena chuckled inwardly. She felt she could write a fine paper herself this morning, in the manner of Miss Caroline Spurgeon, on the chthonic imagery of Norine's apartment, which, if not exactly a cellar, as Kay insisted on calling it, was black as a coalhole and heated by the furnace of the hostess' unslaked desires, burning like quicklime and giving off, Helena said to herself sharply, a good deal of hot air. Drolly, she considered the 'bitch in heat upstairs', surely a totem or familiar, the Fallopian tubes of the landlady (a root system?), the Cerberus in the back yard. 'Oh queen of hell,' she said to herself, 'where does your Corn Mother mourn?' On lower Park Avenue, she discovered, somewhat later in the conversation. Norine's mother lived on alimimony from her father, who had remarried; Norine went to dinner with her at Schrafft's every other Wednesday.

'I'm not the first,' Norine jerked out now, while the curling-iron sizzled. 'Harald tells me stuff he doesn't tell Kay. He had a long *affaire* with a show girl he met last fall; she wanted to marry him.

She has a rich husband and a house in Connecticut, where he and Kay still go sometimes for week-ends. But Harald won't sleep with her any more, though she begs him to. He has a horror of messy relationships. Before he and I went to bed, for instance, we both had to agree that we wouldn't let it affect our marriages.'

'Isn't that easier said than done?' demanded Helena. 'Not for Harald,' said Norine. 'He's a very disciplined person. And I'm fond of Put. Sometimes I get a bit jealous of Kay since I know Harald sleeps with her sometimes, though he doesn't talk about it. But I tell myself that every experience is unique; what he does with her can't alter what he does with me. And vice versa. I'm not taking anything away from her. Most married men perform better with their wives if they have a mistress. In other societies, that's taken for granted.'

'Still,' said Helena, 'you'd rather Kay didn't find out. Or Put, I gather. And you must admit, you had a close call last night. What if Kay had marched in, instead of me?' Norine nodded sombrely. 'Check,' she said. Then she laughed. 'God!' she confided, 'we had another close call the other day. . . .' Helena raised an eyebrow. 'Do you want to hear?' said Norine. 'All right,' said Helena. 'It happened right here,' said Norine. 'One afternoon. About ten days ago. We were fornicating there' – she indicated the couch – 'when there was an awful banging on the door and a voice yelled, "Open up there!"'

Helena shuddered. As she listened to her classmate, her imagination soberly reconstructed the scene, disrobing Norine and Harald and placing them, affrighted in the midst of their 'transports', on the couch. What could the knocking mean? Harald, it seemed, did not wait to find out; he seized his trousers from the collapsible chair she was now sitting on and raced into the bedroom. Norine sat up and wrapped herself in the couch cover as the banging continued. She was sure it was the police – the Red Squad – after Putnam's files. It sounded as though they would break the door down any minute; they must have heard her and Harald whispering. 'Answer it!' hissed Harald from the bedroom. Clutching the black couch cover around her, in her bare feet, Norine opened the door a crack. Two men in plain clothes and a woman burst into the room. 'That's her!' cried the strange woman, a middle-aged type, in jewels and a fur coat, pointing to Norine. 'Where's my husband?'

Before Norine could stop them, the plain-clothes men pushed open the door into the bedroom, where they found Harald buttoning his fly. 'Here he is, ma'am!' they yelled. 'Partially disrobed. In his undershirt. Trousers unbuttoned.' The woman went in to see too. 'But that's not my husband,' she exclaimed. 'I never saw this man before. Who is he?' And she turned angrily to Norine.

At this point in Norine's narrative, Helena laughed. 'The secretary upstairs?' she surmised. 'How did you guess?' said Norine. Helena had grasped the situation. The plain-clothes men were private detectives, matrimonial specialists, and they had picked the wrong apartment. All the time, the woman's husband was upstairs with 'Grace', the secretary, waiting to be caught by his wife and the detectives; it was an 'arranged' divorce case. 'And of course,' Norine continued, 'they weren't really supposed to be fornicating – just to have their clothes "disarrayed". And they were supposed to open the door right away and let the detectives in quietly; otherwise John makes a stink. He keeps telling Margaret they're running a "disorderly house".' '"John" is the landlord?' asked Helena. Norine nodded. 'Actually, he can't say much, because Margaret caught him with the previous tenant and threw her out. But he's pretty stuffy about Grace sometimes – the profit motive, as usual. He uses the house as a sort of showroom for his decorating clients and he's afraid the address will get in the paper in some divorce case. This time, it was all the stupidity of those detectives; they'd been clearly told to raid the top-floor apartment and instead they came to the ground floor. When we didn't open the door and they could hear us inside, they decided there was some funny business, that the husband was reneging on the deal. So, instead of calling up the lawyer, as they should have done, for instructions, they straight-armed their way in here. The wife didn't know what was up when she found me in the coverlet and her husband, she thought, hiding. She'd been told to expect a blonde (it has to be a blonde), so naturally she assumed I was Grace. Probably - she figured her husband had decided to suit the action to the word.' She laughed.

Harald had been 'magnificent'. Very quietly, he had elicited all the facts from the detectives and then given them a tongue-lashing. He had told them they were a pair of stupid goons who had got their training in violence on the New York police force and been 'broken' for extortion or sheer witlessness. He dared them to deny it. They ought to have learned that they could not enter a private residence without a policeman and a search warrant, and in Norine's place, he said, he would bring suit against them for housebreaking, which was a felony, and send them and their lady-client to jail. 'You were hardly in a position to carry out that threat,' commented Helena. 'The detectives must have seen that.' Norine shook her head, which was now frizzed all around in a pompadour. 'They were livid with fear,' she declared.

Luckily, she went on, more prosaically, the house had been empty that afternoon, except for Grace and the man with her on the top floor; otherwise, the banging and shouting would have brought everyone running. 'Where was Nietzsche, by the way?' inquired Helena. 'I should have thought he would have added his voice.' Nietzsche had gone to the country for the day with the landlord and his wife; it was Lincoln's Birthday, which was why Grace had the afternoon off; normally she was raided at night, unless John and Margaret had a dinner party. 'And Kay?' said Helena. 'Kay was working,' said Norine. 'The stores don't observe Lincoln's Birthday. They cash in on the fact that the other wage slaves get the day off. It's a big white-collar shopping spree. When do you think a forty-eight-hour-week stenographer gets a chance to buy herself a dress? Unless she goes without her lunch? Probably you've never thought.' She stared at Helena and lit a cigarette, holding the burning match for a moment, as though to lighten the darkness of Helena's mind.

Helena got up; she was resolved to speak her piece. The careless, cursory tone of 'Kay was working' had made her lips tighten. 'I'm not a socialist, Norine,' she said evenly. 'But if I were one, I would try to be a good person. Norman Thomas is a good person, I think.' 'Norman used to be a minister,' put in Norine. 'That's his big handicap. He doesn't appeal to the modern worker. They smell the do-gooder in him. He's been helpful to Put, but Put thinks the time has come when he's got to break with him. There's a new group of Congressmen in Washington – Farmer-Labourites and Progressives – that Put feels he can work with more effectively. They're closer to the realities of power. A couple of them are coming this afternoon for drinks; probably we'll go to the Village with them afterwards, to a night club – one of them likes to dance.

Put and Bill – did he tell you? – want to start a newspaper syndicate and get out of fund-raising, where the Communists have a pretty formidable edge. Now these Congressmen have a lot of small-town newspapers behind them, in the farm states, that are hungry for real, uncensored labour news and the latest on cooperatives and profit sharing. I've asked Harald and Kay too this afternoon, because Harald has his roots in Veblen – ' 'Norine,' interrupted Helena. 'I said if I were a socialist, I would try to be a good person.' Her voice, though she strove to maintain its careful drawl, began to tremble. Norine, staring, slowly put out her cigarette. 'You say your husband can't sleep with you because you're a "good woman". I suggest you enlighten him. Tell him what you do with Harald. And about the progressive-school teacher with the wife and six children. That ought to get his pecker up. And have him take a look at this apartment. And at the ring around your neck. If a man slept with you, you'd leave a ring around him. Like your bathtub.' Norine sat staring up at her, perfectly impassive. Helena gulped; she had not spoken so fiercely since she was a spunky child and angry with her mother. She hardly recognized some of the language she was using, and her voice was doing curious slides. In her dry constricted throat, a crowd of disconnected sentences seemed to be milling, like a mob she was trying to moderate. 'Get some ammonia,' she heard herself declare all of a sudden, 'and wash out your brush and comb!' She stopped with a gasp, afraid that she might cry from sheer temper, as used to happen with her mother. Swiftly, she walked to the french windows and stood looking out into the garden, endeavouring to frame an apology. Behind her, Norine spoke. 'You're right,' she said. 'Dead right.' She picked up the hand mirror and examined her neck. 'Thanks for telling me the truth. Nobody ever does.'

At these gruff words, Helena jumped. She turned around, slowly in her brown lizard pumps. Gratitude was the last thing she had expected from Norine. Helena was no reformer; she had 'reacted', as Norine would say, against her mother's measured and stately meliorism and bridled at the very notion of changing people, as much as at the notion of being changed. She did not know, now, what had possessed her to fly off the handle – a defensive loyalty to Kay or to a canon of honesty or simply the desire to show Norine that she could not fool all of the people all of the time. But to find

Norine receptive was quite a responsibility to shoulder. 'Go on. Tell me more,' she was urging. 'Tell me what I need to do to change my life.' Helena sighed inwardly and sat down opposite Norine at the table, thinking of her appointment with her father and of how much she would rather be looking at old silver than playing the new broom to Norine's life. But she supposed that at least the Congressmen and perhaps Putnam would thank her if she advised her to begin by cleaning up the apartment.

'Well,' she said diffidently, 'I'd start with a little "elbow grease".' Norine looked absently around her. 'Scrub the floor, you mean? O.K. Then what?' Despite herself, Helena warmed to the opportunity. 'Well then,' she proceeded, 'I'd get some toilet paper. There isn't any in the bathroom. And some Clorox for the garbage pail and the toilet bowl. And boil out that dishcloth or get a new one.' She listened. 'I'd unchain the dog and take him for a walk. And while I was at it, I'd change his name.' 'You don't like Nietzsche?' 'No,' said Helena, dryly. 'I'd call him something like Rover.' Norine gave her terse laugh. 'I get it,' she said appreciatively. 'God, Helena, you're wonderful! Go on. Should I give him a bath to christen him?' Helena considered. 'Not in this weather. He might catch cold. Take a bath yourself, instead, and wash your hair in the shower.' 'But I just curled it.' 'All right, wash it tomorrow. Then get some new clothes and charge them to Putnam. When he makes a fuss over the bill, tear up the budget. And buy some real food – not in cans. If it's only hamburger and fresh vegetables and oranges.' Norine nodded. 'Fine. But now tell me something more basic.'

Helena's green eyes looked around thoughtfully. 'I'd paint this room another colour.' Norine's face was dubious. 'Is that what you'd call basic?' she demanded. 'Certainly,' said Helena. 'You don't want people to think you're a fascist, do you?' she added, with guile. 'God, you're dead right,' said Norine. 'I guess I'm too close to these things. I never thought of that. And you can't be too careful. The Communists are completely unscrupulous. One day they're your bedfellow and the next day they're calling you a fascist. They even call Norman a social fascist. O.K. Go ahead.' 'I'd get rid of that polar bear,' said Helena mildly. 'It's just a dust-catcher, and it seems to have outlived its usefulness.' Norine agreed. 'I think Put's allergic to it, anyway. Next?' 'I'd take some real books out of the library.' 'What do you mean, "real books"?' said Norine, with a wary glance at her shelves. 'Literature,' retorted Helena. 'Jane Austen. George Eliot. Flaubert. Lady Murasaki. Dickens. Shakespeare. Sophocles. Aristophanes. Swift.' 'But those aren't seminal,' said Norine, frowning. 'So much the better,' said Helena. There was a pause. 'Is that all?' said Norine. Helena shook her head. Her eyes met Norine's. 'I'd stop seeing Harald,' she said.

'Oh,' murmured Norine. 'Fill up your time some other way,' Helena went on briskly. 'Register for a course at Columbia. Or write up what you saw in the coal mines. Get a job, even a volunteer one. But, Norine, don't see Harald. Not even socially. Cut it clean.' With this plea, her voice had grown earnest; she resumed in a lighter key. 'In your place, I'd get a divorce or an annulment. But that's something you have to determine – you and Putnam. It's nothing you should discuss with anyone else. If you want to stay with him, then I think you should decide to do without sex. Don't try to have it both ways. Make up your mind which you want: sex or Putnam. Lots of women can live without sex and thrive on it. Look at our teachers at college; they weren't dried up or sour. And lots of women,' she added, 'can live without Putnam.'

'You're right,' said Norine dully. 'Yes, of course you're right. It's a choice I have to make.' But her tone was flaccid. Helena had the feeling that some time back Norine had ceased to listen to the programme she had been outlining or was only listening mechanically and making noises of assent. 'The subject,' she concluded, 'is no longer fully cooperative.' And despite herself, she was vexed and disappointed. Why should she care, she asked herself, whether Norine heeded her advice or not? Except on Kay's account, but it was not only, she admitted, on Kay's account that she minded. She had got carried away by a vision of a better life for Norine. And now, inflamed by her own missionary zeal, she did not want to give that vision up. 'Whatever choice you make, Norine,' she said firmly, 'don't talk about it. That's my principal advice to you. Don't talk about yourself or Putnam to anyone but a lawyer. Not even another doctor. If anybody talks to a doctor, it ought to be Putnam, not you. And as long as you're married to him, resolve not to mention sex. In any form – animal, vegetable, or mineral. No Fallopian tubes.' 'O.K.,' said Norine, sighing, as if this would be the most difficult part.

A weighty silence followed; the dog resumed its barking; the Elevated rumbled on its trestle. In this Homeric contest, Zeus, opined Helena, was taking out his golden scales. Norine coughed and stretched. 'You're a precocious kid,' she said, yawning. 'But you're still in short pants, emotionally. *Si jeunesse savait . . .*!' She yawned again. 'Seriously, I'm grateful to you for trying to help me. You've told me the truth, according to your lights. And you've given me a few damn good ideas. Like having to make a choice between sex and Put. Commit myself one way or the other. Instead of straddling the issue, the way I've been doing. What are you smiling at?' 'Your choice of words.' Norine gave a brief guffaw. Then she frowned. 'That's an example,' she said, 'of what I'd call the limitations of your approach. You're hipped on forms, while I'm concerned with meanings. Do you mind if I tell you that most of your advice is superficial?' 'Such as?' said Helena, nettled. 'Cleaning up the apartment,' replied Norine. 'As if that were primary. Buying toilet paper, buying Clorox, buying a new dress. Notice your stress on bourgeois acquisition. On mere *things*. I ask for bread and you offer me a stone. I grant you we ought to have toilet paper in the bathroom; Put bawled me out for that this morning. But that won't solve the important questions. Poor people don't have toilet paper.' 'Still,' suggested Helena, 'I should have thought that one of your aims was to see they they did have toilet paper.' Norine shook her head. 'You're dodging my point,' she said. 'Your obsession with appearances. You don't touch on the basic things. The intangibles.' 'The "spirit of the apples",' remarked Helena. 'Yes,' said Norine. 'It seems to me your "central problem" is rather tangible,' Helena drawled. She perceived that Norine did not intend to follow any of her prescriptions, unless perhaps she would change the dog's name to Rover – as a conversation-maker. 'No,' Norine replied thoughtfully. 'There's an underlying spiritual malaise. Put's impotence is a sign of a Promethean loneliness.'

Helena picked up her ocelot coat from the studio couch. After her last remark, Norine had sunk into meditation, her chin cupped in her hand, and seemed to have forgotten that Helena was there. 'Do you have to go?' she said absently. 'If you stick around, I'll give you some lunch.' Helena refused. 'I have to meet my father.' She slipped her coat on. 'Well, thanks,' said Norine. 'Thanks a lot.

Drop in this afternoon if you're free.' She put out her big hand with its bitten, dirty fingernails. 'Harald and Kay will be here, if you want to see them again.' Her memory appeared to jog her, and she reddened, meeting Helena's eye. 'You don't understand,' she said, 'Put and I can't just drop them. I have to see Harald socially. He and Put have a lot in common – in their thinking. Probably they mean more to each other than I mean to either of them. And Harald depends on us for intellectual stimulation. I told you – we run sort of a salon. We're being written up this month in *Mademoiselle*. "Put and Norine Blake, he Williams '31, she Vassar '33, keep open house for the conscience of young America." With pictures.' Her laugh jerked out. Then she frowned and ran a hand through her hair. 'That's the element you miss in your analysis. The vital centre of my marriage with Put. We've come to stand for something meaningful to other people, and when that happens you're no longer a free agent. From *your* perspective, you can't see that. And that leads you to over-emphasize sex.' Norine's tone had grown instructive and kindly as she stood looking down on her little visitor. 'You won't repeat what I've told you?' she added, on a sudden note of anxiety. 'No,' said Helena, adjusting her jaunty hat 'But *you* will.' Norine followed her to the door. 'You're a peach,' she declared.

A week later, in Cleveland, Mrs Davison looked up from yesterday's New York *Times*. She was sitting in her morning room, in the corner she called the ingle, to which she always repaired with the mail after the postman's visit. The *Times* came a day late, but Mrs Davison did not mind this, since she only read it for 'background'. The room was done in blue and violet and white chintzes and English furniture; it had a small-paned Tudor bow window of the kind that had made Helena, as a schoolgirl, imagine Sir Walter Raleigh writing on it with a diamond. There was a handsome Queen Anne secretary, with pigeonholes and a secret drawer, where Mrs Davison tended to her correspondence; her collection of patch boxes held stamps of various denominations, like coloured treasures; on a sturdy Jacobean table stood the month's periodicals, arranged in stacks, as in a school library. On the panelled wall above the secretary hung Mrs Davison's 'lares and penates' – faded late-Victorian photographs of the family seat in Somerset, 'a plain gentleman's manor' which her ancestor, a clergyman, had left for Canada. The fireplace was tiled in a pretty blue-and-white heraldic pattern, and next to it sat Mrs Davison in her easy-chair, glancing over the newspaper, her porcelain-handled letter opener in her large polka-dotted lap. 'Helena!' she called in her sonorous windy voice, like the foghorn of a majestic Cunarder. Helena appeared in the doorway. 'Harald has been arrested!' 'My stars!' said Helena. 'For fighting with some private detectives, it appears,' continued her mother, rapping on the paper with the letter opener. 'He and a man named Putnam Blake. Do you know who that would be?'

Helena blanched. 'Let me see it, Mother!' she implored, bolting across the room as though to wrench the newspaper and the awful information it contained from her mother's custody. Harald and Norine must have been surprised again in their illicit embraces and the prospect of submitting to her mother's cross-examination on the subject made her gold freckles stand out dark on her cheek-bones. Her mother, always tantalizing, fended her off. 'You'll muss it, Helena!' she chided, slowly folding the paper. In the midst of her concern, it struck Helena as peculiar that Mrs Davison did not appear to be as shocked as she should have been; rather, her attitude was if that were possible, one of comfortable and dignified alarm. 'I'll read it out to you,' Mrs Davison said. 'Here it is, on page five. And there's a picture too. These newspaper photographs are so *blurry*.' Helena put her small sandy head next to her mother's large grey one, her cheek grazing the hairnet that restrained Mrs Davison's 'puffs'. 'I don't see where you mean,' she said, her eye running apprehensively down the headlines, which all concerned labour disputes. 'There!' said her mother. '"Guests Walk Out in Waiters' Strike, Two Held."' Helena's teeth caught her lip; she gulped down her astonishment and sank on to a footstool, prepared to listen to her mother's reading. 'I don't know, Helena, whether you're aware that a group of waiters has been striking in some of the leading New York hotels. Daddy and I have been interested because of the Savoy Plaza. Daddy's breakfast waiter told him, only last week – ' 'Please, Mother,' Helena interrupted. 'Let's hear about Harald.' Thereupon Mrs Davison commenced to read, with her customary stresses and pauses:

'The striking waiters at the Hotel Carlton Cavendish received support last night from an unexpected quarter. A sympathy strike of guests led by Putnam Blake, publicist, 24, was staged in the candlelit Rose Room while the band played. The striking guests wore evening dress and included, besides Mr Blake, who was taken to the East 51st Street station house, Dorothy Parker, Alexander Woollcott, Robert Benchley, and other literary celebrities. The signal for the walkout was a speech by Mr Blake, urging the seated guests to demonstrate in sympathy with the waiters, whose union was picketing outside the hotel. Service was disrupted for three-quarters of an hour. Mr Blake was charged with disorderly conduct on a complaint by Frank Hart, assistant manager of the Carlton Cavendish; also held on disorderly conduct charges was Harald Petersen, 27, a playwright. Both men, appearing in night court, were released in temporary bail of $25 each. Mr Blake told reporters that he and Mr Petersen intended to prefer charges against Mr Hart and two house detectives employed by the Carlton Cavendish Corporation who, he said, had 'roughed them up' and attempted to hold them prisoners in the hotel basement. Mr Petersen charged that brass knuckles were used. He and his party, Mr Blake said, were exercising their rights in leaving the Rose Room when they discovered that they were to be served by non-union waiters; Mr Hart and the two detectives had acted to restrain them from leaving peaceably. Mr Hart stated that the 'group of troublemakers' had ordered drinks and other refreshments and left without paying. Mr Blake and Mr Petersen denied this; all their party, they said, which consisted of about thirty persons, scattered at individual tables in the luxurious, newly decorated Rose Room, had left 'adequate compensation' for the beverages they had consumed before embarking on the walkout; they had, however, refrained from tipping. It was possible, Mr Blake added, that other guests had quitted the dining-room without paying, in the confusion that ensued when he and Mr Petersen were allegedly attacked by a 'flying squad' of non-union waiters and detectives. In night court, Mr Blake and Mr Petersen were accompanied by their wives, smartly dressed in evening gowns, and by a group of friends in silk hats and tail coats. Their trial will be held March 23. The 'strikers', it was said, included a number of Vassar girls. A similar walkout was staged a few weeks ago at the lunch hour in the Hotel Algonquin, led by Heywood Broun, newspaper columnist. On that occasion, no arrests were made.

'My word!' said Helena. 'Do you suppose Kay's in the picture? Let's see!' The photograph showed a milling scene in the hotel dining-room; a table and some chairs had been overturned. But unfortunately, as Mrs Davison said, it was blurry. They could not find Kay, but they thought they spotted Harald, pale and shadowy in a dinner jacket, an arm raised aloft as a corps of waiters bore down on him. While her mother searched for Dorothy Parker ('She was convent-bred, Helena; did you know that?'), Helena identified Norine, in the centre of the picture, facing the camera, wearing what appeared to be a low white satin evening dress and a jewelled tiara, as though she were in a box at the opera; she had on long white gloves, presumably *glacé* kid, with the hands rolled back over her wrists. A small inset showed Putnam as he was arraigned in night court; it was hard to tell whether the print was smudged or whether he had a black eye; he was dressed in a tail coat, apparently, but his white tie was missing.

Mrs Davison laid down the paper. 'That big photo shows you, Helena,' she observed trenchantly, 'that the whole affair was *staged*.' 'Of course it was staged, Mother,' retorted Helena impatiently. 'That was the point. To get publicity for the waiters' grievances.' 'It was *engineered*, Helena,' said her mother. 'They must have tipped off the newspaper to send a camera-man. Yet that Putnam Blake says in his statement that they left "when they *discovered* that they were to be served by non-union waiters". Notice the inconsistency.' 'That's only *pro forma*, Mother. Probably his lawyers advised him to say that. Otherwise, he might be charged with conspiracy or something. It's not meant, really, to fool anybody.' 'I'm going to call Daddy at the office,' said Mrs Davison. 'He may have missed the story. It's just as his breakfast waiter at the Savoy Plaza told him; outside elements have got hold of the waiters and are *manipulating* them. I'm afraid Harald may be in for some very serious trouble. Letting himself be a party to a charade like that. Do you think you should put in a call for Kay?' Helena shook her head. She did not want to talk to Kay with her mother standing by. 'Not now,' she said. 'She'll be at work, Mother.' 'Well, at least,' returned Mrs Davison, 'they didn't put her in the paper. And Petersen is a common name. It's a wonder to me, by the by, that the *Times* spelled it correctly, We can only hope that Macy's doesn't find out about this; I should hate to have Kay lose her position.'

She rose to go to the telephone, which was on a table in the corner. 'Run along now,' she said, 'while I talk to Daddy.' Mrs Davison's communications with Davy Davison, even on the most trivial matters, always took place in *camera*. In a little while, Helena was summoned back. 'Daddy knows about it already. He's sent out for today's edition. If it's come yet. And for yesterday's *Tribune* and the yellow press. Daddy wonders whether the New York office could help Harald out of this scrape. Find him a reputable lawyer. Who is this Putnam Blake? I never heard Harald speak of him. Neither has Daddy.' She spoke in tones of mild affront; Helena did not remind her that she had not seen Harald for many months. 'He went to Williams,' she said patiently. 'He and another boy run an organization called Common Causes – to help raise money for the "forgotten man" in labour cases. He's married to Norine Schmittlapp, in our class. She's the one in the tiara and long gloves. She was always leading demonstrations at college.' 'Exactly,' said Mrs Davison. 'I knew it! "*Cherchez la femme*," I said to Davy Davison. "You mark my words; you'll find there's a woman behind this."' Helena was taken aback by her mother's astuteness. 'What do you mean, exactly, Mother?' she inquired cautiously.

Mrs Davison patted her hairnet. 'I said to your father that what this fracas reminded me of was the old suffragette demonstrations. Chaining themselves to lamp-posts, and that young woman, Inez Something Something, Vassar she was too, who rode a white horse down Fifth Avenue to demonstrate for the vote. Dressed to kill. It was all in the papers then, when you were a baby. They were very fond of getting themselves arrested. Your father would never let me take part in those shenanigans. Though there were many fine women – Mrs McConnaughey and Mrs Perkin, right here in Cleveland – who were active in the movement.' These two friends of Mrs Davison's, one a Smith woman, the other a Wellesley woman, figured frequently in her conversation and had loomed over Helena's childhood like secular patron saints. Mrs Davison sighed. 'But those suffragette shindigs were all staged too,' she added in a more vigorous and cheerful voice, as though mastering her regrets. 'With the press invited ahead of time. No, as soon as I saw the article' – she picked up the *Times* and tapped it significantly – 'I said to myself: "No man ever planned this."' 'But why?' asked Helena. 'No grown-up man,' said her mother, 'will ever put on a tuxedo unless a woman makes him. No man, whatever his politics, Helena, is going to put on a tuxedo to go out and sympathy-strike, or whatever they call it, unless some artful woman is egging him on. To get her picture in the paper. Don't tell me Harald did this for Putnam Blake's blue eyes. No; she's probably got Putnam Blake and Harald wound round her little finger. That tiara now – probably she wanted to wear that. And those gloves. It's a marvel to me she didn't have an ostrich-feather fan.' Helena laughed and patted her mothers' plump arm. 'Why, you'd think, Helena,' Mrs Davison continued umbrageously but clearly feeling herself to be in 'good vein', 'she was in the receiving line at some charity ball. I'll wager she bought the whole outfit for the occasion. Or did she find it in her grandmother's trunk?' Helena laughed again; she could not help marvelling at her mother's inductive powers. 'A publicity hound,' said Mrs Davison, administering a final tap to the paper. 'What was her field at college?' 'English,' said Helena. 'She did her main work for Miss Lockwood. Contemporary Press.' Mrs Davison smote her forehead. 'Oh, my prophetic soul!' she said, nodding.

Chapter 7

In New York two nights before (the story Mrs Davison read had been reprinted from the previous day's late edition), Hatton, the Protheros' English butler, in his royal-purple wadded dressing-gown of Chinese embroidered silk with *moiré* lapels, had been seated in a wing chair in his bedroom on the top floor of the Prothero town house, reading the *Herald Tribune*, his radio set turned on. He was smoking a pipe, and his feet, in silk socks and red leather slippers, were resting on a footstool. The dressing-gown, the slippers, the wing chair, the radio set – all of Hatton's costume and stage properties, except the pipe he was smoking – had been passed on to him by Mr Prothero, a mature sporty fashion plate of Hatton's age and build. Hatton was somewhat taller, more digni-fied, and less purple in the face; one of the footmen had overheard the Vassar young ladies, Miss Mary's class-mates, declare that the butler looked like Henry James, an American novelist and London diner-out, it seemed, who had moved in the best circles – facts that Hatton himself had unearthed on his day out, in the reference room of the Society Library, not trusting the chauffeur, who ex-changed Mrs Prothero's crime story, picked for her every Friday by the head librarian, to do the job properly. (Mr Prothero's library, as Hatton observed to the younger footman, was more what you might call a gentleman's library; it contained chiefly sporting books – histories of the thoroughbred, stud and yacht-ing registers, memoirs of turf and field, bound in morocco and calfskin – and some volumes of pornography in dummy cases.)

The newspaper Hatton was conning had been glanced at by Mr Prothero this morning and turned over to the butler in almost mint condition, like the dressing-gown and the slippers, which scarcely showed signs of wear. Hatton, in fact, was a sort of double or slightly enlarged replica version of Mr Prothero, and he was not displeased by this, feeling himself to be, on the whole, an improvement on his American master: Mr Prothero's suits showed to better advantage on him because of his greater height; he enjoyed his evening read of the newspaper more than Mr Prothero did the morning's brief, bloodshot stare at the stock-market pages. When valeting Mr Prothero, he could not help seeing him sometimes, as he flicked the brush over his shoulders and adjusted the handkerchief in his pocket, as a sort of tailor's dummy in relation to himself – a mere padded form of wire and cloth on which clothes and other accoutrements were tried in rough stitching by a fitter for the 'man' who was their real and final destination. Mr Prothero, you might even say, broke in his shoes for him. He not only succeeded to Mr Prothero's wardrobe, his chair, newspaper, and radio set, practically as good as new; he 'stood in' for Mr Prothero in household emergencies, such as fire alarms, for Mrs Prothero, a huge, 'delicate' lady, soft as a plump bolster or sofa cushion, had a great fear of fire, and Hatton, trained by her to 'smell smoke', often led the family and the footmen and the maids downstairs to safety in the middle of the night, while Mr Prothero slept. To meet Hatton, like a big wattled purple bird, in the corridors or on the stairways of the tall house late at night (Mrs Prothero also had a fear of 'prowlers') had often confused Miss Mary's house guests, coming back from a ball somewhat the worse for champagne; Hatton was aware of the fact that, seeing him without his livery, they took him for Mr Prothero, whom they might have met during the evening in an identical dressing-gown helping himself from the decanter of whisky in the library. Hatton himself was a total abstainer.

Hatton was not only the 'man' but also the 'man of the house' and a very responsible character. He had been with the family for years, ever since the girls were small, and though he had once had a a secret plan of retiring to England on his savings and marrying a young woman, he had done the distinguished thing of losing all he had in the stock-market crash, four and a half years before. They had sold Hatton out, on the Street, and here too he had outshone Mr Prothero, who, after a short setback in '29, had gone through the depression getting steadily richer without any effort on his part but because of a patent he had bought from a man someone had introduced to him at the Piping Rock Club after a polo game. This fellow, who had looked like a swindler, had killed himself shortly afterwards by diving into an empty swimming-pool. But the patent, which controlled one of the processes in making the new synthetics, turned out to be worth a mint. Making money, Mr Prothero confessed, must be in the blood. He went downtown, now, to an office most weekdays, to provide what he called the window dressing for the firm that administered the patent; they made him a director, though he did not, as he said, understand what the hell they were manufacturing or leasing for manufacture, whichever it was. But he supposed it was his duty, in these times, to put his shoulder to the wheel.

The Prothero family, on both sides (Mrs Prothero was a Schuyler), was dim-witted and vain of it, as a sign of good breeding; none of them, as far back as they could trace their genealogy, had received a higher education, until Pokey, or Mary, as she was called at home, came along; her younger sister, Phyllis, had been dropped from Chapin, to Mrs Prothero's relief, in the sophomore year, and after a few months in Miss Hewitt's classes, had been able to leave school, according to state law, as soon as she turned sixteen. By now, she had had her coming-out party and was ready for marriage at nineteen – just the right age, Mrs Prothero thought, although she would be sorry to lose her, for she was a lonely woman and enjoyed having Phyllis's companionship on her trips to the hairdresser and the Colony Club, where she could sit in the lounge while Phyllis and her friends swam in the pool. Mrs Prothero, poor soul, her staff agreed, was a woman of few resources: unlike most ladies, she did not care for shopping; fittings fatigued her, for she did not believe she could stand long, having suffered from milk leg after the births of the girls; matinees made her cry (there were so many sad plays nowadays), and she had never been able to learn the bidding for contract bridge. She took no interest in interior decoration, the way so many ladies were doing; the furniture, carpets, and pictures in the main rooms of the house had scarcely changed since Hatton had been there. The servants, except for the younger footman and Annette, the girls' maid, had not changed either. Mrs Prothero had a pale, dusty tannish skin – the colour of the upholstery and stair carpets; the paintings in the drawing-room were of white and brown ruminants, cows and sheep, sitting in dark-brown fields. Hatton approved of the paintings, which he understood to be Dutch and valuable, and of the subdued brownish tone of the furnishings, but the women servants said that the place needed livening up. The trouble was that you could not get either Mrs Prothero or the girls to take any notice. Recently, Forbes, the girls' nursery governess, who now looked after the linen and the heavy mending, had taught Mrs Prothero to do petit point, which, as Forbes said, was like having a bit of company in the house, what with Miss Mary away at Cornell, studying to be a vet and never bringing her friends to stay any more, week-ends, the way she had at Vassar, and Mr Prothero at the office, and Miss Phyllis, who had been such a mainstay, off with girls of her own set to lunches and teas and fashion shows.

The Protheros entertained, but only at dinner; Mrs Prothero was not equal to leading the talk at luncheon. Mr Prothero always took his lunch at the Brook or the Racquet or the Knickerbocker, and the girls were told to have their friends to lunch at the Club, to save making extra work for Hatton. That was the Madam's way of putting it, but Hatton had never shirked work, as she ought to know. It was Hatton who planned Mrs Prothero's dinners, bringing her the menus and a diagram of the seating arrangements, before writing out the place cards; the conundrum of seating eight or sixteen had never been unriddled by Mrs Prothero, who always looked up at Hatton with faint surprised alarm when she found another lady opposite her, where she was used to seeing Mr Prothero, at the other end of the long table. Mrs Prothero's life was too inactive to warrant her having a social secretary, except during the two seasons when the girls were coming out. Hatton managed her invitations and her acceptances, told her who was coming to dinner and whom she was going to. He directed her contributions to charity and sometimes, on a night when they were entertaining, was able to suggest a topic for conversation.

Needless to say, he was also in the habit of giving the girls a hand. 'Hatton, you're a genius!' Miss Mary and Miss Phyllis were always shrieking when they did a list or seated a table in consultation with him. 'Infallible social sense,' Mr Prothero often muttered, of the butler, with a wink and a peculiar movement of the cheek muscle that gave him a paralysed appearance. The girls had more confidence too in Hatton's judgement in matters of dress than they had in Annette's or Forbes's; they would come up to his room in their ball gowns, twirl around before him, and ask whether they should wear the pearls or the Madam's diamonds or carry a scarf or a fan. It had been Hatton, in alliance with Forbes, who had seen to it that Miss Phyllis was made to wear a patch over one eye, as well as keep the braces on her teeth; if Hatton had not backed up Forbes, poor Miss Phyllis would be, as Forbes said, a regular Ben Turpin today.

The whole family adored Hatton. 'We all adore Hatton,' Miss Mary would announce in a vigorous whisper, shielding her pursed mouth with one hand, to a young man who was seeing her home, for the first time, from a tea dance or a young lady who was coming, for the first time, to stay; the butler's trained features would remain impassive as he led the way up the stairs, though the pretence of not hearing would have tried an inferior servant, since both the young ladies were not only blind as moles but had loud, flat, unaware voices like the voices of deaf people, so that even when they whispered everyone turned around to look at them and listen to what they were saying. They had inherited this trait, another sign of blue blood, from their grandmother on their father's side.

Hatton, though he took no notice, partly from habit, was not displeased that the young ladies made it a point that nobody who stayed in the house or came to dinner should fail to appreciate him. The slow ceremoniousness of his manners, his strict austere bearing ought to have spoken for themselves, but it was a convention, he understood, among the better class of Americans, to pretend that the service was invisible, which was *their* little way of showing that they were used to being waited on. This offended Hatton's professional pride and had caused him to leave his last place. With the Prothero family, being more of the old school, his exceptional endowment and qualifications were brought into the limelight, and the more unobtrusive he made himself, the more all heads turned surreptitiously to watch his deportment as he entered or left a room. He had only to close a door, noiselessly, or retire into the pantry to know that the family and its guests were discussing him. To be aware of Hatton was a proof of intimacy with the family – a boast, you might say, particularly among the young people. 'Hatton's a wonder,' the tall young gentlemen who were going on to a dance in white ties and tails would confide to each other, profoundly, over the coffee and the brandy when the young ladies had left the dining-room. 'Hatton's a wonder, sir,' they would say to Mr Prothero, at the head of the table. Hatton did not have to be psychic (which Miss Mary liked to let on he was) to surmise, from a glance through the pantry door, the trend of the conversation. The Vassar young ladies upstairs not all being used to society, the footman who served the Benedictine and the crème de menthe sometimes came down with a tale to tell, but with the young gentlemen over the brandy it was always the same.

'Like one of the family,' Mr Prothero would reply. 'Kind of an institution, Hatton is. Famous.' Hatton was not sure that he cared to be described as 'like one of the family'; he had always maintained his distance, even when the young ladies were toddlers. But he did feel himself to be an institution in the household and was used to being looked up to, like a portrait statue raised on a tall shaft in a London square. With this end in mind, he had perfected an absolute immobility of expression, which was one of his chief points, he knew, as a monument and invariably drawn to the attention of visitors. The signals directing attention to his frozen, sculptured face on the part of the young ladies and their friends Hatton was perfectly familiar with and accepted as a form of compliment while not, even inwardly, moving a muscle. When asked about the family he had served so long and with such apparent suppression of self ('Hatton is *devoted* to us,' Mrs Prothero declared, in one of her rare positive assertions of any kind), he would answer, with reserve, that it was 'a good place'. Miss Phyllis, when she was younger, used to pester him to say he liked her, being the ugly duckling, not that the rest were swans, but all Hatton would answer was simply, 'It's a good place, miss.' The same with the master when he was half-seas over and Hatton was guiding him to bed: 'You like us, eh, eh, Hatton? After all these years, eh?' Forbes, a stout party from Glasgow who had been with the family ever since Miss Mary was born, sometimes reminded Hatton that there were better places: a first-class butler, she said, was not supposed to act as a social secretary and valet, besides being a Holmes Protective man and a human fire-alarm system (this was Forbes's joke). 'Beggars can't be choosers,' Hatton, who was fond of a proverb, coldly retorted, but he really meant the opposite: a butler of his capacities could choose to take on extra duties without prejudicing his legend. He was the bigger man for it. Hatton, through doing crossword puzzles, was familiar with the principal myths, and his mind sometimes vaguely dwelt on the story of Apollo serving King Admetus, not that he would place Mr Prothero so high. Yet the comparison occasionally flashed through his head when he was waiting on table, throwing a spacious aureole or nimbus around him as he moved from one chair to the next, murmuring 'Sherry, madam?' or 'Champagne, miss?' Miss Mary, he felt, was aware of the nimbus, for he would find her near-sighted eyes frowningly focused on him, as if observing something unusual, and her nostrils sniffing, a sign of aroused attention she had probably picked up from the Madam; the poor young lady herself had no sense of smell. Miss Mary swore by telepathy; she had a sixth sense, she insisted, to make up for the missing one. She had decided that Hatton had too. 'Are your ears burning, Hatton?' she often asked him when he came to answer the bell in a room where she and her friends were playing one of those mind-reading games, with cards, she had learned at Vassar. He explained to her that it was the job of a good servant to read his master's mind and anticipate his wishes; for him, he added reprovingly, it was all in the day's work, no fun and games about it. 'How did you become a butler, Hatton?' she sometimes asked, seating herself on his bed. 'Yes, how did you, Hatton?' said Miss Phyllis, occupying his footstool. But Hatton declined to answer. 'That is my private affair, miss.' '*I* think,' said Miss Mary, 'you decided to become a butler because you were psychic. Natural selection.' This was over Hatton's head, but he did not allow the fact to be seen. Miss Mary turned to Miss Phyllis. 'It proves my point, Phyl. Don't you get it? Darwin. The survival of the fittest.' Her loud peremptory voice resounded through the servants' quarters. 'If Hatton wasn't psychic he'd be a flop as a butler. *Ergo* he is psychic. Q.E.D.' She scratched her head and beamed victoriously at Hatton. 'Pretty smart, eh wot?' 'Very smart, miss,' Hatton agreed, wondering if this was the Darwin who had discovered the missing link. 'Girls!' came Forbes's voice from below. 'Come down and get into your baths.'

The fact was, Hatton had become a butler because his father had been in service. But he too had come to feel that there was something more to it than this; like Miss Mary said, he had had a vocation or a higher call that had bade him assume the office. This conviction had slowly overtaken him in America, where genuine English butlers did not grow on trees. 'You're the real article, Hatton!' a gentleman who had come to stay in the Long Island house had said to him one morning with an air of surprise. He was like a stage butler or a butler you saw on the films, the gentleman doubtless meant to imply. Hatton had been pleased to hear it; being somewhat younger then and on his own, so to speak, in a foreign country, he had tried to conform to an ideal of the English butler as he found it in films and in crime stories and in the funny papers that Cook read, for the wise man knew how to turn the smallest occasion to profit. Yet he now felt that study alone could not have done it. When the young ladies told him he was a genius, he believed they had hit on the truth: 'out of the mouths of babes'. He had long accepted the fact that he was the brains of the family and the heavy obligation that went with it. The eternal model of the English butler, which he kept before his eyes, even in his moments of relaxation and on his day off, required that he have the attributes of omniscience and ubiquity, like they taught you in the catechism: 'Where is God?' 'God is everywhere.' Hatton was Church of England, and did not mean to blaspheme, but he could not help noticing those little correspondences, as when he had observed, in his earlier situations, that he was expected to be invisible too.

Folding the newspaper, Hatton sighed. One of the duties or accomplishments of the classic English butler, of which he personally was the avatar, was to be well informed on matters that would not at first glance seem to be relevant to the job in hand and also to be a past master of proper names. That was why, at present, he was reading the *Herald Tribune*, on behalf of the family, having already had a hasty look at Cook's tabloid for the murders, and why he had started with the society columns and the sporting pages, to have a go at them while his mind was fresh. Hatton was not a sporting man, except for the races and, back home, the cricket, but duty obliged him to take cognizance of the proper names and lineage of dogs, cats, boats, horses, polo players, golfers, as they appeared in the news, together with all sorts of figures and ratings, since it was these names and figures that were most commonly wanted in the Prothero household. Then there were the society columns, for the Madam and the girls. When a young gentleman got married, it was Hatton who struck his name off Miss Mary's list, and when a young lady announced her engagement, it was Hatton who reminded Miss Mary or Miss Phyllis to buy a wedding present – a thing Miss Mary often neglected or sent Annette to do.

Selecting a green pencil, Hatton made a small check on the society page; this meant: present, Miss Phyllis; a red-pencil check meant: present, Miss Mary. With a new sigh, this time of content, he folded the paper to the obituary page – one of his favourite sections. Yet even here the voice of duty intruded, though not, he saw at a glance, this evening: he would not have to warn Yvonne, Mrs Prothero's personal maid, to look over her mistress's blacks, nor get Mr Prothero ready to be a pall-bearer. He settled down to the obits. Next, he turned to the stock-market pages, which no longer interested him much personally; he had not had a flyer since the fall of '29; but he kept abreast of the market in order to follow the conversation at the dinner table when the senior Protheros were entertaining and the ladies had left the room. In the back of his mind, there was always the thought of picking up a tip from one of the older gentlemen, but he had not yet refound the courage to call his broker with an order.

Relighting his pipe, he studied the entertainment news, to make sure the film he planned to see on his day out was still playing. He read Percy Hammond's review of the play that had opened the night before. Hatton had never been to a proper theatre, only to music hall, but he took an interest in the stage partly because he understood that it was customary to begin a play with a scene between a butler and a parlourmaid with a feather duster. He would have given something to see that. Miss Mary's friend, Miss Katherine from Vassar, had promised to get him tickets some time on his night out, but that was the last he had heard of it. She was the one who had married the actor or whatever he was, something connected with the stage; Miss Mary had gone to the wedding. Hatton had never been partial to Miss Katherine; he did not see eye to eye with Forbes, who called her 'the bonny lass'. Forbes would have changed her tune if she had seen what he had, coming downstairs one night, still tying his dressing-gown sash in his hurry and his bridge-work not in, because the Madam had 'heard a noise, Hatton. Please go and see.' For once, the Madam was right: there the two of them were, in the front hall, on the landing, the 'bonny lass' and her 'fiancé', going right at it. Hatton had not liked the look of him at dinner. 'Harald Petersen,' he was called, like some blasted Viking; Hatton had taken special notice of the spelling as he made out the place card. When Miss Katherine was going to get married, Miss Mary, Hatton recalled, had consulted him as to whether it would be possible for the young lady to have the use of the town house for the wedding, since the rest of the family, except Mr Prothero, would already have gone down to the country. Bearing in mind what he had seen ('Just a bit of kissing,' Forbes said; did you do that on the floor with your skirts up and the 'fiancé' planted on top of you for anybody from the street to see?), not to speak of the tickets, Hatton had said no, the furniture would be in dust covers, and it would upset the master, if he was staying in town that night, to find strangers in the house. 'You're a treasure, Hatton!' Miss Mary had proclaimed. Hatton had not been surprised to read in the paper this last summer that the play Mr Petersen was with had closed, despite Miss Katherine's telling them that it was going to run for years and years; since then, he had not seen the name in the theatrical columns, though he had observed in the real-estate notices that a Mr and Mrs Harold Peterson [*sic*] had taken an apartment in the East Fifties, near Sutton Place. That was them, said Miss Mary, who had been there only the other day. She had not had them to the house, though, since she had been up there at agricultural college; when she gave a dinner party nowadays, it was more for her own sort; she would just phone down to Hatton to have twelve covers and make up the list himself and to be sure and see to it that Miss Phyllis was not home for dinner that night. But if Miss Katherine and Mr Petersen *were* asked again, Hatton had made a mental note to address her as 'madam' when he opened the door. 'Good evening, madam' (not 'miss'), and a small, discreet smile; it was those little touches that counted. 'He called me "madam"; isn't that perfect?' Miss Katherine would whisper to her husband. 'Hatton called me "madam", Pokey; what do you know?'

Hatton turned to the front page, which he had saved for the last; he liked the sense of exercising his intellect which the world and general news gave him. A labour dispute had been occupying a small part of the front page for over a week; the waiters of the

148

principal hotels were on strike. Hatton made it a point to take no sides in American politics; he believed that it was against the law for an alien to interfere in the domestic affairs of a foreign country and consequently refrained from having any thoughts on the subject. 'Who would *you* vote for, Hatton?' Miss Katherine had asked him at the time of the last election, when she was staying in the house. 'I am not an American citizen, miss,' Hatton had replied. Nevertheless, the waiters' strike had enlisted his sympathies, to a certain degree, for they were his fellow-creatures, even if there was a gulf, a very wide gulf, between private service and what you might call common service. For a brief time, while he was getting his training, he had worked at a hotel in London. Hence, he had been following the strike news, and he knew from Cook's *Daily Mirror* that something had happened last night at the Cavendish – another demonstration.

Now his grey eyes imperturbably widened; he shook the newspaper on his lap. When he had finished reading the item and turned to page five for the continuation, he refolded the paper back to page one, selected a blue pencil from his table and slowly drew a border around the story. His hands trembled slightly with suppressed excitement. Then he refolded the paper still again, into a shape that would fit onto a salver, which he would present to Mrs Prothero at breakfast: 'Beg pardon, madam; I thought this would interest Miss Mary.' He then mentally withdrew to the side board or, better, to the serving pantry, within earshot.

'Hatton!' he heard the mistress' voice call in agitation the next morning, and he slowly re-entered the dining-room. 'What *is* this? Why have you brought me this?' Mrs Prothero quivered through all her shapeless, cushiony form. 'Excuse the liberty, madam, but I ventured to think that one of the gentlemen referred to was Miss Katherine's husband.' He bent forward and indicated to his mistress with his pink, manicured forefinger the name of Harald Petersen (spelled 'Harold Petersen'). 'Miss Katherine?' demanded Mrs Prothero. 'Who is she? How do we know her, Hatton?' She turned her head away from the group photograph on page five he was attempting to show her. 'The young lady who came to stay, madam, over the Christmas holidays and on one or two other occasions when Miss Mary was in school at Vassar.' He paused, waiting for Mrs Prothero's otiose memory to begin to work. But Mrs Prothero shook her head, a mass of pale-brown, lustreless, trembling ringlets that, despite all Yvonne's and the hairdresser's labours, resembled a costumier's wig. 'Who were her people?' 'We never knew, madam,' Hatton replied solemnly. '"Strong", she was called. From one of the western states.' 'Not Eastlake?' queried Mrs Prothero, with a momentary, uncertain brightening. 'Oh no, madam. We *know* Miss Elinor, But this other young lady was dark too, and pretty, in a natural sort of way. Forbes, if you remember, took a fancy to her. "A Highland rose," she used to say.' He imitated Forbes's burr. Mrs Prothero gave a faint cry. 'Oh dear, yes,' she said. 'I remember. *Very* pretty, Hatton. But rather uncouth. Or was that the person she married? What was it she always called him?' '"My fiancé"?' supplied Hatton, with a smile in abeyance. 'That's it exactly!' cried Mrs Prothero. 'Still, we oughtn't to laugh at her. Mr Prothero used to recite a poem when she stayed here. "Maud Muller, on a summer's day . . ." And then something about the hay. Oh dear, how did it go? Help me, Hatton.' But Hatton for once was caught napping. 'I've got it!' Mrs Prothero exclaimed. '"Stood listening while a pleased surprise/Gleamed in her long-lashed hazel eyes." Tennyson, I suppose.' 'I daresay, madam,' replied Hatton austerely. 'But we never knew who she was,' Mrs Prothero reminisced, sighing. 'Mr Prothero often used to ask me, "Who's that girl who's always staying here? The Maud Muller girl." And I was never able to tell him. Her people were early settlers out West, I believe she said.' She put on her glasses and peered again at the folded rectangle of newspaper. 'And now, Hatton, you tell me she's in jail. What has she done? Shoplifting, I expect.' 'I believe,' Hatton intervened, 'that it's her husband who was in custody. Something to do with a labour dispute.' Mrs Prothero waved a pale plump hand. 'Don't tell me any more, Hatton. And I beg you not to bring it to Mr Prothero's attention. We had the man to dinner. I remember it distinctly.' She reflected, her pale, dim eyes turning anxiously behind her gold-rimmed spectacles. 'The best thing, I think, Hatton, would be for you to take that article out to the kitchen and burn it in the stove. Without saying anything to Cook, if you please. People in our position can't afford, Hatton – ' She looked up at the butler expectantly, for him to finish her thought.

'Quite, madam,' he agreed, picking up the folded paper and replacing it on the salver. '"People who live in glass houses", Hatton . . . . How does it go? Oh, dear no, I mean another one. "Should be above reproach." Shakespeare, isn't it? *Julius Caesar.*' She smiled. 'We are being quite highbrow this morning,' she went on. 'Quite the intellectuals. We must blame Vassar for that, mustn't we, Hatton? Though you've always been quite a thinker.' Hatton bowed in acknowledgement and retired a few steps. 'Now mind you burn it, Hatton. With your own hands,' his mistress cautioned.

When the butler had left the room, Mrs Prothero gave way; she leaned on a podgy milk-blue elbow and let the tears rise to her eyes. Hatton watched her through the porthole in the pantry door. He knew what the Madam was thinking. She was thinking how brave she had been in the butler's presence, not letting him see how upset she was by that nasty story in the newspaper. Disgraceful. And of how she blamed everyone, starting with the Chapin School, for contriving to send Miss Mary to that college that was always getting in the paper – not that the others were any better, but you heard less about them. Everyone she trusted, starting with the Chapin School, had turned against her on the college issue: the schoolmistress, what was her name, who has helped Miss Mary fill out her own application forms; Forbes, who had lent her the price of the registration fee out of her savings; the Hartshorn girl, who had smuggled her out of the house three days running, it seemed, to take the college entrance exams; and Hatton, Hatton himself, who had got round her and her husband, when Miss Mary was accepted, by announcing that he did not believe a year or two of college would do the young lady any harm. It was like a case in Bar Harbour she had heard about only the other day at the Colony Club. She had told Hatton about it, just to show him that she had not forgotten. An elopement, *that* was, out a french window of one of the big houses and through a parting in the hedge. The staff, as usual, there too (yes, she had said 'as usual' straight out to Hatton) had gone against the family's wishes; the butler had actually crept out at night with a pair of garden shears and cut a hole through the hedge. What if the couple *were* married immediately, by a minister who was waiting in the rectory, so they said? He was only another accomplice. As for her own staff, she had always suspected that someone – Forbes or, more likely, Hatton – had signed her name to the Vassar application forms; Miss Mary swore she had done it herself and was brash as paint about it, but Mrs Prothero still felt that Hatton had guided her hand.

Hatton turned away from the porthole; the Madam's sobs were becoming audible, and he went to ring for Yvonne. When she reached that point, the Madam was quite unreasonable. She was very much mistaken in thinking, as she still did, that he had forged her signature. They had kept their secret from him too; he had known nothing about the whole affair until it was over, and Miss Mary had been accepted. At the present time, he rather shared the Madam's views on higher education, though the Madam was not consistent: why give Miss Mary a plane if you did not want her to fly up every week now to learn to be a horse doctor? But Miss Mary always had her way, except with him.

He compressed his lips and went to take another peek at Mrs Prothero. He was sorry now he had showed her the newspaper story, for what she did not know would not hurt her, poor lady. It had been an excess of zeal that had prompted it, he recognized – a certain over-perfectionism, if that was the term, in the performance of his role. 'Hatton,' he said to himself, 'pride goeth before a fall.' In the dining-room, Mrs Prothero would be reflecting that, thanks to higher education, she had had a jailbird in the house.

'A jailbird!' she repeated indignantly, with a wobble of her receding chin, so loud that Yvonne, coming down the stairs, could hear her. Clutching her wrapper around her and holding Yvonne's arm, she retired upstairs to her bedroom and cancelled the car which was to take her to the hairdresser at eleven. Meanwhile Hatton, who had already told the chauffeur that he would not be needed, was cutting out the newspaper clipping and preparing to paste it in his scrapbook.

In Boston, the next morning, Mrs Renfrew met Dottie for lunch at the Ritz. They were lunching early in order to go to Bird's for the wedding invitations and announcements; later in the afternoon, they had an appointment at Crawford Hollidge for a fitting. Dottie's wedding dress and going-away costume were being made in New York, but on most items, country suits and simple sports things above all, you could do just as well in Boston and at half the price. After Crawford Hollidge, if there was time, they were going to stop at Stearns' to look at linen and compare prices with Filene's. The Renfrews were not rich, only quite comfortably off, and Mrs Renfrew economized wherever she could; she felt it was poor taste, in these times, to splurge when others were doing without. They had had the dressmaker in to see if Mrs Renfrew's wedding gown, which *she* had got from *her* mother, could possibly be made over for Dottie, who was dying to wear it, but there was not enough material in the seams; Dottie, they discovered (and there was progress for you!), was nearly four inches wider in the waist, bust, and hips, though not at all 'hippy' or 'busty'; it was a question of larger bones. Mrs Renfrew's mind this morning was full of measurements – sheets and glove and dress sizes; she was thinking too of the bridesmaids' presents. Silver compacts from Shreve Crump? Tiny sterling cigarette lighters? There would only be the three: Polly Andrews, of course, and Helena Davison, and Dottie's cousin, Vassar '31, from Dedham, who was going to be matron of honour. Since the groom was a widower, both Dottie and Mrs Renfrew felt it was better for the wedding to be quiet, just the matron of honour and the two attendants behind her. Dottie had been pining to have Lakey, but Lakey had written, from lovely Avila, that she could not come back this year. In her letter she said that she was sending a little Spanish primitive of a Madonna (perfect for the Southwest) and that Dottie should have no trouble clearing it through the Customs House, as an antique. Mrs Renfrew hoped that Sam, Dottie's father, whose firm had been clearing Customs since the days of sailing ships, would see to that for them; there was such a great deal to do.

On her way here to meet Dottie, who had gone to Dr Perry for a check-up, Mrs Renfrew had stopped at the Chilton Club to have a manicure and leafed through the day's New York papers in the library, in case she saw anything in the ads for Dottie that could be ordered by mail. Her eye was caught by a photo of some young people in evening dress on one of the inner pages, next to a Peck & Peck ad. She turned back to start the story, reprinted from yesterday's late edition, on the front page. When she saw Harald's name, she immediately made a note to tell Dottie at lunch: Dottie might want to call Kay to get all the gory details. Mrs Renfrew was a cheerful, lively person who always looked on the gay side of things; she imagined it must have been quite an adventure for those radical young people to get dressed up and do battle with the hotel staff, rather like a *Lampoon* prank; Kay's husband, she was sure, when he came up for trial, would be let off after a lecture from the judge, the way the Harvard boys always were when they got in trouble with the Cambridge police force. Apropos of that, she meant to ask Sam to stop at City Hall and pay a parking ticket she and Dottie had got the other day.

It was only because she had so many other things on her mind, such as type faces, sheet sizes (would Brook and Dottie sleep in a double bed? It was so hard to know, with a widower, what to expect), and the bridesmaids' dresses (such a problem, unless Helena could come on from Cleveland early to be fitted), that she quite forgot to mention Harald's fracas till they had finished luncheon and were walking down Newbury Street, side by side, like two sisters, Mrs Renfrew in her beaver and Dottie in her mink. 'Dottie!' she exclaimed. 'I nearly forgot! You'll never guess what I was reading this morning at the Club. One of your friends has run afoul of the law.' She looked quizzically up at her daughter, her blue eyes dancing. 'Try to guess.' 'Pokey,' said Dottie. Mrs Renfrew shook her head. 'Not even warm.' 'Harald Petersen!' repeated Dottie, when her mother had told her. 'That wasn't fair, Mother. He's not exactly a friend. What did he do?' Mrs Renfrew related the story. In the middle of it, Dottie stopped dead, between Arlington and Berkeley. 'Who was the other man?' she asked. 'I wonder who it could have been,' 'I don't know, Dottie. But his picture was in the paper. He had quite a "shiner".' 'You don't remember the name, Mother?' Mrs Renfrew ruefully shook her head. 'Why? Do you think it's someone you know?' Dottie nodded. 'It was a fairly common name,' said Mrs Renfrew, pondering. 'It seems to me it began with B.' 'Not Brown?' cried Dottie. 'It might have been,' replied her mother. 'Brown, Brown,' she repeated. 'I wonder if that was it.' 'Oh, Mother!' said Dottie. 'Why didn't you clip it out?' 'Darling,' said her mother. 'You can't clip newspapers in the Club. It's against the house rules. And yet you'd be surprised, the number of members that do it. Magazines too.' 'What did he look like?' said Dottie. 'Rather artistic,' said Mrs Renfrew. 'Dissipated-looking. But that may have been the black eye. A gentleman, I should think. Now, what did it say he did? Sad to say, Dottie, my memory's going. "Harald Petersen, playwright," and the other one was something like that. Not "ditchdigger", anyway,' she added brightly. '"Painter"?' suggested Dottie. 'I don't *think* so,' said her mother.

All this time, they had been standing in the middle of the sidewalk, with people brushing past them. It was cold; Mrs Renfrew pushed back her coat sleeve and glanced at her watch. 'You go on, Mother,' said Dottie abruptly. 'I'll meet you. I'm going back to the Ritz to buy the paper.' Mrs Renfrew looked seriously up at Dottie; she was not alarmed, having guessed for a long time that some little love trouble had happened to Dottie early last summer in New York. That was why she had sent her out West, to get over it. 'Do you want me to come with you?' she said. Dottie hesitated. Mrs Renfrew took her arm. 'Come along, dear,' she said. 'I'll wait in the ladies' lounge while you get it from the porter.'

A few minutes later, Dottie appeared with the *Herald Tribune*; the *Times* had been sold out. 'Putnam Blake,' she said. 'You were right about the B. I met him at Kay's party. He raises funds for labour. We got an appeal from him the other day for something. And he married Norine Schmittlapp, who was in our class. You can see her in the big picture. The four of them have got very inty this winter.' From Dottie's flat tone, Mrs Renfrew could tell that this was not 'the one'. The poor girl laid the paper aside quietly; then she sank her chin into the palm of her hand and sat thinking. Mrs Renfrew took out her compact, so as not to seem to watch Dottie. As she powdered her pretty, bright features, she considered what to do. Dottie still 'had it bad', as the girls said nowadays; that was all too clear. Her mother's sympathies, like delicate feelers, fluttered out to her; she knew how it felt to yearn for the sight of a certain name long after the man who owned it had passed out of one's life forever. The very prospect of seeing his name and his photograph had got Dottie all 'hot and bothered' again. Yet Mrs Renfrew could not decide whether it would be wiser to let Dottie bear her disappointment in silence or to help her talk it out. The danger of this was that Dottie's flame might only be fanned by talking; if she had the strength to stamp it out alone, she would come through, in the end, a finer person. And yet it made little Mrs Renfrew wince and bite her lips to sit pretending to fix her hair when a few words from her might be balm to Dottie's soul.

Mrs Renfrew had complete confidence in Dottie's judgement:

if Dottie considered this man in New York, whoever he was, unsuitable for her, Dottie must be right. Some girls in Dottie's position might give up a fine young man because he was poor or had a dependent mother and sisters to support (Mrs Renfrew had known such cases), but Dottie would not do that; through her religion, she would find the patience to wait. Whatever the reason, Dottie's heart had made its decision last summer and stuck to it splendidly; it was Mrs Renfrew's guess that the man was married. There *were* cases (the wife hopelessly insane and shut up in an institution and no prospect of her death) in which Mrs Renfrew might have counselled a liaison for Dottie, no matter what Sam Renfrew threatened, but if it had been something of *that* sort, Dottie would surely have told her. No; Mrs Renfrew did not doubt that Dottie had done the wise and brave thing in cutting this man out of her life; it only troubled her that Dottie might be marrying too hastily, 'on the rebound', before her former feelings had had a chance to die naturally. She had come back from Arizona quietly happy and looking fit as a fiddle, but with Brook still out West and the strain of the wedding preparations, she had begun to seem a little over-tired and nervous. It worried Mrs Renfrew, now, to realize that Dottie, with two fittings yet to come on her wedding dress, would be in New York and exposed, probably, at every turn, to memories of this man.

These thoughts, sharp as bird tracks, passed through Mrs Renfrew's pretty little hatted head as she sat, tense with sympathy for her daughter, in the Ritz ladies' lounge. She wondered what Dr Perry or Dr Leverett, the dear old rector, would advise; perhaps Dottie would be able to talk to one of them, in case she had any real doubts about the state of her feelings. She snapped shut her handbag. 'How was Dr Perry today?' she asked smiling. 'Did he give you a clean bill of health?' Dottie raised her head. 'He wants to try some diathermy for my sciatica. But he says I'll be better when I get back into the sun – the great open spaces.' She forced a twinkle into her brown eyes. Mrs Renfrew hesitated; this was neither the time nor the place, but she was a believer in impulse. She looked around the lounge; they were alone. 'Dottie.' she said. 'Did Dr Perry say anything to you about birth control?' Dottie's face and neck reddened, giving her a rough, chapped look, like an ailing spinster. She nodded briefly. 'He says you told him to, Mother. I wish you hadn't.' Mrs Renfrew guessed that Dr Perry had been having one of his gruff days and had offended Dottie's maiden modesty; engaged girls often had the most unaccountable reactions to the prospect of the wedding night. Mrs Renfrew moved her chair a little closer. 'Dottie,' she said. 'Even if you and Brook are planning to have children, you mayn't want them just yet. There's a new device, I understand, that's ninety-per-cent effective. A kind of rubber cap that closes off the uterus. Did Dr Perry tell you about it?' 'I stopped him,' said Dottie. Mrs Renfrew bit her lip. 'Darling,' she urged, 'you mustn't be frightened. Dr Perry, you know, isn't a woman's doctor; he may have been a bit brusque. He'll arrange to send you to a specialist, who'll make it all seem easier. And who'll answer any questions you want to ask – you know, about the physical side of love. Would you rather see a woman doctor? I don't think this new device is legal yet here in Massachusetts. But Dr Perry can fix it for you to have an appointment in New York, the next time we go down for your fittings.'

It seemed to Mrs Renfrew that Dottie shivered in reply. 'I'll go with you, dear,' she added, brightly. 'If you want moral support. . . . Or you could ask one of your married friends – Kay or Priss.' Mrs Renfrew did not know what had done it – the mention of New York, perhaps – but Dottie began to cry. 'I love him,' she said, choking, as the tears ran in furrows down either side of her long, distinguished nose. 'I love him, Mother.'

At last it had come out. 'I know, dear,' said Mrs Renfrew fishing in Dottie's pocketbook for a clean handkerchief and gently wiping her face. 'I don't mean Brook,' said Dottie. 'I know,' said Mrs Renfrew. 'What am I going to do?' Dottie repeated. 'What am I going to do?' 'We'll see,' promised her mother. Her principal object now was to get Dottie's tears dried and her face powdered and take her home, before any of their friends could see her here. 'We'll give up the fitting,' she said. The doorman brought the car around (he and Mrs Renfrew were old friends); Mrs Renfrew put her small foot on the accelerator and in a few minutes they were home and up in Dottie's bedroom, with the door closed, having let themselves in so softly that Margaret, the old parlour-maid, had not heard them. They sat on Dottie's chaise-longue, with their arms around each other.

'I thought I was over it. I thought I loved Brook.' Mrs Renfrew nodded, though she had not yet learned the circumstances or even the young man's name. 'Do you want to marry him?' she asked, going straight to the heart of the matter. 'There's no question, Mother, of that,' Dottie answered, in a cold, almost rebuking tone. Mrs Renfrew drew a deep breath. 'Do you want to "live" with him?' she heard herself bravely pronounce. Dottie buried her head in her mother's strong small shoulder. 'No, I guess not,' she acknowledged. 'Then what do you want, darling?' said her mother, stroking her forehead. Dottie pondered. 'I want to see him again,' she decided. 'That's all, Mother. I want to see him again.' Mrs Renfrew clasped Dottie tighter. 'I thought he'd be at Kay's party. I was *sure* he'd be there. And you know, when I first came in, I only wanted him to be there so that he could hear about my engagement and see my engagement ring and watch how happy I was. I looked awfully well that day. But then, when he didn't come, I started wanting to see him just to see him – not to show him he didn't mean a thing to me any more. Was that first feeling just sort of an armour, do you think?' 'I imagine so, Dottie,' said her mother. 'Oh, it was awful,' said Dottie. 'Every time the doorbell rang, I was convinced it was going to be Dick' – she pronounced the name shyly, looking sidewise at her mother – 'and then when it wasn't I nearly fainted, each time, it hurt me so. And all those new friends of Kay's were terribly nice but I almost hated them because they weren't Dick. Why do you think he didn't come?' 'Was he invited?' asked Mrs Renfrew practically. 'I don't know and I couldn't ask. And it was so peculiar; nobody mentioned him. Not a word. And all the time a drawing by him of Harald was hanging right there on the wall. Like Banquo's ghost or something. I felt sure he'd been invited and was staying away on purpose and that everybody there knew that and was watching me out of the corner of their eye.' 'Your grammar, Dottie!' chided her mother, absently; her sky-blue eyes had clouded over. 'Does Kay know about this?' she asked, taking care to make the question sound casual, so that she would not seem to be reproaching Dottie. Dottie nodded mutely, not looking at her mother, who made a little grimace and then controlled herself. 'If she knew, dear, and knew you were engaged,' she said lightly, 'she doubtless *didn't* invite him. For your sake,' Mrs Renfrew was 'fishing', but Dottie did not bite.

'How cruel,' she answered, which told Mrs Renfrew nothing. 'You mustn't be unfair, dear,' she said mechanically, 'because you're unhappy. Your father would say,' she added, smiling, 'that Kay "showed good judgement".' And she looked questioningly into Dottie's eyes. How far had this thing gone? Mrs Renfrew had to know, yet Dottie did not seem to be aware of the fact that she had left her parent in the dark.

'Then you think I shouldn't see him?' Dottie answered swiftly. 'How can I say, Dottie?' protested her mother. 'You haven't told me anything about him. But I think *you* think you shouldn't see him. Amn't I right?' Dottie stared pensively at her engagement ring. 'I think I *must* see him,' she decided. 'I mean I feel I'm fated to see him. If I don't do anything about it myself. As if it would be arranged, somehow, before I was married, that I would meet him just once. But I think I mustn't *try* to see him. Do you understand that?' 'I understand,' said Mrs Renfrew, 'that you want to have your cake and eat it too, Dottie. You'd like God to arrange for you to have something that you know would be wrong for you to have if you chose it of your own free will.' A look of relief and wonder came into Dottie's face. 'You're right, Mother!' she cried. 'What a marvellous person you are! You've seen right through me.' 'We're all pretty much alike,' consoled Mrs Renfrew. 'Judy O'Grady and the Colonel's lady, you know,' She squeezed Dottie's hand. 'And yet,' said Dottie, 'even if it's wrong, I can't stop hoping. Not hoping, even. Expecting. That somehow, somehow, I *will* see him. On the street. Or on a bus or a train. The day after Kay's party, I went to the Museum of Modern Art; I made believe I was going to see an exhibition. But he wasn't there. And the time's getting so short. Only a month left. Less than a month. Mother, in Arizona, I hardly thought about him at *all.* I'd almost forgotten him. It was Kay's party that brought it all back. And ever since then I've had the most *peculiar* feeling. That he was thinking about me too. Not just that, Mother. Watching me, sort of sceptically, wherever I went, like to Dr Perry today or a fitting; he has the most thrilling grey eyes that he narrows. . . .' She hesitated and broke off. 'Do you believe in thought transference, Mother? Do you remember *Peter Ibbetson*? Because I feel that Dick is listening to my thoughts. And waiting.' Mrs Renfrew sighed. 'Your imagination has got overactive, dear. You're letting it run away with you.' 'Oh, Mother,' said Dottie, 'if you could only see him! You would like him too. He's terribly good-looking and he's suffered so much.' All at once, she dimpled. 'How could you ever have thought that I'd have fallen for someone that looked like that Putnam Blake? Why, he's white as a leper and needs to wash his hair! Dick isn't the unwashed type; he comes from a very good family – descended from Hawthorne. Brown is a very good name.'

Mrs Renfrew put her hands on her daughter's shoulders and shook her gently. 'I want you to lie down now. And I'll bring you a cold compress for your eyes. Rest till dinner. Or till Daddy comes home.' It was just as she had feared; talking about this man had revived all Dottie's feeling for him; having started by crying, she had finished in smiles and dimples. In the bathroom, wringing out two hand towels in cold water, Mrs Renfrew wondered whether it might not be a good thing, however, for Dottie to see this man again. In her own environment, among her own friends. . . . Despite what Dottie said, he was evidently a bit of a rough diamond. If Dottie had not been engaged, she could have asked him to a little party in New York, perhaps at Polly Andrews's place. Or to dine quietly with herself and her mother some night, and to go to a play or a concert afterwards, with some older man present to make a fourth? Six would be better still – less pointed. Dottie could simply telephone him and say that her mother had an extra ticket and could he dine first? But an engaged girl was not free to ask whomever she chose, even with all the chaperonage in the world. And what would Brook say to Dottie's mother if anything were to happen as the result?

Mrs Renfrew sharply wrung out the compress, which had got tepid while she was thinking, and held it afresh under the cold-water tap. For Dottie's own sake, she *had* to know how far the thing had gone. If it had gone the whole way and the man had aroused her senses, the poor child was in a fix. Some women, they said, never got over the first man, especially if he were skilful; he left a permanent imprint. Why, they even said that a child conceived with the legal husband would have the features of the first lover! That was nonsense, of course, old wives' talk, yet the thought stirred Mrs Renfrew's blood a little. She was forty-seven years old and had just had her twenty-fifth reunion (where she had been voted the youngest-looking member of the class) at the time of Dottie's

Commencement, and yet at heart, she feared, she was still a romantic; it excited her foolish fancy to think that a man who took a girl's virginity had the power to make her his forever. She could not make out what Dottie's own heart was dictating. Dottie was independent; she had her own bank account in the State Street Trust. What then was holding her back from seeing this man if she wanted to?

She laid the compress on Dottie's forehead, briskly drew the shades, and sat down on the bed, meaning to stay only a minute, to feel Dottie's pulse. It appeared to be normal. 'Dottie,' she said impulsively, tucking the coverlet around her, 'I think you have to be true to your own lights in this. If you love "Dick"' – she brought out the name with difficulty – 'perhaps you should take the initiative in trying to see him. Is it your pride that's holding you back? Did he hurt you in some way? Did you have a quarrel or a misunderstanding?' 'He doesn't love me, Mother,' said Dottie in a low voice. 'I just excite him sexually. He told me so.' Mrs Renfrew closed her eyes for an instant, feeling something click inside her, rather unpleasantly, at hearing, with finality, what she had already guessed to be the case; then she picked up Dottie's hand and squeezed it warmly. 'So he *was* your lover.' There had only been one night, it seemed; the night she had tried to reach Dottie at the Vassar Club and Dottie did not come in. That was the time. 'But you hardly knew him,' said Mrs Renfrew. 'Dick's a fast worker,' replied Dottie with a twinkle and a cough. 'And what happened afterwards?' said Mrs Renfrew gravely. 'You never heard from him again? Was that it, Dottie?' Compassion for her daughter moved her heart. 'I can't explain,' said Dottie. 'I don't know myself what happened. I ran away, I suppose you could say.' Mrs Renfrew clicked her tongue against the roof of her mouth. 'Was it a very painful experience? Did you bleed a great deal, dear?' 'No,' said Dottie. 'It wasn't painful that way. Actually, it was terribly thrilling and passionate. But afterwards ... Oh, Mother, I simply can't tell you, I can never tell anyone, what happened afterwards.' Mrs Renfrew's sensitive conjectures were wide of the mark. 'He had me' – Dottie suddenly spoke up – 'go to a doctor and get a contraceptive, one of those diaphragm things you were talking about.' Mrs Renfrew was stunned; her wide bright eyes canvassed her daughter's face, as if trying to reassemble her. 'Perhaps that's the modern way,' she finally ventured. 'That's what Kay said,' replied Dottie. She described her visit to the doctor. 'But what were you supposed to do with it then?' asked Mrs Renfrew. 'That was the whole trouble,' said Dottie, flushing. And she told how she had sat for nearly six hours in Washington Square with the contraceptive apparatus on her lap. 'I knew then he couldn't care for me at all or he couldn't have put me through that.' 'Men are strange,' said Mrs Renfrew. 'Your father – ' She stopped. 'I sometimes think that they don't want to know too much about that side of a woman's life. It destroys an illusion.' 'That was your generation, Mother. No. The truth is, Dick didn't give me a thought. I have to be unsentimental, like Kay, and face that. I left the whole caboodle under a bench in Washington Square. Imagine the junkman's surprise! What do you suppose he thought, Mother?' Mrs Renfrew could not help smiling too. She understood now what had made Dottie shed tears in the Ritz. 'So you thought,' she said gaily, 'Dr Perry and I were going to make you go back to the same woman doctor. Like seeing the same movie over. Oh, poor Dottie!' Despite themselves, both mother and daughter began to laugh.

Mrs Renfrew wiped her eyes. 'Seriously, Dottie,' she said, 'it's queer that your "Dick" wasn't home all that time. What do you suppose he could have been doing? I rather agree with Kay that he couldn't have sent you to the doctor just to make game of you.' 'He just forgot,' said Dottie. 'He stopped to have a drink in a bar, probably. That's another thing, Mother. He *drinks*.' 'Oh, dear,' said Mrs Renfrew.

He was a thoroughly bad hat, then, but that was the kind, of course, that nice women broke their hearts over. Mrs Renfrew remembered the gay days of the war, when Dottie was still in short dresses with her hair in a big ribbon, and Sam, home on leave from camp, had christened a member of their set 'the matrimonial submarine'. How attractive he had been, too, to dance with, though all the men disliked him and in the end he had drunk himself into the sanatorium after torpedoing three happy marriages! She nodded. 'You're right, Dottie,' she said firmly. 'If he were serious about you, he would have realized the shock he'd given your feelings and tracked you down through Kay. Or there may be *some* good in him. He may have decided to leave you alone, knowing that he'd ruin your life if you fell in love with him. Had he been drinking when he seduced you?' 'He didn't seduce me, Mother. That's *vieux jeu*. And I *am* in love with him. Do you think if he knew about *that* . . .? He's very proud, Mother. "I'm not in your class," he said. That's one of the first things he told me. If I were to go to him and tell him . . .?'

'I don't know, Dottie,' Mrs Renfrew sighed. It was not clear to her whether she herself was trying to dissuade Dottie from seeking this Dick out or the opposite. More than anything else, she wanted to guide Dottie to discover her own real feelings. There was one simple test. 'Dear,' she said. 'I think we'd better postpone your wedding for a few weeks. That will give you time to know what your real feelings are. Meanwhile, you rest, and I'll get you a fresh compress.' She got up and smoothed down the counterpane, feeling decidedly more cheerful as she began to see that it really would be practicable, and probably the best solution, to put off the wedding for the present. 'Luckily, Dottie,' she murmured, 'we didn't order the invitations today. Just think, if I hadn't stopped at the Club for a manicure this morning, I should never have seen that newspaper, and you would never have told me what you did, and the invitations would be ordered. "For want of a nail. . . ."' 'But what about the dresses?' said Dottie. 'The dresses will still be good a month from now,' replied Mrs Renfrew. 'We'll lay the blame on Dr Perry.' By this time, her active and sanguine mind had raced ahead another step: she was checking off the eventualities in case the wedding should be called off altogether in the end. She and Sam would have to compensate the bridesmaids for their dresses, but that would not amount to much; because of Polly Andrews, they had chosen an inexpensive model. And a few pieces of silver had already been marked, but fortunately in the old way, with the bride's initials, so that they would come in handy some time. No wedding presents would have to be returned, barring Lakey's Madonna, which could wait till Lakey came back. As for the wedding gown, it could either be kept or passed on to one of the younger cousins. At Mrs Renfrew's age, she had learned to cope with disappointments; young people, she had noticed, found it a great deal harder to adjust to a change of plans.

When she came back with a fresh compress, she at first thought Dottie had fallen asleep, for her eyes were closed and she was breathing regularly. Mrs Renfrew raised the window a crack and laid the cold towels gently on Dottie's forehead, noticing with tenderness the strong widow's peak. Then she tiptoed out of the room, thanking her stars that she had found the right remedy; as soon as the pressure of the oncoming wedding had been removed, Dottie had been able to relax. But just as she was closing the door, carefully, Dottie spoke.

'I don't want the wedding postponed. Brook would never understand.' 'Nonsense, Dottie. We'll just say that Dr Perry – ' 'No,' said Dottie. 'No, Mother. I've made up my mind.' Mrs Renfrew came into the room again and shut the door behind her; she had heard old Margaret, who was an eavesdropper, prowling about. 'Darling,' she said, 'you thought you'd made up your mind before. You were very sure you loved Brook and could make him happy.' 'I'm sure again,' said Dottie. Mrs Renfrew advanced into the room with her precise, light step; she had limped as a young girl and overcome it with exercises and golf. 'Dottie,' she said firmly, 'it's cruel and wicked to marry a man you only half love. Especially an older man. It's a kind of cheating. I've seen it happen among my own friends. You promise the man something that you can't give. As long as that other man remains in the back of your mind. Like a hidden card up your sleeve.' She had grown quite agitated, and her golden head, with its silver glister, had begun to tremble a little, as if in memory of that old invalidism which they had called palsy in those days.

To her immense distress, they began to quarrel, in low-pitched, well-bred voices; Mrs Renfrew would not have thought this could happen between her and Dottie. She was telling Dottie that she must see Dick again, if only to make sure. 'If you order me to, I'll do it, Mother. But afterwards I'll kill myself. I'll throw myself off the train.' 'Please don't be melodramatic, Dottie.' 'It's you who're being melodramatic, Mother. Just allow me to marry Brook in peace.' Distractedly, Mrs Renfrew was aware of the oddity of this situation, in which the roles were reversed, and the daughter was hurrying herself into a 'suitable' marriage while the mother was pleading with her to seek out an unsuitable rake. This was, apparently, that 'gulf between the generations' that had been discussed at her class reunion last June; one of the faculty members of Mrs Renfrew's class had stated it as a generalization that this new crop of girls was far less idealistic, less disinterested, as a body of educated women, than their mothers had been. Mrs Renfrew had not believed it, noting to herself that Dottie and her friends were all going out to work, mostly at volunteer jobs, and were not trammelled by any of the fears and social constraints that had beset her own generation. And yet here was Dottie virtually demonstrating what that faculty member had said. Was it a sign of the times? Had the depression done it? Were girls nowadays afraid of taking a risk? She suspected that Dottie, with her poor health and Boston heritage, was terrified of becoming an old maid. That (not the other) was the 'fate worse than death' for Dottie's classmates. Yet marriage, as she had always impressed on Dottie, was a serious thing, a sacrament. Dottie did not love Brook; the certainty of this was beyond any doubt to Mrs Renfrew's eyes, and she felt as though she would be condoning a very grave sin if, knowing what she knew, she let her go ahead unreflecting. Did Dottie even respect Brook? If so, she ought to hesitate.

'You're unwilling to make a sacrifice,' Mrs Renfrew said sorrowfully, her head commencing to tremble again. 'Not even to wait a month to keep from hurting a man who isn't in his first youth. You're unwilling to sacrifice your pride to see "Dick" again and live with him, if you love him, and try to reform him. Women in my day, women of all sorts, were willing to make sacrifices for love, or for some ideal, like the vote or Lucy Stonerism. They got themselves put out of hotels for registering as "Miss" and "Mr" when they were legally married. Look at your teachers, look what they gave up. Or at women doctors and social workers.' 'That was your day, Mother,' Dottie said patiently. 'Sacrifices aren't necessary any more. Nobody has to choose between getting married and being a teacher. If they ever did. It was the homeliest members of your class who became teachers – admit it. And everybody knows, Mother, that you can't reform a man; he'll just drag you down too. I've thought about this a lot, out West. Sacrifice is a dated idea. A superstition, really, Mother, like burning widows in India. What society is aiming at now is the full development of the individual.'

'Oh, I agree; I quite agree,' said Mrs Renfrew. 'And yet it's such a little thing I'm asking of you, Dottie. Bear with your Aged P.' She put in this family joke in a nervous conciliatory manner. 'It isn't necessary, Mother. I truly do know my mind. Because I slept with Dick doesn't mean I should change my whole life. He feels the same way himself. You can fit things into their compartments. He initiated me, and I'll always be grateful to him for making it so wonderful. But if I saw him again, it might not be so wonderful. I'd get involved. . . . It's better to keep it as a memory. Besides, he doesn't want my love. That's what I was thinking about when you were in the bathroom. I can't *throw* myself at him.' 'It often works,' said Mrs Renfrew, smiling. 'Men – unhappy, lonely men, particularly – ' she continued gravely, 'respond to a faithful heart. An unswerving faith, Dottie, moves mountains; you should have learned that from your religion. "Whither thou goest I will go. . . ."' Dottie shook her dark head. '*You* try sitting in the Common, Mother, with a douche bag and whatnot on your lap. And anyway you don't really want me to live with him either. You're only talking, because you want me to "pay the price". Postpone my wedding and upset everybody's plans, just to allow a "decent interval" to elapse. Of mourning for Dick. Isn't it true?' A faint teasing smile came into her brown eyes as she interrogated her mother.

Mrs Renfrew considered the accusation. It was true, she had to confess, that *she* did not want Dottie to 'live with' Dick. But she would want *Dottie* to want to do it. Yet how to express this? Perhaps Dottie was right, and she was only being conventional in wishing to postpone the marriage. It might be the conventional Bostonian in her that felt that Dottie ought to make *some* gesture towards the past. Yet was this enough to account for the deep sad sense of disappointment she had – disappointment in Dottie? It seemed to her, looking at it as charitably as she could, that Dottie was being tempted by Brook's wealth and by the glorious outdoor life he had to offer her, of which she had painted such a vivid unforgettable picture – the desert and the silver mines and the pack trips into the mountains. 'You were "just talking" yourself, Dottie,' she chided, 'when you said you loved Dick. I was only going by what you told me. I don't believe you do love him. But I think you like to say so. Because if you didn't you would be too shamed and degraded.' 'Please, Mother!' said Dottie haughtily.

Mrs Renfrew turned away. 'Try to get some rest,' she said. 'I'm going to lie down myself.' There were tears in her bright-blue eyes as she lay on her chaise-longue, which faced the window, hung with pretty Swiss-embroidered curtains, overlooking Chestnut Street.

She had certainly not married Sam Renfrew for money or for what they called 'security' nowadays, and yet she felt as if she had and as if some dreadful pattern were being repeated in Dottie. Had she and Sam given Dottie false values, despite all their efforts to the contrary? She and Sam had married for love, and there had never been anyone before him, and yet she felt as if, long ago, she had had a lover whom she had given up for this house and the State Street Trust and the golf and the Chilton Club, and it was all being visited on Dottie or on that poor man out in Arizona. The sins of the fathers. This was all perfect *stuff*, she knew, and Dottie, she supposed, might learn to love Brook, especially since her senses seemed to have been awakened; that, at least, was the positive side of all this sad affair – or could be, if Brook were careful. The Arizona climate, too, was 'just what the doctor ordered' for Dottie. A few tears, nevertheless, rolled out of one eye, and she stanched them with the handkerchief of fine Irish linen and lace old Margaret had given her for Christmas. An idea of a lost lover, of someone renounced, tapped at her memory like a woodpecker. Whom could she be thinking of, she asked herself demurely. The matrimonial submarine?

Chapter 8

Libby MacAusland had a spiffy apartment in the Village. Her family in Pittsfield was helping her pay the rent. The job she had been promised by a publisher, just before graduation, had not exactly materialized. The man she had interviewed, who was one of the partners in the firm, had shown her around the offices, given her some books they published, and introduced her to an editor, who was smoking a pipe in his sanctum. Mr LeRoy, a portly young man with a dark moustache and bushy eyebrows, had been very forth-coming as long as the partner was there, but afterwards, instead of settling her at a desk right away (Libby had spied an empty cubby-hole in the editorial department), he had told her to come back in a week or so. Then he said he was going to give her manuscripts to read at home to try her out. They paid $5 apiece for reading a manuscript and writing a summary and an opinion, and she ought to be able, he thought, to do three a week, which was the same as having a half-time job – better. 'If we started you in the office,' he said, 'we could only give you $25 full time. And you'd have your carfare and your lunches to pay.' When he asked her if she needed the work, Libby had let on that she did; she thought if he thought she was pretty desperate he would find her more manuscripts to read.

Anyway, that ought not to have been his business. Her back-ground was perfect for a berth in publishing: fluent reading know-ledge of French and Italian; copy editing, proofreading, and dummying as editor in chief of the Vassar literary magazine; short-story and verse-writing courses; good command of typing – all the tools of the trade. But mindful of the competition, Libby took special pains with her reports for Mr LeRoy, typing them triple-spaced on a kind of sky-blue typing paper that was still manufactured in one of the mills in Pittsfield and stapling them in stiff blue covers. The 'presentation' of her themes had been out-standing at Vassar. She always added a title page with a colophon – her device, the same she used for her bookplate – to her weekly papers and put them between covers; her handwriting was distinctive, with Greek e's and embellished capitals. Miss Kitchel had noticed her immediately in English 105 as 'the artistic young lady with the fine Italian hand'. Her 'effusions', as Miss Kitchel, who was a hearty soul, used to call them, had been printed in the freshman *Sampler*, and she had been invited, while still a freshman, to serve on the board of the literary magazine. Libby's forte was descriptive writing. 'This hopeful beauty did create' (Carew) was the motto beneath her picture in the yearbook.

Her mother's sister had a villa in Fiesole, and Libby had spent a year there as a child, going to the sweetest dame school in Florence, and countless summers afterwards – to be exact, two; Libby was prone to exaggerate. She spoke a breathless Italian, with a nifty Tuscan accent, and had been dying to take her junior year abroad, at the University of Bologna, for she had read a fascinating novel called *The Lady of Laws*, about a learned lady in Renaissance times who had been a doctor of law at Bologna and got raped and carried off by one of the Malatestas (Libby had been an alternate in a debate on censorship with Wesleyan freshman year). But she had misdoubted that being a year away from college might cost her the 'crown' she coveted; she counted on being elected President of Students.

Libby played basketball (centre) and had a big following among the dimmer bulbs of the class; she was president of the Circolo Italiano and had been president of the class sophomore year. She was also active in the Community Church. But running for President of Students, she had been mowed down, as it turned out, by the big guns of the North Tower group, who were more the hockey-playing, ground-gripper, rah-rah Vassar sort and carried off all the class offices senior year. They had asked her to group with them at the end of freshman year, but she had thought Lakey's crowd was snazzier. Came the dawn when Lakey and the others would not even electioneer for her.

It seemed to be Libby's fate (so far) to start out strong with people and then have them lose interest for no reason she could see – 'They flee from me that some time did me seek.' That had happened with the group. Libby adored *Of Human Bondage* and Katherine Mansfield and Edna Millay and Elinor Wylie and quite a lot of Virginia Woolf, but she could never get anybody to talk with her about books any more, because Lakey said her taste was sentimental. The paradox was that she was the most popular member of the group *outside* and the least popular *inside*. For instance, she had put Helena, who was one to hide her light under a bushel, on the board of the literary magazine; then Helena had blandly turned around and sided with a minority that wanted to print 'experimental literature'. She and the arch-enemy, Norine Schmittlapp, had collaborated on an 'Open Letter to the Editor', claiming that the college magazine no longer represented Vassar writing but had become the inheritance of a 'pallid' literary clique. Libby, counselled by the faculty, had let herself run with the current and printed an 'experimental number'; the tide turned *her* way when one of the poems in it proved to be a hoax, written by a cute freshman as a spoof on modern poetry. But in the very next issue a story she had battled for was discovered to be plagiarized, word for word, from a story in *Harper's*. It was hushed up, for the sake of the girl's future, after the Dean had had a talk with *Harper's* about it, but someone (probably Kay) whom Libby had told in strictest confidence betrayed her, and soon the rebel clique was busy spreading the news. It was one thing, they said, to be generously taken in by a hoax and another to print as original writing an unadventurous theft from a stale, second-rate magazine. Libby literally could not understand this last part; one of her highest ambitions was to have a story or a poem published by *Harper's*. And lo and behold, hold your hats, girls, it had happened to her finally a year ago this last winter.

She had been in New York nearly two years now, living first with two other girls from Pittsfield in Tudor City and now alone, in this spiffy apartment she had found. She was avid for success, and her parents were willing; Brother was settled, at long last, in a job in the mill, and Sister had married a Harkness. So Libby was free to try her pinions.

Mr LeRoy had given her stacks of manuscripts to start out with. She had had to buy a lady's briefcase at Mark Cross to lug them all back and forth – black calf, very snazzy. 'You're *made*, Libby!' her room-mates in Tudor City used to gasp when they saw her stagger in with her load. And to pile Pelion on Ossa, she had got herself some book-review assignments from the *Saturday Review of Literature* and the *Herald Tribune Books* – no less. Her room-mates were green with envy because they were only going to Katherine Gibbs Secretarial School themselves. Her family was jubilant; that was why they had let her have the apartment. Libby was obviously dedicated to the idea of a literary career, as Brother reported to headquarters when he came home from a visit to New York. Father had had her first cheque photostatted and framed for her, and it hung above her desk, with a little branch of laurel from the parental garden, to show that she was crowned with bays.

The idea of the book reviews was completely Mr LeRoy's. 'You might try for some reviewing,' he said to her one day when she wanted to know how she could get ahead faster. So with that flea in her ear, she had gone to Miss Amy Loveman and Mrs Van Doren (Irita, the wife of Carl), and they had both let her have a chance. She still had the New York *Times* to crack.

Most of the manuscripts Mr LeRoy gave her were novels; biographies (which Libby doted on) he kept for specialists, and he had not yet tried her on a French or an Italian book – she was too much of a tyro, she supposed. Libby wrote exhaustive plot summaries, for she did not want the whole burden of decision to rest on her, and she laboured far into the night on her critical exegeses, making constructive suggestions. She was eager to get into editing, which was the more glamorous part of publishing – not just copy editing, but creative rewriting. She tried to read creatively too, making believe she was a housewife in Darien or a homely secretary when she sat in the seat of judgement. It stood to reason, she argued, that publishers were in business to reach the public and not to please Libby MacAusland. So she tried to look on every novel as a potential best seller. That was what the editor of the *Herald Tribune Books* thought too; she had told Libby, in the sweetest Southern accent: 'We believe here, Miss MacAuslan', that there's something good in evvra book that should be brought to the attention of evvra reader.'

Yet Mr LeRoy had begun to eye her reflectively when she brought in her reports. It could not be her clothes; she made it a point to dress the way she imagined a publisher's reader should: neat but not gaudy, in a plain skirt and shirtwaist, with sometimes a pleated front or an old cameo brooch of Great-Grandmother Ireton's at the throat – general effect a smitch Victorian, like an 'operative' in a Howells novel (Libby loved old words). If she ever got a regular job in an office, she was going to pin paper cuffs over her real ones. On cold days she wore a sweater and skirt with some gold beads or her pearls, which were not Oriental, only cultured, but as far as Mr LeRoy could tell they might have come from the five-and-ten. It must be something about her reports, she was afraid. He dropped a hint once that she need not go to quite such length in describing a novel that she was turning thumbs down on. But she said she was only too happy to do the job right; the labourer must be worthy of his hire.

She often found him reading a magazine: the *New Masses*, she noticed, or another once called *Anvil* or still another with the peculiar name of *Partisan Review*, which she had tried to read in the Washington Square Bookshop. That was what gave her the idea of slipping words like 'labourer' into her conversation, to remind him that she too was one of the downtrodden. Rumour had it that there were quite a few pinks in the publishing biz. Be that as it might, Mr LeRoy was no Lord Chesterfield, sitting there in his shirt sleeves, phlegmatic and rather porky, tipping back in his desk chair, rubbing his moustache, and Libby sometimes got the feeling that he was not used to feminine women. She had a way of tilting her head to one side and thrusting her chin forward eagerly, with lips slightly parted, like one listening to music, that seemed to embarrass him, for whenever she did this he would stop in the middle of a sentence and frown and wring his eyebrows.

'You don't need to read them all through,' he observed to her suddenly one day, balancing her blue folder on two fingers and puffing at his pipe. 'Some publishers' readers just smell 'em.' Libby shook her gold head in its navy beret emphatically. 'I don't mind, dear sir,' she cried. 'And I'd like to scotch the legend that manuscripts aren't read by publishers. You can swear on the Book these have been. And you can't object if I'm doing it on my own time.'

He got up from behind the desk and began to walk around with his pipe. 'If you're seriously trying to make a living out of this, Miss MacAusland,' he said, 'you must treat it as piece work and rationalize your time like any sweated worker.' 'Don't call me "sweated",' she smiled. 'Odo-Ro-No.' He did not smile back.

'Seriously,' she went on, 'I love doing it. I'm one of those unhappy few mortals that can't put down a novel till I know how it comes out. Words cast a spell on me. Even the worst words in the worst order. I write myself, you know.' 'Write us a novel,' he proposed abruptly. 'You write damned well.' Libby lit herself a cigarette. She said to herself warily that she must not let him deflect her by flattery into a writing career. 'I'm not ready for that yet. Construction is my fatal weakness. But I'm learning. Reading these manuscripts has taught me a lot. When my day comes and I open up the old Remington and type "CHAPTER ONE", I'll profit from their mistakes.' He went back to his desk and knocked out his pipe. 'You do it on your own time, as you say, Miss MacAusland. But the function of the first reader is to save the second reader's time. *And* his own. What you're doing is uneconomic.' 'But I have to make the work interesting to myself,' Libby protested. 'All work ought to be interesting. Even manual labour. Hear, hear!' she added jovially, in the manner she had learned at Vassar. 'Sound of falling bricks,' she muttered, when Mr LeRoy remained silent.

Libby punched out her cigarette. She usually made it a policy to stay fifteen minutes, as if she were paying a call, but it was hard work, often, with Mr LeRoy to stretch the visit that long. Now came the moment she dreaded. Some men in offices stood up to indicate that the interview was over, but Mr LeRoy stayed seated at his desk or else he was pacing around restlessly anyway. He sometimes acted as if he had forgotten what she had come for, which was to get a fresh supply of manuscripts. He would let her put her coat and gloves on without seeming to notice that she was ready to make her adieux and without a single glance at the desk drawer where, she had discovered, the incoming manuscripts were kept. It was a big drawer, like a bin; lowering herself to pun, Libby called it the loony bin, because the suspense of waiting each time for him to open it drove her crazy. Sometimes she had to remind him, but generally she found that if she waited long enough he remembered. Each time, though, she felt her whole career hanging by a thread for what was probably only a minute by the clock but, measured by her heart's beat, eternity. Finally he would fish out a couple of manuscripts and toss them on the desk. 'Here, have a look at these.' Or, peering into the drawer, 'There doesn't seem to be much here this week, Miss MacAusland,' he would say, coughing. When Libby, arching her neck, could see that the drawer was practically full. Some day, she feared – and she used to tell it to herself as a story – the drawer would remain closed. She would put on her coat (simple navy blue with a velvet collar) and go out into the wintry streets with her empty briefcase; after that, she could never see Mr LeRoy again – her pride would not let her.

In fact, Libby usually repaired to Schrafft's for a malted after a session with Mr LeRoy. On this day of evil omen, she tottered out of the office in a shaken condition, with one measly manuscript to show for her trouble. Total blackness; ice and desolation. 'The function of the first reader is to save the second reader's time.' Fanning her brow with the tea menu, she called on herself to face the truth: he had been letting her down gradually for months, preparing her for the final blow, hint by hint, like an author preparing the reader! How much kinder if he had simply said to her, 'I'm afraid you haven't worked out, Miss MacAusland. Sorry.' Nothing would have been simpler than that. She would have understood. After all, publishers could not farm out manuscripts as a charity. 'Thank you, Mr LeRoy, for your frankness,' she would have told him. 'Do come and have tea with me some time.'

After a while, sucking at her malted, Libby began to realize what a solipsist she was: all that was in her own mind. The trouble was, she had been looking at their interviews from *her* point of view, which was one of secret, mad apprehension concentrated on that drawer. But from Mr LeRoy's point of view, it was all in the day's work. She was one of many readers he had to distribute manuscripts among. And he could not *make* manuscripts out of thin air, if authors did not send them in. Moreover, he had to be fair; he could not favour her over older readers who probably depended on it for their livelihood. You could see he was fair from his eyebrows, which always looked so perplexed. When he talked to her today like a Dutch uncle, it was because he was trying to teach her the trade, curb her 'instinct of craftsmanship', which was too creative for the marts of commerce. He probably had not the faintest inkling of the tumults of hope and fear he stirred up in her girlish bosom. He took it for granted she was on the payroll. When he said there wasn't much this week, the emphasis in his mind was on 'this week'. And what she had said to herself just now was perfectly true: nothing would have been easier for him than just to tell her that she had been found wanting – *if* he thought so. He must have to tell some poor soul that every day. Each time he rejected a manuscript. Why had she never considered that?

It struck her that it would be a fascinating exercise in narrative point of view to tell the story of their relation first from her standpoint and then from Mr LeRoy's. What would stand out, of course, would be the complete contrast. It would show how each of us is locked in his own private world. 'The Fatal Drawer', you could call it. Or 'The Secret Drawer', which would give the idea of secret, closed lives and would be an evocation of secret drawers in old desks, like Mother's desk at home. Tapping on her glass, Libby summoned the Irish waitress and borrowed a pencil; she began scribbling notes on the back of the menu. She had an inspiration that she wanted to catch on the wing. What if the heroine (never mind her name) had been enthralled, all through her childhood, by a secret drawer in her mother's (grandmother's?) desk, which she had never succeeded in opening? That would give a sort of poetic depth to the story and help explain the heroine's psychology: the granite Victorian house in the shadow of the mills, the tall hedges, the monkey tree in the garden, the summerhouse or pergola where the lonely child had tea, and the Queen Anne secretary in the dark hall at the top of the stairs, beyond the curving banisters. . . . Later, when the heroine met the publisher, you could have her imagine all sorts of grisly things, like making her suspect that his precious drawer was really bulging with manuscripts and that a not-so-bad-looking girl she had seen waiting outside with a cardboard briefcase was a rival for Mr LeRoy's favours. When really it would turn out that the girl was an author whose manuscript was going to be given to Libby to pass on. That would be clear when you got the story from Mr LeRoy's angle.

Libby was chock-full of ideas for stories, which she generally wrote down in her diary. Every writer ought to keep a diary, Mrs M. A. P. Smith said. Libby had been keeping hers faithfully for the last three years, noting her impressions and new words and her dreams. And titles for stories and poems. '"The Drawer"'! she exclaimed now. That was it, of course – the first rule for good writing was to strike out adjectives. Libby signalled for the hostess. 'You don't mind if I take this?' she queried, showing her the menu and pointing to the briefcase. The hostess of course was delighted: all the world loves a writer, Libby had found. The old French waiters at the Lafayette Café had got so they gave her a regular table when she dropped in, *toute seule*, on Sunday afternoons, to read or take notes at the marble-topped table and watch the odd characters playing checkers or reading the newspapers, which were rolled up on wooden poles the way they were in France.

Libby was not all work and no play; she was managing to have a splendiferous time for herself without overspending her allowance. During the winter, she would go up to ski in the Berkshires on those week-end cut-rate excursions the New York Central ran; the trains were full of skiers, and she had made a lot of new friends that way. Most of them were flabbergasted when they heard she had broken into print. Last winter she had discovered a beauteous young man who taught English at one of the private schools and who knew, it turned out in the spring, a nifty picnic spot that could be reached for five cents on the subway: Pelham Bay Park; you took the Lexington Avenue Express to the end of the line and then got out and walked. Libby would pack a lunch of cucumber sandwiches, hard-boiled eggs, and big fat strawberries, and they would throw in a leather volume of poetry to read aloud after they had eaten and were lying on a steamer blanket in a sheltered spot overlooking the water. Libby was crazy about the Cavalier Poets, and he doted on the Elizabethans, especially Sidney and Drayton ('Since there's no help, come let us kiss and part. – Nay I have done, you get no more of me . . .'). He told Libby she looked just the way he imagined Penelope Rich (Penelope Devereux that *was*, the sister of the Earl of Essex), the 'Stella' of Sidney's 'Astrophel and Stella'. 'Stella' had blonde hair and dark eyes, from which came killing darts, like Libby's. The combination of brown eyes and gold hair was the Elizabethan *ne plus ultra* of womanly beauty. This spring, Libby could hardly wait for the first pussy willows for those picnics to start again. He was full of the most intriguing comparisons, which sometimes introduced her to complete new realms of reading. For instance, when he came last spring to pick her up one Saturday morning at the Tudor City apartment for their picnic, wearing heavy shoes and carrying a student's bookbag, she was in the kitchen buttering bread for their sandwiches. Whereupon he started reciting:

> 'Werther had a love for Charlotte
> Such as words could never utter.
> Would you know how first he met her?
> She was cutting bread and butter.'

Her room-mates nearly popped, they were so impressed, having only gone to Smith and Holyoke. That was a parody by Thackeray of Goethe's *Sorrows of Werther*, which Libby had promptly devoured in the library. She often demanded of herself, placing her index finger on her forehead dramatically to indicate deep thought, whether this delirious young man could be in love with her, though he didn't have a bean, except his teacher's salary. This Christmas he had taken her skating in Central Park twice, which was the only time he had put his arm around her, to hold her up on the ice, but unfortunately he had had a cold most of the winter and just taught his classes and afterwards had a hot lemonade and went to bed.

Then she had other heavy beaux – a young actor she had met at Kay's who took her to the theatre in cheap seats they got at Gray's cut-rate ticket place in the bowels of the earth underneath the New York *Times* building; they always stopped outside to read the illuminated ribbon of news (the snappy comparison was Libby's) that ran around the *Times* building. And a young man from the Yale Music School who took her to Harlem to hear jazz. And there was this Jewish boy she had met on the ski train, with a lisp and curly eyelashes (from a very nice family who had changed their name legally), who took her dancing at the Plaza; he was studying politics and had been a poll watcher for the Democratic party at the Congressional elections last fall. She knew some young lawyers downtown, former flames of Sister's, who sometimes took her to the opera or a concert in Carnegie Hall. Or to the Little Carnegie Playhouse, where they showed foreign movies and you could get free demi-tasses and play ping-pong in the lounge. Libby was a whiz at ping-pong, as you might guess from her height and her long arms; Brother had taught her a wicked serve. On Sundays she sometimes went to church, with a Buchmanite boy she knew, to hear Sam Shoemaker, who was rector at Calvary; at college, she had been steamed up about the Oxford Group.

Right next to her apartment, practically, was the Fifth Avenue Cinema, where you could see foreign movies too and have a demitasse on the house; she went there mostly with other girls – Kay, when Harald was working, which he was again, Polly Andrews, Priss, when Sloan was at the hospital (so sad, she had lost her baby in the sixth month of pregnancy), and some of the old North Tower gang, whom she had rediscovered on the ski train. On her list too for manless evenings were two girls she had met in her career of crime as a book reviewer – the editorial secretary of the *Saturday Review of Literature*, Libby would have you know, and the editor's assistant on the *Herald Tribune Books*. One of them had gone to Smith, Class of '30, and the other had gone to Wellesley, ditto, and they both lived alone in the Village and had taken a big shine to Libby. The girl from the *Tribune* lived on Christopher Street, and she and Libby often forgathered for cocktails at Longchamps on Twelfth Street and then they might go on to Alice MacCollister's on Eighth Street or to the Jumble Shop, where there were lots of artists and writers that this girl pointed out and Filipino waiters. Libby usually tried to stand treat to cocktails. 'I asked *you*,' she would gaily insist. She had both girls to a mulled-wine party she gave in January, to which she also invited their bosses, who unfortunately couldn't come. Kay said you should not invite the boss and her secretary to the same occasion; that cheapened your invitation. She also thought that Libby should have invited Mr LeRoy, but Libby did not have the nerve. 'He pictures me in a garret,' said Libby. 'I don't want to destroy his illusions. And besides, how do I know whether he's married?' 'A flimsy excuse, MacAusland,' replied Kay.

Libby was too much of a lady (she preferred the old word, *gentlewoman*) to presume on a business acquaintance. Why, when she was making friends with the *Trib* and the *Saturday Review* girls, she would just poke her head in their door and wave till she was sure of her welcome. Now, of course, she would sally right in for a chat and a peek at the new books, so that she would know, when it was her turn, what to ask the editor for; it paid to ask for a specific book. Some reviewers followed the *Publishers' Weekly* religiously. There was a whole science to getting books for review; Libby honestly thought she could write an article on the subject. First, you had to know that the editors had 'days', like hostesses, when they were at home to reviewers. Tuesday was the 'day' at the *Tribune* and Wednesday at the *Saturday Review*. The *Times* was

Tuesday too, though, so far, Libby had just sat there, ignored, in the waiting-room, till the office boy came and said there was nothing this week. The book-review editors were like kings (or queens), she always fancied, holding levees, surrounded by their courtiers, while petitioners waited eagerly in the anteroom and footmen (that is, office boys) trotted back and forth. And, like kings, they had the power of life and death in their hands. She had got to know the other reviewers or 'clients', as the Romans would have called them, quite well by sight – middle-aged bohemian women with glasses or too much rouge and dangly earrings and worn briefcases or satchels; pimply young men in suits that looked as if they were made of paper. And their shoes! Half-soled and with broken laces tied in frayed knots; it broke Libby's heart to study their shoes and the red, raw ankles emerging from cheap imitation-lisle socks. It reminded her of going to the eye doctor (she had to wear reading glasses), where you waited for hours too, and seeing all the poor people with cataracts patiently camping there. Among the book reviewers, there was a great deal of jealousy and spite; the young men with acne and eroded teeth always looked her up and down contemptuously and then positively hissed when she got ushered in ahead of them. Yet a lot of these would-be reviewers were dishonest; instead of reviewing the book, *their* object was to walk off with an armful and sell them to some little second-hand man without even looking at them. Which was unfair to the honest reviewer and even more so to the author and the publisher; any book that got published deserved the courtesy of a review. These 'raiders', which was Libby's name for them, were supposed to be much more prevalent at magazines like the *New Republic* and the *Nation*, where no attempt was made to 'notice' every book that came out. At the *Nation* and the *New Republic* they said too that you had to run a gauntlet of Communists before getting in to see the book editor – all sorts of strange characters, tattooed sailors right off the docks and longshoremen and tramps and bearded cranks from the Village cafeterias, none of them having had a bath for weeks. This was the effect of 'proletarian literature', which was all the rage right now. Why, even up at Vassar, they were teaching it in courses; Miss Peebles gave it after 'Multiplicity' in Contemporary Prose Fiction. Kay said that Libby ought to try the *Nation* and the *New Republic*, for they had a high standing among thinking people like her doctor father, but Libby said, '*Mon ange*, it's the *sitting* that interests me; I don't want to get fleas!'

Book reviewing, moreover, was only a means to an end: it got your name known in publishing circles, where they read every review, no matter how short. And it was there that Libby was going to make her way, come hell or high water, and despite her bouts of discouragement, when it seemed to her that she could not face another 'Blue Monday' watching Mr LeRoy scratch his moustache as he looked through her reports. Monday was her established 'day' with Mr LeRoy, a day she had fixed herself and never varied from, unless it was a holiday; men were creatures of habit.

After that grim session when he had given her such a scare, Libby decided that she must have another string to her bow. 'You write damned well. . . .' This put the bee in her bonnet of talking to him about doing translations; the idea was really Kay's originally. Kay said Harald said that Libby's problem was to become a specialist in something. Otherwise, she was just competing with all the English majors who graduated every June and who had all been class poet or editor of their literary magazine. Libby should use her foreign languages – particularly her Italian, having lived there – to carve a field for herself. She should offer to do a sample chapter free, then, if they liked it, translate the book, setting aside an hour a day for the purpose. The literary exercise would be good for her style, and meanwhile she would be becoming an expert – a kind of technician. Other publishers would send her Italian books to read and editors would come to her to review Italian authors; she would meet scholars and professors and become an authority. In a technological society, Harald said, it was all a question of having the right tool.

Libby did not exactly feature herself as a translator; editing was much more exciting, because you worked with people. Besides, Harald's project, like most of his ideas, was too long-term to stimulate her imagination. At the same time, she felt that she could not allow her relation with Mr LeRoy to stand still. It dawned on her that this might be a way of moving into the foreign-book line. They paid more ($7.50) for reading foreign books, she had discovered. So the very next time she saw Mr LeRoy, she did not even wait for him to riffle through the manuscript bin; she took the bull by the horns and said she wanted him to let her have a chance at reporting on a French or an Italian novel; she was going to try her hand at translating. 'I'll do the report and then if we want to publish the book, I'll do you a sample chapter.'

Mr LeRoy, she thought, rather squirmed at that 'we', which she had put in on purpose to sound professional. But by the strangest coincidence, that very day he had had an Italian novel back from his regular Italian specialist, a professor at Columbia, with a report that ended 'Suggest you get another opinion'. It was fate, plainly, that Libby had happened in at that moment, and Mr LeRoy clearly felt that too. 'OK,' he said. 'Take it home with you.' He reflected. 'Your Italian is pretty fluent?' '*Fluentissimo.*' It would not pay her, he warned, to try to set up as a translator if she were not completely at home in the language; speed was of the essence. Libby left the office slightly daunted; something in Mr LeRoy's attitude made her feel he was giving her her last chance.

Back in her apartment, she saw the trap he had laid for her. The conversation in the book was mostly in Sicilian dialect. Libby, who was used to the pure Tuscan, nearly passed away. In fact, she was not even sure it was Sicilian; the characters seemed to be peasants and small landowners, and the village they inhabited could be any-where. She thought of dashing up to Vassar to consult Mr Roselli, but, woe was her, he was on sabbatical leave, and the other mem-bers of the department, who were not her particular friends, would probably broadcast the fact that she had fled back to college for help. A small voice told her to return the book to Mr LeRoy and admit that it was too hard for her, but she could not face the thought; this would give him an excuse to tell her that she was through.

Libby took a stance in the middle of her living-room, one hand clapped to her brow, the other holding the book outstretched in a declamatory manner. 'Lost, lost, all lost,' she exclaimed. 'Farewell, sweet maid.' She then staggered to the couch and reopened the book – 521 pages! It fell from her pale, limp hand, the leaves sadly fluttering. One of the big features of living alone was that you could talk to yourself all you wanted and address imaginary audiences, running the gamut of emotion. She rose from the sofa now, shaking her head, and went to contemplate herself in the mirror, scrutinizing her features as if for the last time. Then, shifting mood, she gave herself a nudge in the ribs and went to feed her lovebirds some lettuce, reminding herself that she still had a week in which to cope. 'Be brave!' she clarioned, popping on her hat, and stamped out to

Alice MacCollister's to dinner, where she saw a girl she knew, eating with a man. Stopping by their table on the way out, Libby instantly confided her problems with this Italian novel, which she showed them, having brought it along, with her pocket dictionary, to work on during dinner. 'We *saw* you!' the girl said. 'Gosh, it must make you feel important to have a job like that!' 'I may not have it long,' Libby prophesied. 'Five hundred and *twenty*-one pages of the thickest Sicilian. And me nurtured on Dante.'

She did not get her report done till late the following Sunday, though she stayed home nearly the whole week-end and did not even do the *Times* crossword puzzle. Her summary of the plot was short. Some features of the action had baffled her, despite some heavy work with the atlas and the dictionaries in the Public Library. She described the book as a 'study of the agrarian problems of modern Italy, seen against the background of a feudal past. Don Alfonso, the protagonist, representative of the old order, is at odds with the mayor of the village, who stands for progress and innovation. The peasants, who are sharply characterized and who speak a rich, racy idiom redolent of the sty and the barnyard, are divided between the point of view of Don Alfonso and that of the mayor, Don Onofrio. Don Onofrio's daughter, Eufemia, is drawn into the political struggle and is stabbed by accident during a tumultuous meeting in the piazza. The peasants treat her as a saint and attempt to venerate her remains. The parish priest intervenes. The *cara-binieri* appear, and order is finally restored, after a "miracle" worked at the tomb of Donna Eufemia. This occurs just as the obsequies of Don Alfonso, the last of his race, are being performed and suggests an intended symbolism. There is much curious folk-lore, well presented, particularly the tapestry or, better, mosaic of pagan belief, Christian superstition, and primitive animism seen darkly glittering in the minds of the peasants, as in some ancient, dim-lit, bat-flittery church with its uneven pavement marked by the worn, sunken tombs of Norman Crusaders and the clerestory upheld by defaced pillars ravaged from Greek temples. The political "slant" of the author is not sufficiently defined. Where does he stand in the struggle? With Don Alfonso or with the mayor? He does not say, but it is important that we, as readers, should know. The place assigned the "miracle" tends to make us believe that he stands with the mayor; *ergo*, with present-day Italy and Il Duce.

The *carabinieri* enter as virtual deliverers. If we attempt to peer into the cauldron of boiling *minestra* which this tale constitutes, we are driven back by the steam of pungent, scalding language. But this reader, at any rate, could not escape the suspicion that the author has written an apologia for the corporate state. For this reason, I would register a negative opinion on the book's chances here.'

Libby had often heard her aunt in Fiesole say that Mussolini was doing the Italians a great deal of good; and she had been thrilled herself as a little girl by the Blackshirt rallies in the Piazza della Signoria. But she had tried to look at the novel from Mr LeRoy's point of view, what with Ethiopia and Haile Selassie and the League, and she felt pleased, on the whole, with her 'effort' when she brought it in to him on Monday, especially with the way she had managed to *suggest* that the book was laid in Sicily without actually naming it, in case she might be wrong.

She sat there lacing her fingers as he glanced through her report. 'Sounds like a damned opera,' he remarked, raising his eyes from the first sentences. Libby just waited. He went on reading and suddenly shot her a quizzing look from under his bushy brows. He put her blue folder down, pulled the silk cord abstractedly, raised one pained eyebrow as if he had *tic douloureux*, and slowly lit his pipe. 'Oh me oh my!' he commented. He was chuckling. 'What book did you read?' he demanded and handed her the first reader's report. '. . . a too-little-known classic of militant Italian liberalism tempered with Chekhovian pity and ironic detachment . . . The author, whose place in Italian letters was made by this one novel, died in 1912. . . .'

Libby was speechless. 'Sound of hollow laughter,' she said finally, venturing a peal of same. 'I can explain,' she went on. 'It's not important,' he said. 'I can see how you were misled. Probably customs and manners haven't changed much in Italy in the last fifty years.' 'The words out of my mouth!' ejaculated Libby, almost bounding out of her chair with relief. 'Time has stood still in the *Mezzogiorno*. That's what I was going to say. I thought the author was trying to emphasize the backwardness. *You* know, that it was part of his thesis. Oh, did you ever hear anything so funny? But I'll have to redo my report. ''In the light of recent discoveries'' – ha, ha. If you'll just give it back to me . . .' She turned her bright face anxiously to him, realizing that she had become horribly nervous, which was the effect his musing silences had on her.

He sighed. 'Miss MacAusland,' he said, 'I'm going to have to give it to you straight. I think you'd better look for some other kind of work. Have you ever thought of trying for a job with a literary agent? Or on one of the women's magazines? You've got a real writing talent, believe me, and plenty of drive. But you're not cut out for straight publishing.' 'But why?' said Libby quite calmly; now that the blow had fallen, she felt an actual relief; she was only curious as to what he would say – not concerned. He puffed on his pipe. 'I don't know that I can explain it to you. I've tried in my own mind to figure out exactly what's wrong. You just don't have the knack or maybe the common sense or the nose or whatever it is for picking out a publishable manuscript. Or let's say you're not hard-boiled enough. You're essentially a sympathizer. That's why I see you with a literary agent. You keep telling me you want to work with authors. Well, that's what agents do, work hand in glove with them, especially on magazine stuff. Encourage them; ride them; tell them what to cut; hold their hand; take them out to lunch.' 'But publishers do that too,' put in Libby sharply. She had often pictured herself, in a snappy hat and suit, taking authors out to lunch on the expense account and discussing their work over coffee. 'Those rumours are greatly exaggerated,' said Mr LeRoy. 'You probably think I lunch every day with famous authors at the Ritz. As a matter of fact, I eat at least two lunches a week alone in the Automat. I'm dieting. Today, I lunched with an agent – a damned smart one, a woman. She makes three times what I do.' Libby's well-arched brows manifested surprise and incredulity. 'That's another thing, Miss MacAusland.' He leaned forward. 'Publishing's a man's business. Book publishing, that is. Name me a woman, outside of Blanche Knopf, who married Alfred, who's come to the top in book publishing. You find them on the fringes, in publicity and advertising. Or you find them copy editing or reading proof. Old maids mostly, with a pencil behind their ear and dyspepsia. We've got a crackerjack here, Miss Chambers, who's been with us twenty years. I think she was Vassar too. Or maybe Bryn Mawr. Vinegary type, with a long thin nose that looks as if it ought to have a drop on the end of it, a buttoned-up sweater,

184

metal-rimmed glasses; a very smart, decent, underpaid, fine woman. Our galley slave; pardon the pun. No. Publishing's a man's business, unless you marry into it. Marry a publisher, Miss MacAusland, and be his hostess. Or make connexions with an agent. Or work your way up in the slicks.'

'What a picture you conjure up,' said Libby thoughtfully, her chin cupped in her hand. 'I wonder ... Would you let me do an interview with you for the *Vassar Alumnae Magazine*?' Mr LeRoy put up his hand. 'I don't think that would be in keeping with the firm's policy,' he said stuffily. 'Oh, but I wouldn't have to name you, if you didn't want. I could just take a few notes now. Or, better, if you were free some day for a cocktail ... ?' But he rudely brushed this aside. 'We're having sales conference this week, Miss MacAusland. And next week, let's see — ' he glanced at his desk calendar – 'next week I have to be out of town.' He cleared his throat. 'You can write what you want of course, but I'd rather not be involved in it.' 'I understand,' said Libby.

She started to get up then, till it dawned on her that she was just tamely accepting her dismissal without having heard one adequate reason. He was only talking in generalities, not telling her frankly where she had failed, so that she could have a chance to correct it. And if she did not think of something fast, she would have no excuse, like the interview, for seeing him again. What did you do in a case like that?

She lit a cigarette. 'Couldn't you try me at something else? Writing blurbs, for instance. I'm sure I could write blurbs.' He cut her short. 'I fully agree that you could write very passable jacket copy. But that's one of the mechanical trades in this business. No honour attaches to it. Everybody pitches in. I do it; all the editors do it; my secretary does it; the office boy does it. It comes down to this, Miss MacAusland; we really have no work that you're uniquely qualified to do. You're one of thousands of English majors who come pouring out of the colleges every June, stage-struck to go into publishing. Their families back them for a while; a year is about the limit. Till the girls finally find somebody to marry them and the boys go into something else.'

'And your opinion,' said Libby, 'is that I'm just one of those. Those anonymous hordes.' 'You're more persevering,' he said, with a glance at his watch and a sigh. 'And you say your family isn't supporting you. Which makes your perseverance more redoubtable. And you do seem to have some eerie relation to literature. I wish you luck.' And with that, he was standing up and vigorously shaking her hand across the desk. Her lighted cigarette dropped on the rug. 'Oh, my cigarette! Oh, horrors!' she cried. 'Where is it?' 'Never mind,' he said. 'We'll find it. Miss Bisbee!' he called, to his secretary, who promptly poked her head in the open doorway. 'There's a lighted cigarette in here somewhere. Find it, will you? And see that Miss MacAusland gets her cheque in the mail.' He grabbed up Libby's coat and held it for her; the secretary was on her hands and knees scrabbling around the floor; Libby's head was reeling with the shock and confusion. She took a step backward and, girls, can you imagine it, she fainted kerplunk into Mr LeRoy's arms!

It must have been the overheated office. Mr LeRoy's secretary told her afterwards that she had turned quite green and the cold sweat had been standing out on her forehead. Just like the summer day her aunt was with her when she passed out cold in the Uffizi in front of 'The Birth of Venus'. But Gus LeRoy (short for Augustus) was convinced it was because she was hungry – she confessed she had not eaten any lunch. He insisted on giving her $10 out of his own pocket and a dollar for a taxi besides. Then the next morning he rang her up and told her to go to see this literary agent who needed an assistant. So that now, lo and behold, she had this snazzy job at $25 a week, reading manuscripts and writing to authors and having lunch with editors. She and Gus LeRoy were the best of friends; he was married after all, she learned from her boss.

Chapter 9

Gus LeRoy met Polly Andrews at a party given by Libby in May the following year. It was 1936, and half the group were married. Of the old crowd, Libby had invited only Priss, who couldn't come, and Polly and Kay; the others, she had rather lost sight of. She was serving a May *bowle*, made of Liebfraumilch and fresh strawberries and sweet woodruff. There was a special store where you could get the woodruff, dried and imported from Germany; it was over on Second Avenue, under the El, a dusty old German firm with apothecary jars and old apothecaries' scales and mortars and pestles in the window. Polly could not possibly miss it, Libby said on the phone; it was right around the corner from where she lived, and she could stop for the woodruff for Libby any day on her way home from work. If she brought it the day before the party, that would be in plenty of time; it only had to steep overnight. Polly worked as a technician at Cornell Medical Centre, giving basal metabolism tests chiefly, which meant that she had to be at the hospital the first thing in the morning, when the patients woke up. But she got off early in the afternoons, which Libby didn't, and took the Second Avenue El home quite often – she lived on Tenth Street, near St Mark's Place, almost catercorner from St Mark's-in-the-Bouwerie, where the rector, Dr Guthrie, had such beautiful liturgy, though Polly never took advantage of it and slept Sunday mornings.

The herbal firm was nine blocks from Polly's place; trust Polly, who could be prickly in her mild, smiling, obstinate way, to let that transpire when she appeared with the woodruff at Libby's apartment. But they were nine short blocks, dear, Libby retorted, and Polly could use the fresh air and exercise. When she heard Polly's description of the shop's display of pharmacopoeia – all the old herbs and simples and materia medica in big stoppered glass jars with the Latin names written in crabbed Gothic lettering – she was sorry she had not gone herself, in a taxi. But to reward Polly for her pains, Libby had taken them both out to dinner at a new place in the Village, and afterwards they had come back to the apartment and got the *bowle* started and everything organized for the party. Polly had a passion for flowers (she did wonders that evening with Libby's mountain dogwood), and she was efficient in the kitchen. Libby had persuaded her to make Mr Andrews's famous chicken-liver *pâté*, a recipe he had brought back from France, and, having splurged on chicken livers at the market, she stood by watching Polly *sauter* them and laboriously push them through a sieve. 'Aren't you doing them too rare?' she suggested. 'Kay says *she* always cooks everything fifteen minutes longer than the recipe calls for.' Libby was scandalized by the amount of fresh print butter Polly mixed in afterwards, *plus* brandy and sherry – no wonder the Andrews family was insolvent. But Polly was sweet to do it and tenacious about having her own way, once she started on something. All the Andrews were like that. Mr Andrews, Polly said, clung to making his own stock and boiling it down for the glaze, but Polly consented to use Campbell's consommé to line the mould, thank heaven; otherwise, they would have been up till dawn. As it was, Libby was completely exhausted by the time Polly left. Just pushing those livers through a sieve had taken nearly an hour. She would not hear of Polly's washing up; a coloured maid was coming the next afternoon to clean and serve at the party.

Fortunately, Polly could take the Eighth Street bus home; it was a long walk from Libby's place, just west of Fifth Avenue, and you had to pass some pretty sinister lofts and warehouses. Polly's apartment, though in a fairly decent block, was not as attractive as Libby's, which had high ceilings and a fireplace and windows almost down to the floor. In fact, it was flattery to call Polly's an apartment. It was really a furnished room and bath, with a studio bed, which Polly had covered with a pretty patchwork quilt from home, and some worn Victorian chairs and a funny old marble-topped table with lion's-claw feet, and a two-burner hot-plate and some shelves covered with bright-blue oil-cloth in one white-curtained-off corner, and an icebox that leaked. At least it was clean; the family were professional people (actually, the wife was Vassar, Class of '18), and Polly had made friends with the other lodgers – two refugees, one a White Russian and the other a

German-Jewish socialist – and always had funny stories to tell about them and their violent discussions. Polly was a sympathetic soul; everybody she met told her their troubles and probably borrowed money from her. Yet, poor girl, her family could not afford to send her a cent. Her Aunt Julia, who lived on Park and Seventy-second, had given her some china and a chafing-dish, but she did not realize how the other half lived; for one thing, she had heart trouble and could not climb Polly's stairs. In her day, St Mark's Place had been a nice neighbourhood, and she did not know that things had changed. Still, Polly's apartment would be perfectly suitable if she did not have this habit of letting herself be imposed on by strangers. The German-Jewish man, for instance, Mr Schneider, was constantly bringing her little presents, coloured marzipan in the shape of fruits (once he brought her a marzipan hot dog, which for some reason delighted Polly), chocolate-covered ginger, a tiny pot with a St Patrick's Day shamrock, and in return Polly was helping him with his English, so that he could get a better job. This meant that almost every evening he was tapping at her door. Libby had met him one night – a dwarf, practically, with frizzy grey hair in a mop and a thick accent but old enough (Libby was glad to see) to be Polly's father, if Mr Andrews had not been almost old enough himself to be her grandfather. You found the most curious visitors at Polly's, most of them ancient as the hills: Ross, her Aunt Julia's maid, who you had to admit was a sketch, sitting there doing her knitting, having brought Polly some lamb chops from her aunt's butcher on Park Avenue; the White Russian, poor devil, who liked to play chess with Polly; the iceman. Well, that was a bit exaggerated, but Polly did have an awfully funny story about the Italian iceman, a veritable troglodyte, coming in one day with the ice on his shoulder this last March and saying 'Tacks' over and over and Polly offering him thumbtacks and him shaking his head and saying 'No, no, lady, *tacks*!'; it turned out, believe it or not, that he was having trouble with his income-tax return, which he whipped out of his back pocket with his horny hand – only Polly would have an iceman who paid income tax. Naturally, she sat down and helped him with the arithmetic and his business deductions and dependants. Yet when one of her friends asked something of her, she might suddenly flush up and say, 'Libby, you can perfectly well do that yourself.'

To look at, she was one of those 'gentle ray of sunshine' girls – very fair, with almost flaxen hair, the colour of pale straw or rough raw silk, big blue eyes, and milk-white skin, bluish, like skim milk; she had a soft, plump chin with a sort of dimple or cleft in it, plump white arms, and a wide, open brow. Some people thought she looked like Ann Harding in the movies, but she was not as tall as Ann Harding. She had taken to wearing her hair in braids around her broad head; she thought it was neater, for the hospital, all coiled around like that. The trouble was, it make her look older. When Priss was having her last miscarriage, in New York Hospital, in semi-private, Polly had stopped in to visit her every day, which was easy for *her* since she worked there; seeing her in her white coat and low-heeled shoes and those matronly braids, the other patient thought that Polly must be at least twenty-six. She had been on the Daisy Chain (that made four in the group – Libby herself, Lakey, Kay, and Polly – which was sort of a record), but Libby had never agreed that Polly was beautiful. She was too placid and colourless, unless she smiled. Kay had cast her as the Virgin in the Christmas pantomime senior year, which she directed, but this was to give her a pickup from having broken her engagement to the boy with the bad heredity. Actually, behind the placid exterior, Polly was rather emotional but very good fun, really a delightful companion, with an original point of view. All the Andrews were original. Polly had majored in Chemistry, thinking that she might be a doctor, but when Mr Andrews lost his money, naturally she had to give that up; luckily, the college Vocational Bureau had got her placed at New York Hospital – Cornell Medical Centre. All the group hoped she would meet some ravishing young doctor or pathologist who would want to marry her, but so far this had not happened or if so, no one knew about it. About herself, Polly was very reserved. It sometimes sounded as if she saw nobody but her aunt and those strange inhabitants of her rooming-house and other girls with jobs, some of them pretty dreary – the type, as Kay said, that had bulbs of paper narcissi growing in their windows in a dish from the five-and-ten. This capacity for making lack-lustre friends, especially of her own sex, was Polly's *faiblesse*. The Chem majors at college were a case in point, worthy souls, no doubt, but the science majors as a group (credit Kay for this observation too) were about the lowest stratum at Vassar. They were the ones, as Kay said, you would not remember when you came back for your tenth reunion: pathetic cases with skin trouble and superfluous hair and thick glasses and overweight or underweight problems and names like Miss Hasenpfeffer. What would happen to them afterwards? Would they all go home and become pillars of their community and send their daughters back to Vassar to perpetuate the type or would they go into teaching or medicine, where you might even hear of them some day? 'Dr Elfrida Katzenbach is with the Rockefeller Institute – Congratulations, Katzy', you would read in the alumnae news and 'Who was she?' you would ask yourself. Astronomy and Zoology were a little different – Pokey had majored in Zoology and, would wonders never cease incidentally, last year she had up and married a poet, a sort of distant cousin who was in Graduate School at Princeton – her family had bought them a house down there, but Pokey still commuted by plane to Ithaca and was still planning to be a vet. Anyway, Astronomy and Zoology were different – not so dry, more descriptive; Botany too. Next to the Physics and Chem majors in dreariness came the language majors; Libby had narrowly escaped that fate. They were all going to be French or Spanish teachers in the high school back home and had names like Miss Peltier and Miss La Gasa. Polly had her followers among them too, who were even invited up to stay in Stockbridge, to talk French with Mr Andrews. Polly was a democrat (all the Andrews voted for Roosevelt, being related to the Delanos), though Lakey used to say that the democracy was all on the surface and that underneath Polly was a feudal snob.

Be that as it might, Libby saw Polly as often as she could and almost always asked her to her parties. The trouble was, Polly, though wonderful company when you were alone with her, did not shine at big gatherings. Her voice was very low, like her father's, who virtually whispered his mild remarks. If you did not explain her family background (a nest of gentlefolk with a few bats in the belfry; Mr Andrews's sisters had all been painted by Sargent), people were inclined to overlook her or ask after she had gone home who that quiet blonde girl was. That was another thing; she always left early unless you gave her something to do, like talking to a bore, to make her feel useful. All you had to do was tell her to go rescue some stick who was standing in a corner, and Polly would engage him in animated conversation and find out all sorts of wondrous things about him that nobody had ever suspected. But if you told her someone was a great catch, she would not make the slightest effort – 'I'm afraid I must make my excuses, Libby' (all the Andrews talked like that).

But the minute you started a game, be it poker or 'Pin the Tail on the Donkey', Polly was in her element, delighted to sort chips or cut out pieces of paper or make blindfolds; she was always the court of authority or the umpire – the person who decided the rules and kept everybody in order. That was the Andrews family again. Having lost their money and had so much trouble, they kept cheerful by doing charades and playing games. Anybody who stayed with them in that rambling old farmhouse, with its big fireplaces and attics and storerooms, was immediately drafted to be 'It' after dinner and hastily told all the rules, and woe to him or her who was not quick to catch on. Some nights they did charades, very complicated ones, in costumes in the barn with kerosene stoves to keep warm. Some nights they played 'Murder', though that made Mr Andrews very nervous, they discovered, for it seemed he had had violent spells in the hospital and trembled if he had to do the carving at the table on one of his darker days. Some nights they played 'Cache-Cache', which was just the French version of good old 'Hide and Seek' with slightly different rules that they had learned in their château in France. Or 'Ghosts', which the family had re-named 'Punkin' because Mr Andrews sometimes burst into quiet tears or laughed strangely when he missed a question and had to say 'I'm one-third of a ghost'; so now instead they said ' one-third of a punkin', after 'pumpkin head'. Then they played 'Geography', which Mr Andrews was a perfect fiend at, having travelled so much and knowing all the Y's and K's like Ypres, which he called 'Wipers' and Yezd and Kyoto and Knossos. And a new version of 'Ghosts' that they called the 'Wily Austrian Diplomat' game ('Are you a wily Austrian diplomat?' 'No, I am not Metternich'). Polly's family, being brainy, liked these guessing games almost best, next to charades, but they played silly ones too, like 'I packed My Grandmother's Trunk'. And on rainy days there were chess and checkers and parcheesi; the family had had to give up Monopoly (some kind friend had sent them a set), again because of Mr Andrews, poor lamb, who was always reminded of his investments. When they had to make a joint decision, like where to send young

Billy to college or what to have for Christmas dinner, they would solemnly do the '*sortes Virgilianae*' in full concourse assembled with Mr Andrews' old *Aeneid*; the idea was that the children became voting members of the family when they were able to construe Latin – think of that! Then the children got up treasure hunts, with homemade pincushions and calendars and a single amaryllis bulb for prizes, to take the place of paper chases, because they could not afford riding horses any more – only a few cows and chickens; one winter they had tried a pig. Polly used to hunt and ride sidesaddle, and she still had her riding-habit and boots and bowler, which she took with her down to Princeton when Pokey remembered to ask her (Pokey had her own stables and hunted week-ends); she had had to let out the coat, because she was a little fatter now than she was at eighteen, but they said she still looked very pretty, with her white skin and pale hair in the full-skirted black riding-costume with a stock. Black was Polly's colour.

Weekdays, she dressed very plainly, in an old sweater and plaid skirt and low-heeled shoes. But for parties, like today, she had one good black crêpe dress, with a low scalloped neckline and a fringed sash, and she had two wide-brimmed black hats, one for winter and one for summer. The summer one, which she was wearing today, was a lacy straw trimmed with black lace. The crêpe of her dress was getting a little rusty (black crêpe did that, alas), but it set off her full white neck, fleshy chin, and bosom; she had done her hair low on her neck, in a big knot, which was much more becoming. Harald Petersen said she looked like a Renoir. But Libby thought a Mary Cassatt. Libby herself was in high-necked brown taffeta (brown was *her* colour) with topaz earrings to bring out the gold lights in her hair and eyes. She thought Polly, who did not have any good jewellery left, might have worn a white rose in her corsage.

Libby had balanced her guests carefully: a little bit of Vassar, a little bit of publishing, Sister and her husband, who were just back from Europe, a little bit of Wall Street, a little bit of the stage, a lady author, a man from the *Herald Tribune*, a woman from the Metropolitan Museum. *E cost via*; she had not asked anybody from the office, because it was not that kind of party. A rather mixed bag, Sister commented, narrowing her amethyst eyes, but Sister had always been critical of Libby's aspirations. 'Noah's Ark, eh?'

chuckled Sister's husband. 'Bring on your menagerie, Lib!' He never failed to tease her about leading 'the literary life'. Libby usually played up to this, but today she had other fish to fry. She wanted Sister and her husband to impress her latest flame. His name was Nils Aslund; she had met him this winter on the ski train. He was the ski jumper at Altman's and a *genuine Norwegian baron*! Her brother-in-law, who was getting too fat, nearly choked on a gob of Mr Andrews' *pâté*, when Nils came in, wearing the most beautiful Oxford-grey suit, and bent to kiss Sister's hand – you only did that with married women, Nils had explained to her. He had the most heavenly manners and a marvellous figure and danced divinely. Even Sister had to admit he was pretty snazzy, after talking to him for a while. His English was almost perfect, with just the trace of an accent; he had studied English literature at the University, and imagine, before he knew Libby, he had read her poem in *Harper's* and remembered it. They had the same interests; Libby was almost certain he was going to propose, which was partly why she had decided to have this party. She wanted him to see her in her setting; hence the dogwood, girls. She had never let him come up to the apartment before; you never knew, with Europeans, what they might assume. But at a party, with some of her family present, that was different. Afterwards, he was going to take her to dinner, and that was where, she expected, if all went well, he was going to pop the question. Her brother-in-law must have smelled a rat too. 'Well, Lib,' he said, 'is he gainfully employed?' Libby told him that he was in charge of the ski run at Altman's; he had come to America to study business. 'Seems a funny place to start,' said her brother-in-law, thoughtfully. 'Why not the Street?' He chuckled, 'You certainly can pick 'em. But seriously, Lib, that rates him socially about on a par with a golf pro.' Libby bit her lip. She had been afraid of this reaction from her family. But she mastered her vexation and disappointment; if she accepted Nils, she decided, she could make it a condition that he find some other work. Perhaps they could open a ski lodge in the Berkshires; another Vassar girl and her husband had done that. And still another couple had a ranch out West. It was just a question of waiting till his father died, when he would go home and run the ancestral estate. . . .

With all this on her mind, it was no wonder that Libby, at the height of her party, forgot to keep an eye on Polly and see that she was circulating. When things calmed down a bit, what was her amazement to discover her deep in conversation with Gus LeRoy, who had said, when he arrived, that he could only stay a minute. Libby never did find out who had introduced them. They were standing by the window, looking at Libby's lovebirds. Polly was feeding them bits of strawberry from her glass (the poor birds would be tight as ticks on Liebfraumilch), and Gus LeRoy was talking to her a mile a minute. Libby nudged Kay. Polly's blue-white breasts were rather in evidence, which was probably the source of the attraction, and her strawy hair, which had a tendency to be untidy, it was so fine, was slipping a little from its pins in the back, at the nape of her neck.

Libby started to tell Kay Gus LeRoy's history. Her baron was hovering nearby, and she signalled to him to join them. 'We're prophesying a romance,' she explained. Gus came from Fall River where his family had a printing business. He and his wife were separated, and there was one child, about two and a half years old, Augustus LeRoy IV. The wife taught at a progressive school and was a Communist Party member; she was having an affair with somebody in her cell – that was why Gus had left her. Up to now, he had been pretty pink himself but never a Party member, and he had brought several important authors who were Communist sympathizers to the firm, but now the Communists were turning a cold shoulder on him because he wanted to divorce his wife and name this other man, which they called a 'splitting tactic' or something. 'Nils is a Social Democrat,' she added, smiling. 'No, no,' said the baron. 'As a student, I was. Now I am neutral. Not neuter.' He gave his jolly, boyish laugh and looked sidelong at Libby. The reason Libby had heard all this, she continued, flashing a reproachful look at Nils, was that there was an open Communist right in her office – a very homely girl, built like a truck, with nothing to do but drink by herself in the evenings or go to Party meetings. This girl or woman (she must be almost thirty) knew Gus LeRoy's wife. 'Oh well, homely women!' said the baron, making a disdainful face. 'For them it's like the church.' Libby hesitated. The story that popped into her mind was a bit off colour, but it would point a moral to Nils. 'I beg to differ, dear sir. You should hear the horrible thing that happened to this girl the other night. Quite another pair of gloves from the Girls' Friendly Society or the Altar Guild of St

Paul's. I had to take over this girl's work for her till they let her out of the hospital. Four teeth knocked out and a fractured jaw. That was what she got for being a Communist.' 'Picketing!' cried Kay. 'Did you hear that Harald led a picket march the other day?' Libby shook her head. '*Quite* another pair of gloves,' she repeated. 'This girl – I won't tell you her name – being a Communist, is very sympathetic to the workingman. Point two: she drinks. You should smell her breath some mornings. Well, one night – actually it was over a month ago; you remember that cold spell we had late in March? – well, she was coming home in a taxi, having had one too many in a bar somewhere, and she started talking to the taxi driver and commiserating with him about his lot, naturally, and they both mentioned how cold it was. She noticed – anyway, that's how she told the story – that he didn't have an overcoat or extra jacket on. So, as one comrade to another, she asked him up for a drink, to get warm.' Kay caught her breath; Libby nodded. Several other guests drew near to listen; Libby had quite a reputation as a storyteller. 'Maybe she thought being so homely was some protection,' she pursued. 'But he had other ideas. And he assumed she did too. So when he had had the drink, he made overtures. She was very startled and pushed him away. The next thing she knew, she came to on her floor, in a pool of blood, with her teeth all over the place and her jaw broken. He was gone, of course.' 'Did – ?' 'No,' said Libby. 'Apparently not. And nothing was stolen. Her purse was lying right beside her on the floor. My boss wanted her to go to the police. So did the hospital. They had to wire her jaw together, and it will take her *years* to pay for the dental work. But she wouldn't do a thing about it. It's against Communist principles, it seems, to call the police against a "worker". And she said, between her clamped jaws, that it was her own fault.' 'Quite right,' said Nils firmly. 'She was in the wrong.' 'Oh, I don't agree at *all*,' cried Kay. 'If every time someone misunderstood you, they had a right to knock your teeth out . . .? Or if every time you tried to be nice, it was taken the wrong way?' 'Girls should not try to be nice to taxi drivers,' said Nils. 'Old Europe speaking,' retorted Kay. 'I'm always nice to taxi drivers. And nothing has ever happened.' 'Really? Never?' said Sister, looking rather pityingly at Kay. 'Well, actually,' said Kay, 'once one did try to get into the back of the cab with me.' 'Heavens!' said Libby. 'What did you do?' 'I talked him out of it,' said Kay.

The baron laughed heartily; he had evidently caught on to the fact that Kay was an inveterate arguer. 'But, Kay, my child, what had you done to encourage him?' said Libby. 'Absolutely nothing,' said Kay. 'We were talking, and all of a sudden he said I was beautiful and that he liked the perfume I was wearing. And he stopped the cab and got out.' 'He had good taste. Don't you think so, Elizabeth?' Nils spoke of Kay, but he looked deeply into Libby's eyes with his bright burning blue ones till her knees nearly knocked together.

After that, discussion was general. Kay wanted to tell about Harald's picketing. 'His picture was in the tabloids,' she declared. Libby sighed, because of Sister and her husband. But the story, it turned out, was fascinating – not the usual kind of thing at all. It seemed that Harald had been directing a play for a left-wing group downtown. It was one of those profit-sharing things, cooperatives but run really by Communists behind the scenes, as Harald found out in due course. The play was about labour, and the audiences were mostly theatre parties got up by the trade unions. 'So when Harald found out that these Communists in the management were cooking the books, he organized the actors and threw a picket line around the theatre.' The man from the *Herald Tribune* scratched his jaw. 'I remember that,' he said, looking curiously at Harald. 'Your paper played the story down,' said Kay. 'So did the *Times*.' 'Because of advertising?' suggested the lady author. Harald shook his head and shrugged. 'Go on, if you must,' he said to Kay. 'Well, the audience couldn't cross a picket line, obviously, even if most of the actors hadn't been in it. So the management had to agree right then and there to show its books every week to a committee of the actors, which Harald is head of. Then they all marched into the theatre.' 'And the show went on!' concluded Harald, with an ironical flourish of his hand. 'So you won,' said Nils. 'Very interesting.' In practice, Kay said, the actors were still only getting the $40 Equity minimum, because the show was not doing too well. 'But in principle,' Harald said dryly, '"'twas a famous victory".' His skeletal face looked sad.

He was not drinking, Libby noted; perhaps he had promised Kay. His own play, poor man, had not been done after all, because the producer's wife had suddenly sued for divorce, just as they were casting, and withdrawn her money; a lawsuit was going on, which

Harald's play was somehow tied up in. Harald had never been a special favourite of Libby's. They said that he was constantly sleeping with other women, and that Kay either did not know about it or did not mind, she was still so dominated by him intellectually. But he had thoroughly charmed Nils today, talking a little bit of Norwegian to him and reciting a few lines of *Peer Gynt* (you pronounced it 'Per Gunt'), in which Nils had joined. 'A delightful fellow, Petersen,' Nils said to Libby. 'You have such charming friends.' And even Sister remarked that he was an ugly-attractive man.

All this time, Polly and Gus LeRoy had been standing by the window, paying no attention to the conversation. Their wine glasses were empty. Polly was very temperate because of the alcoholism in her family (one of her uncles had ridden a horse, while drinking, into the Copley Plaza in Boston), but usually she made an exception for wine and for odd liqueurs like Goldwasser and the one that had a tree growing in the bottle. Libby floated up to them and took their glasses to refill. 'I think he's asking her to dinner,' she reported to Kay. 'And mark my words, she'll refuse. She'll find some bizarre reason for having to go home.'

Sure enough, before long, Polly was 'making her excuses' and wondering if she could have a little of the *bowle* to take home with her to that Mr Schneider. Libby threw up her hands. 'Why?' she wanted to know. 'He can perfectly well go around the corner to Luchow's if he wants a glass of May wine. Why do you have to bring it to him?' Polly coloured. 'I'm afraid it was my idea. I told him about your *bowle* when I brought the woodruff home. And he and Mr Scherbatyeff had a violent nationalistic argument about what to put in white-wine punches. Mr Scherbatyeff' – she gave her quick humorous smile – 'favours cucumber rind. Anyway, I offered to bring them home a sample of yours. If you can spare it, Libby.' Libby glanced at the punch bowl, calculating; it was still a third full, and the guests were thinning out. 'It won't be good tomorrow,' put in Kay, tactlessly. 'The strawberries will go bad. Unless you strain it. . . .' 'If you have a cream bottle I can take it in,' persisted Polly, 'or an old mayonnaise jar.' Libby bit her lips. Unlike Polly, she had no patience with the kind of German refugee who was homesick for the old country and the 'good old German ways'. She and Polly had argued about this before, and Polly said it was their *country*, Libby, but Libby said they would have to adapt to America. And, frankly, she thought it was a bit unseemly for a German Jew to be such a supporter of German products; why, there were people who believed that even Americans should boycott Nazi goods. Libby would probably be citicized herself for having served Liebfraumilch at her party. Gus LeRoy, she noticed, had got his hat and was standing there – waiting to say good-bye to her, she supposed.

She was afraid her irritation showed. 'Here,' she felt like saying, 'Polly has a chance to go out to dinner with you at some nice place, and instead she's going home to those lodgers, because of a silly promise she made! Isn't that perverse?' Besides, no man, not even a parlour pink, liked a girl who carried things around in old cream bottles stuffed into paper bags. Libby turned to Polly. 'You can't take it home on the bus. It'll spill.' Gus LeRoy stepped forward. 'I'm taking her in a taxi, Miss MacAusland.'

Libby fanned herself. 'Come into the kitchen,' she said to Polly. She had to talk to her alone. 'Now, Polly,' she said, 'I don't mind giving you the *bowle*. After all, you got the woodruff for *me*. But don't, please don't, take Gus into that place of yours and introduce him to all those weird characters. For my sake, if not for your own, don't.' What Libby meant was that the quaint life of Polly's rooming-house was all very well to dilate on to other girls, when you were having a bite alone, but a man would think, to hear about it, still more to see it in the flesh, that you were desperate for company if you had to fall back on that. A man, any man, wanted to imagine that you were courted by all sorts of glamorous rivals. . . . Libby frowned. No, that was not exactly her thought. What was it about those roomers, about the brownstone house itself, the very carpet on the stairs, Polly's little tray of gold-speckled liqueur glasses with the worn gold rims, Mr Scherbatyeff's smoking jacket, that Libby's feminine instinct told her would cook a girl's goose with any normal member of the opposite sex? As though a visit to that house would betray something horribly personal, like a smell, about Polly. The smell of poverty? But Gus LeRoy might like that. No; the smell of having seen better days. That was it. That was what they all – the house, the lodgers, and Polly herself, alas – had in common. Having seen better days and not making those crucial distinctions any more, not having any real ambition.

Hoarding a few sepulchral joys, like the pomander balls Polly made for Christmas presents – oranges stuck with cloves and rolled in orrisroot and tied with ribbons to hang in your closet or perfume your drawers. Actually, those pomander balls were quite snazzy; they were a very original present and cost practically nothing. Libby had written down the recipe in her Florentine-leather recipe book, and she was going to get Polly to help her make some herself for next Christmas. But somehow it would be all right for Libby to do it, whereas for Polly . . .? It would even be all right, strangely enough, for Libby to live in that rooming-house, not that she would; she could say she was gathering material for a story. . . .

'I wasn't planning to, Libby,' answered Polly, rather stiffly. 'Anyway, let's forget about the *bowle*. Please.' 'Now don't be trying,' said Libby. 'Here, Ida,' she called to the maid, 'get Miss Andrews that little glass cocktail shaker. Go and fill it from the punch bowl, and make sure it's clean, please. Perhaps Miss Andrews would like some of the *pâté* too. You're sure?' – she turned swiftly to Polly. 'Now what are you going to do? He's going to drive you to your door. . . .' By dint of close questioning, Libby established that Polly intended to leave the *bowle* at her house and then she and Gus LeRoy were going to have dinner at that famous Yiddish restaurant right around the corner from Polly's – the Café Royal, where all the stars from the Yiddish Theatre went and the journalists from the Jewish newspapers. 'Whose idea was that? His?' 'Mine, I'm afraid,' said Polly. 'It's not the *quietest* place.' 'Nonsense,' said Libby. 'It's just the thing. Pluperfect.' She thought it clever of Polly, since Gus was so hard to talk to, to pick out a place where you could just look at the other patrons and not try to make yourself heard. She herself had been in transports when Polly took her there one night, frankly turning around and rubbernecking and getting Polly to tell her who the celebrities were (every *one* of them was a 'name' to his co-religionists, which showed you the emptiness of fame) and uttering cries of delight when the food came, till Polly told her to stop, claiming that it would hurt their feelings to be looked at as curiosities, when anyone could see that that was why they came here – to show off. 'No, it's perfect,' she said thoughtfully putting her index finger to her cheek. 'Now what are you going to have to eat? That wonderful scarlet bortsch *we* had, with the boiled potato popped into it . . . ?' 'I haven't thought, Libby,' said Polly, taking the cocktail shaker, filled, from the maid. 'No, no,' said Libby. 'Ida will wrap it up for you. You just go to my dressing-table and straighten your hair a bit.' She lightly pushed some of Polly's silvery hairpins back into the knot at the nape of her full neck and then stood back so that she could examine her profile: Polly was going to have to watch her chin line. 'Help yourself to some of the perfume in my atomizer.' As Polly was leaving, with Gus LeRoy behind her awkwardly fingering his moustache and then leaping forward to settle Aunt Julia's old silver-fox tippet over her almost bare shoulders, Libby stepped in and extracted Polly's promise to bring back the cocktail shaker tomorrow evening, because Libby might be needing it; that way, Libby would be able to hear the post-mortem.

Kay and Harald said good-bye; they were going to have a ham-burger before the performance. Harald went every night, to check on the house and see that the actors were still playing their parts as he had directed them. Kay sometimes went with him and sat in one of the actors' dressing-rooms. 'She snorts like an old war horse,' explained Libby, 'at the smell of the grease paint. You can't keep her out of the greenroom. At college, she was a director.' There was one of those silences that come towards the end of a party. A few guests still lingered, not realizing, obviously, that Libby had a dinner date with Nils. 'Oh, don't go yet,' she urged the woman from the Metropolitan, who obediently sat down again; Libby hated the feeling of a room emptying too quickly, as though every-one were afraid of being the last to leave. It was still light out, a perfect May evening. The greenish-white dogwood grew paler in the shadowed corner; the tall Rhine wine bottles glimmered green and gold on the damask-covered punch table; there was a smell of strawberries and lilies of the valley in the room – Nils had brought her a little bunch. Ida was ready to go, with her black satchel; Libby paid her off and in a fit of spring madness told her to take the rest of the *pâté* home. 'You are generous,' said Nils. 'With your maid and your friend. The Liebfraumilch girl.' So he too had noticed Polly's display of bosom. Libby laughed uncertainly. The way he had said 'generous' made her slightly uneasy. The Metropolitan Museum woman leaned forward 'Speaking of Liebfraumilch, do any of you recall that amusing Tintoretto in the National Gallery? 'The Milky

Way"? Such an unusual conceit.' Everyone looked blank. 'When will we be alone?' Nils murmured into Libby's ear.

This happened sooner than Libby had anticipated. All at once, the other guests, seeing him whisper to her, got up and left. One minute they were there, and the next they were gone. He turned to her. 'I'll get my wrap,' she said quickly. But he seized her hand. 'Not yet, Elizabeth. Why do you let them call you that horrible nickname?' 'You don't like it?' 'I like Elizabeth,' he answered. 'I like her very much. Too much.' He pulled her to him and bent back her head and kissed her. Libby responded; she had dreamed of this moment so often that she knew just how it should be – her head falling back, like a chalice, to receive his lips, her nostrils contracting, her eyes shut. Nils's lips were soft and warm, contrary to her imaginings, for she always thought of him in a ski sweater, fair and ice-cold, his blond hair windswept under the peak of his cap. The thin skin of his face was very tight-drawn, over reddened high cheekbones, and she would have supposed, with all that outdoor life, that his lips would be hard and taut. He brushed his mouth back and forth gently over hers. Then he tilted her chin, looked into her eyes and kissed her passionately, taking her breath away. Libby staggered back a little and released herself. 'Elizabeth!' he said, and again he pulled her to him and kissed her very gently, murmuring her name. In a minute – or hours, she could not really tell – she could feel his large teeth pressing hard against her closed mouth. She broke away, staggering back a second time. She tried to laugh. 'Quiet,' he said. She pulled the chain of the big brass table lamp, for it was getting dark, and leaned against the table, supporting herself with the palm of one hand while with the other she nervously pushed back her hair. He came and stood beside her, encircling her shoulders with his arm, so that she could rest against him, her forehead brushing his cheek; he was four inches, she reckoned, taller than she was – a perfect difference. Standing like that, at rest, Libby felt utterly comfy; time slipped by. Then he slowly turned her to him, and, before she knew it, he had his tongue in her mouth and was pushing it against hers. His tongue was very firm and pointed. 'Give me your tongue, Elizabeth. Give me a tongue kiss.' Slowly and reluctantly, she raised the tip of her tongue and let it touch his; a quiver of fire darted through her. Their tongues played together in her mouth; he tried to draw hers, sucking, into his mouth, but she would not let him. A warning bell told her they had gone far enough. This time he let her go of his own accord; she smiled glassily. 'We must go,' she said. He ran his beautifully manicured hand up and down her arm in its long tight taffeta sleeve. 'Beautiful Elizabeth. Lovely rippling muscles. You're a strong girl, aren't you? A strong passionate girl.' Libby felt so flattered that she allowed him to kiss her some more.

Then he went and pulled down the blinds and led Libby towards the sofa. 'Come, Elizabeth,' he said disarmingly, 'let's read some poems together and drink some wine.' Libby could not resist this; she let him take the *Oxford Book* from her poetry shelf and pour them two brimming glasses of Liebfraumilch from a fresh bottle, which he uncorked. He came and sat beside her on the sofa. 'Skoal,' he said. 'Rhine maiden!' Libby giggled. 'Shakespeare,' she said unexpectedly, 'died of an overdose of Rhenish wine and pickled herring.' Nils looked through the book, frowning; Libby's favourite lines were underscored, and the margins were peppered with exclamation points and question marks. 'Ah, here it is!' he cried. And he began to read aloud. 'The Passionate Shepherd to His Love'; '"Come live with me and be my Love,/And we will all the pleasures prove. . . ."' Et cetera; Libby felt a tiny bit embarrassed; that poem was such a chestnut – she had known it by heart since she was sixteen. When he had finished, he leaned over and kissed her hungrily. 'Oh, but I wager you don't know the answer, sir,' she said laughing and extricating herself. '"The Shepherdess Replies." Sir Walter Raleigh.' And she began to recite from memory. '"If all the world and love were young,/And truth in every shepherd's tongue . . ./Then these delights my mind might move/To live with thee and be thy Love."' Her voice faltered as he gazed at her. '. . . "Thy coral clasps and amber studs . . ."' How did it go? The upshot was that Raleigh, speaking for the shepherdess, refused the shepherd's kind invitation. 'Give me the book,' she begged. Nils demanded another kiss in payment – a longer one. She was limp when he let her have the book. His hand stroked her hair as she thumbed through the index, looking for Raleigh; the pages, irritatingly, stuck together. She tried to ignore his hand, which had reached the back of her neck and was toying with the collar, and concentrate on finding the poem. All at once, she heard one of the snaps at the back of her dress open.

At that faint sound, all Libby's faculties stood alert; her spine stiffened. Her eyes goggled. Her Adam's apple moved as she swallowed. She realized he was planning to seduce her. The book fell open of its own accord on her lap. This must be the Continental approach. Those barons and counts used manoeuvres so obvious that you would not think they would try them. Oh, poor Nils, how he was dropping in her estimation. If he only knew how old-fashioned he seemed! Another snap surreptitiously opened. Libby could not decide whether to laugh or be angry. How to show him his mistake, without hurting his feelings, so that they could still go out to dinner? Her senses had stopped fluttering, like a clock ceasing to tick; her blood was perfectly mute. As if he were aware of the change in the temperature, he turned her head to him and stared into her eyes. Libby swallowed again. When he drew her to him and kissed her, she kept her teeth gritted. That ought to give him the hint. 'Ice Maiden,' he said, reproachfully. 'That's enough, Nils,' she said, trying to sound more friendly than she felt. She plunked her feet firmly on the floor, closed the book, and started to get up. But suddenly he had her in a vice of iron and bore her backward on the sofa. 'Kiss me,' he said roughly. 'No, not that way. Give me your tongue.' Libby thought it wiser to comply. He was frighteningly strong; she remembered with horror having heard that athletes had uncontrollable sex urges and something, too, about Scandinavians being the most ferocious Don Juans. Who had said that – Kay? This kiss actually hurt her; he was biting her lips. 'Please, Nils!' she cried, opening her eyes wide, to see his eyes staring at her like two blue pinpoints and his lips drawn back across his teeth like a wild animal about to charge. He had changed into a totally different person, very cruel-looking. Libby would have been fascinated if she had not been so scared. He was holding her down with his body, while his hands sought to caress her. The more she wriggled, the more determined he got. As she struggled, the snaps opened at the back of her dress; a hook tore loose from her brassière. Then she heard a fearful sound of ripping material – her brand-new dress bought at Bendel's spring sale! With one hand, he tore the bodice open, clear away from the sleeve, which remained dangling on her arm; with the other, he held her pinned down by her wrist, which he twisted when she tried to move. He buried his head in her neck and started pulling at her skirt.

Libby was moaning with terror. She considered screaming for help, but she had never spoken to the people in the other apartments, and she could not bear to be found by strangers in her torn clothes and general disarray. Dimly she thought of Polly and those lodgers, who would have rescued Polly in a second if anybody had attempted anything. She wondered if she could faint, but what might not happen while she was unconscious? The doctors at Vassar used to say that a woman could not be forced against her will. They advised girls to kick a man in his testicles or jab him there with your knee. When she started to try that, aiming with her knee at what she hoped was the right place, Nils gave a crowing laugh and slapped her lightly across the face. 'Bad girl.' The transformation of Nils was the most painful aspect.

'Are you a virgin?' he said suddenly, stopping right in the middle of his fell design. Libby nodded speechlessly. Her only hope, she now felt, was to throw herself on his mercies. 'Oh, what a bore!' he said, half relaxing his hold. 'What a bore you are, Elizabeth!' He grimaced. 'Libby, I should say.' With a shake, he disengaged himself. Libby had never been so hurt in her whole life. She lay there, gulping, in her ruined dress, looking piteously up at him out of her big, brown affrighted eyes. He pulled her skirt down roughly over her glove-silk bloomers. 'It would not even be amusing to rape you,' he said. And with that he rose from her sofa and calmly went into her bathroom. Libby was left alone with the *Oxford Book of English Verse*. She could hear him go to the toilet without even running the water or shutting the door. Then, whistling, he let himself out of her apartment. She heard the latch click and his step on the stairs, and that was that.

Libby tottered to her feet and headed straight for the mirror. She looked like the Wreck of the Hesperus. Moreover, she was hungry; he had not even waited till after dinner. And she had let Ida take the *pâté*. '"You are generous,"' she said to herself in the mirror. '"Beautiful Elizabeth."' Her feelings were in the strangest turmoil. Nils, of course, could not have meant that she was a bore; he had to vent his chagrin at finding out that she was a virgin. His code as an aristocrat had made him stop then. It was the code that was a bore to him. He wanted to rape her and go berserk like the old Vikings. At least that would have been something dramatic and conclusive. She would have lost her honour. But she would have found out what it was like when a man did it to you. Libby had a little secret; she sometimes made love to herself, on the bath mat, after having her tub. She always felt awful afterwards, sort of shaken and depleted and wondering what people would think if they could see her, especially when she took herself what she called 'Over the Top'. She stared at her pale face in the mirror, asking herself whether Nils could have guessed: was that what made him think she was experienced? They said it gave you circles under your eyes. 'No,' she said to herself, shuddering. 'No.' Perish the thought. Nobody could guess. And no one would ever guess the shaming, sickening, beastly thing that had happened, or failed to happen, this evening. Nils would not tell. Or would he?

Chapter 10

Priss Hartshorn Crockett was nursing her baby. That was the big news. 'I never expected a breast-fed grandson,' said Priss's mother, laughing and accepting a martini from her son-in-law, Dr Sloan Crockett, the budding paediatrician. It was the cocktail hour in Priss's room at New York Hospital – terribly gay. Over the week-end, Sloan stopped in every afternoon and shook up martinis for visitors. He had done his residency at the hospital, so that he could get ice from the diet kitchen and generally break the rules.

'You never expected a *g-grandson*, Mother,' pointed out Priss with her slight nervous stammer from the bed. She was wearing a pale-blue bed jacket, and her thin ashy hair was set in waves; the student nurse had done it for her that morning. On her lips, which were dry, was a new shade of lipstick, by Tussy; her doctor had ordered her to put on lipstick and powder right in the middle of labour; he and Sloan both thought it was important for a maternity patient to keep herself up to the mark. Priss, whose personality was confessed to be rather colourless, looked unreal to herself sitting up in bed all bedecked and bedizened – like one of those New York children dressed in furs and trailing satins and their mothers' slippers to beg in the streets at Hallowe'en. Little Ella Cinders, Sloan called her, after that funny in the paper. She would have been more comfortable in the short cotton hospital nightshirt that tied in back, but the floor nurses every morning made her struggle into a satin-and-lace 'nightie' from her trousseau. Doctor's orders, they said.

The nurses treated Priss as a special pet because she had been in Obstetrics and Gynaecology three times with miscarriages before she had made the grade. To be sure of coming to term this time, she had quit her job with the League of Women Shoppers and stayed in bed or on the sofa for the first five months of pregnancy – her uterus was retroverted. Even so, in the last month she had had a kidney complication; they had rushed her to the hospital and fed her intravenously till the inflammation went down. But now, as Mrs Hartshorn said, the nativity had been accomplished. Glory be, on the Feast of St Stephen, the day after Christmas, Priss had been brought to bed with a seven-and-a-half-pound son; delivery had been normal, though labour had been protracted – twenty-two hours. Her room was full of holly, mistletoe, azaleas, and cyclamen, and there was a little Christmas tree by her bedside. The child was to be called Stephen, after the first martyr.

He was in the nursery now, behind the plate-glass window at the end of the corridor – roaring his head off; his feeding time was six o'clock. Priss was drinking an eggnog, to help her lactate; liquids were very important, but she had lost her taste for milk during pregnancy, doing nothing and having to force herself to drink that quart a day that the doctors insisted on if she were not to lose her teeth building the baby's bones. Now, to tempt her, the nurses flavoured her milk with egg and sugar and vanilla and gave her fruit juices on the hour and ginger ale and Coke – every kind of liquid but alcohol, for if she drank a martini, Stephen would have gin for his dinner.

Sloan rattled the ice in the silver shaker and chatted with Priss's brother, Allen, who was down for the holidays from Harvard Law. Those two were great friends, both being staunch Republicans, unlike Priss and Mrs Hartshorn. Liberalism seemed to run in the female line: Mrs Hartshorn and her dead husband had had a running battle over Wilson and the League, and now Priss and Sloan were at swords' points over Roosevelt and socialized medicine. It had been a red-letter day for Sloan and Allen when the Supreme Court killed the Blue Eagle and put Priss out of a job. Working for the League of Women Shoppers had never seemed as exciting to her; it was more like a volunteer thing, which had made it easier for her to resign to have Stephen.

Priss had been good about that, though she missed her work and fretted about finances, since Sloan was just getting established in practice (with an older paediatrician), and they had depended on her salary for cigarettes and concerts and theatres and contributions to charity and their library membership – Priss was a great reader. Her mother could not help very much, because she still had her two youngest in college (Linda was at Bennington), which was quite a bit for a poor widow woman, as Mrs Hartshorn gaily called herself, to swing. She had been sending Priss her maid, the faithful Irene, to do the housework mornings, and most evenings Lily, the cook, would nip over with a casserole for Priss to heat, so that Sloan would have one good hot meal, at least, in his daily round. When Priss came home from the hospital, Irene, who had had children of her own, was to move in for two weeks and sleep on an army cot in the baby's room (the dining-room as *was*) to save the cost of a practical nurse.

This was Mrs Hartshorn's present to the young parents; to the newborn himself she was giving an English pram, a mad extravagance, and, come the spring, she was going to send them Linda's old crib, which was shut up in the attic in Oyster Bay, and her high chair and odds and ends, though high chairs, they said, were out now. For the time being, Stephen would sleep in a laundry basket on the baby-carriage mattress – quite a clever idea that Priss had got from a pamphlet on child care issued by the Department of Labour.

'Yes, my dear, no pun intended,' said Mrs Hartshorn to Polly Andrews, who had dropped in to see Priss. Allen guffawed. 'Why not the Department of the Interior?' Priss winced at her brother's witticism. 'The pamphlet's an excellent home manual,' she said earnestly. 'Sloan thinks so too, believe it or not, Allen.' 'Some of your friend Madam Perkins' work?' retorted Allen. In the bed Priss grew tense, preparing an answer; her lips moved voicelessly, in spasms. 'No politics today,' said Mrs Hartshorn firmly. 'We've declared a moratorium. Priss has to think of her milk.'

Lakey, she went on to Polly, had sent the most exquisite christening robe from Paris, fit for a dauphin – a great surprise, because she had not written for ages; she was doing her doctorate at the Sorbonne. And Pokey Prothero Beauchamp, who had had twins herself the year before, had sent a baby scales, a most thoughtful gift. Everyone had been frightfully kind. Dottie Renfrew Latham had arranged, from way out in Arizona, for Bloomingdale's to deliver a sterilizer, all complete with bottles and racks, instead of the conventional baby cup or porringer. That would come in handy later on, when Priss's milk ran out.

Mrs Hartshorn glanced at her daughter and lowered her voice.

'Just fancy little Priss being the first of your set to do it, Polly. She's so flat there she's never had to wear a brassière. But Sloan says it's not the size that counts. I do hope he's right. The miracle of the loaves and fishes, *I* call it. All the other babies in the nursery are on bottles. The nurses prefer it that way. I'm inclined to agree with them. Doctors are all theory. Nurses see the facts.' She swallowed her martini in a single draft, like medicine; this was the style among advanced society women of her age. She wiped her lips and refused a 'dividend' from the silver shaker. 'Which way progress, Polly?' she demanded, in a slightly louder voice, shaking her white bobbed locks. 'The bottle was the war-cry of my generation. Linda was bottle-fed. And you can't imagine the difference. For us, the bottle spelled the end of colic, and the frantic young husband walking the baby all night. We swore by the bottle, we of the avant-garde. My mother-in-law was horripilated. And now, I confess, Polly, I'm horripilated myself.'

Her son-in-law pricked up his ears and gave a tolerant smile. He was a tall young man with glasses and an Arrow-collar profile who had worked his way through medical school; his father, an army surgeon, had died of influenza during the war, and his mother was a housemother at a girls' school in Virginia. Priss had met him at her cousin's coming-out party junior year, through another cousin, a medical student, who had been ordered to bring some extra men.

'Medicine seems to be all cycles,' continued Mrs Hartshorn. 'That's the bone I pick with Sloan. Like what's-his-name's new theory of history. First we nursed our babies; then science told us not to. Now it tells us we were right in the first place. Or were we wrong then but would be right now? Reminds me of relativity, if I understand Mr Einstein.'

Sloan ignored this excursion. 'By nursing Stephen,' he said patiently, 'Priss can give him her immunities for at least the first year. He won't be liable to chicken pox or measles or whooping cough. And he will have a certain protection from colds. Of course, in some cases the mother's milk disagrees with the child. You get a rash or stomach upsets. Then you have to weigh the advantages of breast-feeding against the negative side effects.'

'And psychologically,' appended Polly, 'isn't the breast-fed baby supposed to have a warmer relation with his mother than the bottle-fed baby?' Sloan frowned. 'Psychology is still a long way from being a science,' he declared. 'Let's stick to measurable facts. Demonstrable facts. We can demonstrate that the breast-fed infant gets his mother's immunities. And we know from the scales that Stephen is gaining. An ounce a day, Cousin Louisa.' This was his name for Mrs Hartshorn. 'You can't argue with the scales.'

The sound of a baby's crying made itself heard in the silence that followed this speech. 'That's Stephen again,' said Mrs Hartshorn. 'I recognize his voice. He yells louder than any other baby in the nursery.' 'Shows he's a healthy young fellow,' replied Sloan. 'Time to worry if he didn't cry for his dinner. Eh, Priss?' Priss smiled wanly. 'Sloan says it's good for his lungs,' she said, grimacing. 'Develops them,' agreed Sloan. 'Like a bellows.' He drew air into his chest and released it.

Mrs Hartshorn looked at her watch. 'Can't the nurse bring him in now?' she wondered. 'It's quarter of six.' 'The *schedule*, Mother!' cried Priss. 'The reason babies in your time had colic wasn't because they were breast-fed, but because they were picked up at all sorts of irregular times and fed whenever they cried. The point is to have a schedule and stick to it absolutely!'

There was a knock on the half-open door. More visitors were arriving: Connie Storey and her husband and young Dr Edris, who had been Sloan's room-mate in medical school. The conversation grew louder, and the room was full of cigarette smoke. Mrs Hartshorn opened a window and tried to produce a *courant d'air*. What was the point of keeping the infant behind glass if he were then brought in to nurse in a smoke-filled room? 'Not to mention our germs,' she added, exhaling with a certain complacency, as though her germs were especially vigorous and well-pedigreed. Sloan shook his head. 'A baby needs to build up some immunities before going home from the hospital. If he's never been exposed to germs, he gets sick the minute he gets home. I think we overdo the sterility business, don't you, Bill? Just a bit?' 'Depends,' said Dr Edris. 'You can't impress it too much on the average mother.' Sloan smiled faintly. '"Boil baby's rattle every time he drops it"', he quoted. 'Don't you believe in boiling everything, Sloan?' anxiously demanded Priss. 'That's what the child-care pamphlet says to do.' 'You goop,' said her brother. 'That pamphlet was written for slum women; by a Vassar graduate, I bet.' 'Rattles are out anyway,' Priss replied stoutly. 'Everyone knows they're unsanitary and likely to break.' 'A dangerous toy,' agreed Sloan. There was a silence. 'Sometimes Sloan likes to play the heretic,' smiled Priss. 'You should hear him *épater* the floor nurses.' Mrs Hartshorn nodded. 'A promising sign in a doctor. Inspires confidence,' she observed. 'Though goodness knows why. We all trust a doctor who doesn't believe in medicine.'

In the middle of the general laugh, a nurse tapped at the door. 'Excuse us, ladies and gentlemen. Feeding time.' When the room was cleared of guests, she closed the window Mrs Hartshorn had opened and then brought the baby in on her shoulder. He was wearing a long white nightgown and his face was red and swollen; she placed him next to Priss in the bed. It was exactly six o'clock. 'Which one is it tonight, dear?' she demanded. Priss, who had managed to lower one shoulder of her nightgown, indicated her right breast. The nurse swabbed it with cotton and alcohol and laid the baby to suck; as usual, he made a face at the alcohol and pushed the nipple away. The nurse settled it firmly in his mouth again; then she went about the room emptying ash-trays and collecting glasses to take back to the diet kitchen. 'You had quite a party tonight.'

To Priss, this sounded like a criticism, and she did not reply. Instead, she gritted her teeth. The baby's mouth always hurt her nipple at the beginning, like a bite. Her breasts were very sensitive, and she hated to have Sloan touch them in love-making; she had hoped that nursing the baby would get her over that. People said that nursing was very satisfying, sensually, to the mother, and she had thought that if she got in the habit with a baby, she would not mind so much with a grown man. Though she had not told Sloan, this was one of her principal reasons for agreeing to breast-feed Stephen: so that she could give Sloan, who was entitled to it, more fun in bed. But so far nursing, like most of sex, was an ordeal she had to steel herself for each time it happened by using all her will-power and thinking about love and self-sacrifice. The nurse was watching her now, to make sure that the baby was drawing at the nipple properly. 'Relax, Mrs Crockett,' she said kindly. 'Baby can sense it if you're tense.' Priss sighed and tried to let go. But naturally the more she concentrated on relaxing, the more tense she got. 'Bless braces, damn relaxes,' she joked feebly. 'You're tired this evening,' said the nurse. Priss nodded, feeling grateful that someone knew and disloyal, at the same time, to Sloan, who did not know that it wore her out to have company, especially mixed company that sat there discussing her milk.

But as the baby (she wished the nurse would call him 'Stephen', not 'Baby') commenced to suck rhythmically, making a little noise like a snore, Priss grew somewhat easier. She did not *enjoy* the sucking, but she liked his fresh, milky smell, which made her think of churns and dairies, and his pale fuzz of hair and his warmth. Soon she was unaware of his sucking, except as a hypnotic rhythm; the nurse put the bell in her hand and tiptoed out. Priss was almost asleep when she came to, with a start; Stephen was almost asleep himself. His little mouth had ceased to tug, and the noise he was making *was* a light snore. She joggled him a little, as she had been taught to do, but her nipple slipped out of his mouth. He turned his round soft head away and lay sleeping with his cheek flat on her chest. Priss was terrified; she tried to turn his head and thrust her breast into his mouth. He resisted; his little hands rose and beat feebly at her breast to push it away. She shifted her position and looked at her watch. He had only been nursing seven minutes, and he was supposed to nurse fifteen to get the milk he needed to carry him through till the next feeding, which would be at ten o'clock. She had been cautioned before not to let him fall asleep. She rang the bell, which turned the light on outside her door.

No one came; she listened; there was complete silence in the corridor. Not even the sound of a baby crying came from the far end at the nursery. They were all being fed, obviously – all but poor Stephen – and the nurses were all busy, giving them their bottles. She was always fearful of being left alone with Stephen and usually she contrived to keep a nurse with her, making conversation. But since yesterday there were two new babies in the nursery and two new mothers to care for, so that Priss had become an 'old' mother, who ought to be able to look after herself. But this was the first time she had been left entirely alone; normally the nurse popped her head in the door from time to time, to see how things were going. Priss was afraid the nurses knew that she was afraid of Stephen – her own flesh and blood.

Still no one came; another three minutes had passed. She thought of Sloan, who would be in the Visitors' Lounge with her mother and Bill Edris, talking and enjoying himself; it was against the hospital rules for the husband to watch the mother nurse, and this was one rule that Sloan did not care to break. Perhaps a passing interne would notice her light. She raised her arm to look at her watch again; two more minutes gone. She felt as though she and Stephen were marooned together in eternity or tied together like prisoners in some gruesome form of punishment. It was useless to remind herself that this frightening bundle was her own child and Sloan's. Rather, she felt, to her shame, that he was a piece of hospital property that had been dumped on her and abandoned – they would never come to take him away.

Just then Stephen woke. He gave a long sigh and turned his head, burying it in her breast, and at once went back to sleep again. Priss could feel his nose pressing against her shrinking skin, and the idea that he might suffocate made her suddenly cold with fear. That was always happening to babies in their cribs. Maybe he had already suffocated; she listened and could not hear his breathing – only the loud noise of her own. Her heart was pounding with a sort of stutter. She tried to move his head gently, but again he resisted, and she was afraid of accidentally touching the soft part of his skull. But at least he was still alive. Gratefully, she tried to collect herself and make an intelligent decision. She could telephone down to the switchboard and get them to send help. But two things deterred her: first, her shyness and dislike of being a nuisance; second, the fact that the telephone was on the right side of the bed and she would have to move Stephen to reach it, but moving Stephen was just the problem. She was scared to. Scared of what, she asked herself. Scared that he might cry, she answered.

'Priss Hartshorn Crockett!' she said sternly to herself. 'Are you ready to let your newborn baby die of suffocation because you're shy and/or because you can't bear to hear him cry? What would your mother think?' Determined, she half sat up, and this abrupt movement dislodged the baby, who slipped to her side in a little heap, woke up and began to cry furiously. At that moment, the door opened.

'Well, what's going on here?' exclaimed the student nurse, who was Priss's favourite, she was glad it was not the other one, at any rate. The girl, in her blue-striped uniform, picked up Stephen and cuddled him in her arms. 'Have you two been having a fight?' Priss replied with a weak chime of laughter; humour was not her strong point, but now that she saw the baby safe in the nurse's strong bare arms, she laughed with relief. 'Is he all right? I'm afraid I lost my head.' 'Stephen's just plain mad, isn't he?' the girl said, addressing the baby. 'Does he want to go back to bed?' She picked up his blanket and wrapped him in it; she patted his back to 'bubble' him. 'No, no!' cried Priss. 'Give him back, please. He hasn't finished nursing. I let him go to sleep in the middle.'

'Oh, my!' said the girl. 'You must have been scared, all right. I'll stay with you this time till he finishes.' The baby belched, and the girl unwrapped him and laid him, under the covers, on Priss's breast. 'Somebody should have come in to bubble him,' she said. 'He swallowed a lot of air.' She gently slid the nipple into his mouth. The baby pushed it away and began to cry again. He was evidently angry. The two girls – Priss was the older – gazed at each other sadly. 'Does that happen often?' said Priss. 'I don't know,' said the girl. 'Most of our babies are bottle babies. But they do that sometimes with the bottle if the holes in the nipple aren't big enough; they get mad and push the bottle away.' 'Because the milk doesn't come fast enough,' said Priss. 'That's my trouble. But I wouldn't mind if he pushed a *b-bottle* away.' Her thin little face looked rueful. 'He's tired,' said the student nurse. 'Did you hear him this afternoon?' Priss nodded, looking down at the baby. 'It's a vicious circle,' she said gloomily. 'He wears himself out crying because he's famished and then he's too exhausted to nurse.'

The door opened again. 'You left Mrs Crockett's light on,' the older nurse chided the student. 'You should remember to snap it off when you come in. What was the trouble here, anyway?' 'He won't nurse,' said Priss. The three women looked at each other and sighed jointly. 'Let's see if you have any milk left,' said the older nurse finally, in a practical tone. She moved the baby's head slightly to one side and squeezed Priss's breast; a drop of watery liquid appeared. 'You can try it,' she conceded. 'But he'll have to learn to work for his supper. The harder he works, of course, the more milk you produce. The breast should be well drained.' She squeezed Priss's breast again, then clapped 'Baby's' head to the moist nipple. While both nurses watched, he sucked for another minute, for two minutes, and stopped. 'Shall we prime the pump again?' said Priss with a feeble smile. The older nurse bent down. 'The breast is empty. No sense in wearing him out for nothing. I'll take him now and weigh him.'

In a moment the student nurse was back, breathless. 'Two ounces!' she reported. 'Shall I tell your company they can come back?' Priss was overjoyed; her supper tray appeared while she was waiting for her family to return, and she felt almost hungry. 'We've heard your vital statistic,' announced Mrs Hartshorn. 'Is two ounces a lot?' asked Allen dubiously. 'An excellent average feeding,' declared Sloan: Priss's milk was highly concentrated, though the volume was not large; that was why the baby was gaining steadily, despite the little fuss he made before meals. Then they all trooped out for the evening, to let Priss have her supper in peace. Sloan was carrying the cocktail shaker; they would not need it any more in the hospital, for next week-end Priss would be home.

Priss picked up the last number of *Consumer Reports*; she was hoping they would have an article on bottled baby foods. She knew she was letting herself slip, mentally, in the hospital; she *lived* on the bulletins the nurses brought her of how many ounces Stephen had taken – they weighed him before and after each feeding. If the nurse forgot to come and tell her, she nearly died, imagining the worst and not having the gumption to ring and ask. The other important event was the regular morning weighing, before his bath, which showed his over-all gain for the day. Nothing but these figures and her own fluid intake interested Priss now; she was always having to ring for the bedpan because of the gallons of water she imbibed. The nurses were awfully cooperative, though they disapproved, she knew (except the student), of her breast-feeding Stephen. They thought Sloan and her obstetrician, Dr Turner, were barmy. But they too were impressed, *nolens volens*, by the evidence of the scales. The child *was* growing.

If it had not been for the bulletins, Priss would certainly have lost faith. Sloan and Dr Turner did not have to hear Stephen crying. The nurses and Priss had to hear it. At eight o'clock that night, right on the dot, down in the nursery Stephen started to cry. She knew his voice – the whole floor knew it. Sometimes he would whimper and then go back to sleep for a while, but when he began noisily, as he was doing now, he might cry for two solid hours – a scandal. It was against the rules for the nurses to pick him up; they were allowed to change him and give him a drink of water, and that was all. The babies were not supposed to be 'handled'. And if they gave him a second drink of water, he might not nurse properly when feeding time finally came.

Sometimes merely changing him would quiet him for the time being. Often the drink of water would quiet him. But not always. A lot depended, Priss had discovered, on when he got the water; if they gave it to him too soon, he would sleep briefly and wake up again, howling. If he woke up midway between feedings, the nurse usually let him cry, after changing him, for an hour, and then gave him the water, so that, tired from crying and with a deceptively full stomach, he would often sleep through until the next feeding. That was the best, for then he was fresh when he was brought in to nurse and would draw with might and main from the nipple. But if he woke up shortly after a feeding, it was horrible: after an hour's cry he would get his water, sleep, wake up and cry again without stopping – his record, so far, was two hours and three-quarters.

Priss's ear was attuned to every detail of this routine; she could tell when he was getting his water, when the nurse was just changing him or turning him over. She could tell when he fell asleep from sheer exhaustion, by the way his cries subsided and finally trailed off. She could recognize the first sleepy whimperings, and her imagination shared the nurse's hesitation as to whether to pick him up and change him at once or whether to leave him alone, hoping that he would not wake fully. She knew too that one of the nurses (she was not sure which) used to break the rules and pick him up and rock him in her arms; this was indicated by a sudden respite, a fairly long silence, and then a fierce renewal of crying as he was set back in his basket again. She could never make up her mind how she felt towards the nurse who did this: thankful or disapproving.

The nights were the worst. There were nights when, hearing him start at three or four in the morning, she would have welcomed anything that would let him stop and rest – paregoric, a sugar-tit, any of those wicked things. During her pregnancy, Priss had read a great deal about past mistakes in child rearing; according to the literature, they were the result not only of ignorance, but of sheer selfishness: a nurse or a mother who gave a crying child paregoric usually did it for her own peace of mind, not wanting to be bothered. For the doctors agreed it did not hurt a baby to cry; it only hurt grown-ups to listen to him. She *supposed* this was true. The nurses here wrote down every day on Stephen's chart how many hours he cried, but neither Sloan nor Dr Turner turned a hair when they looked at that on the chart; all they cared about was the weight curve.

Sloan had warned Priss repeatedly against listening to the nurses: they meant well but they were in a rut. They also liked to think they knew better than the doctor. It irritated him to have Priss dwell on how long Stephen had 'vocalized'. If 'it bothers you so much,' he had said to her sharply the other day, 'you can get them to give you some cotton for your ears.' That was not Priss's point, but she had considered doing what he said because she knew that worrying was bad for her milk supply; the nurses were always telling her that. But she was too much of a liberal to 'turn a deaf ear' to a hungry baby; that would be like those people who were blind to bread lines and picket lines. If Stephen howled, she wanted to know it. Moreover, being a worrier, she would *imagine* that Stephen was crying if she had ear stoppers in. Sloan replied that this was ridiculous, but that since she refused to be rational, she would have to suffer.

Poor Sloan was impatient with suffering; that was why, probably, he had become a doctor. But he hid his idealism behind an armour of hardness; otherwise, he could not go on practising, seeing all the pain he saw. She had often formulated this theory about Sloan when they had words about crossing a picket line or boycotting Spain and Japan ('Little Captain Boycott', he called her, to their friends), but now, in the hospital, it struck her as peculiar that nurses, who heard more crying than doctors did, did not develop an armour against it. And she did *not* think that it was only for their own peace of mind that the nurses had begun muttering among themselves (she had heard them) that they would like to see Dr Turner spend just one night in the patient's place.

They blamed Dr Turner, because he was Priss's doctor, but it was really Sloan who had the bee in his bonnet. Lying in bed tensely listening to Stephen's mournful cry, Priss suddenly did not understand why Sloan was so strong for breast-feeding. Was it entirely for the reasons he gave – the medical reasons? Or because he had a stubborn streak and felt that Mrs Hartshorn, the nurses and Priss were all against him? Or was it something worse? It crossed her mind that Sloan, who was just starting in practice, might regard her nursing Stephen as a sort of advertisement. He liked to make a point of his differences with dear old Dr Drysdale, who had taken him into his office and who had practically introduced the bottle into New York society. Dr Drysdale prided himself on being ultra-scientific, but Sloan said that all that boiling and sterilizing was inefficient and wasteful (not to mention the cost of the equipment), when you could tap nature's resource; the baby could be weaned from the breast directly to the cup. Any mother could nurse, he maintained, just as any woman could keep her weight down during pregnancy – Mrs Hartshorn had been astonished at how little Priss had gained, even with being on the sofa. Priss had been proud of keeping her girlish figure and proud as Lucifer of nursing Stephen, but now her pride was deflated by the thought that Sloan was using her to prove his theories, like a testimonial in a magazine. And it was true that the tale of her nursing had spread far and wide: everybody and his brother in this wing of the hospital seemed to have heard that poor little Mrs Crockett, a chestless wonder, was breast-feeding; outside, in the Cosmopolitan Club, her mother's circle were all talking about it. 'Well, you've certainly started something!' Kay Strong Petersen had commented. 'Every pregnant alumna who's heard about you wants to nurse.'

It was unlike Priss to be bitter, but it galled her to feel, as she did tonight, that she was a party to a gross deception – one of those frauds on the public that the government Bureau of Standards was always out to uncover. At nine o'clock, when the maid brought in her fruit juice, Stephen was still crying, steadily, like a buzz saw; Priss was trying to do a crossword puzzle but could not concentrate. At the opening of the door, the screams from the nursery came louder; a weaker voice had joined Stephen's. The idea that her child disturbed the other infants greatly troubled Priss, though the nurses tried to reassure her: newborn babies, they said, quickly got accustomed to a familiar noise. Still, Priss could not refrain from framing an apologetic sentence to the maid. 'Oh, dear, Catherine,' she said (she had made a point of learning the maids' names), 'do you hear him? He'll wake up the whole hospital.' 'Hear him?' replied Catherine, who was Irish. 'He'll wake the dead. When are they going to let him have a bottle, for God's sake?' 'I don't know,' said Priss, closing her eyes in pain. 'Ah, don't take it so hard,' the maid said jauntily, straightening Priss's covers. 'He's exercising his lungs.' Priss wished everyone would not say that. 'It's not my place to ask,' said Catherine, moving closer to plump Priss's pillows, 'but I've been wondering. What put it into your head to nurse?' Priss felt her neck redden. 'Im-m-munities,' she stammered. The maid looked at her curiously. 'You know,' said Priss. 'Like vaccination. He can't get any diseases I've had, like mumps or chicken pox or measles.' 'Always something new,' said Catherine, shaking her head. She poured Priss fresh water. 'They're always inventing something, aren't they?' Priss nodded. 'Would you like your radio on, now? A little music? You won't hear him, over the music.' 'No, thank you, Catherine,' said Priss. 'Can I crank you up a bit, Mrs Crockett?' 'No, thank you,' Priss repeated. The maid hesitated. 'Good night, then, and cheer up. Look on the bright side. They used to say it developed the bust.'

Priss could not help treasuring this last remark; she saved it to tell her mother tomorrow, in the brogue, if she could without stuttering. At the same time she had to admit that she had been secretly hoping that Stephen *would* be a bust-developer and she had made Dr Turner laugh when she asked him anxiously whether she wouldn't need a nursing brassière. Her mood lightened; outside, silence reigned – Stephen must have had his drink of water while she and the maid were talking.

This calm was broken by the head floor nurse, Miss Swenson, who was going off duty. She came in and closed the door. 'I want to tell you, Mrs Crockett, that I'm going to speak to Dr Turner in the morning. To recommend that Stephen be given a supplementary bottle.' The nurse's casual tone did not fool Priss. *A supplementary bottle* – the phrase sounded horrid, as if Miss Swenson had said, 'I'm going to recommend a dose of strychnine.' The very word *bottle* made Priss bristle, no matter what adjectives were attached. She braced herself against her pillows and prepared to give battle. Miss Swenson went on smoothly, as if she had not noticed the effect of her announcement on Priss. 'I know this will be a great relief to you, Mrs Crockett. We all understand what you've been through. You've been a wonderful patient, a remarkable patient.' Even in her shock, Priss recognized that Miss Swenson, whom she had always liked, was speaking with real earnestness. 'But why?' she brought out finally. 'The scales . . .'

Miss Swenson, who was in her thirties with blonde hair in a bun, came to the bedside and took her hand. 'I know how you feel, my dear. Torn. Most nursing mothers cry when I have to tell them that I recommend a supplementary bottle. Even when the child is failing to gain weight. They want to keep trying. You're exceptionally brave not to break down.' 'You mean this happens often?' asked Priss. 'Not very often. But we have one or two younger doctors who like to have the mothers nurse as long as they're able. Not all the mothers agree, of course. There's still a prejudice against breast-feeding, especially – and this will surprise you – among ward patients. They feel that a bottle baby is socially superior.' 'How interesting!' Priss exclaimed. 'And we see that same attitude with our Jewish private patients. Even when they have plenty of milk, and the doctor encourages it, they don't want to nurse; they have the idea it's lower East Side.' 'How interesting,' Priss repeated thoughtfully. 'Oh, being a nurse one sees a great deal. And the class differences are quite extraordinary. For example, on a surgical floor you'll find that all the female private patients and many of the male patients after an abdominal operation have postoperative urinary retention. While in a ward of Negro men you won't get a single case. It's simply a question of modesty; the upper class has been trained to feel embarrassment about the lower part of the body and after an operation when the abdomen has been opened, their inhibitions get to work and they can't urinate.'

'Fascinating,' breathed Priss. She often wished she had studied sociology. But she did not want to be distracted from the main point. 'Do higher-income women have a lower milk supply?' She did not like to use the words *upper class*. Miss Swenson avoided answering this blunt question; probably she was afraid of depressing Priss with the thought that her case was statistically pretty hopeless. She looked at her watch. 'I want to explain the supplementary bottle to you, Mrs Crockett.' To Priss's surprise, she found that this phrase no longer sounded like a death knell. 'But if he's gaining the right amount . . .?' she protested, nevertheless. 'He's an unusually hungry baby,' said Miss Swenson. 'Your milk is quite adequate from a nutritional point of view, but it doesn't give him enough volume. What I suggest, Mrs Crockett, is this. After his six o'clock evening feeding, starting tomorrow, we'll give him a small amount of formula in a bottle. Your milk supply is at its lowest then, I've noticed. At ten he gets enough volume from you to hold him. On a full stomach he'll sleep through till two; so will you, poor girl. In fact, with the supplementary bottle we may even be able to train him, before you leave the hospital, to sleep right through till six in the morning, so that you'll have an unbroken night. We like to do that anyway for our mothers, before they go home; once the baby has the habit of the two o'clock feeding, it's hard for the mother to break it herself. A baby works like a little clock, and we like to have it set right before the mother takes over.'

Priss nodded. How wonderful, she thought, of the hospital to plan ahead for the mothers. None of this would have been possible a few years before. 'If he's still fretful, even with one supplementary bottle,' Miss Swenson went on, 'we may have to give him more. Some babies take a supplementary bottle after each time at the breast. But in Stephen's case I don't think this will be necessary. You may even find that your flow of milk increases, once Stephen is more comfortable.'

When Miss Swenson left, Priss was a changed woman. What impressed her, she said to herself, was the empirical spirit here, the willingness to try without prejudice different methods and *mixtures* of methods till they found one that worked, which was often a compromise, like the New Deal. She was sure Miss Swenson was a Democrat. She was so relieved that Sloan had got his training here, instead of at Columbia and Presbyterian. This hospital, she mused, half fancifully, was like an up-to-date factory: no baby was sent out until he was in good working order, tried and tested and guaranteed to run without friction for at least the first few months. Why, they even gave demonstrations, for mothers who were not lucky enough to afford an Irene or a practical nurse, on how to bathe a baby and bubble him and fold his diapers, and the ambulatory mothers who wanted to were allowed to go into the diet kitchen and see the formulas made! And these new babies who ate and slept regularly, on a schedule, like little clocks, as Miss Swenson said, were going to grow up into a new kind of man, who perhaps (it did not do to be *too* optimistic) would no longer want to make wars and grab property. And nowadays everything was being made so easy for those babies' mothers: the infants were trained to the toilet in the very first months, by just being set gently on the potty when their regular time came, and as for washing diapers, there was this new thing called Diaper Service that came every day with fresh diapers and took away the soiled ones in a sanitized can.

That night Stephen broke all his previous records – three solid hours, from 3.0 a.m. till 6.0 a.m. Dr Turner, when he came into Priss's room the next morning, scolded her for the circles under her eyes and advised her to put on some rouge. But he was very sweet about the bottle, acting as though Miss Swenson's suggestion was what he had decided to prescribe himself, after looking at the chart. The weight curve, he said thoughtfully, was not the whole picture. Priss did not remind him that he had said the exact opposite, standing in the same spot, two days before, on Saturday. He departed humming, having picked one of Priss's roses for his buttonhole.

The fly in the ointment was Sloan. She was afraid he would see red at the words *supplementary bottle*. Dr Turner promised to talk to him; if *she* did it, Priss thought, she would find herself stammering and using some sickly euphemism like 'Tonight Stephen is going to get some formula for dessert.' It was odd how hospitals got you talking that way. One thing Priss was resolved on: neither she nor anyone else was ever going to talk baby-talk to Stephen. Or use expressions like 'Wee-wee' or 'Number Two'. She had not yet decided what to say instead.

At lunch time, Sloan appeared; he was angry. A muscle twitched by his eye. He was more angry at Dr Turner and the nurses than he was at Priss, whom he treated as an innocent party. They had high-pressured her, he said, into accepting the bottle. 'But Sloan,' she argued, 'it does sound like a good idea. Stephen will be getting the best of both worlds, don't you see?' Sloan shook his head 'Prissy, you're a layman. Turner's a woman's doctor. When you leave the hospital, he doesn't follow through. Except for your check-up. He doesn't see what happens when a child that's been nursing starts getting a bottle. Neither do these maternity nurses. That's what the paediatrician sees. Every darned time.' He sat down in the armchair and ran his hand through his blond hair; Priss saw that he was truly upset. 'What happens, Sloan?' she said gently. 'It's simple,' he said, wiping his glasses. 'When a child gets an ounce of formula, without half trying, from a bottle, he stops nursing so eagerly from the breast. Why should he? The child is a reasonable being. When he stops sucking for all he's worth, the

223

mother's milk supply goes down. Then they give him another "supplementary bottle". Then another. Within a week he's getting a bottle with each breast-feeding. At that point he starts rejecting the breast. Too much trouble. Or the paediatrician steps in and calls a halt. If the mother's milk is down to an ounce a feeding, it's not worthwhile to go on. Especially with the headache of boiling the bottles and the nipples and making the formula for six daily feedings – it's a duplication of labour. I tell you, Priss, if Stephen starts on a bottle tonight, you won't be home a week before your milk gives out, and you'll have a full-time bottle baby!'

Priss nodded meekly. She seemed to have no mind of her own. In no time, he had convinced her that it would be all over with her nursing if they gave Stephen that bottle. Why, it would be like starting him on drugs or liquor; right away, he would get a taste for it. She saw what Sloan was fighting and how Miss Swenson and Dr Turner had deceived her. For herself, she felt sad and beaten, as though she had lost her reason for living if she could not nurse Stephen. It was silly how much she had counted on it. 'Does it make that much difference, Sloan?' she said earnestly. 'Haven't you and I got a wee bit hipped on this nursing?'

'No,' he said, in a dead voice. 'It doesn't make so much difference. We wanted to give Stephen the best possible start, that's all. If you'd been able to nurse him even a month or two . . .' 'I'm sorry,' said Priss. 'It's not your fault,' he said. 'It's this damned hospital. I know them. They wouldn't let you try. You would have come through with flying colours. Just one more day would have done it. Two more days.' 'What do you mean?' 'Stephen would have settled down and stopped crying for the moon. Your milk supply has been building. Look at the chart. That's what I told Turner. Nobody here has the guts to go through with an experiment. A baby yells and they hand him a bottle. You can't make any progress in medicine unless you're willing to be hard. It's the same with your friend Roosevelt and those soft-headed social workers in the White House. The economy would have recovered by itself if they'd left it alone, instead of listening to the whimpers of the down-and-outs. Recovery! There hasn't been any recovery. The economy is sick and pumped full of formula.' He gave a sudden boyish laugh. 'Pretty good, that, wasn't it, Prissy?' 'It was funny,' she said primly, 'but I don't admit the comparison.'

'Good old Priss,' he said fondly, still pleased with his pun. 'Never give an inch.' 'What did you tell Dr Turner?' she said. He shrugged. 'What I just told you. He said it was no use trying to experiment under present-day hospital conditions. The nursing staff is against you. It's a conspiracy.'

'What do you mean, Sloan, exactly, when you say "experiment"?' 'To prove that any woman can nurse,' he said impatiently. '*You* know; you've heard it a hundred times.' 'Sloan,' she said coaxingly, 'be fair. Stephen cries about ten hours a day.'

Sloan raised a finger. 'In the first place, ten hours is exaggerated. In the second place, what of it? In the third place, the nurses pick him up and fuss over him when he cries.' Priss could not answer this. 'Of course they do,' said Sloan. 'So that naturally he cries some more. Already, in the second week of life, he's learned to cry to get attention.' He folded his arms and stared, frowning, at Priss.

'We'll fix that,' he said, 'when we get him home. You're not to let Irene pick him up, except to change him. Once you've established that he's not cold or wet, back he goes in his basket.' 'I agree with you utterly,' said Priss. 'I've already had a talk with Irene. She understands that babies are treated differently now. But what about the bottle?' 'He'll get one supplementary bottle,' Sloan said. 'For the time being. When we get him home, I have a little idea to try.'

Priss felt a chill; he alarmed her. Ever since she had been in the hospital, her feelings for Sloan had been undergoing a change. Sometimes she thought she was not in love with him any more. Or perhaps it was a thing that happened to many women: now that her baby was born, she felt divided in her interests. She had begun to see that she might have to defend Stephen against Sloan, and the more so because Sloan was a doctor and therefore had a double authority. She found that she was checking what Sloan said against what the nurses said, against what the Department of Labour pamphlet said, against *Parents' Magazine*. When Sloan declared that the baby should sleep in an unheated room, she was amazed to find that the Department of Labour agreed with him; the nursery in the hospital, of course, was heated. There was a side of Sloan, she had decided, that she mistrusted, a side that could be summed up by saying that he was a Republican. Up to now this had not mattered; most men she knew were Republicans – it was almost part of being a man. But she did not like the thought of a Republican controlling the destiny of a helpless baby. In medicine, Sloan was quite forward-looking, but he was enamoured of his own theories, which he wanted to enforce, like Prohibition, regardless of the human factor. She wondered, really, whether he was going to make a very good paediatrician.

'What's your idea, Sloan?' she asked, trying not to sound anxious. 'Oh, a thought I had.' He got up and strolled to the window. 'I wondered how Stephen would do on a three-hour cycle.' Priss's eyes nearly popped out of her head. 'The four-hour cycle isn't sacred, Prissy,' he said, coming to her bedside. 'Don't look so severe. Some of the new men are trying a three-hour cycle. The point is to find the right one for the individual baby. All babies aren't alike, you know.' Priss pondered the implications of this, which did not sound like Sloan exactly. It occurred to her that he had been doing some homework in the latest medical journals. 'Obviously,' he went on, 'you can't try out the three-hour cycle in a hospital; the routine isn't geared to it. You'd have all the nurses up in arms. But if a baby's unusually hungry and cries a great deal, it can easily be tried at home.' Priss's heart was touched. She took back everything she had just thought. He had been worrying about Stephen too, though he had not showed it. Probably he had been reading far into the night. But, like all doctors, he would not admit openly to having made a mistake or even to having changed his mind. 'It's even simpler, Priss, with the breast than it would be with the bottle. You could give him the breast every three hours for a week or two, then revert to the four-hour schedule. The main thing is to have a regular cycle, whatever the length of the intervals.' 'But would I have enough milk?' The vision of Stephen leaving her breast hungry eight times a day was rather daunting. 'Your milk ought to be stimulated by nursing more frequently,' he said. 'Anyway, I'd like to try it.' Priss could not see the harm, provided her milk held out. But she felt it her duty to put a last question. 'You're sure you're not turning the clock back? I mean, the next thing would be feeding the baby every two hours and then every time he's hungry. And before we knew it, we'd be back to Mother's day.' Sloan laughed. 'Or Grandmother's day,' he said. 'Don't be silly.'

You would never guess what happened after Sloan left. Priss had just finished giving Stephen his afternoon feeding when she got a telephone call from Julie Bentkamp, another classmate, who was an editor of *Mademoiselle*. Julie had heard from Libby MacAusland, who was now a high-powered literary agent, that Priss was nursing her own baby. She thought that was very exciting and she wondered whether Priss would like to write an article on how it felt for *Mademoiselle*. Priss said that she couldn't think of it; she was sure it was against medical ethics for a doctor's wife to write a piece like that. A few minutes later, Libby herself rang up – the same old Libby. She said that if Priss wrote it, she was positive she could resell it to the *Reader's Digest*. 'You could write it under a pseudonym,' she pointed out. 'Though personally I should think Sloan would welcome the advertisement. Let me call him and ask him.' 'Doctors don't advertise,' said Priss coldly. 'That's just the point, Libby.' Priss was annoyed; this was the 'high-pressure salesmanship' that she hated. Who could have told Libby, she asked herself – an idle question. What she feared was that Sloan, if Libby got at him, instead of being stuffy, would urge her to do it; she tried to imagine old Mrs Drysdale, Dr Drysdale's wife, writing such a thing even when she was young. . . . 'I'll ask Sloan for a drink,' Libby went on. 'Now that he's a lonely bachelor. With Julie. I'm sure we can talk him into it. You should see Julie now; she's a knockout.' 'If you d-dare, Libby – ' cried Priss. 'The thing is,' said Libby, 'you must be sure to put in your bust dimensions. Not in so many words. But you have to let the reader know that you're not a perfect thirty-six. Otherwise the reader would miss the point.' 'I understand, Libby,' said Priss. 'And put in that you were Phi Beta Kappa at college and worked for the government. If Sloan agrees, of course, they'll run a picture of you in the contributors' column.' '*I'm not going to do it*,' said Priss. 'I only know how to write reports on economics. My style is too dry.' 'Oh, I'll rewrite it for you,' said Libby airily. 'I'll do all the descriptive parts and the emotions, if you want. If you just tell me honestly what it's like.' '*I'm not going to do it*,' Priss repeated. 'Under any circumstances.' 'You can have a nurse for six months with the profits if we sell it to the *Reader's Digest*. A nanny with a cap – do they wear streamers? – to take the baby to the park . . .' Priss held the receiver away from her ear; finally there was a silence. Then Libby's voice resumed in a different tone. 'Why not?' Priss hesitated. 'It's in poor t-taste,' she stammered. 'I don't see that,' said Libby. 'I don't see that at all.' Her voice grew louder and louder. 'Is it in poor taste to talk about it? Why, it's the most natural thing in the world. In Italy, the women do it in public, and no one thinks a thing about it.' 'I'm not going to do it in public,' Priss said. 'And if it's so natural, why are you so excited about putting it in a magazine? You think it's unnatural, that's why.' And she hung up the telephone. It *was* unnatural, she said to herself forlornly. Accidentally, she had put her finger on the truth, like accidentally hitting a scab. She was doing 'the most natural thing in the world', suckling her young, and for some peculiar reason it was completely unnatural, strained, and false, like a posed photograph. Everyone in the hospital knew this, her mother knew it, her visitors knew it; that was why they were all talking about her nursing and pretending that it was exciting, when it was not, except as a thing to talk about. In reality, what she had been doing was horrid, and right now, in the nursery, a baby's voice was rising to tell her so – the voice, in fact, that she had been refusing to listen to, though she had heard it for at least a week. It was making a natural request, in this day and age; it was asking for a bottle.

Chapter 11

Polly Andrews and Gus LeRoy had been having a love affair for nearly a year. She still lived in a furnished room-and-bath and went to work every morning at Medical Centre, and he shared an apartment with another man just around the corner – a book designer who, like Gus, was separated from his wife. Every night after work Gus came to Polly's for drinks, unless he had to go out with an author, and after drinks she cooked them dinner on her hot-plate. Afterwards they went to a movie or to a meeting about the Spanish Civil War or silicosis or the sharecroppers or they played Polly's phonograph, but every week night he went home to sleep because it was simpler that way – he had his shaving things there and his pipes and the manuscripts he was reading; it did not disturb him if the book designer had women in the other bedroom, so long as Gus could have his corn flakes and coffee the next morning in his bathrobe without having to make conversation with a third party.

Saturdays he worked till noon, but they had Saturday afternoons together, to go for walks in the Italian section or in Chinatown or to the Hispanic Museum or the Barnard Cloisters. Coming home, they usually marketed, if Polly had not done it Saturday morning; Gus would buy wine on University Place, and they would walk past Wanamaker's with bags of groceries all the way to St Mark's Place and cook in Polly's landlady's kitchen if the landlady and her husband had gone to their week-end cottage in New Jersey. Or else Gus would take Polly to a French or Spanish place for dinner and dancing. Saturday nights, he stayed at Polly's, in her narrow bed, and Sunday mornings they had a late breakfast together and read the papers. Sunday afternoons he spent with his little boy, taking him to the Bronx Zoo or to ride on the Staten Island Ferry or climb up the Statue of Liberty or walk across the George Washington Bridge or visit the Aquarium at the Battery or the Snake House in the little zoo on Staten Island; it was Polly who planned their expeditions, but she would not go along. 'Not until we are married,' she said, which always made Gus chuckle because the phrase sounded so old-fashioned, as though she were refusing him her favours until she had a wedding ring. But that was the way she felt. So Sunday afternoons Polly saw her old friends, and Sunday evenings, when Gus brought young Gus home, he stayed for a glass of beer with his wife and afterwards fixed himself a sandwich in his kitchen. Sunday night, they had agreed, was his 'night off' from Polly, which she used to do her laundry and wash her hair.

It was Sunday night now, and Polly's underwear, stockings, and girdle hung in her bathroom. In the living-room her English ivy and Delicious Monster had just had their weekly bath too, and her blouses were pinned to a stout cord festooned across her window; she was brushing her long damp hair with an Ogilvie Sisters hairbrush and rubbing it with a towel. On another towel a white wool sweater was stretched out to dry. Doing her laundry, Polly had found, was a working-girl's cure for depression, and Sunday nights she was depressed. The soapsuds, the steam, the smell of damp lamb's wool, the squeak of her clean hair gradually made her feel, though, that somehow it would 'all come out in the wash'. If she ironed six white blouses in her landlady's kitchen, mended her stockings, and started on a diet to lose five pounds, Gus would decide that they could not wait any longer to get married.

Five afternoons a week, before coming to Polly's, he had an hour with his psychoanalyst. The psychoanalyst said it was a principle of analysis that the patient should not change his life situation while undergoing treatment; this would upset the analytic relation. Therefore Gus had not done anything about getting a divorce. When he was 'ready' for a divorce – the analyst's expression – he assumed he would go to Reno for six weeks. But Reno divorces were expensive, and Polly did not know how Gus was going to pay for one, when his savings were being spent on psychoanalysis and half his salary was made over to his wife for temporary maintenance and child support. Polly had her doubts too that Gus's wife would agree to give him a divorce. She had promised him one when he was finished with his analysis, but Polly suspected that she and the analyst were in cahoots to wear him out by attrition. He had been in analysis three months when he met Polly at Libby's May wine party, and the analyst was quite taken aback when he heard they had started a serious relationship – he felt that Gus had broken his promise. As if a man could control falling in love!

Polly's family did not have an inkling of what was going on, but her friends guessed there must be a married man in the picture because she was so silent about how she was spending her time. The theory was that it must be one of the doctors at the hospital. Polly was reticent about their love, not because she was ashamed but because she could not bear the thought of advice and sympathy. The only people who knew for certain were the people who could not avoid knowing: the book designer, Polly's landlady and her husband, the two lodgers, and Ross, her Aunt Julia's maid, who had been in the habit of dropping in evenings to give Polly 'a hand' with her knitting or sewing. Not even Miss Bisbee, Gus's secretary, knew. Polly would not go to literary cocktail parties with Gus ('After we're married,' she said), partly from a dread of meeting Libby but mainly from that same sense of propriety that made her balk at spending Sundays with little Gus and his father, so long as his father and mother were man and wife. Polly hated questions – the questions young Gus would ask and the questions his mother would put to him, the questions her appearance at cocktail parties would solicit from the people in Gus's office. 'When are you going to get married?' was what everyone immediately wanted to know when they saw a girl and a man in love. It was what Ross had asked, straight off, and Mr Schneider, who did not believe in marriage, and the landlady, who belonged to a nudist group in New Jersey, and Mr Scherbatyeff. And a truthful answer to this question led everyone at once to ask another one, as if in a single voice: why was Gus going to a psychoanalyst? What was the matter with him?

It was a question that, strangely enough, no one had ever asked about her father, when he had been 'put away' in Riggs, poor darling, though her father's disease had a name – melancholia – which would have made it easy to answer queries. If only Gus had talked to himself or refused to talk or engaged in weeping fits or what the doctors called bizarre behaviour, no one would have asked what was wrong with him! But the trouble here was just the opposite. Polly could not see that there was anything the matter with Gus. He was one of the most normal men she had ever met, at least to the naked eye, which was all she had to judge with. No loathèd melancholy or black bile or antic disposition. He liked to dance cheek to cheek and play tennis and drive a car – he had an old Hupmobile jacked up in a garage in Brooklyn. Like most New Englanders, he was cautious with the pennies, but he always went to the best shops when buying presents – he had given Polly a beautiful handbag, some carved lapis lazuli earrings, and a soft blue sweater from Brooks Brothers; every week, practically, he brought her flowers, and when they went out to dance on Saturday he bought her violets or a camellia. On the other hand, he did not care what he wore; he had two rather threadbare suits bought off the rack at Wanamaker's, a tweed jacket, flannels, and some bow ties. He had Blue Cross hospital insurance and went to the dentist three times a year to get his teeth cleaned. He watched his waistline and checked up on young Gus's visits to the paediatrician, who was one of the best younger men in the city, like Gus's analyst, who had been Brill's favourite pupil. Though he was only thirty, he was a second father to his authors, very patient in listening to their troubles and getting them lawyers, theatre tickets, discount books, an apartment, a secretary, a girl friend – whatever they needed. He had been active in starting the local of the Book and Magazine Guild in his office, though he could not be a union member himself because he was considered part of management. He smoked union-made cigarettes when he did not smoke a pipe and tried to look for the union label on whatever he bought; unlike Priss, however, he was a secret believer in name brands, like Arrow shirts and Firestone tyres and Teacher's Highland Cream and Gillette razors. He could not be persuaded by the consumer movement that something at half the price was just as good. It tickled him to watch Polly mix her powder and cold cream at home, to save money; she failed to count the cost of her labour, he pointed out.

His liking for name brands was what had sold him on Communism years ago, when he graduated from Brown spank into the depression. Shaw had already converted him to socialism, but if you were going to be a socialist, his room-mate argued, you ought to give your business to the biggest and best firm producing socialism; i.e., the Soviet Union. So Gus switched to Communism, but only after he had gone to see for himself. He and his room-mate made a tour of the Soviet Union the summer after college and they were impressed by the dams and power plants and the collective farms and the Intourist girl guide. After that, Norman Thomas seemed pretty ineffectual. Gus never took any notice of the little splinter groups, like the Trotskyites, which Polly's friend Mr Schneider, across the hall, belonged to, or the Lovestoneites or the Musteites – every big movement, he said, had its share of cranks. Yet he had not joined the Party when he and his room-mate got back. He did not want to hurt his father, the owner of a job-printing business in Fall River that had been in the family for four generations. The LeRoys were respected by the mill-owning families whose wedding and funeral announcements, visiting cards, dance programmes, 'Keep Off' signs, and foreclosure sale notices they had been printing since the Civil War; in their shop below the presses on Main Street they also sold school supplies, Christmas cards, Valentines, and gift-wrapping paper. If Gus became an active Communist, those flinty mill-owners were perfectly capable of boycotting the LeRoy shop. Besides, the American Communists did not seem to Gus as responsible as the Russian ones. Instead, he married a Party member – a Jewish girl he had met on a double date at a dance at Webster Hall; she taught the first grade at the Downtown Community School.

Kay Petersen, Polly knew, would say that Gus's attraction to Communism – and in particular to Communist women – was a sign of emotional instability. But Polly herself did not think so; she could not see the Party as the Scarlet Woman in Gus's life. Moreover, he was phlegmatic in his sympathy. He never took part in demonstrations or marched in May Day parades or referred to the police as Cossacks; the only part of the *Daily Worker* he read was the sports page. He did not argue with the infidels, including herself, and in fact did not seem to care about spreading the faith, unlike poor Mr Schneider, who was always trying to convert her to Trotskyism and just now was extremely exercised about the Moscow trials, which he brought up every time he met Gus on the stairs. They were too far away, Gus said, to judge the rights and wrongs of – history would have to decide. To him they seemed insignificant in comparison with the war in Spain, which was something he was really excited about.

He was busy commissioning books on Spain – reports from the battle front, an anthology of Loyalist war poetry, a study of the International Brigade, a new translation of *Don Quixote*. He had tried to get Hemingway to do a book on El Campesino, but unfortunately he was already signed up with Scribner's, and Vincent Sheean, his other idea, did not answer his cables. He hoped for a great novel to come out of the Abraham Lincoln Battalion, and at one point this winter, when they were recruiting for it, he decided to join up himself and slipped off one day during his lunch hour to have a physical, without even telling his analyst. The picture of Gus as a brave volunteer in a beret appealed to Polly; she thought he would have made an excellent officer. But when his wife heard about it (he was going to leave his life-insurance policy to take care of Gus Fourth), she grew very indignant and accused him of irresponsibility. In Gus's case, she said, enlisting would be an escape mechanism, which would make his action politically invalid. According to her, the truth was that he was unwilling to finish his analysis and instead was running away from his real problems, which concerned her and their son, and incidentally who was going to pay the child support while Gus was fighting the fascists or hanging around cafés in Madrid? Hearing this, Polly was sorry for his wife, in the same way that she was sorry for a person like Libby, who was always lying to herself. But then, trying to be fair, she wondered whether it was really the money or whether the money was not an excuse his wife gave herself for worrying that Gus might be killed; perhaps his wife in her way loved him more than she did, who would be quite willing to let him risk his life for a cause.

Polly sympathized warmly with the Spanish Republicans and when asked about the reason for her allegiance, she would answer smiling, 'I'm a Basque.' This was a reference to the fact that there was a Catholic strain in Polly's ancestry; on her mother's side she was an Ayer and related to Lord Acton. Politically, she and Gus were opposites; her heart hastened to the losers in any battle, and she loved small sects with quaint doctrines, like Döllinger's Old Catholics, who denied the infallibility of the Pope, the Dukhobors, who went to Canada to escape the Czar's military service, the virtuous Anabaptists, the Chassidic Jews, who danced and leapt for joy in Polish villages; she championed 'lost' races like the Basques, with their mysterious language; she was partial to extinct and extirpated species, like the passenger pigeon, on which she had done a paper for Zoology. Not since Bonnie Prince Charlie had she cared so much for a cause as she did now for the Loyalists in Spain. She and Gus were both very generous with contributions to the Republican war effort, though Gus gave for aeroplanes and Polly gave for ambulances and medical supplies. Normally, she said smiling – that is, in peacetime – she was a pacifist, but in Gus's place she would have volunteered, and she was surprised he had listened to the analyst, who told him that he would be more use to the Spanish cause in New York than in Madrid. This might be true, but Polly could not imagine consenting to weigh yourself in the balance like that, as though you were an ingot you were hoarding. It was this side of Communism that Polly did not cotton to.

But if Polly was surprised that Gus had listened to the analyst, she was more surprised that the analyst had talked to him. 'I thought they weren't supposed to give you advice,' she said frowning. The analyst, Gus had told her, was utterly neutral; he only listened to the patient and asked an occasional question. The patient was meant to interrupt himself. 'That's the theory,' Gus answered. 'But he's a human being,' he explained. 'If he sees a patient about to commit suicide, naturally he steps in, as a human being.' 'I should think he would step in as a doctor,' Polly said mildly. Gus shook his head. 'Unh-unh,' he said. 'That's what they have to watch out for. The patient's always trying to involve the analyst, qua analyst, in an unorthodox situation. To coax him out from behind his barrier. But the analyst has to stay behind that barrier – Rule One. If he can't, he has to terminate the analysis. But the patients are cunning as hell. Dr Bijur might figure, for instance, that my signing up with the Lincoln Battalion was just a trap to get him interested in my personal decisions. A play for attention.' He wrung his eyebrows. 'Christ, Polly, maybe it was. Maybe I was just playing soldier.' 'But were you?' cried Polly. 'I believed you. Weren't you sincere, Gus?' 'How do I know?' said Gus, spreading his hands. 'Good Lord!' said Polly. There it was again, that curious thing, of treating yourself as if you were a dense, opaque object. Or as if you were not you but someone else, whose motives you could only guess at. Was this strange, flat objectivity what was the matter with Gus or was it an effect of the treatment?

She did not pursue the subject. Rule Two, she knew, was that the patient was not supposed to discuss his illness with his friends or family, and this was almost the longest conversation she and Gus had ever had about his analysis – since the very first one, when he had broken it to her, after they had already slept together several times, that he was going to Dr Bijur. Polly was a conscientious girl and she would no more have tempted Gus to talk to her about his analysis than she would have pressed sugar on a diabetic, and the result was that she was totally in the dark about what to him, no doubt, was the most vital part of his life. For if it were not the most vital part of his life, why would he be going to talk for an hour a day about it to a stranger?

In retrospect, Polly sometimes wondered whether she would have let Gus come up to her room and make love to her if he had told her ahead of time he was 'in analysis'. He had told her he was married and living apart from his wife (which she already knew anyway from Libby), but not a peep about the analyst. Polly could see why; at first he did not know her well enough to tell her, and when he did know her well enough it was because they had been to bed together and then it was too late for Polly to have any choice. The die was cast, for, having let him love her, she loved him. But *if* she had known beforehand, she doubted that she would have lost her virginity with an 'analysand'; she would have been afraid to.

Polly had always known that sex would mean a great deal to her. That was why she had been leery of men. She could tell from conversations with other girls in college that necking did not shake them to their foundations the way it did her when she was engaged. Several times then, she had nearly gone the limit, as they used to call it, but something had always saved her – once a campus policeman but mostly the boy himself, who had scruples. When she had broken her engagement and had to go to the infirmary, it was sex principally that tortured her. After that, she had firmly suppressed her desires, to the point of avoiding movies with kissing in them; she did not want to be 'aroused'. She decided she wanted a cool, starchy independent life, with ruffles of humour like window curtains. They told her she had a sweet nature, and she made friends easily, as she could get birds to eat from her hand. Having considered her own case carefully, as well as the hereditary 'taint', she concluded that she had best live for friendship, not for love or marriage. She saw herself in later years, large and soft, as an abbess, framed in a wimple, or as an Episcopal deaconess tending the altar, dusting the organ, and visiting the sick of a parish. As it happened, she was an unbeliever, but time, she supposed, might remedy that. Her immediate danger, she saw, was that she was on the verge of becoming a 'character', and she resisted being pasted, at twenty-six, which was not yet old, in an album. Already some of her friends were treating her as a 'find' they had pounced on in a thrift shop – a slightly cracked piece of old china.

It was true, she did not care for people with drive or those most likely to succeed, which had made her rather a misfit at Vassar; the only way she could like assured, aggressive girls like Libby and Kay was to feel sorry for them. She was horribly sorry for Libby, to the point where she could hardly bear seeing her; Libby's red open mouth, continually gabbling, was like a running wound in the middle of her empty face. But Libby had no suspicion, of course, that there was anything about her to pity, which was just what made her pitiable; *she* thought she was sorry for Polly and was doing her a favour every time she made some imposition on her. If Polly stopped seeing her, then poor Libby would have no one to imagine that she was being charitable to, because Libby could not be charitable to anyone who was really miserable but only to someone like Polly who was quite happy as she was. But this being quite happy as she was, alas, was what made her a 'character' in the eyes of her incredulous friends; the Andrews family were regarded as eccentric because they had lost their money and survived. Polly could laught at this notion, but for most people, evidently, it *was* eccentric or possibly a pose to be jolly when your money was gone. And to wear your aunt's old Paris clothes, made over, with a twinkle, was original, though Polly did not know how you were expected to wear them – in the deepest gloom? If Polly had come to prefer the company of odd ducks, it was possibly because they had no conception of oddity, or, rather, they thought you were odd if you weren't. Mr Scherbatyeff, for example, looked on Libby as an incredible phenomenon and kept asking Polly to explain her.

There was only one point on which all Polly's acquaintances, odd or not, agreed, and that was that she ought to be married. 'You pretty girl. Why you no marry?' said the iceman, adding his voice to the chorus. 'I'm waiting for the right man,' said Polly. And this, despite the wisdom she exercised on herself, was secretly the case. If she made it difficult for him to find her, that was part of the test he had to pass. 'How are you going to *meet* anybody,

Polly?' her classmates cried. 'Living the way you do and never going out with a soul?' She was familiar with the arguments: that the way to meet a man was through other men, that you did not have to love a man or even to like him a lot to agree to go to dinner and a theatre with him, that he only wanted your company, which was little enough to give. But Polly's own strong desires made her doubt this, and she did not think it right to start a relation you were not prepared to go further with; it did not seem to her honest to use a man to meet other men. So she had stubbornly refused all attempts to arrange male friendships for her – the extra man invited to dinner and prodded into gallantry. 'Dick will take you home, Polly. Won't you, Dick?' 'No, thank you,' Polly would interpose. 'I'll take the First Avenue bus. I live right next to the bus line.' Even Mr Schneider and Mr Scherbatyeff had been guilty of similar efforts; a series of young Trotskyites had been produced by Mr Schneider, to meet Polly and drink a glass of 'schnapps' in his room, while Mr Scherbatyeff had served up a nephew who was learning the hotel business in Chicago. Above all, Polly had declined to be coupled with Libby's awful brother, known as 'Brother', who was always eager to take her out.

'It is your pride, little girl, that makes you act so,' said Mr Schneider one evening when she had reproached him for trying to find her a 'man'. 'Maybe,' said Polly. 'But don't you think, Mr Schneider, that love ought to come as a surprise? Like entertaining an angel unawares.' The deep cleft in her chin dimpled. 'You know how it is in mystery stories. The murderer is the least obvious suspect, the person you never would have guessed. That's the way I feel about love. The "right man" for me will never be the extra man specially invited for me. He'll be the person the hostess never in her born days would have chosen. If he comes.' Mr Schneider looked gloomy. 'You mean,' he said, nodding, 'you will fall in love with a married man. All the other suspects are obvious.'

Sure enough, it had been like that with Gus. 'You two are the *last* people,' Libby had said the next day, 'that I would have expected to hit it off. Did he ask you out again?' Polly had answered no, truthfully – he had only taken her phone number – and Libby was not surprised. 'He's awfully hard to talk to,' she remarked. 'And not your cup of tea at all. I've been thinking about you, Polly. You're the type older people find attractive. Older people and other girls. But a man like Gus LeRoy would be blind to your looks. That's why I nearly went kerplunk when you walked out of here with him last night. You might not think so to talk to him, he's so quiet, but he's the *dernier cri* in publishing; you should see the authors on his list. Authors that are personally devoted to him and that he could take with him tomorrow if he left Ferris. Of course a lot of them are Communists; they say he's a secret Party member and has orders to bore from within at Ferris. But, like it or lump it, some of our best authors are Communists this year.' She sighed. Polly was silent. 'Did he talk about me?' asked Libby suddenly. 'A bit,' said Polly. 'Oh, what did he say? Tell me all.' 'He said you were doing awfully well as an agent. I think he used the word "crackerjack".' Libby was disappointed. 'He must have said more than that. Does he think I'm attractive? He must or he wouldn't have come to my party. I'm afraid I rather neglected him. Did he mention that? I had eyes only for Nils. You know, the baron.' She sighed again. 'He proposed last night.' 'Oh, Libby,' said Polly, laughing, 'you can't marry the ski jumper at Altman's! I hope you refused.' Libby nodded. 'He was in a rage. Berserk. Will you promise not to repeat it if I tell you what happened?' 'I promise,' 'When I turned him down, he tried to rape me! My new Bendel dress is in ribbons – did you like it? And I'm a mass of bruises. Let me show you.' She opened her blouse. 'How horrible!' said Polly, staring at the black-and-blue marks on Libby's thin chest and arms. Libby rebuttoned her blouse. 'Of course he apologized afterwards and was no end contrite.' 'But how did you stop him?' said Polly. 'I told him I was a virgin. That brought him to his senses at once. After all, he's a man of honour. But what a Viking! Lucky you, out with Gloomy Gus. I don't suppose he even tried to kiss you?' 'No,' said Polly. 'He called me "Miss Andrews" with every other sentence.' She smiled. 'Poor fellow,' she added. 'Poor fellow!' exclaimed Libby. 'What's poor about him?' 'He's lonely,' said Polly. 'He said so when he asked me to have dinner with him. He's a nice, solid man and he misses his wife and child. He reminded me of a widower.' Libby raised her eyes to heaven.

Polly was telling the truth. She had begun by being sorry for Gus. And the way he had called her 'Miss Andrews' all through dinner had amused her – as though there were a desk between them instead of a restaurant table. That desk, she had fancied, was part of him, like an extra limb or buttress; he had a special desk voice, judicious, and a habit of tilting back in his chair that had immediately made her see him in his office. He had told her, as a joke on himself, the story of Libby fainting on his carpet. 'I thought the girl was starving, Miss Andrews, so help me God.' He looked ruefully from under his eyebrows at Polly, who burst into laughter. 'When did you find out different?' she asked finally. 'Not for quite a while. Her boss told me, as a matter of fact. Seems the MacAuslands are among the powers-that-be in Pittsfield. Is that true?' 'Yes,' said Polly. 'They own one of the principal mills. That's how I first knew Libby. My family live in Stockbridge.' 'Mill-owners?' Polly shook her head. 'Father was an architect who never built anything except for his relations. He lived on his investments till the crash.' 'And now?' 'Mother has a tiny income, and we have a farm that we work. *They* work,' she corrected herself. 'And what do you do, Miss Andrews?' 'I'm a hospital technician.' 'That must be interesting. And rewarding. Where do you work?' And so on. Exactly, Polly thought, like a job interview. This whole desk side of Gus, which impressed Libby, had touched Polly's heart. She sometimes felt she had fallen in love with a desk, a swivel chair, and a small scratchy moustache.

Still, to fall in love with a desk and be presented with a couch was daunting. She often now tried to picture him on the psychiatric couch and failed. Did he smoke his pipe and fold his arms behind his head? Or did he chain-smoke cigarettes, dropping the ashes into an ashtray on his chest, as he sometimes did in bed? Which voice did he use – the desk voice, which creaked like the creaking of the swivel-chair, or a softer, lighter voice that matched his boyish smile, slim ankles, soft red lips, and the ingenuous way he had of wrinkling his nose at her, bunny-like, to signify warm affection?

When he had first told her about the analyst, his voice had trembled, and there were tears in his eyes. He had got out of bed, wearing Polly's Japanese kimono, a relic of Aunt Julia's Oriental travels, which came down just to his knees; nervously, he lit a cigarette and flung himself into her armchair. 'There's a thing I've got to confess to you. I'm being psychoanalysed.' Polly sat up in bed, clutching the sheet to her in an instinctive movement, as though a third person had entered the room. 'Why?' she demanded. 'Oh, Gus, why?'

Her voice came out like a wail. He did not tell her why, though he seemed to think he had. What he told her was how he had happened to start going to the doctor.

It was all his wife's idea. After Gus had walked out on her because she had been 'running around' with a Party organizer. Esther – that was her name – had decided she wanted him back. She had tried all the old methods – tears, threats, promises – without shaking Gus's determination not to return home. Then one day she came to see him in his office in a calmer frame of mind and with an entirely new proposal, which was that they should both go to analysts, to see whether their marriage could be saved. To Gus, after the scenes he had been through, this had seemed a reasonable offer, and he was struck, above all, by the change in his wife's attitude. She pointed out that analysis would help her in her work with children; quite a few of her fellow teachers were being analysed for no other purpose than that, and the school principal strongly recommended it for the whole staff. It would probably help Gus too, in his work with authors, make him better able to deal with their conflicts, so that even if he and she decided to divorce when they were finished, they would have gained a great deal from it professionally. Gus told her he would think it over, but before she left his office he had already resolved to give it a try. He too would have liked to save his marriage, on account of little Gus, and his hopelessness about it had been based on the notion that neither he nor Esther could be changed. If he had not been hopeless, he would have gone back long ago, for he missed Esther and there was no one else in his life. The idea of gaining an 'insight' – a word Esther used freely – attracted him too, Polly could see; he was grateful for the insights of Marxism and, manlike, was eager to add a new tool to his thinking kit.

All this Polly understood. What she could not understand was why he kept on going to the doctor now, when there *was* someone else in his life. Now that he no longer had a doubt about divorcing Esther, why didn't he stop? Was it because of the promise he had given? But if so, that implied to Polly's mind that there still was a possibility that the analysis might return him to Esther, all mended, like some article that had been sent for repair. Or was he continuing to go, as she sometimes felt, from sheer inertia? Or because the doctor had discovered something seriously wrong with him, as when you went to get a cavity filled and learned you had a huge abscess?

Gus had asked her if she minded that night when he had broken the news. 'Of course not,' she had answered, meaning that she loved him just the same and always would. But in fact she did mind, she had found. It gave her a very unpleasant feeling to have Gus come to her every day 'fresh from the couch'. She wished he could have his 'hour' in the morning, before work, or at lunchtime. This way, she could not help wondering what they had been talking about, whether it was her, horrible thought, or Esther, horrible thought too. She hoped it was about his childhood; it was all right if it was about his childhood. The odd thing was that he never seemed shaken or upset when he arrived from the analyst's; he was always as matter-of-fact as if he had come from the barbershop. He was much more excited on certain Fridays when he got excused from the analyst to audit a meeting of the Book and Magazine Guild. In his place, Polly was sure she would have been in turmoil if she had just spent an hour ransacking her unconscious.

Or indeed her conscious. Gus was not allowed to read Freud while he was in analysis (another rule), but Polly in her lunch hour had been perusing the literature available in the psychiatric section of the Medical Centre library. Though the psychiatrists at the hospital were violently anti-analytic, at least they had the books of Freud and his principal followers. She was trying – rather slyly, she felt – to find out which of the neuroses or psychoneuroses Gus could be suffering from. But he did not seem to fit any of the descriptions of hysteria, anxiety hysteria, compulsion neurosis, anxiety neurosis, character neurosis. He was most like a compulsion neurotic, in that he was set in his ways, punctual, and reliable, but she noticed that he did not do any of the things that compulsion neurotics were supposed to do, like being sure to step on the cracks of the sidewalk or *not* to step on them, as the case might be. On the other hand, anxiety patients had difficulty making decisions, and it was true that Gus had been of two minds about enlisting to fight in Spain and had vacillated a bit about leaving his wife. But a real anxiety patient, according to the books, was one who could not make up his mind whether to take the B-MT or the IRT to work, for instance, and Gus always took the bus. Moreover, with all the neuroses, the patient's sexual life was supposed to be disturbed.

Polly had no point of comparison, but Gus's sexual life, so far as she could see, was completely unruffled; he was always eager to make love and seemed to have had a lot of practice, for he did it very authoritatively and had taught Polly how with great tenderness, like a man teaching a child to fly a kite or spin a top or button its buttons – he was obviously a good father. It was bliss, Polly thought, making love with him.

The more Polly read and studied Gus, the more convinced she became that the only thing wrong with him was that he was spending $25 a week going to a psychoanalyst. And she asked herself whether that could be a disease, a form of hypochondria, and whether you would have to go to an analyst to be cured of it.

But if she could not match dear Gus, like a paint sample or snippet of material, with any of the charted neuroses, the opposite, she found to her dismay, was true of herself. She seemed to be suffering from all of them. She was compulsive, obsessional, oral, anal, hysterical, and anxious. If her sexual life was not disturbed now, it certainly had been. A sense of guilt transpired from her Sunday-night washing ritual, and she allayed her anxiety by the propitiatory magic of ironing and darning. The plants on her window sills were the children she could not have. She was addicted to counting; she collected buttons, corsage pins, string, pebbles, hat pins, corks, ribbons, and newspaper clippings; she made lists, including this one, and was acquiring a craving for drink. The fact that she viewed this alarming picture with humorous fascination was itself a very bad sign, proving a dissociation from herself, a flight into fantasy and storytelling from an 'unbearable' reality. The whole Andrews family, Freud would say, lived in a world of myth.

Joking aside – and there were times when, reluctantly, she had to put joking aside – Polly realized that she was in a deplorable state. Whatever the clinical name for it. Sunday nights she knew that she was terribly unhappy. Again. Love had done this to her, for the second time. Love was bad for her. There must be certain people who were allergic to love, and she was one of them. Not only was it bad for her; it made her bad; it poisoned her. Before she knew Gus, not only had she been far happier but she had been nicer. Loving Gus was turning her into an awful person, a person she hated.

That person came to a head on Sundays, like a boil, because Sundays Gus saw little Gus and his wife. She was perfectly conscious of the connexion, unlike the patients she read about who could not seem to put two and two together. She was jealous. On top of that, she was conscience-stricken, for, to be truthful, she did not approve of divorce where there were children. Unless the parents came to blows in front of them or one of them was an evil influence. Look at what her own mother had suffered from her father. And yet they were together. Esther had committed adultery repeatedly and she did not sound like a pleasant woman, but Gus had loved her enough to have a child by her. If Polly were not the 'other woman', she would advise Gus to go back to her. At least on a trial basis. No, that was equivocating. Forever.

At that word, Polly's blood ran cold. She wrapped a dry towel round her damp head and began to darn a hole in the toe of a stocking. It was not she who had asked Gus to marry her, but the other way around. Yet that was no excuse. She was acting like Cain in the Bible and pretending that the divorce was Gus's business and she had nothing to do with it; she was not Gus's keeper. But she was. She told herself that it had never entered anyone's mind but Esther's that Gus should go back to her. That was not true, though. It had entered Polly's. Not all at once, but gradually. During the week she forgot about it, but on Sundays, when Gus was not there, it came creeping back. As if, once she had entertained it, she could never turn it away. And in this it behaved exactly like a temptation. She longed to tell Gus about it, but she was afraid that he would laugh at her or perhaps that he wouldn't. This thought was her Sunday secret. And the whispering of conscience (if that was what it was), far from directing her mind to good resolves, made her still more jealous – just short of the point where she mentally slew little Gus. Here something stayed her hand, always, and instead she slew Esther and lived happily ever after with little Gus and his father.

Polly put down the darning-egg. She went to the window and felt her blouses to see whether they were dry enough yet to iron. They were. She wrapped them in a towel and coiled up her hair and stuck two big pins through it. If she ironed, she said to herself, Gus would call to say goodnight to her, as he sometimes did. She had come to feel that this call was a reward she earned, for if she moped and did not do her ironing or mend her stockings and step-ins, often, as if he knew, he did not call.

She had discovered a sad little law: a man never called when you needed him but only when you didn't. If you really got absorbed in your ironing or in doing your bureau drawers, to the point where you did not want to be interrupted, that was the moment the phone decided to ring. You had to mean it; you had to forget about him honestly and enjoy your own society before it worked. You got what you wanted, in other words, as soon as you saw you could do without it, which meant, if Polly reasoned right, that you *never* got what you wanted. Practically every other Sunday Polly gaily found she could do without Gus if she had to; climbing the stairs with a stack of blouses still warm from the iron, she would feel quite happy and self-sufficient and think that it might be almost a deprivation to get married. And she wondered if Gus, a block away, puttering around his kitchen, smoking his pipe, listening to the news on his radio, was thinking the same thing. Whether they were not, really, a bachelor and an old maid who were deceiving themselves and each other about the urgency of their desire to mate.

But this was the *other* Sunday. Tonight she needed him and so probably he would not call. It was late, and the house was still. She pondered knocking on Mr Schneider's door, to ask him to keep her company in the kitchen while she ironed. Though she had banished the bogies for the time being, the prospect of the lonely kitchen, in the basement of the house, and of the labour of putting up the heavy ironing-board seemed infinitely wearisome to her. And she was afraid of being alone with her thoughts there, out of the protection of her own four walls.

Yet if she summoned Mr Schneider, he would be bound to start talking politics with her, and this, she felt, would be disloyal to Gus. If it were not the Moscow trials, it would be the war in Spain. Mr Schneider was hipped on a group called the 'Poum' and he also favoured the Anarchists, both of whom, according to Gus, were sabotaging the war. But according to Mr Schneider, it was the Russian commissars who were sabotaging the revolution and thereby losing the war to Franco. Mr Schneider said the Communists were murdering Anarchists and Poumists, and Gus said they were not and if they were it was because the others were traitors and richly deserved their fate. Polly could see how Gus as a practical man would logically support the Russians, who were the only ones who were sending help to Spain, but she could not control her instincts, which went sneaking over to Mr Schneider's side of the argument. Besides, Mr Schneider was a better arguer than she was, who could only repeat lamely what Gus told her, which meant that Gus was worsted by proxy every time she let Mr Schneider get started. Gus saw no harm in letting Mr Schneider 'blow off steam', but Polly felt it was wiser to avoid the occasions of sin, for the truth was that she half-liked listening to Mr Schneider go on. It was a kind of eavesdropping, hearing what the Party did not want people like herself to hear. Listening to Gus and then to Mr Schneider describe the same set of events was like looking at the war in Spain through a stereopticon – you gained a dimension, seeing it from two sides. This was her justification for listening, and she thought that if someone like Mr Schneider could get Roosevelt's ear it might persuade him to lift the embargo, for if the Americans sent arms, then the Russians would no longer be in control. But really she was not so much interested in the fine points of the Spanish Civil War as in Gus, and what Mr Schneider gave her, without meaning to, was another perspective on him. In this perspective, Gus appeared credulous – 'the Stalinists and their dupes', Mr Schneider was fond of saying. But if Gus were a dupe, she ought not to want to know it.

Yet wanting to know was consuming her. She blamed the psychoanalyst for that. It was the psychoanalyst who had made Gus a mystery man, at least to her, and often, she suspected, to himself. The idea that there was another Gus who came out like a ground hog every afternoon at five o'clock was becoming more horrible day by day. At first she had minded the psychoanalyst because he was an obstacle to their getting married; now she hated him because, the longer Gus went, the more she speculated about what passed between the two of them. She was sure Gus told the doctor things he did not tell her. Perhaps he told the doctor that he was no longer so keen on marrying her or that he dreamed every night of Esther – how did she know? Or perhaps the doctor told him that he *thought* he loved Polly Andrews but his dreams proved he didn't. He could not be going to an analyst all this time unless he had a 'conflict', but what was the conflict between?

Most of all, though, she hated the doctor because, thanks to him, she had seen things in herself that she hated. If there was another Gus, there was also another Polly. Not only a jealous Polly who engaged in murderous fantasies, but a suspicious, spying Polly. The worst was that itch to know. When she mentally slew Esther, she was not unduly disturbed, because the real Polly would not kill Esther even if she could do it by cosmic rays or by pressing a button. But the real Polly would give anything to be present, in a cloak of invisibility, in Dr Bijur's office. Why did she *have* to know? Feminine curiosity. Pandora's box, the source, according to the Greeks, of all the evils in the world. Bluebeard's closet. Yet Pandora's box at least had been primed with genuine troubles, nasty little winged creatures that she let loose on humanity, and Bluebeard's closet had been full of bloody corpses – the moral of those tales was that it was best to remain in ignorance. Polly did not approve of that moral; no science major could. It was another fable, she feared, that fitted her case – the story of Cupid and Psyche. Gus on the analytic couch, all innocent trust, was the sleeping Cupid, and she was Psyche, with her wax taper, trying to steal a look at his face, though she knew it was forbidden. What had Psyche expected – an ugly monster? Instead, she saw a beautiful god. But when the hot wax of her curiosity seared him, he woke up and flew away sadly. The moral of that story was that love was a gift that you must not question, because it came from the gods. What Polly was doing, to her sorrow, was like looking for the price tag on a priceless present. The penalty was that love would leave her. But she could not stop; that was the trouble with sins of thought. Once Psyche got the urge to see what Cupid looked like, she was done for, poor girl; she could not keep from wondering and speculating between his nightly visits – he came at the end of the business day, just like Gus. It showed gumption, Polly thought, on Psyche's part, to take a candle and get it over with.

For her own part, she wished she could say 'Choose between me and the analyst.' But she could not. She was too soft and pliant. Besides, she had kept hoping that the analysis would end soon. But lately, as though by reverse serendipity, she had been hearing stories that cast a new light on that. Kay Petersen knew a woman who had been going eight years. Why, at that rate, when the wedding bells rang, Polly would be too old, practically, to have children, and Gus would be on home relief. The only bright spot Polly could see was that Gus's savings would run out before long. Analysts, apparently, did not extend credit; they were worse than the telephone company and Consolidated Edison put together.

Cheered by this thought, Polly went softly down to the kitchen and put up the ironing-board. In his room, Mr Schneider had begun playing his fiddle. She was in the middle of her third blouse when the phone rang on the landing. It was Gus. He wanted to know if he could see her for a minute this evening. Polly unplugged the iron and hurried up to her room to put on lipstick and powder. Before she had time to do her hair properly the doorbell rang. He kissed her, and they climbed the stairs together.

'Looks like a laundry,' he commented, entering. 'You've been washing your hair.' He approached her, sniffing, and dropped a kiss on her topknot. 'Smells good,' he said. 'Nice shampoo.' 'Camomile rinse,' said Polly. She poured them each a glass of New York State sherry. He glanced around her room. It was the first time he had been here on a Sunday evening. She waited, wondering why he had come; he did not take off his tweed topcoat but walked to her street windows with his glass, looked out idly, and pulled the shades.

'I had a talk with Esther this evening.' 'Oh?' 'We talked about my analysis.' 'Oh?' The second 'Oh?' was more cautious. Had he come to tell her that he and Esther had decided to call off the analysis? 'She asked me how it was going. Hers is going great. She dreamt she went to her analyst's funeral' "You're telling me," he said, "that the analysis is finished." Next week she's having her last hour.' 'Well!' said Polly brightly. Gus coughed. 'My own news wasn't so good, Polly. I had to tell her I was blocked.' He fingered the avocado plant that Polly had grown from a seed. 'Oh,' said Polly. 'Blocked?' He nodded. 'What does that mean, exactly?' 'I don't dream,' he said, flushing. 'It's funny, but I've stopped dreaming. Completely.' 'Is that so serious?' 'It's a hell of a note,' said Gus. 'But why? There are lots of people who don't dream. I remember a girl at college who used to pay me to wake her up in the morning yelling "Fire" to make her dream for a paper she was writing on Freud. That was part of Student Self-Help.' She smiled. Gus frowned. 'The point is, Polly, if I don't dream, I've got nothing to say to Bijur.' 'Nothing?' 'Nothing. Literally. Not a damn word.'

He drained his sherry despondently. 'Every day it's the same story. I go in. "Good afternoon, doctor." I lie down on the couch. "Any dreams?" says Bijur, picking up his notebook. "No." He puts down the notebook. Silence. At the end of fifty minutes, he tells me the hour's over. I hand him my five bucks. "So long, doctor," and I leave.'

'Every *day*?' cried Polly. 'Just about.' 'But can't you talk about something else? The weather. Or a movie you've seen. You can't just lie there without making a sound!' 'But I do. It's not a social occasion, honey. You're supposed to dredge up stuff from your unconscious. If I don't have a dream to warm the motor, I'm stuck. I can't start free-associating in a vacuum. So I just lie there. Once last week I fell asleep. I'd had a rough day at the office. He had to tap me on the shoulder to let me know the hour was up.'

'But you can free-associate to *anything*,' said Polly. 'The word "fire" for instance. What does it make you think of?' 'Water.' 'And water?' 'Fire.' She could not help laughing. 'Oh dear.' 'You see?' he said darkly. 'That's what I mean. I'm blocked.' 'Have you tried talking about not talking?' 'Bijur suggested that. "Why do you suppose you refuse to talk?" he asked me. "I don't know," I said. End of conversation.' He grimaced. 'I've never liked the idea of talking to somebody who doesn't answer, who just sits there behind you, thinking.'

'How long has this been going on?' 'About a month. Longer, off and on.' Polly's face crinkled into smiles. 'If you only knew what I'd been imagining!' 'About my analysis?' She nodded. 'I never thought I'd tell you. I was afraid you talked about me.' 'Why should I talk about you?' 'Well, I mean, sex . . .' said Polly. 'You goop,' said Gus tenderly. 'The patient doesn't talk about real sex. He talks about sexual fantasies. If he has any. I haven't since I was a kid.' He paced about the room. 'You know, Polly, what's wrong with me? I'm not interested in myself.' 'But, Gus,' she said gently, 'I think that's an admirable thing. Doesn't everybody strive for self-forgetfulness?' She was about to say 'Look at the saints' and corrected herself. 'Look at Lenin,' she said instead. 'Did he think about himself?' 'He thought about the masses,' Gus answered. 'But frankly I don't think much about the masses either.

Not in those terms.' 'What *do* you think about?' she asked curiously. 'Sales conference. Dust jackets. Bookstore reports. Agents. A talk I have to give to the League of American Writers.' He brooded.

'I don't think your doctor ought to take the money,' she said virtuously. 'It's unethical.' Gus shook his head. 'According to him, it's all grist to the mill. He told me that, when I wondered whether I shouldn't quit – stop wasting his time. He said most patients expressed their resistance through talking. I express mine by silence. But my silence, he claims, is valuable. It shows the treatment is working and I'm fighting it.'

Polly lost patience. Seeing Gus so upset and so humble made her angry. She asked the question she had resolved never to ask. 'Tell me,' she said, trying to sound casual, 'what *are* you being treated for? What's supposed to be the matter with you? What's its name?' 'Name?' He sounded surprised. 'Yes,' prompted Polly. '"Compulsion neurosis", "obsessional neurosis", "anxiety neurosis" – one of those.' Gus scratched his head. 'He's never said.' 'Never *said*?' 'No. I think maybe it's against the rules to tell the patient the name of what's the matter with him.' 'But aren't you curious?' 'No. What's in a name, anyway?' Polly controlled herself. 'If you went to a doctor with a rash,' she said, 'wouldn't you feel entitled to know whether he thought it was measles or prickly heat?' 'That's different.' Polly tried another tack. 'What are your symptoms, then? If I were writing your chart, what would I put down? The patient complains of . . .?' Gus seemed suddenly irritated. 'Get the hospital out of your mind, Polly. I went, I told you, because Esther and I agreed. Because our marriage had broken up, over my jealousy. Esther wanted a free relationship; I couldn't take it.'

A feeling of alarm came over Polly. 'Oh,' she said. 'But that's natural, surely?' He knitted his brows. 'Only in our culture, Polly. You understand, don't you, that there's a conflict in me between Fall River and Union Square?' 'There is in almost everybody, isn't there? I mean of our generation. Maybe not exactly Union Square.' She hesitated. 'What if there were nothing the matter with you, Gus? What if you were just normal?' 'If there were nothing the matter with me, I wouldn't be blocked, would I?' He sat down wearily. Polly touched his shoulder. 'What did

Esther say?' He closed his eyes. 'She said I was sabotaging the analysis. Because of you.' 'So she knows about me.' 'Jacoby told her.' That was the book designer. Gus opened his eyes. 'Esther thinks I'd unblock if I stopped seeing you for the time being.'

Polly stiffened. Her first impulse was to laugh; instead, she waited, warily watching Gus. 'The way Esther looks at it,' he went on, flushing, 'I'm throwing a monkey wrench into the analysis to keep from getting well. Because the part of me that's weak and evasive clings to you for support or refuge. The fact that you work in a hospital makes me see you as a nurse. If I got well, I'd have to leave my nurse.' He looked at her inquiringly. 'What do you think of that?' 'I think,' Polly said with a tight throat, 'that Esther ought not to practise medicine without a licence. Isn't it up to Dr Bijur to tell you these things, if they're true? He should be the one to recommend that you stop seeing me for the time being.'

'He can't, Polly. He's my analyst. We've been over that before. He can't advise me about my life-decisions. He can only listen when I report them.' 'At least,' remarked Polly, 'this will give you something to talk about in your next session.' 'That's a nasty crack,' said Gus. 'Have I deserved that, Polly?' He wrinkled his nose appealingly. 'I love you.' 'But you've already decided, haven't you?' she said steadily. 'You're going to do what Esther says. That's why you came to see me tonight.' 'I wanted to talk to you about it before I saw Bijur. And I have a lunch with an author tomorrow. But I haven't decided anything. We have to decide this together.' Polly folded her hands and stared at them. 'Hell,' said Gus. 'I don't suggest I believe what Esther said. But I might be game to try it as an experiment. After all, she knows me pretty well. And she has a good head on her shoulders. If we agreed to stop seeing each other for a week or so and I unblocked, that might prove something. And if I didn't unblock, that would prove she was wrong, wouldn't it?' He smiled eagerly. 'She knows you *very* well,' observed Polly.

'Hey!' he said. 'That isn't like you. Poll. You sound catty, like other women.' 'I am like other women.' 'No.' He shook his head. 'You're not. You're like a girl in a story book.' He looked around the room. 'That's how I always think of you, as a girl in a story book or a fairy tale. A girl with long fair hair who lives in a special room surrounded by kindly dwarfs.' For some reason, this friendly allusion to the lodgers was the thing that undid her. Tears streamed from her eyes; she had never thought he liked the two 'dwarfs'. 'And that's why you're going to let me go,' she said. 'Because I'm part of a fairy tale. I'm unreal.' She brushed away her tears and poured herself another glass of sherry.

'Whoa!' he said. 'I'm not going to let you go. This is just a temporary tactic. In the interests of the over-all strategy. Please understand, Polly. I made an agreement with Esther, and she's going to hold me to it. If I don't finish the analysis, no divorce.' 'We could wait,' she said. 'You could quit the analysis and we could wait. Living in sin. You could move in here or we could find another place.' 'I couldn't do that to you,' he said emphatically. 'You weren't built to live in sin. I would never forgive myself for what it'd do to you.' 'Is that Union Square speaking?' 'No, that's Fall River. Granite Block.' She smiled mistily. 'So you do understand,' he said. 'And you know I love you.'

Polly reflected, turning the gold-speckled glass in her hand. 'I know. I must be crazy, but I know. And I know something else. You're going to go back to Esther. You think you're not, but you are.' He was struck. 'Why do you say that?' Polly waved a hand. 'Little Gus, the Party, the psychoanalyst. You've never really left her. To leave her, you'd have to change your life. And you can't. It's all built in to you, like built-in furniture. Your job too. Your authors. Jacoby. I've always known we'd never get married,' she added sadly. 'I don't belong with the built-in furniture. I'm a knick-knack.'

'Are you condemning me, Polly?' said Gus. 'No.' 'Is there something you think I should have done different?' 'No.' 'Tell the truth.' 'It's just a silly thing,' She hesitated. 'Nothing to do with us. I think you should have listened to Mr Schneider about the Moscow trials.' 'Oh for Christ's sake!' said Gus. 'I told you it was silly,' she said. 'No, Gus, listen. I think you *should* go back to Esther. Or I *think* I think you should.' What she meant, she supposed, was that he would be doing the right thing, for him, but that she wished he were different. A better man or a worse one. A few minutes ago, she had suddenly realized a fact that explained everything: Gus was ordinary. That was what was the matter with him.

He was looking at her piteously, as if he felt naked before her eyes; at the same time, she observed, with surprise, that he still had his topcoat on, like someone who had come on business. 'It's been awfully tough, Polly,' he burst out. 'These Sundays. You don't know. With the kid always asking, when I bring him back, "Are you going to stay this time, Daddy?"' 'I know.' 'And Jacoby, with his drawing-board and his dames. Not that he hasn't been damn decent.' It was a minute before Polly recognized that he was taking her at her word: he was going home. As soon as he could with honour. And he was glad and grateful, as if she had 'released' him. This was not what she had meant at all; she had meant that sometime in the future, eventually, he would go back. 'I've loved you so much,' he said. 'More than anyone, ever.' He sighed. '"Each man kills the thing he loves," I guess.' 'I'll be all right,' she whispered. 'Oh, I know *that*,' he said loudly. 'You're strong and wise – too good for me.' He turned his head and looked around the room, as if in farewell to it. '"Like the base Indian threw a pearl away, richer than all his tribe",' he muttered into her neck. Polly was embarrassed. They heard Mr Schneider tune up his fiddle again. Gus kissed her and gently disengaged himself, holding her at arm's length, with his hands on her shoulders. 'I'll call you,' he said. 'Towards the end of the week. To see how you're doing. If you need anything, call me.' It came to her that he was going to leave without making love to her.

This would mean they had made love *for the last time* this morning. But that did not count: this morning they did not know it was for the last time. When the door shut behind him, she still could not believe it. 'It *can't* end like this,' she said to herself over and over, drumming with her knuckles on her mouth to keep from screaming. The fact that he had not made love to her became a proof that he would be back; he would remember and come back, like someone who has forgotten some important ceremony, some-one who has taken 'French leave'. When the church clock struck one, she knew he would not come; he would not disturb the house by ringing the bell so late. Yet she waited, thinking that he might throw pebbles at her window. She undressed and sat at the window in her kimono, watching the street. Towards morning she slept for an hour; then she went to work as usual, and her sufferings, as if punching a time clock, did not begin again until after five.

On the way home on the bus her mind automatically started to make a market list – bread, milk, lettuce – and then stopped with a jerk. She could not buy food just for herself. But if she did not buy food, this said that she knew Gus would not come tonight. And she did not know it; she refused to. To know it was to let fate see that she accepted it; if she accepted it, she could not live another minute. But if she bought food for two, this told fate that she was counting on his coming. And if she counted on it, he would never come. He would only come if she were unprepared. Or would he come only if she were prepared? With her lamp trimmed like the wise virgins? Christianity would tell her to buy food for two, but the pagans would say, 'Don't risk it.'

Getting off the bus, she stood in front of the A. & P. while other shoppers brushed past her; she was glued to the spot. It was as though this decision – to market or not to market – would settle her whole future. And she could not decide. She took a few steps down the street and turned back uncertainly. She read the weekly specials in the window; they had oxtails at a bargain, and Gus liked oxtail soup. If she made oxtail soup tonight, it would be ready for tomorrow. But what if he never came again? What would she do with the soup? Oxtail soup with sherry. She had sherry. Supposing she were to compromise and get eggs? If he did not come, they would do for breakfast. At the word 'breakfast' she let out a little cry; she had forgotten about the night. She read the specials again.

It occurred to her that there was something familiar about this panic of indecision, as if she had experienced it before, quite recently, and then she remembered. It was those cases she had read about in the hospital library – the anxiety patients who could not make up their minds about what to buy for dinner or which subway line to take to work. This was what it meant, then, to be a neurotic. To be a neurotic was to live, day in, day out, in a state of terror lest you decide the wrong thing. 'Oh, poor people!' she exclaimed aloud, and the pain of her own suffering turned into an agonized pity for those others who had to endure steadily something she had only experienced now for a few moments and which was already unendurable. A beggar came up to her, and again her will was paralysed. She wanted to give him money, the money she would have spent in the A. & P., but she remembered that Gus frowned on giving money to beggars, because charity, he said, helped perpetuate the capitalist system. If she disobeyed Gus's will, he would never come tonight. While her mind veered this way and that, the man went on down the street, shuffling. He had decided for her. But this thought made her act. She ran after him, opening her pocketbook, and stuffed two dollar bills into his hand. Then slowly she walked home. She had given the money freely, on a quick impulse, not as a bargain, and she did not expect any result from it.

Under her door was a letter for her. She picked it up, not daring to look at it, for she knew it would be from Gus. She took off her coat and hung it up, washed her hands, watered her plants, lit a cigarette. Then, trembling, she tore open the letter. Inside was a single sheet of paper, a short letter, in handwriting. She did not look directly at it yet but put it on the table, glancing at it sidewise, as if it could tell her what it said without making her read it. The letter was from her father.

Dear Polly:
   Your mother and I have decided to get a divorce. If it suits you, I would like to come to New York and live with you. That is, if you are not otherwise encumbered. I could make myself useful, do the shopping and cooking for you. We might look for a little flat together. Your mother will keep the farm. My mental health is excellent.
Your obedient servant and loving father,
Henry L. K. Andrews

Chapter 12

It was an ill wind that blew nobody good. Had Gus not decided to go back to Esther (and he did, the following week), Polly would have had to turn her father away. In fact, if the letter had arrived on Saturday, instead of Monday, she would have been in a terrible quandary. On Saturday there was still Gus. What *could* she have done? Probably she would have telephoned her mother and begged her to keep Mr Andrews on the farm – not to rush into a divorce. Or she might have suggested mental treatment. The irony of this was not lost on her from the very first minute. She took cold comfort from the thought that, thanks to Gus, she could wire her father to come ahead. On hearing the news, everyone took for granted that her parents' separation must have been a dreadful shock to her, but the sad truth was that all Polly felt then was a wan gratitude that her father was coming. It was with a start finally that she remembered her mother and wondered how she was taking it.

Long afterwards, Polly admitted that it had all worked out for the best. She was happy, living with her father, far happier than she had been with Gus. They suited each other. And his arrival, three days after his letter, was occupational therapy for her – just what a doctor would have prescribed.

Mr Andrews himself, when he got off the train, was in fine fettle – a small white-haired old man with a goblin head and bright blue eyes; he was carrying a case of fresh farm eggs, which he would not entrust to the redcap, and a bouquet of jonquils. He had not been so well in years, he declared, and Kate was well too, never better. He attributed it all to divorce – a splendid institution. Everyone should get a divorce. Kate already looked ten years younger. 'But won't it take a long time, Father?' said Polly. 'All the legal side. Even if Mother consents.' But Mr Andrews was sanguine. 'Kate's already filed the papers and served me. The process server came to tea. I've given her grounds, the best grounds there are.' Polly was slightly shocked at the notion that her father, at his age, had been committing adultery. But he meant insanity. He was delighted with himself for having had the foresight to be loony and to have the papers to prove it.

Low-spirited as she was during the first days, Polly was amused by her father. She was startled to hear herself laugh aloud the night he came; it was as if the sound had come from someone else. She told herself that she was going through the motions of living, now that she had someone to live for, but before long she found she was looking forward to coming home from work, wondering what they would have for dinner and what her father had been up to in her absence. He was immensely proud of the divorce and talked about it to everyone, as if it were some new process he had discovered, all by himself. For the time being, Polly had taken for him a room on the third floor; on week-ends, they were going to look for an apartment. But then Mr Andrews had a better idea. Having made friends with the landlady, he persuaded her to turn the top-floor rooms into an apartment for him and Polly – the lodger in the one that was rented could move downstairs to Polly's place. He designed the new apartment himself, using the hall to gain space and to make a little kitchen, long and narrow, like a ship's galley. All spring and early summer he and Polly were busy with the remodelling, which did not cost the landlady very much since Mr Andrews gave his services free, did some of the carpentry himself (he had learned at the workshop in the sanatorium), and found a secondhand sink and plumbing fixtures in the junk yards he haunted, looking for treasure. Polly learned to paint, well enough to do the bookshelves and cupboards; she sewed curtains from old sheets, with a blue and red border, the colours of the French flag, and she got to work with upholstery tacks and re-covered two of the landlady's Victorian chairs.

The apartment, when it was finished, was delightful, with its old marble fireplaces and inside shutters; if Mr Andrews and Polly were ever to leave it, the landlady could rent it for much more than she was charging them. Carried away with his success, Mr Andrews wanted to redo the whole house into apartments and make the landlady's fortune – a project Polly vetoed, thinking of Mr Schneider and Mr Scherbatyeff, who could not afford apartment rentals and would have had to move. Mr Andrews had to content himself with the plan of making Polly a little winter garden or greenhouse for her plants, outside the back windows, which had a southern exposure; he wanted this to be Polly's Christmas present and spent a good deal of his time at the glazier's.

The change in Mr Andrews amazed everyone who knew him. It could not be just the divorce, his sister Julia said, nor dear Polly's good heart and youthful spirits. Something else must have happened to Henry. It was Polly's mother who provided the information, during a visit she made to New York, where she stayed with her ex-sister-in-law on Park Avenue. 'They changed the name of his illness, did you know that, Polly? They don't call it melancholia any more. They call it manic-depressive psychosis. When Henry heard that, he felt as if he'd been cheated all these years. He'd only had the "depressed" phase, you see. He cheered up extraordinarily and began to make all these projects. Beginning with the crazy notion that we ought to get a divorce. At first I went along with it just to humour him. You know, the way I did when he insisted on being baptized into the Roman faith by the village curé and then baptized all you children himself. I knew those baptisms were otiose, since you'd all been christened as infants in the Episcopal church. Well, I assumed the divorce bug would pass, like the Romanism bug. But he got more and more set on it and on coming to New York. So I finally said to myself, "Why not? Henry may have a good idea, after all. At our time of life, there's no earthly reason to stay together if we don't feel like it." And I've been a new woman myself ever since.' Polly looked at her mother, pouring tea at Aunt Julia's table. It was true; she was blooming, like an expansive widow, and she had had a new permanent wave. 'Excuse me, madam,' said Ross, who was passing biscuits, 'but why couldn't you and Mr Henry just live apart, the way so many couples do?' 'Henry said that wouldn't be respectable,' replied Mrs Andrews. 'It would be like living together without marriage – living apart without a divorce.' 'I see,' said Ross. 'I never thought of it that way.' She gave Polly a wink. 'I can run the farm much better myself,' Mrs Andrews went on to Polly, lighting a cigarette and oblivious of Polly's blush. 'With just your brothers' help. Henry was always interfering, and he's never cared for domestic animals. He was only interested in his pot-herbs and his kitchen garden. Now that he's gone, we've bought some Black Angus and I'm going to try turkeys for the Thanksgiving market – I've been to see Charles & Company and they took an order. If Henry were there, he'd insist on Chinese pheasants or peacocks. And peacocks are such an unpleasant bird! Quarrelsome and shrill.'

'Do you mean that Father is in a "manic" state?' 'I suppose so, my dear,' Mrs Andrews answered comfortably. 'Let's only hope it lasts. He's not giving you any trouble, is he?' 'No,' said Polly, but the next day she had a talk with the second psychiatrist-in-charge at the Payne Whitney Clinic, whom she had known as a young resident. She often had to give metabolism tests to manic-depressive patients, but she had not known that her father's 'melancholia' – which she connected with *Il Penseroso* and with Dürer's engraving – was part of the same syndrome. In her experience, the manic patients were frequently under restraint, in straitjackets, and she was amazed at her mother's unconcern.

Yes, said the young doctor, Mr Andrews's behaviour did indeed reveal some of the typical manic symptoms, but in a mild form. It was possible that a trough of depression would follow, but, given the mildness of the manic elation, it need not be severe. At her father's age, the cycle often lengthened or abated altogether 'How old is he?' 'About sixty.' The doctor nodded. 'After the climacteric, many manic-depressive patients spontaneously recover.' Polly told him her mother's idea: that her father had changed his symptoms when he learned the new name of his disease. The doctor laughed. 'That isn't possible, is it?' said Polly. 'With these nuts anything is possible, Polly,' he declared. 'Insanity is a funny thing. We don't really understand anything about it. Why they get sick, why they get well. Changing the name may make a difference. We've noticed that now that we no longer speak of dementia praecox, we get fewer dementia-praecox patients. It tempts you to think sometimes that all mental illness has an hysterical origin, that they're all copying the latest text-books. Even the illiterate patients. Could your father be hysterical?' 'I don't think so,' said Polly. 'Though he used to cry a lot. But very quietly.' 'Would you like me to see him?' Polly hesitated; she was feeling greatly relieved, without knowing why. 'You might come for sherry some afternoon. Or for Sunday lunch, if you're off duty. Very informal. Father's a good cook and he loves to entertain.'

This was true. Polly's social life had become much more active since her father had been sharing an apartment with her. The chief problem was restraining his expenditures. He had discovered the new A. & P. self-service market and was an enthusiastic patron, confident that he was saving money with every purchase he made. He shopped in quantity, saying that it saved time; the big economy-size package appealed to him; he took advantage of 'special offers' and never missed a sale. He was also fond of the Italian fish and vegetable markets on lower Second Avenue, where he bought all manner of strange sea creatures and vegetables Polly had never seen before. Every Sunday at lunch they entertained, using chafing-dishes Aunt Julia had put away as old-fashioned, and the guests sometimes stayed the whole afternoon, playing games or listening to the phonograph. Polly now had great trouble finding time to do her laundry and wash her hair.

Shortly after his arrival, Mr Andrews had taken up ping-pong; as a young man, he had played tennis very well, and now he had found a bar on First Avenue with a long back room where there was a ping-pong table. Every day he played with the 'regulars' and on Saturday afternoons he would take part in tournaments, in which he insisted that Polly play too. In this way, she met a number of young men, some of whom would turn up for Sunday lunch or for her father's Friday-night bouillabaisse. The guests often brought a bottle of wine. When Mr Schneider came, he brought his violin. Or there would be a chess tournament, which Mr Scherbatyeff presided over. 'I hear you have a *salon*,' Libby said enviously on the telephone. 'Why don't you invite me? Kay says Norine Blake says you and your father are the *succès fou* of the year.

But the red-letter day in Mr Andrews's life was the day he became a Trotskyite. Not just a sympathizer, but an organizational Trotskyite! It was Mr Schneider, of course, who was responsible. Once the apartment was finished, Mr Andrews had time to kill while Polly was at the hospital, and behind her back Mr Schneider had been supplying him with reams of books and pamphlets about the Moscow trials. At first her father had found them heavy going; he had never taken much interest in politics, being a pessimist in the tradition of Henry Adams. But his attention was slowly fixed by the element of mystery in these trials – her father had a passion for puzzles, rebuses, mazes, conundrums. He concluded that Trotsky was innocent. The figure of the whiskered war commissar wearing a white uniform and riding in his armoured train or reading French novels during Politburo meetings captured his imagination. He demanded that Mr Schneider recruit him to the Trotskyite group. And unlike the village curé in France, who had required him to take instruction before being 'received', the Trotskyites, apparently, had accepted him as he was. He never understood the 'dialectic' and was lax in attendance at meetings, but he made up for this by the zeal with which, wearing a red necktie and an ancient pair of spats, he sold the *Socialist Appeal* on the street outside Stalinist rallies. He proselytized at Aunt Julia's tea table and at his ping-pong bar.

Polly was embarrassed by her father's behaviour; she felt that his style of dress and upper-class accent were giving the Trotsky-ites a bad name: the Stalinists would laugh at this 'typical convert' to the doctrine of permanent revolution. And just as Gus had not made a Stalinist of her, her father could not make her a Trotskyite. She felt that neither Mr Schneider nor her father would be so en-thusiastic about the Old Man, as they called him, if he were actually in power. She did not approve of revolutions, unless they were absolutely necessary, and she thought it peculiar, to say the least, that her father and his friends were eager to make revolutions in democratic countries like France and the United States instead of concentrating on Hitler and Mussolini, who *ought* to be over-thrown. Of course, as her father said, it was pretty hopeless to make a revolution against Hitler for the time being, since the wor-kers' parties had all been suppressed; still, it seemed rather unfair to penalize Roosevelt and Blum for not being Hitler. Fair play, replied her father, was a bourgeois concept and did not apply against the class enemy. Polly would have been horrified to hear her parent talk this way if she had thought he believed what he was saying. But she was sure that he did not, and furthermore the idea of his 'seizing power' made her smile, it was so unlikely. She won-dered whether the Trotskyites were not all a little touched. 'Do you belong to a cell, Father?' she asked him, but he would not say, claiming that he was under discipline. It struck her that becoming a Trotskyite had merely given him one more thing to be snobbish about. He now looked down his nose at Stalinists, progressives, and New Dealers, as well as on the middle class and the 'moneyed elements', whom he had always derided. Some of his worst prejudices, she told him, scolding, were being reinforced by his new adherence. For example, coming from Massachusetts, he had a plaintive aversion to the Irish, and he was elated to hear that Marx had called the Irish the bribed tools of imperialism. 'Look at that bribed tool of imperialism!' he would whisper, of the poor policeman on the beat.

Eventually, of course, he learned about Gus ('That Stalinist', he called him) from Mr Schneider or Mr Scherbatyeff or the landlady – Polly never knew exactly. The people in the house believed that Polly had sent Gus away when she knew her father was coming, but Polly was too honest to let Mr Andrews think that she had sacrificed love to family duty, and one night she told him the true story. The fact that Gus had been unequal to getting a divorce increased Mr Andrews's contempt for him. 'Are you still pining for that Stalinist publisher?' he asked, if Polly was quiet.

Polly no longer pined, but she felt that her fate was sealed the night she got her father's letter. Fate had sent her father as a sign that it would be kind to her so long as she did not think of men or marriage. Gus had called her, as he promised, at the end of that first week; when the buzzer had rung, her father had gone to the telephone. 'A man wants to talk to you,' he reported, and Polly, feeling weak, went to the phone on the landing. 'Who was that?' said Gus. 'That was my father,' said Polly. 'He's come to stay with me.' There was a long silence. 'Does he know?' said Gus. 'No.' 'Oh, good. Then I guess I'd better stay away.' Polly said nothing. 'I'll call you again next week,' he said. He called, to say that he was moving back to his apartment. 'Is your father still there?' 'Yes.' 'I'd like to meet him some time.' 'Yes,' said Polly. 'Later.' After he had hung up, she remembered that she ought to have asked him if he had 'unblocked'.

Once he had moved, she lost hope of running into him on the street some morning or evening; his own apartment was on the other side of town, in Greenwich Village. Yet she wondered about this hope, for she remembered, quite clearly, the thrill of fear that had gone through her when her father had called her to the telephone. *She had been afraid that Gus would tell her he wanted her back.*

If he had, what would she have done? At the same time, paradoxically, she still felt their love affair had not quite finished: it lived somewhere underground, between them, growing in the dark as people's hair and fingernails grew after their death. She was sure she would meet him again somewhere, some day. This presentiment too was tainted with dread.

When her father became a Trotskyite, he took a defiant pleasure in the thought that the two might meet – on opposite sides of a picket line. And her father's side would be the *right* side. She imagined her father trying to sell him a copy of the *Socialist Appeal* outside some rally for Spain. Gus would shake his head brusquely, and he would be *wrong* because he was afraid to read what the other side said, and Mr Schneider was not afraid to read the *Daily Worker* from cover to cover every day. If it came to the picket lines, she was a Trotskyite too.

But when the two did meet, it was not in the political arena. It was in the ping-pong bar one Saturday afternoon. Polly, luckily, had stayed home to listen to the Metropolitan Opera on the radio. 'I met that Stalinist,' Mr Andrews said, coming home with a shopping-basket full of groceries. 'LeRoy. Beat him two sets out of three.' Polly was pleased; she would have hated it if Gus had beaten her father. 'What was he doing there?' 'He came in with a chap called Jacoby, another Stalinist. A book designer. Your friend has taken up ping-pong to lose weight, he says. They're probably infiltrating that bar.' 'How did you know he was he?' said Polly. 'I didn't. He knew I was I.' He laughed gently. 'I'm well known there. Eccentric Henry Andrews. Decayed gentleman. Used to play tennis with Borotra. Now lives with his beautiful daughter, Polly, on East Tenth Street. Trotskyist agent and saboteur.' 'Oh, Father!' said Polly impatiently. 'You think they came there because of you?' 'Of course.' 'Did you talk about politics?' 'No, we talked about you.' 'You didn't—?' Mr Andrews shook his head. '*He* brought you up. He asked if I had a daughter Polly. Then a great many other tiresome questions. How were you? What were you doing? Did you still have the same job? Were you still living in the same place? I told him your mother and I were divorced.' 'What did he say?' 'That it must have been a shock for you.' 'What did you think of him?' 'Ordinary,' said Mr Andrews. 'Sadly ordinary. A dull dog. Not a bad fellow, though,

Polly. He took losing well, at any rate. I think he was in love with you. That makes him worse, of course. If he dropped you because he was tired of you or wasn't really attracted, I could sympathize. But this poor chap is a dangerous neurotic.'

Polly laughed. 'So you saw that, Father. I never could. He always seemed so normal.' 'It's the same thing,' said her father, putting the groceries away. 'All neurotics are petty bourgeois. And vice versa. Madness is too revolutionary for them. They can't go the whole hog. We madmen are the aristocrats of mental illness. You could never marry that fellow, my dear. He probably knew that himself.'

'I can never marry,' said Polly. 'Nonsense,' said Mr Andrews. 'I intend to find you a husband. For purely selfish reasons. I need a son-in-law to support me in my old age. I don't want to crawl back to Kate.' 'You'll stay with me. I'll take care of you.' 'No, thank you, my dear. I don't want to be the companion of an embittered old maid.' Polly was hurt. 'If you sacrifice your youth to me, you'll be embittered,' said Mr Andrews. 'Or you ought to be. But if I find you a nice husband, you'll be grateful. Both of you. You'll keep a spare room for me and take me as a tax deduction.'

Polly bit her lip. When her father used the word 'selfish', he was speaking the truth. He was selfish; both her parents were selfish. Loving him, she did not mind. Selfish people, she felt, were more fun to be with than unselfish people. If her father had been mild and self-effacing, she would have hated living with him. Instead, he was mild and self-willed. He liked contriving little surprises for her and doing her little courtesies, but it was he who planned their life, like a child playing house. He was hard to circumvent, once he had an idea in his head, and he was quite capable of gently forcing her to marry to provide a home for his old age. And in fact he had a point; she did not know how else she would be able to support him. She could not give him back to her mother – the divorce had taken care of that. It was not that she felt 'saddled' with him; only she did not see how her salary would keep both of them in the style her father liked or how she would ever earn a great deal more than she did. Her mother helped by sending eggs and poultry from the farm – 'my alimony payments', her father called them. Aunt Julia helped; she had given them bed linen and blankets and, as usual, she gave Polly clothes, which Polly and Ross fixed over. But with her father on the scene, Polly had less time for dressmaking and moreover she needed more dresses; if people were coming, he would not let her appear in just a blouse and skirt — 'Put on something pretty,' he would say. That he was thinking of her and not of himself made his thoughtlessness harder to bear.

It was the same with the household money. Every week Polly gave him an allowance, and every week he overspent it and had to ask her for more. And again it was not for himself, but for treats for her and their friends. Knowing him, as the autumn days passed Polly grew afraid of Christmas. She had decreed that all their presents had to be homemade, and by that she meant little things like penwipers. During her vacation, on the farm, she had made jellies out of crabapples and mint and thyme and rosemary, which she intended as presents for their friends and relations, and she was going to make her pomander balls again; at work, she was knitting a muffler for her father and for her mother she had brought a length of cerise jersey, on which she was sewing bows of coloured velvet ribbon for an evening scarf — she had got the idea from *Vogue*. But to her father 'homemade' meant that greenhouse, which he declared he was going to putty together with his own hands; he claimed at first that the sun would heat it, but lately he had been deep in conference with a plumber about how to maintain a temperature of fifty degrees, night and day. And of course he justified it all as an economy: Polly would have flowering plants from cuttings all winter long for the house, and they could force hyacinths and crocuses for Easter to give their friends. In the long run, it would 'pay for itself', an expression he had grown attached to.

Polly did not want that greenhouse, much as she loved flowers, any more than her mother would have wanted peacocks, and she was trying to divert his inventive powers to making simply some glass shelves that he could run across the window like a plant cupboard. Her father said that was a commonplace of modern design, and in the end, Polly supposed, she would have to ask the landlady to put her foot down. She hated to go behind her father's back, but that was what young Dr Ridgeley said she must do when it came to money matters.

They had talked again about her father, after Jim Ridgeley had come to lunch one Sunday, and he had asked her, straight off, whether Mr Andrews had become very openhanded lately. This, it seemed, was one of the signs of the onset of a manic attack. It would be wise, he suggested, to close her charge accounts and to warn tradespeople against giving her father credit. Polly did not have any charge accounts – only a DA at Macy's, and besides, she felt Jim Ridgeley was looking at her father too clinically. He did not understand that a person who had had an independent income for most of his life could not grasp, really, what being poor meant. Polly grasped it, because she was 'a child of the depression', but her father still felt that prosperity was just around the corner. That was why, to him, the 'economies' he made were a kind of play – an adventure, like when the power failed in the country and you used candles and oil lamps and drew your water from the well. Her father, in financial matters, always expected the power to come on again. This was a delusion, but a delusion shared by many people, including, Polly noted, quite a few of her class-mates.

As for the delusion that spending was saving, this too, Polly observed, was quite widespread; all the advertisements tried to make you feel that. Many people too, as they grew older, became obsessed, like her father, with bargains. No matter how much money they had. Aunt Julia had reached that stage and was always buying useless articles because she had seen them at a sale. Every January, for example, she 'replenished' her linen closet at the white sales, even though the sheets and towels and pillow cases she had bought the previous January had never been used. Yet Aunt Julia was perfectly sane.

Except for a big item like the greenhouse, Polly excused her father. It was not his fault that two could not live as cheaply as one. Their problem, she decided, was to find another source of income. Last week, she had gone to the Morris Plan and borrowed some money on her salary, and the experience had frightened her. She felt as if she were taking the first step downward into vice or ruin. The interest rate shocked her and confirmed her instinct that there was something actually immoral about the transaction – a kind of blackmail; the interest, she sensed, was hush money. No questions asked. And in fact it was to avoid questions that she had gone to the Morris Plan people, whose ad she had seen on the bus. She could have asked Aunt Julia, but Aunt Julia would have exacted 'a serious talk' from her, wanted to see her budget – where was the money going – and would at once have started blaming her father. And supposing his carelessness about money *were* a part of his illness, he ought not to be reproached for it, Polly felt – only protected. She did not mention the loan to him.

But how was she going to pay it back? To pay it back, they would have to spend even less than they had been doing, but the reason for the loan was that already they were spending more than their income. Aunt Julia's Christmas cheque would not make up the difference. There were so many little things that added up: when they had calculated the rent on the apartment, they had forgotten that, with an apartment, they would have to pay the gas and electricity too.

Polly had been casting about in her mind for ways of supplementing her pay. She thought of needlework or of marketing her herbal jellies and pomander balls through the Woman's Exchange. She and her father could make plum puddings or fruit cakes. But when she figured out one day at lunch the profit on a jar of rosemary jelly that would retail, say, at twenty cents a jar, she saw that with the cost of the jars, the sugar, the labels, and the shipping, she would have to make five hundred jars to earn $25, and this on the assumption that the fruit and herbs and cooking gas were free. She tried the pomander balls. What could they retail for? Fifty cents? That was too high, but it took her an evening to make six of them, and there was the cost of the oranges and the orris root and the cloves and the ribbons, not to mention the sore thumb she got from pushing in the cloves. It would be the same with needlework. For the first time, she understood the charms of mass production. Her conclusion was that it was idle to think that a person could make money by using her hands in her spare time: you would have to be an invalid or blind to show a profit. She had a vision of herself and her father, both blind or bedridden, supported by a charity, happily weaving baskets and embroidering tablecloths. Useful members of society.

For weeks she had been preoccupied with money-making schemes. She sent in solutions to the contests in the *Evening Post*. She asked her father whether he would like to dictate a cookbook to her, giving his favourite French receipts; Libby could market it for them. But the notion of sharing his receipts did not appeal to her father, and he did not like Libby. She wondered whether, if someone gave them the capital, she and her father could open a small restaurant. Or whether she could make a cucumber skin cream and sell the formula to Elizabeth Arden. She glanced through the alumnae notes of the Vassar magazine for inspiration, but most alumnae described themselves as happy with their 'volunteer work' or heading a Girl Scout group; a few were doing part-time teaching, one was a cowgirl, and one was walking dogs. It occurred to her that her father might be called to do jury duty, which made her smile; he would be such an unusual juror. This led to the picture of him as a professional mourner – but did they have them in America? – or a member of an opera claque. He could sit in the evenings with children, for he was a very good storyteller: why had no one thought of that as an occupation? She could quit her job, and he and she could hire out as cook and chambermaid.

These visions, Polly recognized, were all utopian, when not simply humorous. But when she tried to think more practically, she was appalled by the images that crept into her mind. Just now, on this Saturday afternoon, when her father had been talking to her about marriage, a picture of Aunt Julia's will appeared before her. They were gathered together, the relations, in Aunt Julia's library, the corpse was in the drawing-room, and the lawyer was reading her will to them: Henry Andrews was the chief beneficiary.

'I wouldn't count on Julia,' her father said quietly. Polly jumped. He had this uncanny faculty – which Polly had observed in some of the mental patients in the hospital – of sitting there silently, reading your thoughts. 'Julia,' her father went on, 'is a queer one. She's likely to leave everything she's got to a charity. With a pension to Ross. The Animal Rescue League. Or the Salvation Army. To be used for Santa Claus uniforms.' He gave his plaintive laugh. 'In my opinion, Julia is senile.' Polly knew what her father was thinking of. His sister had always been a temperance woman, because of the history of alcoholism in the family; her uncles and all her brothers, except Henry, had succumbed to the malady. But until recent years she had served wine at her dinners, even during Prohibition, though she herself drank only ginger ale. The law, she said, did not extend to a gentleman's private cellar. But since repeal, illustrating the Andrews' perversity, she had banned wine from her table and served ginger ale, cider, grape juice, and various health drinks described by her brother as nauseous; he insisted that he had been served coconut milk. 'Throughout the meal.' Her latest crime, however, was more serious. She had emptied the contents of her husband's cellar down the sink in the butler's pantry. 'I might have sold it,' she said. 'I had the man from Lehmann appraise the contents. It would have brought me a pretty penny. But my conscience forbade it. To have sold it would have been trafficking in death. Like these munitions-makers you read about – profiteers.' 'You could have given it to me,' said Henry. 'It wouldn't be good for you, Henry. And anyway you have no place to keep it. You know yourself that fine wines deteriorate if kept in improper conditions.' In fact, Ross had saved a number of bottles of Mr Andrews's favourite claret and brought them down to Tenth Street, but Mr Andrews was incensed. 'It was typical of Julia,' he said now, 'to have the cellar appraised before scuttling it. I wouldn't be surprised to learn that she had several different appraisers in. To enter her virtue in the ledger at the highest bid. It will be the same with her will. There'll be a long preamble explaining what she intended originally to leave to her survivors and explaining that she finally decided that it would not be good for them to have it. "My husband's money brought me a great deal of unhappiness. I do not wish to transmit this unhappiness to others."'

Polly smiled. She hoped her father was right, for if he was, she would be able to forget about Aunt Julia's will. Counting on it was close to wishing for her death. Not that Polly had done that, but she feared she might if things got very bad. Or even if she did not, it was still wrong to see the *good side* of the loss of a relation.

'No,' said her father. 'I must find you a husband. Invest my hopes in grandchildren – not in the death of an old woman. Though I still trust that I can get her to leave a small legacy to the Trotsky-ites.' 'You're crazy,' said Polly, laughing. 'You can't seem to get it through your head that Aunt Julia's a Republican.' 'I know that, my dear,' said Mr Andrews. 'But Julia has been convinced by what she reads in the papers that we Trotskyites are counter-revolution-ary agents bent on destroying the Soviet Union. Walter Duranty and those fellows, you know, have made her believe in the trials. If what they write wasn't true, she says, it wouldn't be in the New York *Times*, would it? And of course I've added my bit. The Trotskyites, I've assured her, are the only effective force fighting Stalin. Roosevelt is playing right into his hands. And Hitler has his own axe to grind.' 'You're a crook, Father,' said Polly, kissing him. 'Not at all,' said her father. 'It's true. And I've saved Julia from being a fascist.'

This conversation, by entertaining her, made Polly forget her worries for the moment. That was the trouble with her father. When she was with him, she could not remember to worry. And when she did remember, it was with a start of fear at the thought that she could have forgotten. At night she had terrible dreams about money, from which she would awake sweating. Once she dreamed that Christmas had come and the whole apartment had turned into a greenhouse as big as the Crystal Palace because she had forgotten to tell the landlady to countermand it. Another night she thought that she and her father had become nudists because he said they would economize that way on clothes, and an Irish policeman arrested them. But at the hospital one day she found a solution to their troubles. It was a solution she had never thought of because, like the purloined letter, it was staring her right in the face. She was taking blood for a transfusion from a professional donor, and the thought popped into her mind: 'Why not I?' That week she sold a pint of her blood to the laboratory. The next week she did it again and the week after. She knew it was not dangerous; professional donors did it all the time, and the internes sometimes did it. Besides, she was unusually healthy and well nourished this year because her father was an excellent dietitian – she was bursting with iron and vitamins, and if she looked anaemic, it was only that she was naturally pale. Yet she told herself that it would be wiser, in the future, to make her donations at Bellevue or at another laboratory, where nobody knew her, so as not to cause talk among her colleagues. The next time, though, she was in a hurry, for it was the week before Christmas and she had used her lunch hour to buy candy canes and paper to make chains for Christmas-tree decorations – her mother had sent them a tree from the farm. So she went to her own laboratory as usual, saying that this would be the last time.

That day, as luck would have it, she was discovered by Dr Ridgeley, who had come in to look at a patient's blood sample. 'What are you doing?' he wanted to know, though he could see quite clearly from the apparatus, which still hung beside the couch where she was resting, as you were made to do after giving blood. 'Christmas money,' said Polly, smiling nervously and letting her clenched fist relax. His eyes got quite big and he turned and went out of the room. In a minute, he came back. He had been consulting the records. 'This is your fourth donation, Polly,' he said sharply. 'What's the trouble?' 'Christmas,' she repeated. But he thought it was her father. 'Did you do what I told you?' he said. 'Shut down your charge accounts? See that he doesn't get credit?' 'I don't have any charge accounts. He doesn't use credit.'

'That you know of,' said Dr Ridgeley. 'Look here, Polly. Allow me to put two and two together. If I see a manic patient and meet a member of his family selling her blood in a laboratory, I conclude that he's been on a spending spree,' 'No,' said Polly. 'We're just short of money over the holidays.' She got up. 'Sit down,' he said. 'Your father, my dear girl, is severely ill. Someone ought to see that he gets treatment.' 'Goes to the hospital, you mean? No, Dr Ridgeley.' She refused to call him 'Jim' now. 'He's sane, I swear to you. His mind is completely clear. He's just a little bit eccentric.' 'These spending sprees, I told you,' he said impatiently, 'are symptomatic. They indicate that the patient is way up on the manic curve. The next stage is often an outbreak of violence, with megalomania. Commonly with a sense of mission. Is your father interested in politics?'

Polly paled; she was dizzy, which she tried to attribute to blood loss. 'Everyone is interested in politics,' she muttered. 'I'm not,' said Jim Ridgeley. 'But I mean, does he have some special angle? Some pet formula to save the world? A discovery he's made in recent months?' To Polly, this was magic. 'He's a Trotskyite,' she whispered 'What's that?' he said. 'Oh, don't be so ignorant ' cried Polly. 'Trotsky. Leon Trotsky. One of the makers of the Russian Revolution. Commander of the Red Army. Stalin's archenemy. In exile in Mexico.' 'I've heard of him, sure,' said Jim Ridgeley. 'Didn't he used to be a pants-presser in Brooklyn?' 'No!' cried Polly. 'That's a legend!' A great gulf had opened between her and this young man, and she felt she was screaming across it. In fairness, she tried to remember that a year ago she too had probably thought that Trotsky had pressed pants in Brooklyn; a year ago, she had been almost as ignorant as this doctor. But this only made her realize how far she had travelled from her starting-point, the normal educated centre, where Jim

Ridgeley doggedly stood in his white coat and which now seemed to her subnormal and uneducated. Yet he had guessed her father was a Trotskyite without even knowing what one was. She begun explaining to him that the Trotskyites were the only true Communists and that, right now, they were in the Socialist Party. 'You've heard of Norman Thomas, I hope.' 'Sure thing,' replied the doctor. 'He ran for President. I voted for him myself in '32.' 'Well,' said Polly, relieved, 'the Trotskyites are part of his movement.' As she spoke, she was aware of a slight dishonesty. The Trotskyites, she knew from her father, had entered the Socialist Party 'as a tactic'; they were not really Socialists like Norman Thomas at all.

He sat down on the leather couch beside her. 'Be that as it may,' he said, a phrase Polly disliked, 'they're a small sect with a mission. Is that right?' 'In a way,' said Polly. 'They believe in permanent revolution.' And in spite of herself, she smiled. The doctor nodded. 'In other words, you think they're nuts.' She tried to be honest. Forgetting about her father, did she think Mr Schneider was a nut? 'On many points, I think they're right. But on that one point – permanent revolution – I can't help feeling that they're a bit out of touch with reality. But that's just my idea. I may lack vision.' He smiled at her quizzingly. 'You have wonderful eyes,' he said. He leaned forward. For a startled moment, she thought he was going to kiss her. Then he jumped to his feet.

'Polly, you ought to commit your father.' 'Never.' He leaned down and took her hand. 'Maybe I feel strongly because I'm falling in love with you,' he said. Polly pulled her hand away. She was not as surprised as she ought to have been. In the back of her mind, she feared, she had been angling to make Dr Ridgeley fall in love with her. That was why she had consulted him about her father! Just like other women, she had had her eye on him, having guessed that he liked her quite a bit. Sensing nothing but that about him, she had 'thrown herself in his way'. But now that she had heard what she had been hoping to hear, she was scared. He sounded like the hero of a woman's magazine story. The idea that she had probably been using her poor father as a pawn to lure this young man forward made her smile disgustedly at herself. At the same time, inside her, an exultant voice was crowing 'He loves me!' But another voice said who was Jim Ridgeley after all, what did she know about him? She stared at him coldly. 'If you won't do it,' he said in a different tone, 'your mother should.' 'She can't,' Polly answered triumphantly. 'You forget. They're divorced.' 'Then the nearest of kin.' 'His sister,' said Polly. 'My Aunt Julia.' He nodded. 'She's senile,' said Polly, in that same tone of childish triumph. She did not know what had got into her, some mischievous demon that was prompting her to lie. 'And your brothers?' 'They'd never do it. Any more than I would. You'll have to give up, Dr Ridgeley.' 'Stop playing,' he said. 'It's a dangerous game.' '*My father is not dangerous*,' said Polly. 'You leave him alone.' 'He's dangerous to you now,' he said gently. 'You shouldn't be giving your life blood for him.' 'I suppose you think I have a father complex,' she answered coldly. He shook his head. 'I'm not a Freudian. You feel protective towards him. As if he were your child. This may be because you haven't yet had any children.'

Suddenly Polly began to cry. He put his arms around her, and she pressed her wet cheek against his stiff white coat. She felt completely disconsolate. Nothing lasted. First, Gus, and then on top of that, father. She had been so happy with him and she would be still, if only they had some money or if he were just a *little* different. But it was true, he was like a child who could never change, and gradually she had got to know that, just as gradually she had got to know that Gus would never marry her. But she ought to have faced facts in both cases from the beginning. She had welcomed her father because she needed him and had deliberately not noticed his frailties, just as she had done with Gus. And with her father, there was probably a little element of trying to be superior to her mother: *she* could make him happy, if her mother couldn't. This meant she had given in to him, where her mother had had the strength not to. They should *never* have taken the apartment, her mother could have told her that; that was the beginning of the *folie de grandeur*. She could not control her father; she was inert. The same with Gus. If she had given him a strong lead, he would have married her. Now she was glad she hadn't, but no credit was due her. She had just let things follow their natural course, and the ordinary streak had come out in him. Which her father had seen right away, just as everyone else, apparently, could see her father's loony streak.

'I had an *awful* love affair,' she said, still weeping. 'The man threw me over. I wanted to die, and then my father came. I thought finally I had a purpose in life, that I could take care of him. And now I can't seem to do it. It's not his fault; I just don't earn enough for the two of us. And I can't ship him back to my mother. And I won't put him in an asylum. He really and truly isn't certifiable. You said yourself he might "spontaneously recover". Of course, I could go to my aunt. I guess that's what I'd better do.'

'Go to your aunt?' 'Ask her for money. She isn't senile. That was a lie. And she's very rich, or used to be – nobody really knows how much she has left. But you know how funny rich people are about money.' 'That might solve your problem temporarily,' he said, sounding like a psychiatrist. 'But you must face the fact that your father may get worse. What will you do with him when you marry, Polly?' 'I can't marry,' she said. 'You know that. At least, I can't have children, with my heredity. I've come to terms with that finally. It would be selfish to have children – wicked.'

'Was it wicked to have you?' he said smiling. Polly rushed to her parents' defence. 'They didn't know, then, about my father's melancholia. That happened later.' He still smiled, and Polly saw the point. Would she wish not to have been born? Unhappy as she was, she could not say that. Even when she had wished to die, she had not wished never to have been alive. Nobody alive could do that. 'What strange set ideas you have!' he said. 'And you a medical technician. It isn't as if you had a family history of idiocy. Or hereditary syphilis.' 'I always thought,' said Polly, 'that from a scientific point of view I ought to be sterilized.' 'Good God!' he replied. 'What bunkum! Where did you learn that?' 'At college,' said Polly. 'I don't mean the professors taught it in class, but it was sort of in the atmosphere. Eugenics. That certain people ought to be prevented from breeding. Not Vassar women of course' – she smiled – 'but the others. I always felt like one of the others. There was a lot of inbreeding in my family – people marrying their cousins. The Andrews' blood has run thin.' '"The blood of the Andrews",' he said, glancing at Polly's arm, where a pad of cotton still lay at the point the vein had been opened. 'How dare you be a blood donor? You ought to be exposed.' He laughed heartily. 'I'll prove to you that I have confidence in the blood of the Andrews. Will you marry me?' Polly feared this was a line he used with all the young nurses and technicians, and yet if he asked them all to marry him, how did he edge out of it afterwards? He was quite good-looking, tall and curly-haired, and that in itself suddenly made her suspicious. In real life, it was only homely men who fell in love with a bang and did not leave you to guess about their intentions. 'Are you always such a "fast worker"?' she heard herself say in the teasing tone she took with her father in his wilful moments. 'No,' he said. 'I've never been in love before. I'm thirty-one years old. And I don't want to waste time.' Polly's misgivings lessened. Perhaps he had been too busy working to fall in love till now. But she laughed gently. '"Waste time",' she chided. 'How long do you imagine you've been in love with me?' He looked at his watch. 'About half an hour,' he said in a matter-of-fact voice. 'But I've always liked you. I picked you out when you first came to the hospital.' So she had been right, Polly said to herself. Her confidence increased. But she was frightened now in a new way. He was different from Gus, straightforward, and she liked that, yet she found herself wanting to parry his onslaught. He was all too ready to commit himself, which meant he was committing *her*. 'But we have nothing in common,' she started to object, but this sounded rude. Instead she said, 'Even if I were to marry, I could never marry a psychiatrist.' To her surprise, she discovered she meant this, from the bottom of her heart. Looking for what was wrong with Jim Ridgeley, she had found it, alas. A psychiatrist would have a desk side far more wooden, even, than Gus's. 'Good,' Jim Ridgeley said promptly. 'I'm going to get out. It was a mistake I made in medical school. I thought it was a science. It ain't. I'm leaving here the first of the year.' 'But what will you do then?' said Polly, thinking that if he left at the first of the year, she would miss him. 'General medicine? But you'd have to start all over again, with your internship.' 'No. Research. There are discoveries to be made in treating mental illness, but they won't be made in the consulting-room. They'll come from the laboratory. Brain chemistry. I have a job lined up with a research team; I share an apartment with one of them. You can work with us too – as a technician. There's no future for you here.' 'I know that,' said Polly. 'But what attracts you about mental illness, Jim?' 'The waste,' he said promptly. 'Of human resources. I'm impatient.' 'I can *see* that,' she murmured. 'Then I suppose I have a bit of the do-gooder in me. Came by it naturally. My father's a minister. Presbyterian.' 'Oh?' This news was pleasing to Polly; it would be nice, she reflected, to have a minister in the family. 'If you like, he can marry us. Or we can go down to City Hall.'

The more serious he sounded, the more Polly tried to joke. 'And what about *my* father?' she said lightly. 'You can use him as a guinea-pig, I suppose. To test your brilliant discoveries on. He could be my dowry.' He frowned. 'He can live with us and keep house,' he said shortly. 'Do you mean that?' 'I wouldn't say it otherwise,' he replied. 'And after we're married, I can keep an eye on him. To tell the truth, Polly, I think most of our patients would be better off at home. It's a mistake to isolate them in hospitals. The Victorian system was better, with mad Auntie upstairs. More human. The fault lies mostly with the families. They want to get their mad relation out of the house and into what's known as "the hands of competent professionals". I.e., sadistic nurses and orderlies. The same with old people; nobody wants old people around any more.' 'Oh, I agree!' exclaimed Polly. 'I like old people. It's awful the way they're junked, like old cars. But if that's the way you think, why did you say he should be committed?' He hesitated. 'The old difference between theory and practice. I didn't like the idea of your being alone with him.' '*He's not dangerous*,' repeated Polly. 'They would never have sent him home from Riggs if he were dangerous.' 'Nonsense,' he said. 'Most homicidal lunatics who go berserk and murder ten people are found to have been just released from a mental hospital. Your father was let out of Riggs because you had no money to keep him there. If you had, he might be there still.' 'You're very cynical,' said Polly. 'You get that way in psychiatry,' he answered. 'That's why I'm getting out of it. If you stay, you have your choice of becoming a cynic or a naïve fraud. But let's grant that your father isn't dangerous; you probably know more about it than a doctor. He may still be dangerous to himself. If he dips into a depressed phase. He was suicidal at one time, wasn't he?' 'I'm not sure. He talked about it, and Mother was afraid.' 'Well.' He looked at her; his eyes were a light brown, with green flecks. 'Maybe,' he said, 'I told you to commit him partly to see what you'd say.' 'Oh!' exclaimed Polly. 'You were testing me! Like a fairy tale.' She was disillusioned. 'Maybe,' he repeated. 'It's a habit you fall into as a doctor. Watching for the reflexes. But I already knew what you'd answer. I knew you'd say no. I think what I wanted to see was whether I could scare you.' 'You did,' said Polly. 'No, I didn't. Not fundamentally. Nothing could persuade you to distrust your father. You're not a distrustful girl.' 'Oh, but I am!' said Polly, thinking of how she had been with Gus. 'I *know* my father, that's all.'

Polly found she had agreed to marry Jim without ever being aware of saying Yes. That night they had dinner and danced, and he took her home. They kissed a long time in his car in front of her apartment. When she went upstairs, finally, she still did not know whether she loved him or not. It had all happened too quickly. But she was relieved that she was going to marry him, and she wondered whether this was immoral. In the old days, people used to say that gratitude could turn to love – could that be true? She had liked kissing him, but that might be just sex. Sex, Polly had concluded, was not a reliable test of love. What bothered her most was the thought that she and Jim had so little in common – a phrase she kept repeating anxiously to herself. Outside the hospital, they had not a single common acquaintance. And as for those old friends, the characters in books – King Arthur and Sir Lancelot and Mr Micawber and Mr Collins and Vronsky and darling Prince Andrei, who were like members of the family – why, Jim seemed hardly to recall them. When she mentioned Dr Lydgate tonight, he confessed he had never read *Middlemarch* – only *Silas Marner* in school, which he hated. He could not read novels, he said, and he had no preference between Hector and Achilles. At least they both knew the Bible and they both had been science majors, but was that enough? He was more intelligent than she was, but he had not had a Vassar education. And she was insular, like all the Andrews. Why else would they have kept marrying their cousins if not to share the same jokes, the same memories, the same grandparents or great-grandparents even? What would Jim talk about with her brothers, who were only interested in farming now and either discussed feeds and beef-cattle prices or swapped lines from Virgil's *Georgics*, the way other bumpkins swapped dirty stories? They would have bored Polly stiff if she had not known them all her life. And then there were all the old cousins and second cousins who would come out of their holes for her wedding at the smell of champagne. Not that she would have champagne; Aunt Julia's greatest 'sacrifice' had been dumping the champagne she had been saving for Polly's wedding. What would a psychiatrist make of the whole Andrews clan? Polly's mother still described *her* feelings on meeting them as a young bride from New York. Like Queen Victoria, she had not been amused. Over the years she had grown to be like them herself, though without knowing it. 'Your father and I,' she now said, 'have never been compatible. I was too normal for Henry.' But no one would guess that, seeing her on the farm dressed in overalls with a finger wave in her majestic coiffure. These thoughts had never troubled Polly when she had dreamed of marriage with Gus, which proved, perhaps, she decided, that she had never believed in that marriage. This time, she was trying to be realistic.

When she came in, her father, who was a night owl, was still awake. She felt sure he would notice the change in her, though she had combed her hair and put on lipstick in the car, and she was reluctant to confess to him that she had got engaged in a single night. Luckily, his mind was elsewhere. He had been waiting for her to come home to tell her, as he said, an important piece of news. 'He's going to get married,' she exclaimed to herself. But no; he had got a job. In a thrift shop on Lexington Avenue, where he was going to be assistant to the manageress, who ran it for a charity. The pay was not much, but he had only to sit in the shop afternoons and talk to customers; he would have his mornings to himself.

'Why, that's wonderful, Father!' said Polly. 'How did you ever get it?' 'Julia arranged it,' he said. 'Julia's on the board. The position's usually kept for "reduced gentlewomen", but she lobbied me through. I believe I'm being exchanged for a club membership. "Henry knows wood" was her slogan.' 'That's wonderful,' Polly repeated. 'When do you start?' 'Tomorrow. This afternoon the manageress explained my duties to me and itemized the stock. A preponderance of white elephants. The stuff is all donated. "The Antimacassar", it's called. I advised them to change the name to "The Dust Catcher".' 'Is it all bric-à-brac?' said Polly. 'By no means. We have second-hand furs, children's clothes, old dinner jackets, maids' and butlers' uniforms. A great many of those, thanks to the late unpleasantness.' This was his name for the depression. Polly frowned; she did not like the thought of her father selling old clothes. 'They come from the best houses,' he said. 'And there are amusing French dolls and music boxes. Armoires, *étagères*, jardinières. Whatnots, umbrella stands, marble-topped commodes. Gilt chairs for musicales. Gold-headed canes, fawn gloves, opera hats, fans, Spanish combs, mantillas, a harp. Horsehair sofas. An instructive inventory of the passé.'

'But what made Aunt Julia think of finding you a job?' 'I asked her for money. This spurred her to find work for me so that, as she nicely phrased it, I "would not have to beg". Had I asked her to look out for a job for me, she would have told me I was too old.' 'Was this one of your deep-laid plots?' 'Quite the reverse. It was unintentional. But now that it's happened, I find myself pleased to be a bread winner. For the first time in my life. I've joined the working class. And of course Julia plans to exploit me.' 'How?' 'Well, "Henry knows wood". I'm to keep a sharp eye out in the event that a bit of Sheraton or Hepplewhite pops in from an attic. Then I'm to set it aside for her quietly.' 'You can't do that!' said Polly firmly. 'That would be cheating the charity.' 'Exactly my sister's design. As she confided in me, "Some of our younger members have no notion of the value of old furniture." Through another of her charities, she says, she picked up a rare Aubusson for a song.' Polly made a shocked noise. 'But where is it?' Mr Andrews laughed. 'In her storeroom. She's waiting for its former owner to die. It might be embarrassing for Julia if the lady dropped in to call and found the rug underfoot.' 'But why would anyone give a rare Aubusson away?' 'The revolution in taste,' said Mr Andrews. 'It's the only revolution they're aware of, these ladies. Their daughters persuade them that they must do the house over in the modern manner. Or they say, "Mother, why don't you buy a flat in River House and get rid of some of this junk? I warn you, John and I won't take a stick of it when you die."'

It occurred to Polly while he was talking that if she had known this afternoon that he had found work, she might not have sold her blood at the hospital, and in that case she would not be engaged at this moment. It was another of those kinks in time or failures to overlap, like the one that was responsible for her father's being here now. The idea that she had nearly missed being engaged terrified her, as though *that*, not this, were her real fate, which she had circumvented by accident, like those people who *ought* to have gone down on the *Titanic* and for some reason at the last minute did not sail. This fear showed her that already she must be in love.

The announcement of Polly's engagement did not surprise any

of her friends. They had always known, they said, that there was 'somebody' at the hospital. It was only logical that Polly should marry one of the young doctors. 'We were counting on it for you, my dear,' said Libby. 'We all had our fingers crossed.' It was as if her friends wanted to rob her of the extraordinariness of her love. The implication was that, if it had not been Jim, it would have been Dr X in obstetrics or Dr Y in general surgery. And it could never have been anybody else. She had made the great discovery that Jim was good, and this filled her with wonder – most good people were rather elderly. She no longer puzzled over his love for her; she accepted it as Christians accepted the fact that God loved them, even though they were unworthy. Nor did she ask herself any longer whether she was in love with him – how could she fail to be? Yet when she tried to communicate this to others, they seemed bewildered, as if she were talking a foreign language. Even her mother did not appear to understand. 'Why, yes, Polly, he's very attractive. And intelligent, I expect. You're very well suited to each other.' 'That's not what I mean, Mother.' 'I suppose you mean he's a bit of an idealist. But you were bound to marry someone like that. A worldly man wouldn't have attracted you.'

Only Mr Schneider and the iceman seemed to feel as she did. The iceman wanted to be assured that her *fidanzato* was 'a good man'. Mr Schneider went further. 'I understand what you are feeling,' he said. 'As Socrates showed, love cannot be anything else but the love of the good. But to find the good is very rare. That is why love is rare, in spite of what people think. It happens to one in a thousand, and to that one it is a revelation. No wonder he cannot communicate with the other nine hundred and ninety-nine.'

What did surprise Polly's friends – though not Mr Schneider – was that Mr Andrews was going to live with the young couple. One by one, her group mates appeared to advise her against this – Pokey Beauchamp made a special trip by plane up from Princeton. Dottie, who was in town with her husband for the theatres and staying at the Plaza, went so far as to talk to Polly's mother. Even Helena Davison drawled a warning over cocktails in the Vassar Club lounge. Priss Crockett came to lunch in the coffee shop at the hospital. As a paediatrician, Sloan, she said, was terribly opposed. 'When you have children, you will have to think of them. Supposing your f-father – ?' 'Goes mad again,' said Polly. 'Would that be so terrible for them, Priss? He was mad off and on when we were children, my brothers and I.' That was different, Priss allowed; in those days, people did not know any better than to expose young children to mental illness – Polly and her brothers had been lucky, that was all. But even if Mr Andrews were normal, Polly's friends thought she would be making a terrible mistake – a mistake that this generation, at least, had learned to avoid. You did not have your relations to live with you if you wanted your marriage to succeed; it was the one thing on which you put your foot down. Opinion was unanimous on the point. If Polly wanted to fly in the face of experience, she was practically dooming her marriage from the start.

'And you mean to say your doctor *accepts* it?' the young matrons of Polly's circle cried, shocked. 'Yes,' said Polly. This astonishing news planted a grave doubt in her friends' minds. 'If he really loves you,' argued Kay, 'I should think he would want to be alone with you, to have you all to himself. Harald would *never* have let my father come to live with us. Wild horses wouldn't have persuaded him to share me.' Polly did not reply that rumour had it that she and Harald were on the verge of breaking up. 'What would you suggest I do with my father?' she demanded quietly instead. But no one seemed to have an answer for this; the attitude was that love, if it *were* love, would find a way. 'There must be *something* you and Jim could do with him, if the two of you put your heads together,' Kay declared. 'Why can't he live with your aunt Julia?' 'He doesn't like her,' said Polly. 'But she had a *huge* apartment,' said Kay. 'He could have his own quarters. And servants to look after him. He'd be much better off than crowded in with you. What are you going to do with him when you entertain? At your aunt's he could have a tray.' To this concert of opinion, Polly opposed a mute obstinacy, but she began to wonder whether marriage was not more of an ordeal that she had supposed. Hearing her friends hammer at her about making a success of marriage summoned up a picture of failure; in her ignorance, Polly had thought that you 'lived happily ever after', unless your husband was unfaithful, but the Class of '33 seemed to feel that you could not relax for a minute in your drive to make your marriage 'go'. Polly was quite willing to make sacrifices, having learned to do so in a big family, but that was not what her classmates meant. It was very important, they thought, for a woman to preserve her individuality; otherwise she might not hold her husband. What you were supposed to sacrifice, apparently, was 'encumbrances' like your father. 'At least,' remarked Libby, 'you're not going to take him with you on your honeymoon?' 'Of course not,' said Polly impatiently. But soon Polly's mother wrote, anxiously, wanting to know whether it was true that Henry was going to accompany them on the honeymoon – Louisa Hartshorn had heard it at the Cosmopolitan Club.

The only person who was deaf to the general concern was Mr Andrews, who had taken it for granted from the outset that he would live with the newlyweds. For him, the problem was architectural: finding an apartment that would house the three of them and not cost too much to fix over. He was looking at railroad apartments on the upper East Side, near Jim's laboratory; he had seen one on the top floor of an old-law tenement where it would be possible to make skylights to introduce light into the inner rooms. They were going to be married in the spring – on the farm, the plan was; Jim's parents would come from Ohio, and his father would perform the ceremony. It was Dottie's hope that Mr and Mrs Andrews might be reconciled by the occasion and make it a double wedding. 'Your father could be Jim's best man, and your mother could be your matron of honour. And then vice versa. Terribly original.' She twinkled. 'Don't you love the thought, Polly?'

When Jim heard this, he told Polly that they had better get married right away at City Hall and get it over with. Polly agreed. So as not to hurt anybody's feelings, they did not even take her father as a witness. They were married by a magistrate, and that night they went to Key West for their honeymoon, sharing a lower berth. From the station they sent telegrams announcing what they had done. Polly's friends were greatly disappointed that they had not had a chance to give her a shower or any kind of send-off. But they understood that a gay wedding, under the circumstances, would have been more than she could bear. The group was awfully sorry for Polly and would have sent her a floral tribute by telegram if only they had known her address. But naturally she and Jim were lying low, enjoying the last days the two of them would have alone together ever, probably, in their lives. In Dottie's suite at the

Plaza, a few of the girls and their husbands drank a toast to her *in absentia*. 'To her happiness!' they said loyally, clicking glasses. She deserved it if anyone did, the girls affirmed. The men's sympathies went to Jim Ridgeley, whom they did not know, but as Brook, Dottie's husband, continued to refill the champagne glasses, they concurred among themselves that he must be an odd gent to take a situation like that lying down.

Chapter 13

Early one morning in March Polly appeared at the Payne Whitney Clinic, Women's Division, to give a metabolism test to a mental patient who had been admitted the night before. When she came back from her honeymoon, she had stayed on at the hospital; she hoped she might be pregnant, since they had taken no precautions. If that were the case (and it was still too early to be sure), there would be no point in starting a new job that she would have to leave in October. Jim came to the hospital every day and had lunch with her in the staff dining-room, where they held hands under the table. In the evenings Polly's classmates were busy separating them at a series of 'folk suppers' given in their honour. Having joined the ranks of the married, Polly and Jim were not permitted to sit together, but had to balance plates on their laps at opposite ends of a room. These parties, at which everyone was half a couple and lived in an elevator building, gave Polly a vast sense of distance. All the husbands, it went without saying, were 'doing awfully well' in fire insurance or banking or magazine work, and her classmates, except for a few rebels, who were not necessarily the same rebels as in college, were 'taking their place in society'. Yet there were nights when Polly felt, watching them and listening, that she must be the only girl in the Class of '33 who was happy.

It was plain to Polly that many of her married classmates were disappointed in their husbands and envied the girls, like Helena, who had not got married. In June the class would have its fifth reunion and already it had its first divorcees. These hares were discussed wistfully by the tortoises of the class. It was felt that they at least had 'done something'. Norine Blake's divorce – she had gone to a ranch outside Reno and now called herself 'Mrs Schmittlapp Blake.' – had earned her a place of renown in alumnae affairs equal to that of Connie Storey, who had become a model for

284

Bergdorf, or of Lily Marvin, who dressed windows for Elizabeth Arden, and outranking poor Binkie Barnes, who was working as a C.I.O. organizer, and Bubbles Purdy, who was studying to be a preacher. Within the group itself, only Libby had made her mark. Kay, once so vital, had ceased to be a pace-setter. Last year rumour had had it that she, who had been the first of the class to be married, would be the first to be divorced – quite a record. But she was still toiling at Macy's as a junior executive in personnel, and Harald was still writing plays that were as yet unproduced. From time to time, he had a job as a stage manager or a director of a summer theatre, and Kay's family was helping them in their hours of need. Opinion at the fork suppers was divided as to whether Kay was a drag on Harald or vice versa. No one had seen them recently, it seemed, except Dottie, who had made a point of it this winter, and Helena, who had had them to dinner at the Savoy Plaza when her parents were in town. The two of them, Dottie reported, were now running with a fast, poker-playing set, where she was known as 'Mrs Pete' and Harald as 'Mr Pete'; the women were older than Kay, had deep, drawling voices, and called all the men 'Mr', including their own husbands. The game was dealer's choice, and it cost a quarter to open; Harald was a real gambler, but Kay was just a greenhorn who held her cards so that anyone could see them and had a craze for deuces-and-one-eyed-Jacks-wild. For her part, Helena told Polly that her mother, who was a great amateur diagnostician, had announced that Kay was on the edge of a nervous breakdown.

'The patient is quite refractory,' the nurse warned Polly that morning in the corridor, as she unlocked the door. 'She may not cooperate.' The woman in the bed was Kay. She had a huge black eye and contusions on her bare arms. At the sight of Polly in her starched white coat, she burst into copious tears. She was comparing their positions, Polly realized with sympathy, trying to remember whether she had ever seen Kay cry before. Rather than ask questions, which might have upset Kay more, Polly got a washcloth and bathed her swollen face. When she saw that Kay, contrary to what the nurse had said, did not offer any resistance, she found her pocketbook in a bureau drawer, took a comb from it, and gently combed her hair. She did not offer her a mirror because of the black eye. In a few moments, Kay's sobs subsided; she sat up. 'What are you going to do to me?' she asked curiously, eyeing

Polly's big cylindrical tank. 'I've come to give you a basal metabolism test, that's all,' answered Polly. 'It doesn't hurt.' 'I know that,' said Kay impatiently. 'But I haven't had any breakfast!' This protest was so like Kay that Polly was reassured. To her surprise, except for her appearance, her friend seemed completely herself. 'You'll have your breakfast afterwards,' she told her. 'We give these tests on an empty stomach.' 'Oh,' said Kay. 'Heavens, I'm glad you're here! You don't *know* the terrible things they've been doing to me, Polly.' Last night the nurses had taken her belt away from her. 'I can't wear my dress without a belt.' They had taken her nightgown sash too ('Look!') and they had tried to take her wedding ring, but she would not let them. 'We had a frightful struggle, practically a wrestling match, but then the head nurse came and said to let me keep it for the night. Score one for me. After that, they made me open my mouth and looked in to see if I had any removable bridges, though I'd already told them I hadn't. If I had had, they probably would have yanked them out. I must say, I was awfully tempted to bite them.' She gave her loud Western laugh. 'I wish now I had.' She glanced quickly at Polly for approval – which Polly feared was a very bad symptom. Kay was *proud* of battling with the nurses, as if she thought she were still a student standing up to the Dean or Prexy. Did she not understand about straitjackets? It was almost as if she did not grasp where she was. Then it occurred to Polly that Kay was simply embarrassed. 'I gather,' Kay went on in a different tone, 'that they think I want to commit suicide. They keep peering at me through those slats in the door. Did they expect me to hang myself with my belt? And what was I supposed to do with my wedding ring?' 'Swallow it.' Polly's answer was prompt; she thought the nurses would have done better to explain to Kay. 'That's just routine,' she said, smiling. 'They take away everybody's belt and wedding ring. I'm surprised they let you keep yours. And all the rooms on this floor have peepholes.' 'Like a jail,' said Kay. '"Judases", don't they call them?' Tears came into her eyes again. 'Harald betrayed me. He put me in here and left me. He pretended it was the regular hospital.'

'But what happened? Why are you here?' 'First tell me where I am.' 'You don't know?' said Polly. 'I suppose it must be an insane asylum,' Kay answered. 'Though the nurses keep saying, "Oh no, dear. Nothing like that. It's just a place for nervous people to rest." I made *such* a fool of myself last night when they brought me in here. I asked where the telephone was, right away. I felt like talking to somebody. They said there were no telephones in the rooms. So I said, "Why not?" but they wouldn't give a reason. I ought to have guessed then, but instead I decided that this must be some cheap wing of the hospital, a glorified ward, and that Harald had put me in here to save money – you know how he is. Then I asked for a radio, and they wouldn't let me have one. "Why not?" I said. They alleged that it was against the rules. That was *very* peculiar, I said: I had a friend who had a baby right here in New York Hospital a year ago, and *she* had had a radio. I remembered it distinctly.' She grinned. 'They must have thought I was crazy. Right after that, they took my belt away.' 'They do think you're crazy,' Polly interposed. 'You're in the Payne Whitney Clinic. It's a private mental hospital, attached to Cornell Medical Centre. This is the admissions floor, where they sort the patients out.'

Kay drew a deep sighing breath. She closed her eyes. 'All right. Now I know. I had to hear it from somebody to believe it.' 'But tell me how you got here,' urged Polly softly, stroking her friend's bent head. Kay opened her eyes. 'Will you believe me?' she said. 'Somebody's *got* to believe me.' 'Of course, I'll believe you,' said Polly warmly. She had come to the shocked conclusion that there must have been some mistake – as sometimes happened in hospitals. Petersen was a common name, at least in the form of 'Peterson', which was the way it had been spelled on Kay's chart. How awful if Kay had come in with an appendix and they had sent her here through a mix-up! But that left the black eye to be explained. 'It was Harald,' said Kay dully. 'He beat me when he'd been drinking. When was it? It seems so long ago, but it must have been yesterday morning. Yes, yesterday morning.' 'He was drinking in the morning?' 'He'd been out all night. When he came in at seven in the morning, I accused him of being with a woman. I know it was silly of me, to accuse him when he'd been drinking. I ought to have waited till he was sober.' Polly checked a laugh; Kay's self-criticism was always revealing. 'But I was a bit hysterical, I guess. We'd had some people in for cocktails, and we all got quite high. Then when they left, about seven-thirty, and I was making dinner, I needed a cucumber pickle for a sauce. So I sent Harald out to get one at a delicatessen, and he never came back. I realize it was stupid; I could have used India relish. But the recipe called for a cucumber pickle. Anyway, he didn't come back till morning. I ought to have pretended to be asleep – I see that now. Instead, I confronted him. I said he'd been with Liz Longwell – you don't know her, but we play poker with them. She was Bryn Mawr, '29, and her husband's away, trying a case in Washington. Whereupon Harald said he was tired of my dirty mind, and he hit me. You know, I saw stars, the way they do in the funny papers. It was silly, but I hit him back. Then he knocked me down and kicked me in the stomach. What should I have done, Polly? Picked myself up and waited for him to be sorry the next day? I know that's the right technique, but I haven't got the patience. I jumped up and ran into the kitchen. He ran after me, and I picked up the bread knife. I purposely didn't take the carving knife because he'd just sharpened it and I didn't want to scare him too much. Just enough to bring him to his senses. I waved it and said, "Don't you come near me!" He knocked it out of my hand. Then he pushed me into the dressing-room and locked the door. I waited there for a while, trying to get control of myself and hear what he was doing. Finally, I heard him snore. It never occurred to him that it was getting late and that I had to go to work. I knocked on the door; then I pounded; then I took time out to put on my clothes and pounded some more. I was crying and sobbing. And not a sound came from the other room; he'd even stopped snoring. I couldn't see through the keyhole because he'd left the key in the lock. He might have been dead.

'Finally I heard the doorbell ring. Two elevator boys were there, asking what was happening. Harald got up and talked to them through the door, telling them to go away. But they could hear me crying inside; I couldn't stop.' 'Oh, poor Kay!' 'Wait!' said Kay. 'You haven't heard what happened next. The elevator boys went away, and the next thing I knew the police had come. Harald opened the door, as cool as you please. He'd lain down on the bed in his clothes and after that little bit of sleep he must have seemed sober, though he had liquor on his breath. The police came in – there were two of them – and wanted to know what was going on. I was so terrified I'd stopped crying. But then through the door I could hear Harald telling them that we were rehearsing a scene from a play.'

Polly caught her breath. 'Did they believe that?' 'At first they didn't. "We'd like to hear your wife's story", they said. "She's dressing," said Harald. "When she's dressed, she'll confirm what I'm telling you." Then he offered to make a pot of coffee, which was an excuse to get them to follow him into the kitchen. He put on the percolator and left them there at the table in the dinette. Then he came into the living-room and quietly unlocked the dressing-room door. "Are you almost dressed, darling?" he called. "Some gentlemen from the police want to talk to you." I had to make up my mind fast; I knew he was counting on me to back him up and the very thought that he could, after what he'd done, made me mad. But I had to help him. After all, he has a police record, though they didn't seem to know that. I washed and put on a lot of powder and came out. This black eye didn't show then. I backed up his story. My husband, I explained to them, was a playwright, and I'd been trained as a director; we were doing a scene from a play he'd written.'

'What did they say?' 'First they said it was a funny time of day to be rehearsing a play, but I explained he'd been working late at the theatre – the elevator boys had seen him come home – and that I was doing the woman's part with him before going to work at the store. Then they asked to see the script. I was sure we were done for. But Harald – I must say this was masterful of him – thought very fast and whipped one of his old plays out of the cupboard. At the end of the second act there's a violent scene between a man and a woman. He handed it to the lieutenant, open at the right place, and asked whether he'd like to hear us do it. The lieutenant said no. He read about half a page; they finished their coffee and left, telling us not to rehearse again in a residential building. "Hire a hall," said the lieutenant, with a big wink at me. Harald promised them tickets to the play when it was produced.'

'You must have carried it off very well, Kay,' declared Polly admiringly. 'That's what I thought,' said Kay. 'But as soon as they were gone, instead of thanking me for saving him from being arrested, Harald started abusing me again. He said that as usual I'd got everything twisted and that it was he who saved *me* from being arrested. Did I deny having attacked him with a butcher knife? It was a bread knife, I told him. "A small point," said Harald. When I said that I'd just waved it, he smiled in his superior way. "You should have seen your face, my dear. It's a sight I'll never forget.

'I met Murder on the way. It had a face like my wife Kay.'" 'Did he really quote Shelley?' Polly marvelled. 'Was that what it was? Yes, he did,' Kay replied, rather proudly. 'Harald is awfully well read. Anyway, he said that if I didn't remember lunging at him with the knife, I was suffering from amnesia and ought to have psychiatric treatment. At that I started crying again; it seemed so hopeless to argue with him. I ought to have just gone to work, realizing that he was tired and still under the influence of liquor. But I cried and cried, which gave him an excuse to say I was hysterical. He put on his hat and coat. He was going to Norine Blake's, he said, to see if she would let him sleep a few hours in peace in her bedroom – she still has the same place she used to have with Put. "If you go to her, I'll never forgive you," I said very dramatically, barring the way. He just stood there and looked at me, up and down. This was more of my insane jealousy, he said. I had sunk so low as to suspect my best friend. "Doesn't that tell you something, Kay, about yourself?" Well, I did feel rather cheap, though I hadn't meant sex. I'd never suspect Harald of sleeping with Norine – she's not Harald's type. But I was jealous of his going there – giving Norine a chance to tell everybody that Harald had come to her because at home I didn't give him any rest. To me, that was more disloyal than adultery. But he went just the same, saying that he would send Norine over to calm me down – I could hardly accuse him of fornicating with her if she were with me. I didn't particularly want to see Norine but I agreed that she could come.

'In a little while she turned up and said that Harald had begged her to quiet me, that he was frightened by the state I was in. I admitted that this wasn't the first fight we'd had; we've been fighting all the time lately.' 'Has he beaten you before?' asked Polly gravely. 'No. Well, yes. But a long time ago, and I've never told anybody about it. Norine said that I ought to go to a hospital for a few days to get a complete rest; I couldn't rest so long as Harald and I were cooped up in this two-room apartment. If I would rather, she said, I could come and stay with her. But I didn't want to do that. She's such a terrible housekeeper, and besides it would be like a proof that Harald and I had separated. She made tea, and we talked, and at lunchtime Harald came back with some sandwiches from the delicatessen. That made me think of the cucumber pickle and my sauce, and I started crying again. "You see?" Harald said to Norine. "At the sight of me she bursts into tears." I didn't explain about the pickle, because Norine would have thought I was crazy, sending him out because of a recipe. She thinks my cooking is compulsive. We talked all afternoon, and they convinced me that I ought to go to a hospital, where I could just rest and read and listen to the radio. Then when I was rested, Harald and I could decide what we wanted to do about our marriage. The thing, though, that really settled it was my hospital insurance. As soon as Norine heard I had Blue Cross, she was on the telephone, checking up with her doctor about whether I could use it if I had a private room. He said yes, if I paid the difference. So before I knew it, she had it all fixed up for me to go to Harkness. I didn't *want* to go to Harkness; New York Hospital is so much more attractive – I loved the room Priss had with those rough-weave yellow curtains and pure white walls; it had such a modern feeling. Harald said to humour me, and Norine called her doctor back; he told her he didn't practise at New York Hospital but he could get another doctor to admit me. We waited, playing three-handed bridge, till they called and said they had a room for me. By that time, it was night. I packed a bag, and Harald took me in a taxi; when we asked at the main door, they rang up and sent us around to this other building. We thought it must be an annex. Harald brought me in and went into an office to fill out forms while I waited in the lobby. A nurse came and took my bag and said that Harald could go now; the doctor would see me in a minute, and then I'd be taken to my room.

'By then, I was looking forward to it; I did feel awfully tired, and at the thought of a milk shake in bed and an alcohol rub and nurses looking after me and not having to get up in the morning, I was glad that Harald and Norine had persuaded me. Maybe it would help to get away from Harald for a little while, though he could come in the afternoon and make cocktails, like Priss's husband – you remember. Sitting there in the lobby, I was just beginning to wonder where the gift shop was and the florist and the circulating library when a tall doctor came out of an office to talk to me. He seemed awfully curious to know how I'd got the black eye. I laughed and said I'd run into a door, but he didn't get the joke. He kept on pressing me till finally I said, "I won't tell you." I didn't see why he should know what had happened between

Harald and me. "We shall have to ask your husband then," he said. "Ask him!" I said, sassily, and I rather wondered what Harald would say. But by then of course Harald was gone. The doctor had the nurse take me upstairs into this depressing room, so drab, with no private bath, no telephone, no nothing. I decided, though, not to make a fuss then, but to go to bed and ask to have my room changed the next morning. While I was thinking that, the nurses got to work and searched me. I couldn't believe it. They went through my pocketbook too and took my matches away. If I wanted a cigarette, they said, I would have to get a light from a nurse. "But what if I want to smoke in bed?" Against the rules, they said; I could only smoke in the lounge or if a staff member was with me in my room. "I'd like a cigarette now," I said. But the nurse said no; I was to go to bed immediately. By this time, of course, I'd caught on to the fact that this couldn't be the regular hospital, but I kept getting these shocks. I was determined not to let them scare me but to act as naturally as I could. When the nurse left, I climbed into bed and was just starting to read the morning paper, which I'd never got around to, when suddenly the light went out. I told myself it must be the bulb and I rang. Eventually the nurse opened the door. "My light's out," I told her. "Can you fix it, please?" But it seemed she'd turned it out herself, from a switch outside the door. I told her to turn it on again, and she refused. So there I was, alone in the dark.'

Polly squeezed her hand. 'All that was routine,' she said. 'For the admissions floor. Until a psychiatrist has seen a new patient, they take precautions.' 'But I saw that doctor last night.' 'He wasn't one of the regular psychiatrists. Just a resident, probably, on night duty.' 'Why was he so inquisitive about my black eye? That's the part I still can't understand.' 'The assumption is that any injury is self-inflicted. When you wouldn't answer him, he thought you were trying to hide that.' 'But why should I want to give myself a black eye?' 'Patients do,' said Polly. 'Or they may get one throwing themselves in front of a car or down the stairs or off an embankment. When you see the psychiatrist this morning, after you've had your breakfast, you must tell him the truth about your eye. Even so, he'll probably want confirmation from Harald.' 'Confirmation from Harald!' Kay repeated indignantly. 'What if he were to lie? Anyway, I don't want to see a psychiatrist. I want to get out of here. Right away.' 'You can't get out,' said Polly. 'Until you see a psychiatrist. If you tell him the whole story, he may be able to release you. I'm not sure, Kay. You'd better send for Harald right away. I'll phone him as soon as we get this test done. I'm afraid that if he committed you, he will have to take you out himself. Otherwise, the procedure's rather long.' 'Harald committed me?' cried Kay. 'He must have,' said Polly. 'Unless you committed yourself. Did you?' 'No.' Kay was positive. 'That must have been those forms he filled out in the office,' she said. The two girls' eyes dilated. 'But that means,' Kay said slowly, 'that he knew what kind of place this was when he left me.' Polly did not speak. 'Doesn't it, Polly?' Kay urged, her voice rising. 'I said to you just now that he betrayed me. But I didn't mean it, I swear. I thought we *both* thought it was part of the regular hospital.' 'Perhaps,' suggested Polly hopefully, 'Harald didn't realize what he was doing.' 'No.' Kay shook her head. 'Harald never signs anything without knowing exactly what it is. He prides himself on that. He always adds up the bill himself in a restaurant and makes the waiter tell him what each item is. Sometimes I could go through the floor. And he reads all the fine print in a lease. So he knew.' She sank her chin in her hand; her black eye stood out livid in her face, which had slowly drained of colour. She looked gaunt and old. Polly glanced at her watch. 'Come!' she commanded. 'Let's do your metabolism. Afterwards, we can talk.'

Polly wanted time for reflection. While Kay was breathing into the big cylinder and she herself was watching the gauges, the room was still. She was very worried for Kay. The grim thought flitted across her mind that Harald, for some reason of his own, wanted Kay out of the way for a period and had deliberately put her in here, using Norine as a cat's-paw. Or could Harald and Norine be lovers who were plotting Kay's destruction? But such things did not happen in real life, not any more. And what could they gain by such a manoeuvre? Grounds for divorce? But if Harald wanted a divorce, Kay would surely give it to him.

Almost worse was to think that Harald and Norine had persuaded themselves that Kay really was a mental case. They might have chivvied her in here with benevolent intent. If Harald imagined he was acting from laudable motives, poor Kay was a cooked goose. Remembering the bread knife, Polly shuddered. A man who could convince himself that Kay was dangerous could readily convince a psychiatrist – the burden of proof rested on the patient, and how could Kay prove what had been in her mind?

But there was another possibility, a more cheerful one. Supposing Harald had had no notion of putting Kay in Payne Whitney but when he found that this had happened, through some administrative mistake (which Polly might be able to check up on), he had signed the commitment papers as a sort of sardonic joke? That would be quite in Harald's style. Polly nodded to herself. She could just imagine him yielding to a prankish impulse and signing with a flourish while raising a baleful eyebrow and mentally shaking an owlish forefinger. But in that case he would surely be back this morning to take Kay out. He might be here already, waiting downstairs, with a bouquet, to move her grandly to that room with the rough-weave yellow curtains.

This idea relieved Polly's mind. Given Harald, it was the most natural explanation. She smiled. It occurred to her that the whole thing was a little bit Kay's fault; if she had agreed to go to Harkness Pavilion, she might be listening to a radio now while a student nurse rearranged her pillows and offered her a mid-morning fruit juice with a glass straw.

The metabolism test was finished. It was an unexpected boon to be able to tell Kay that she had a perfect score. The figures worked out to zero, which was extremely rare. No doubt this explained her energy. Her organism was in absolute balance. Polly knew that this was not a proof of sanity; nevertheless, she felt it was a good omen. And Kay glowed as if the machine had paid her a compliment. 'Wait till I tell Harald!' she exulted. Polly must be sure to impress on him that Kay was the first patient in all her experience to score zero.

While the maid was serving Kay's breakfast, Polly slipped out to inquire whether Harald, by any chance, was waiting downstairs. The nurse said no message had come through. 'Call and check up, please,' said Polly. 'Mrs Petersen is an old friend of mine.' She went back into Kay's room. In a moment, the nurse appeared. 'No, Mrs Ridgeley.' 'No what?' said Kay. 'No, I don't have a ten o'clock appointment on my calendar,' Polly lied quickly. Since Kay had not shared her hope, there was no reason for her to share her disappointment. 'I'm going to call Harald,' she said. 'Wonderful,'

Kay answered, putting jam on her toast. The result of her basal metabolism seemed to have restored her natural optimism. 'We're feeling better this morning, aren't we?' said the nurse. 'Finish up, dear, and I'll help you dress.'

There was no answer at Kay's apartment. All the better, Polly said to herself; Harald must be on his way. Nevertheless, she called Jim at his Centre and told him briefly what had happened. He promised to come early and stop in to see Kay before lunch. 'If she's still here, of course,' appended Polly. 'She'll be there,' said Jim. 'Now don't be cynical,' said Polly. In her room, Kay, wearing a brown dress, which did need a belt, was packing her bag. 'Did you get him?' she said. Polly explained that he must be on his way to the hospital. The nurse winked at Polly. 'Mrs Petersen doesn't seem to like us here,' she jested. 'She'd rather go home to hubby.' 'She doesn't want me to pack,' Kay said to Polly. 'I've been explaining to her that it's all a mistake. I'm meant to be in New York Hospital.' The nurse smiled delicately. What Kay did not know was that one of the commonest delusions among the patients was that they were here through a mistake. 'I'll be running along now, Mrs Ridgeley,' the nurse said. She turned to Kay. 'Mrs Ridgeley has her own work to do. You mustn't keep her here talking.' Polly came to Kay's support. 'I'll stay with her a few minutes,' she said. 'Her husband will be coming to take her out.' 'I *see*!' said the nurse, with a slight sniff. She evidently felt that Polly was erring in encouraging the patient's false hopes.

'He really will come, you think?' said Kay, when they were alone. 'Of course,' said Polly. She lit cigarettes for them both. They looked at their watches. 'He ought to be here in fifteen minutes,' Kay said. 'If he'd just left when you called.' 'Twenty,' said Polly. 'It's a five-minute walk from the First Avenue bus.' 'Maybe he took a taxi.' They smoked. Kay's volubility had deserted her, and Polly's attempts to introduce impersonal topics failed. They were both concentrating on Harald and willing him to come soon. Kay picked up yesterday's paper, to read Lucius Beebe. 'Harald's met him,' she said. Suddenly they heard screams from the far end of the corridor and the sound of running, rubber-soled feet. 'Oh, my God!' said Kay. 'It's nothing,' said Polly. 'One of the patients has got "excited", that's all. The nurses will take care of her.' 'What will they do?' said Kay. 'Send her upstairs,' said

Polly. 'The violent wards are up above, on the seventh and eighth floors. When a patient in isolation shows signs of improvement, they send her down here on trial, to see how she does with the group of new patients. But quite often she has to be removed. That's probably what's happening now.' They could hear sounds of a scuffle. 'Will they use a straitjacket?' Kay wanted to know. 'If they have to,' said Polly. They listened. A new voice, closer to Kay's room, had begun to howl like a dog. More feet came running, and Polly could distinguish the heavier tread of a doctor or of a male orderly from the violent floors. Kay clung to Polly. They heard a man's voice give an order. Then all was quiet. 'Do they have padded cells up there?' Kay whispered. 'Yes,' said Polly. 'I think so. But I've never been up,' She was inwardly furious, for Kay – why had this had to happen this morning? Jim was right when he criticized the hospital for what he called the bedlam on the admissions floor; it was callous to bring the very sick into contact with people who were tottering on the brink of sanity. New patients with nothing more than a mild nervous breakdown or very young, almost children, were terrified by what they heard and saw in their first days. Polly had just been given a living illustration of this; Kay was still trembling. 'I remember at college,' she said, 'when we used to visit the state asylum for Psych. I never thought then – ' Her eyes filled with tears; she did not finish her sentence. 'Polly!' she said. 'What if he tells them I'm crazy?'

But Harald had not come when, at the end of half an hour, Polly had to go. The nurse came to say that she was wanted right away in the main building for a blood analysis. 'Go ahead,' said Kay. 'I'll be all right. I've got some books to read.' Polly lingered. 'I wish I could leave you some matches. . . . But I don't want to get you in trouble. . . . If the psychiatrist comes – ' She broke off. What she had started to say was 'Be careful.' Instead, she said, 'Don't worry. Whatever happens, Kay, Jim will be here before lunch.' Kay nodded and produced an unconvincing smile. She watched Polly pack up her equipment. 'Go on,' she said. 'What are you waiting for?' Polly wheeled her tray out the door. The corridor was empty. All the doors were ajar; the other patients must be at morning exercise. There was nothing else to do – those were the regulations – but Polly felt horrible doing it: 'Am I my sister's jailer?' said her conscience. What were those fearsome lines in Dante that her father quoted when they locked him up in Riggs? *'E io senti chiavar l'uscio di sotto/all'orribile torre. . . .'* She took the key and locked Kay in.

On the other side of the door, Kay heard the key turn and knew that Polly had turned it. She did not blame her. She did not even blame the perfidious Harald. Soon in her office, she supposed, Polly would be trying to call him. But Kay had lost hope that he would answer. Probably he had not spent the night in the apartment; he was with a woman somewhere. Nor did she think he would turn up at the hospital. The thing she had been dreading for five years had happened: he had left her. Not the way other husbands did, after long discussions and lawyers and dividing up the furniture. She had always known that Harald, one day, would simply disappear. Neither she nor his parents nor anyone who had known him would ever see him again. He would surface, like a submarine, in the Middle West or South America with a different identity. He had been a mystery to her from the beginning and he would vanish mysteriously into nowhere. To leave her locked up in a mental hospital, like somebody tied up in a closet by robbers, would be just the kind of thing he would relish. Eventually, she supposed, she would have to have him declared dead, and he would relish that too. She could hear the cock's crow of his laughter, like that of the Pathé rooster, coming from the four corners of the earth.

And to the day she died, she would never know whether he had been unfaithful to her. She would not even have that last satisfaction. To deprive her and tantalize her was his whole aim. She had tried to bind him with possessions, but he slipped away like Houdini. If he left her, he would not even take his typewriter, which she had got him for Christmas at a discount. That was another thing. He knew she admired him and wanted him to be a success, but he circumvented her as if on purpose. Sometimes she felt that he was postponing being a success till he could wear out her patience; as soon as she gave up and left him, his name would mock her in lights.

She had really thought of leaving him. Last year Norine had had a pet plan, that they should both hitch-hike to Reno. Norine said that if Kay gave Harald his freedom, it would liberate his creative energies. The idea had half-tempted Kay, as a glorious sacrifice, though she had insisted they go on the train. But she did not tell Harald for fear he would agree, which would take all the zest out of the project. Then Harald had said to her, smiling, one night when they had company, 'I hear, Kay, you're planning to divorce me.' And again she had been unable to tell whether he would have minded or not. He had an air of being secretly amused, but, question him as she would, she could never make him say what was funny, if there *was* something funny, about her wanting to get a divorce.

Probably he did not take it seriously because he thought she loved him. There he was making a mistake. She had loved him at first, she reckoned, but he had tormented her so long with his elusiveness that she did not know, honestly, now whether she even liked him. If she had been sure of him, she might have found out. But things had never stood still long enough for her to decide. It sometimes struck her that Harald would not let her be sure of him for fear of losing his attraction: it was a lesson he had learned in some handbook, the way he had learned about those multiplication tables. But Kay could have told him that he would have been far more attractive to her if she could have trusted him. You could not love a man who was always playing hide-and-seek with you; that was the lesson *she* had learned.

Well, Harald might say, if that was so, why was she grieving? Why did she feel now as if her heart was broken? Kay tried to answer this question. She was grieving, she decided, for a Harald-That-Never-Was, not for the real Harald. But if she lost the real Harald, who was not such a muchness, she lost her only link with the Harald-That-Never-Was. Then it was really finished – her dream. She lay on the bed, thinking. There was something else. She had always despised failures, but if Harald had left her she was one.

At eleven-thirty there was a knock. A young psychiatrist with glasses had come to talk to her. 'We were hoping to see Mr Petersen this morning,' he said with an air of disapproval, so that Kay felt she ought to apologize. He took notes while she told him her story. When she had finished, breathlessly, and was waiting to hear his verdict, he sat for a few minutes in silence, riffling through his notebook. 'Why do you place such importance on your belt?' he suddenly demanded. 'The night nurses reported that you first became very unruly when they asked you to give it to them. And I have a note here that you spoke about it to Mrs Ridgeley too and to Mrs Burke, the day nurse.' 'Polly told you that?' Kay exclaimed, hurt and bewildered. 'Mrs Ridgeley wondered whether we couldn't make an exception and give you your belt back. But of course, as Mrs Ridgeley should know, we can't make an exception until we've seen your husband.' Again he looked at her accusingly, as if it were her fault that Harald had not come. 'It's not my fault –' she began. 'Just a minute,' he said. 'I see that you've used the expressions "his fault", "my fault", and their equivalents thirty-seven times in the course of our talk. I wonder if you'd like to give me your thoughts on that.' Kay was dumbfounded. 'I don't understand,' she said. 'I was promised that when I saw a psychiatrist, I could go to the regular hospital.' 'No one in authority could have given you such a promise,' he replied sharply. 'I'm afraid that's your own fantasy, Mrs Petersen.' Kay flushed. It was true that Polly had only said maybe.

The psychiatrist frowned at Kay's suitcase. 'I wanted to avoid this discussion,' he said. 'Which will be quite unprofitable for both of us while you're in a state of great emotional tension and your judgement is affected. You're in no condition, just now, to make an important life-decision. You have a black eye, which you claim your husband gave you. I have no way of knowing whether this is true. In any case we're better equipped here to take care of you than they are across the way. There seems to be nothing wrong with you physically except the eye. We'll begin tests later on in the day to make sure; in the course of your stay here you'll have a thorough medical and dental check-up. But you appear to be in good health. The regular hospital is designed for patients who are physically ill. It's not a rest home or a sanatorium. If you feel you're not in need of psychiatric treatment, you can go home or go to a hotel.'

'All right, I'll go to a hotel,' promptly retorted Kay. He raised a finger. 'Not so fast. *If* your husband consents. Let me be open with you. You can't leave here till we've had a talk with Mr Petersen. He committed you last night, and we would be negligent if we released you on your own say-so. After all, we know nothing about you. And on your own account you did threaten your husband with a knife.' Kay opened her mouth. 'I don't say you are danger-ous,' the doctor intervened. 'If we thought so, you would be on

299

one of the violent floors. You are here for your own protection, believe me.' 'But what if Harald never comes?' The doctor smiled. 'That seems very unlikely. Don't go borrowing trouble, Mrs Petersen. But I'll answer your question. In that eventuality, the head of the hospital, after making a careful study, can release you if he thinks it's warranted.'

'And if Harald insists I stay here?' 'I think you and your husband, with our help, will reach a harmonious agreement about what's best to be done.' These words chilled Kay's bones. 'But supposing Harald contradicts what I've told you?' 'We have experience in getting at the truth.' 'And if you believe me, instead of him, will you let me out?' 'Under those circumstances, the head of the hospital can release you.' 'I demand to see the head of the hospital!' 'Dr Janson will see you in due time.' 'When?' For the first time, the psychiatrist looked human. He laughed. 'You're certainly a persistent woman.' 'I always have been,' Kay agreed. 'Tell me honestly, do you think I'm insane?' He considered. 'Frankly,' he said, 'you've made a favourable impression on me.' Kay beamed. 'That is not to say,' the psychiatrist warned, 'that you don't have severe emotional difficulties. Possibly of an hysterical character. My advice to you is to relax. Have a good lunch and get to know the other patients. You'll find some of these women very interesting. They come from good homes too. Some of them are highly cultured. Later in the afternoon you can have hydrotherapy – you'll enjoy it. And you can go to art class or weaving. Do you like to work with your hands?' Kay did, but she refused to admit it. 'Kindergarten,' she said scornfully. 'Our other patients –' began the doctor. 'I'm *not* your other patients!' interrupted Kay. He got up. 'Good-bye, Mrs Petersen,' he said coldly. She had not meant to sound so rude. He closed his notebook. 'When your husband comes, I'll be happy to have a talk with him. And I'll see you tomorrow.' 'Tomorrow!' He nodded. 'I shall strongly recommend your spending at least another night in the hospital. Even if the interview is completely satisfactory.' He removed a metal rod from the pocket of his white coat. 'Excuse me,' he said and tapped her knee. Her leg jerked. 'Just a formality,' he said. 'Your reflexes are normal, as I expected.' He shook hands. 'Oh, one thing. Mrs Ridgeley is much concerned about you. I've given permission for Dr Ridgeley to see you when he comes.' He went out briskly.

When Jim Ridgeley came, Kay was in the dining-room with the other patients. The psychiatrist had left orders that she was to join them in the lounge for recreation before lunch. Immediately, a squabble had broken out as to which of them was to sit next to Kay at table, which the nurse in charge had settled by placing her between a grey-haired woman, who said she was a manic-depressive, and a pretty girl of about Kay's own age, who told Kay she had been brought to the hospital in a straitjacket. 'I was on the seventh floor for a long time; now I'm better,' she confided. 'My husband's coming to take me home soon.' At this a noisy towheaded girl burst into loud laughter. 'She hasn't got a husband,' the grey-haired woman whispered to Kay. 'He's left her.' Across the round table from Kay sat a catatonic with a boyish bob; she was the only one whose face did not move a muscle when Kay, replying to a question, announced that she was here through a mistake. Some laughed; others looked anxious. 'You mustn't say that,' the pretty girl whispered. 'Even if it's true. They'll never let you out if you say that. They may even send you back to the seventh floor.'

Just then, Jim Ridgeley put his head in the dining-room. 'Hello, Kay,' he said. He surveyed the women at the several tables, who were eating their soup, and nodded to those he recognized. He looked cross and rumpled. 'Have Mrs Petersen's lunch brought to her in her room,' he said to the nurse at Kay's table. 'I want to talk to her.' 'Oh, not fair!' shouted the towheaded girl. 'Dr Ridgeley's *my* sweetie,' said a fat woman, clowning. 'Why have you left me, Dr Ridgeley?'

He hurried Kay into her room. 'This is a crime,' he said. 'They have no business keeping you here.' He was late because he had been arguing with the psychiatrist who had seen Kay. 'What did he say?' 'In a word that he couldn't "take the responsibility" for your release. He wants to pass the buck to Harald, who of course can't be found.' 'Have you tried?' 'Polly's been trying all morning. She finally sent him a telegram. If he doesn't show up this afternoon, I'm going to send out a police call for him.' His anger surprised and pleased Kay; she had forgotten how it felt to have a champion. The last champion she had had was her Dads, back home.

'Look,' said Jim. 'It's not going to be easy to get you out of here unless Harald cooperates. If I were still on the staff, I could swing it. But I'm not, and my departure wasn't a popular move. They're standing on technicalities. Harald could sue them, I suppose, if they let you out and you murdered him.' He laughed. 'That's the kind of reasoning. Old Janson is a fuss-budget. They can't get the idea that a mental home isn't a healthy place for a girl who's upset. They love it here themselves.' He studied Kay. 'If it weren't for that shiner of yours, I'd pass you out with me as a visitor.' Kay looked up from her lunch tray in alarm; she had a strong feeling for legality. 'Polly said you were impulsive,' she remarked. He nodded. 'Let's think,' he said. 'Your father's a doctor, is that right?' 'An orthopaedic surgeon. But he's in general practice too.' 'Supposing I phoned him?' said Jim. 'He could hop on a train tonight. They'd certainly release you to him.' 'But it takes three days to get here,' objected Kay. 'Anyway, I couldn't bear it. That Dads should know. If he thought I was in a place like this . . .' Her tears started again. 'Or if he heard about the black eye and the police. . . . It would kill Dads. He thinks our marriage is a big success and he just worships Harald.' 'From afar, I assume,' Jim remarked dryly.

'I've always been Dads' favourite child,' Kay continued, wiping her eyes. 'He trusts me completely. And I've made him believe in Harald.' Jim stood looking out the small barred window. 'What exactly do you find to believe in?' he asked, not turning around. 'Why, he's a genius,' said Kay. 'I mean, if you knew the theatre –' She broke off. 'Doesn't Polly think he's a genius?' she asked anxiously. 'She hasn't said,' Jim answered. He swung around to face Kay. 'You know, Kay, there's one point on which I question your sanity.' 'Harald,' she supplied in a low voice. He sighed. 'I suppose you love him.'

'It sounds more interesting that way,' Kay answered candidly. 'But I don't think I do. In a way, I think I hate him.' 'Well, that's refreshing,' he said. 'Of course, I hardly know him, Kay. But if you hate the guy?' 'Why don't I leave him?' One reason she never confided in anyone was the fear of having to answer this question. But perhaps a psychiatrist could help her. 'I can't explain,' she said miserably. 'Do you think I could be a masochist?' He smiled. 'No. Even Hopper – the psychiatrist you saw – was struck by your "lack of affect" in response to your husband's brutality.' 'He believed me then!' exclaimed Kay. 'That means a lot to you,' he commented sympathetically. 'Were you given to lying at one time?' Kay nodded. 'Awful,' she said. 'But only to build myself up. Or to get something I wanted.' 'But you'd never bear false witness against your neighbour.' 'Oh, no!' she said, shocked. 'And I've reformed. Ask Polly. The thing is – I might as well tell you – Harald isn't very truthful. And I've had a reaction against that. Maybe it's just a reaction against Harald.' He reflected. 'Do you think your marriage could be a sort of fish story?'

Kay met his eyes. 'How did you guess?' she said. 'I suppose it is. Could that be why I can't run out on it? If I did, everybody would know it was a failure. You don't realize, Jim, I'm a sort of legend in Salt Lake City. "The girl who went east and made good."' '"Made good"?' 'By marrying Harald. The theatre. It all sounds so glamorous to Mums and Dads and the girls I went to school with. You see, I wanted to be a director myself. Or an actress. But I really have no talent. That's my tragedy.'

Jim looked at his watch. 'See here, Kay. Everybody's at lunch. I'm going to try to pass you out. Nobody knows you're a patient except the staff on this floor. You walk down the hall with me to the elevator. If we meet a nurse, OK; I'll turn you over to her. If we don't, we can make a getaway. The elevator men are all friends of mine. You'll have to leave your suitcase. Polly can bring it later. Where's your coat? I'll carry it till we get in the elevator.'

Kay's methodical nature was jarred by the interruption of her train of thought; now that she had started, she was eager to go on discussing Harald. But Jim's enthusiasm caught her for a moment. Polly was lucky; he was quite a knight errant. 'I can't let you do that. Why, it might get you disqualified. They'd be furious when they found out I was gone.' 'Baloney. They'll be relieved and grateful, for a *fait accompli*. Besides, we can let them think I forgot to lock you in and you walked out on your own initiative.' Kay made a grimace. The thought of taking the blame for what was solely his idea did not appeal to her. To be publicly rescued was one thing, but to figure in the records as an escaped lunatic was another. 'No,' she said stiffly. 'I don't want to run away. I want to leave with flying colours. With the hospital acknowledging their mistake.' 'You don't know hospitals,' said Jim. But he saw he could not persuade her. She feared she was a disappointment to him – would Polly, in her place, have agreed? Kay strongly doubted it.

He stood up, looking frustrated. He was a man, she could tell, who liked to get things done. 'We'll have you moved off this floor at least,' he said, setting his jaw. And he explained to her that the hospital worked by a system of promotion. The patients graduated from one floor to the next, going downward. The star patients, those who were pronounced 'convalescent', i.e., almost ready to leave, were on the fourth floor, which was more like a college dormitory. The windows were not barred; the patients were not locked in; they were allowed to wear their belts and wedding rings and had regular visiting hours; they could turn off their light when they wanted, and the only rule was – just like college – that they could not smoke in their rooms. As he painted this picture of privilege, Kay brightened. 'Do you really think you can get me on the fourth floor?' 'This afternoon. Providing they have a bed.' 'You mean I can skip the fifth? Do they let patients do that?' 'Not as a usual thing. But this isn't a usual case, is it?' Kay smiled happily; she had always wanted to skip a grade in school, she confided.

Sure enough, within a half-hour, the nurse came to move her to the fourth floor. Unfortunately, the other patients were in their rooms, napping, so they could not see her go. Kay tried not to savour her triumph and to think, rather, with sympathy of those she was leaving behind, who would be months, probably, getting the double promotion she had achieved in a single day. Yet she could not help preening herself on this very point as she sauntered down the corridor. It was only the memory of the pretty girl that made her feel a little bit sad.

Her new room was very much nicer, though it too did not have a telephone and the walls were an institutional tan. Unpacking her toilet articles, Kay decided that she would not mind staying in Payne Whitney if only her sanity were established. At four o'clock she had an appointment for a general medical examination; tomorrow morning she would see a gynaecologist. And it was all 'on the house', said the new nurse, who had dropped in to get acquainted. At five, Kay would have hydrotherapy. The patients were kept pretty busy in the daytime, but in the evenings they played bridge until it was time for their hot chocolate or Ovaltine. There was a ping-pong table; twice a week they had movies, which the male patients were taken to also. The hospital had a beauty parlour, and occasionally there were dances. Frankly, said Kay, it would give her the creeps to have a male patient for a partner. The nurse agreed, but the women, she said, were a lovely group – she would hate to see them go home.

Just before supper, Harald was announced. Immediately, Kay started to tremble. 'You don't have to see him dear, if you don't want to,' the nurse told her. But Kay declared she was ready. She promised herself not to cry and not to accuse him, but the first words that sprang from her lips were 'Where have you been?' In answer, he handed her a florist's box, from Goldfarb's, containing two red camellias, her favourite flower. He had not come because he had been unable to face her after what he had done. He had been walking the streets. He had seen the dawn come up on the East River, and all day he had been roaming the city, thinking about Kay.

Kay fought down her desire to believe him. The day of reckoning, she told herself, had come, she must not let herself be bought off by two camellias. 'You committed me,' she said coldly. 'Didn't you?' Harald did not deny it. 'But how could you? How *could* you?' 'I know,' he said, groaning. 'I know.' He could not explain what had made him do it. 'I was tired,' he said. 'Obviously there'd been a mistake. But there we were, and it was late. If I hadn't signed, where would I have taken you? They had a room reserved for you here. And they told me it was just a formality. An acquiescent devil inside me wanted to believe that. Ha!' When he had left the hospital, he had stopped in a bar and then had gone home and slept for a few hours, anaesthetized, but his conscience had wakened him, and while it was still dark he had gone out into the streets. He had walked the whole city and twice crossed the Brooklyn Bridge. Standing on a pier in the North River, he had considered shipping on a freighter as a seaman and disappearing for good, into the Canal Zone or Australia. 'I knew it!' cried Kay. Then he had walked to the Bronx Zoo and studied the apes, his ancestors, in the monkey house – then back, to Wall Street, where he had watched the ticker tape. He raised his right foot to show her the hole in his shoe sole. Finally he had taken the subway to Fifty-ninth Street, stopped at Goldfarb's, and come here. 'Have you eaten?' Kay demanded. He shook his head. 'Did you see the psychiatrist?' 'Yes, my poor girl; I've made a full confession. You can leave whenever you want. *Mea culpa.*' He was silent for a moment. 'The psychiatrist told me, Kay, that you refused to give up your wedding ring.' He took her hand and gently pressed his lips to the gold-and-silver band. 'I accepted that as a sign that some day you might forgive me. Was I wrong?'

This was the most abject apology she had ever had from Harald; Kay could not believe her ears. It almost made it worth while to have been shut up in an institution. 'Tonight?' she said. 'Can I leave tonight?' 'If you wish. And you're not too tired.' Kay hesitated. She remembered that in the morning she had an appointment with a gynaecologist. And she was curious to see the other patients. Now that she was here, it seemed a pity, in a way, not to stay. 'I saw a catatonic schizophrenic this morning,' she announced. 'I sat across from her at lunch. It was fascinating. She was completely rigid and had to be fed like a doll. And there was this pretty girl next to me who looked completely normal but they'd brought her in in a straitjacket. She liked me. They fought over which ones should sit next to me. As if I were a new girl at school.' Harald smiled. 'What else did you do?' 'I had hydrotherapy. And a medical exam. I talked to Polly's husband.' She felt herself colour. 'He wanted me to escape. And, oh, I have to tell you about my metabolism. . . .'

Harald listened. There was a discreet knock on the door. 'Supper in five minutes, Mrs Petersen.' They started. 'What should I do?' Kay said. A vague sense of disappointment came over her at the thought of going home; it was like having to leave a party too soon. 'Would you like to stay here for the night?' said Harald. She deliberated. She did not want to hurt his feelings. 'We agreed you needed a rest, you remember,' he encouraged her. 'And you can't go to work until your poor eye heals. Anyway, you've asked for a week's sick leave.' 'I know.' 'Your Blue Cross covers psychiatric hospitals. I made a point of finding out in the office. If I were you, I'd stay here a week or two. You can have daily talks with the psychiatrist. It's all included in the treatment. With your background in psychology, it ought to be fruitful for you. It'll give you a tool you can use in your personnel work, to study the other women here. And you may get a line on yourself.' 'But there's nothing wrong with me,' said Kay. 'I thought that was established.' Her willingness to stay in the hospital was rapidly diminishing when she heard Harald proposing it. 'Jim Ridgeley said it was a crime I was here,' she said hotly. 'Oh, please, Kay, no reproaches!' replied

Harald. 'If you can't forgive me, simply say so and I'll go.' Kay caught herself up; she did not wish to drive him away. 'I'd stay,' she said cautiously, 'if it was understood that I wasn't a mental case like these other people. I don't mind talking to the psychiatrist if it's clear that I don't really need to. I mean, of course everybody needs to, but . . .' She floundered. 'But everybody doesn't have Blue Cross,' supplied Harald.

Kay tested him. 'If I say no, will you take me home?' 'Of course.' 'All right, I'll stay,' she decided. 'Then I'd better go and have supper. You'll come tomorrow, won't you?' Harald promised. 'In any event,' he remarked, 'the psychiatrist will probably be wanting me.' 'Wanting you?' Kay bridled. 'They like to get other points of view on the patient. Incidentally, he'd like to talk to a few of your friends. Shall I have Norine come in the morning? She can drop in to see you afterwards. And who else? Helena?' Kay stared at him. 'If you tell my friends,' she said, 'I'll kill you.' Hearing what she had said, she clapped her hand to her mouth. 'Of course I didn't mean that,' she gasped. 'But I beg you, Harald, don't tell Norine. Don't let her talk to the psychiatrist. I'll do anything you want if you keep Norine away from here.' Heavy sobs began to shake her. 'Oh, don't be childish,' Harald said impatiently. 'Save it for the psychiatrist.' This brutal tone, so soon after his apology, cut her to the heart. The nurse knocked again. 'Are you coming to supper, Mrs Petersen?' 'She's coming,' Harald answered for her. 'Go wash your face. Good-bye. I'll see you tomorrow.' The door shut.

Slowly Kay pinned the camellias to her dress. She reminded herself that she was free to leave. It was her own choice that she was staying. Unlike the other patients, she had never for a minute been out of her mind. But as she advanced to the dining-room, a terrible doubt possessed her. They were using psychology on her: it was not her own choice, and she was not free, and Harald was not sorry – the psychiatrist had coached him, that was all.

Chapter 14

Priss Crockett, who brought Stephen to play in Central Park every morning, was surprised one June day, when she arrived pushing the stroller and followed by Stephen, to see a familiar figure seated on a bench with a baby carriage. It was Norine Schmittlapp, wearing a smart pair of slacks and black sunglasses. The hood of the carriage was down, and on the carriage mattress, which was covered with a rubber sheet, lay a naked infant, male. Priss halted; it was 'her' bench Norine was occupying. She was uncertain whether Norine would recognize her; it must be five years since they had met. Norine had changed; she had put on weight and her hair was blondined. 'Hi,' said Norine, looking up briefly. 'Join us. This is Ichabod.' She joggled the baby carriage. Her tinted gaze sought out Stephen, who was pulling an educational toy along the walk. 'Is that yours?' Priss presented her young. 'Say how do you do, Stephen, to the lady.' She did not know how to introduce Norine, who evidently had remarried. Norine shook Stephen's hand. 'Norine Rogers. Glad to know you.' On her engagement finger was a huge diamond in a platinum setting, and the baby carriage was an English model with a monogram. 'Do you come here every day?' she asked Priss.

They were neighbours, it seemed. She had just moved into a brownstone, between Park and Madison, that she and her husband had bought; Priss's apartment was on Lexington and Seventy-second. 'But you're lucky,' said Priss enviously. 'You must have a back yard. You don't need to come to the Park.' She herself found it quite a chore, mornings, to push the stroller all the way from Lexington and get back in time to put Stephen's baked potato in the oven for a twelve o'clock lunch. Norine said that her back yard was still full of glass bricks and cement-mixers. They were doing the house over, putting in a ramp where the stairs had been and a wall of glass bricks on the street side. Priss realized that Norine's house must be the one the whole neighbourhood was discussing; she wondered what Rogers Norine could have married. 'My husband's a Jew,' Norine threw out. 'His people changed the name from Rosenberg. Do you mind Jews? I'm mad for them myself.' Before Priss could answer, she continued, talking in the rapid-fire way Priss remembered, as if she were dictating a letter. 'Freddy's whole tribe converted. When they changed their name. He's a confirmed Episcopalian. I was hell-bent to have him go back to the old Orthodox faith. With a prayer shawl and phylacteries. The real Mosaic law. The Reformed rite is just a nineteenth-century compromise. But an Orthodox Jew can't marry a shiksah.' Priss was surprised to hear this. Norine nodded. 'They frown on exogamy. Like the Papists. The Episcopalians have a taboo on divorce; Freddy's minister wouldn't marry a divorced woman. So we got a Lutheran pastor in Yorkville. Freddy's parents expected to see a framed picture of Hitler in the dominie's parlour.' She laughed. 'Are you interested in religion?' Priss confessed that she was more interested in politics. 'I'm burned out on politics,' said Norine. 'Since Munich. My passion's comparative religion. Society is finished if it can't find its way back to God. The problem for people like us is to rediscover faith. It's easy for the masses; they never lost it. But for the élite it's another story.'

Her eyes fixed on Stephen. 'This your only offspring?' Priss explained that she had had a series of miscarriages, but she still hoped to have more children, for it would be sad for Stephen to grow up as an only child. 'Adopt some,' said Norine. 'It's the only way. If the élite can't breed, it has to graft new stock or face extinction. Do you know that the Vassar graduate has only 2.2 children?' Priss was aware of this statistic, which had caused concern in alumnae circles – Vassar women were barely replacing themselves while the rest of the population was multiplying. 'What does your husband do?' Norine demanded. 'He's a paediatrician.' 'Oh,' said Norine. 'What school?' Priss began to tell her where Sloan had been trained. Norine cut her off. 'What school of thought. Behaviourist? Gestalt? Steiner? Klein? Anna Freud?' Priss was ashamed to say that she did not know. 'He's a medical doctor,' she said apologetically. Then she essayed a personal question of her own.

'What does *your* husband do, Norine?' Norine chuckled. 'He's a banker. With Kuhn, Loeb. He comes from old money-lending stock. From Frankfurt originally. But they had a Diaspora and they're scattered all over the place. The black sheep of the family became a Zionist and went to Palestine. They never mention his name. Freddy's parents were trying to pass,' she went on sombrely. 'Like so many rich German Jews. They sent him to Choate and Princeton, where he had a searing experience with one of the clubs. When the club found out "Rogers" was "Rosenberg", he was asked to resign.' Priss made a clucking sound, to which Norine replied with a short laugh. It was as if this incident gave her a peculiar kind of relish.

Priss glanced at little Ichabod, who, she observed, had been circumcised, and felt guiltily glad that Stephen did not have a Jewish father. It struck her, awful as it sounded, that if you wanted to give your child the best start in life, you would not marry a Jew. But Norine, she supposed, was dauntless on his behalf; Priss felt in awe of a person who could fasten a name like that on a baby. 'Aren't you afraid he'll be called "Icky" in school?' she said impulsively. 'He'll have to learn to fight his battles early,' philosophized Norine. 'Ichabod the Inglorious. That's what the name means in Hebrew. "No glory."' She rocked the carriage.

'How old is he?' 'Three months.' Priss wished Norine would raise the hood of the carriage; she feared the mid-morning sun was too strong for his little head, which had scarcely any hair yet. 'Isn't he awfully young for a sun bath?' Norine scouted the thought; she had been exposing him to the sun daily since she had brought him home from Mount Sinai. Nevertheless, she slightly raised the hood, so that his face was in the shade. 'It's O.K. here,' she observed contentedly. 'No nursemaids or English nannies. The place I was yesterday, they made an awful stink because he was nude. They were afraid their starchy girls would get ideas from his little prick — weren't they, Ichabod?' Her big hand patted his penis, which stiffened. Priss swallowed several times; she glanced uneasily in the direction of Stephen, who, happily, was chasing his ball in the grass. She was always terrified of arousing Stephen; she hated retracting his foreskin when washing him, though Sloan said she should, for hygienic reasons. But she would almost rather he was dirty than have him get an Oedipus complex from her handling him. Lately, without telling Sloan, she had been omitting this step from his bath.

'Have you got a watch?' Norine asked, yawning. Priss told her the time. 'Are you nursing?' she asked, stealing an envious look at Norine's massive breasts. 'My milk ran out,' said Norine. 'So did mine!' cried Priss. 'As soon as I left the hospital. How long did *you* nurse?' 'Four weeks. Then Freddy slept with the girl we had looking after Ichabod, and my milk went on strike.' Priss gulped; the story she had been about to relate, of how her milk had run out as soon as they gave Stephen a supplementary bottle, was hastily vetoed on her lips. 'I ought to have seen it coming,' Norine went on, lighting a cigarette. 'We hadn't had real sex together for a coon's age. You know how it is. At the end of your pregnancy it's *verboten* and it's *verboten* for a month after the kid's born. Freddy got very randy. And he felt he had a rival in Ichabod. Then we hired this Irish slut. Straight off the boat. She was a cousin of Freddy's mother's waitress. A real Mick. Eyes put in with a sooty finger and no sexual morals. In the old sod, she'd been sleeping with her uncle; she told me that. Naturally Freddy couldn't keep his hands off her. She had a room next to the nursery, where Freddy slept on a cot; I kept Ichabod in bed with me at night – it bushed me to get up for those 2.0 a.m. feedings – and Freddy said he disturbed him.' Priss was sorely tempted to put in a word of guidance – did Norine not know that under no circumstances, not even in a crowded slum home, should a baby be permitted to sleep with an adult? But her shyness and fear of stammering impeded her. 'Freddy,' Norine continued, 'was sneaking into her room. I found out when I was making her bed. There was Freddy's semen on the sheet. What got me was that she hadn't had the grace to use a towel. I pulled the sheet off the bed and confronted Freddy with it while he was eating his breakfast and reading the *Wall Street Journal*. He said it was partly my fault. Instead of treating her like a servant, I'd waited on her hand and foot, so that she felt she had a right to sleep with the master: she was just as good as me. Making her bed, for instance. It was up to her to make her own bed. He's right; I'm no good with labour. He had to put her out of the house himself. While he did, I washed the sheet in the washing-machine; he said I should have left it for the laundress. We quarrelled, and it affected my milk.'

'They say a shock can do that,' said Priss. 'But at least Ichabod got his im-munities.' Norine agreed; the damage, she said absently, would be psychic. She reached into the carriage and found a rubber pacifier, which she thrust into his mouth. Priss gazed at this article, nonplussed. 'Is that to keep him from sucking his thumb?' she asked. 'You know, Norine, paediatricians today think it's better to let them suck their thumbs than try to break them of the habit. What I did with Stephen was distract him gently every time he put his thumb in his mouth. But that p-p-pacifier' – the word seemed to stick in her throat – 'is awfully unsanitary. And it can change the shape of his mouth. You really ought to throw it away. Sloan would be shocked if he saw it. It can be just as habit-forming as thumb-sucking.' She spoke earnestly, amazed to see a girl of Norine's education so ignorant. Norine listened patiently. 'If a kid sucks his thumb,' she said, 'it's because he's been deprived of oral gratifi-cation. He needs his daily quota of sucking time, and he can't get it from the bottle. So you give him a rubber tit. Don't you, Ichabod?' She smiled tenderly at Ichabod, who indeed wore a look of bliss as he drew on the rubber teat. Priss tried to avert her eyes from the spectacle. For a child to find heaven in a dummy breast was the worst thing she could think of – worse than self-abuse. She felt there ought to be a law against the manufacture of such devices.

Stephen approached the carriage. 'Wass sat?' he asked curiously. His hand went out to touch the pacifier in the baby's mouth. Priss snatched his hand away. He continued to stare eagerly, evidently interested by the noises of content Ichabod was making. 'Wass sat?' he repeated. Norine removed the pacifier from the baby's mouth. 'You wan't to try it?' she said kindly. She wiped it with a clean diaper and offered it to Stephen. Priss swiftly intervened. She reached into the stroller and drew out a lollipop wrapped in waxed paper. 'Here!' she said. 'That "pop" belongs to the baby. Give it back to Mrs Rogers. This is yours.' Stephen accepted the lollipop. Priss had discovered that a system of exchange worked very well with him; he would docilely trade a 'bad' thing, like a safety-pin, for a 'good' thing, like a picture book, and often seemed to be unaware that a substitution had taken place.

Norine observed this little drama. 'You've got him trained,' she said finally, with a laconic smile. 'I suppose he's trained to the toilet too.' 'I'm afraid not,' said Priss, embarrassed. She lowered her voice. 'I'm at my wits' end, honestly. Of course, I've never punished him, the way our mothers and nurses did, when he has an "accident". But I almost wish I could spank him. Instead, I've done *everything* you're supposed to. You know. "Observe the time of day when he has his movement and then gently put him on the toidey-seat at that time every morning. If he doesn't do it, take him off, without any sign of displeasure. If he does do it, smile and clap your hands."'

Norine had touched on her most sensitive point. As the wife of a paediatrician, she was bitterly ashamed that Stephen, at the age of two and a half, was not able to control his bowels. He not only made evil-smelling messes in his bed, at naptime, but he sometimes soiled his pants here in the Park, which was why she sought out this isolated bench, rather than take him to the playground. Or he did it – like last week-end – in his bathing-trunks on the beach at the Oyster Bay clubhouse, in front of the whole summer colony, who were sunning and having cocktails. Sloan, even though he was a doctor, was extremely annoyed whenever Stephen did it in public, but he would never help Priss clean Stephen up or do anything to relieve her embarrassment. Last week-end, for instance, it was her young sister Linda who had come to her rescue when Stephen had got away from her and capered down the beach with his full bathing-trunks. Linda had captured him and carried him into the clubhouse, where she helped Priss by washing out his pants while Priss washed him. Meanwhile Sloan had sat under an umbrella ignoring the whole episode.

Afterwards he had told her that she and her sister had made an unnecessary hullabaloo. Yet it was the only sphere where he could say she had failed with Stephen. He did not wet his bed any more; he ate his vegetables and junkets; he was obedient; he hardly ever cried now, and at night he went to sleep at his appointed time surrounded by his stuffed animals. She could not see where she had erred in training him. Neither could her mother. Together, they had retraced the whole history, from the first mornings she had set him on the new toidey-seat strapped to the regular toilet. Immediately, he had changed the time of his movement. It jumped from nine o'clock to ten to seven and all around the clock, with Priss and the young girl she had had helping her chasing it in vain. Whenever they judged, from his expression, that he needed to 'go', they would clap him on the toidey, so that he would associate the two ideas. But no matter how long they lay in ambush for him or how patiently they waited once he was on the seat, he usually disappointed them. Often, as soon as they took him off, he would do it in his crib.

When he was smaller, Priss had tried to think that he did not understand what was wanted of him, and Sloan had authorized her to grunt and make pushing grimaces, to encourage him to imitate her. But her grunts produced no results except to make her feel foolish. She tried leaving him on the toidey alone, so that he would not suppose it was a game the two of them were playing. She tried leaving him there longer, but Sloan said five minutes was enough. On the rare occasions when – by pure chance, it seemed to Priss – he 'performed', she moderated her pantomime of approval, so that he would not sense it as a punishment when she did not smile or clap.

Sloan's belief was that Priss's nervousness was to blame, just as it had been with her nursing. 'He senses your tension when you put him on the toilet. Relax.' Yet Sloan himself would have been far from relaxed if he had had to clean up Stephen's bed when he had fouled his toys and stuffed animals. Sloan always said that the right way was to avoid even the appearance of censure when that occurred. 'Just be matter-of-fact. Act as though nothing had happened.' But that would be a lie. By this time, Stephen must know, though she had never reproached him by word or sign, that she did not really like him to do Number Two in his bed. In fact, it had become clear to her that not only did he know but enjoyed the knowledge. Particularly on a day when she would lead guests to his room after a luncheon party and find that 'it' had happened. Seeing the ladies flee from the scene of the crime, he responded with gurgles and crows. Priss suspected there was a streak of rebellion tucked away in Stephen, which expressed itself by thwarting her in this particular way. As if he had read a hand-book on paediatrics and knew that this was one naughty action for which he could not be punished; instead, he could punish her.

This thought was too morbid to be discussed, even with her mother. Could a two-and-a-half-year-old plot and carry out a scheme of revenge? And for what? Alas, in her darkest moments, Priss feared she knew. For the bottle he had got too late, for the schedule he had been held to, on the minute: six, ten, two, six, ten, two. Perhaps even for this 'sucking' Norine talked about that he had missed. For never having been picked up when he cried, except to have his diaper changed or be given a drink of water. For the fact, in short, that his father was a paediatrician. Everyone, including Mrs Hartshorn, who had begun as a sceptic, now exclaimed over how well the new regime had worked; they had never seen a two-year-old so strong, so big, so well behaved and self-sufficient. Priss's friends, when they came to dinner, were amazed to observe that Stephen went to bed without any discussion. Priss sang to him; he had his arrowroot cookie, his drink of water, and his kiss. Then he was tucked in, and out went his light. He did not call out to have it turned on again or ask for his door to be left open. 'He was trained as an infant,' Sloan would say, passing the hors-d'oeuvre. 'Priss never went in to him, once he'd been stowed away for the night. And we accustomed him to noise. He's never had a pillow.' Not one of Priss's friends could match that; they had tried to follow the broad principles, but they had weakened on some detail, with the result that their young disturbed the parents' cocktail hour with pleas for drinks of water, light, attention generally; they were afraid of the dark or had food crotchets or refused to take naps. The point, Sloan said, was to have the force of character to stick to the system absolutely, except in cases of illness or on trips. Stephen had got a good start in life because Priss had never compromised. This was what Priss endeavoured to think herself, encouraged by her friends' admiration. Yet at times she furtively wondered whether when Stephen made messes in his pants he was not getting his own back for being alive at all.

'I hope you'll be luckier than I've been,' she said sadly to Norine. 'Have you started toilet training yet? Sloan has a theory that we waited too long. If you begin early enough, he says, there's no reason a baby should be harder to train than an animal.' Norine shook her head. She did not plan to train Ichabod. He needed the fun of playing with his own excrement, just as he needed sucking. 'When he's ready to use the toilet, he'll ask for it. Probably when he starts nursery school. The pressure of the group will encourage him to give up his anal pleasures. You'll find, when you put yours in nursery school, that he'll make the great renunciation.' She did not plan to wean Ichabod either – that is, from the bottle. He would wean himself when he was Stephen's age, and, if he did not, *tant pis*.

'Where in the world did you get such ideas?' Not, Priss was certain, from a reputable paediatrician; Norine must have got hold of some quack. They were based on anthropology, Norine explained. Scientists had been watching the habits of primitive peoples and drawing valuable conclusions. The Pueblo Indians, for instance, who were the *crème de la crème* of the Indian world, did not wean their children till they were two or three years old. Most primitive peoples did not bother about toilet training at all. 'But they have no toilets,' said Priss. Norine nodded. 'That's the price of our culture. If you have a flush toilet, you make a fetish of it. Have you read Margaret Mead? A great woman, that.'

Needless to say, Ichabod was not on a schedule. He created his own schedule. He was picked up whenever he cried and was fed 'on demand'. 'What about baby foods? Are you going to give him baby foods?' Norine did not know. But she was against feeding a baby a restricted diet. 'Babies are tough,' she said. 'They'll choose their own diet if you offer them a variety of foods.' Priss said that she thought girls today were perhaps making it too easy for themselves by opening a jar of baby food, instead of puréeing fresh vegetables at home and pressing beef in the ricer for beef juice. The question did not appear to interest Norine. Indeed, the discussions that raged in paediatric circles – how soon to start orange juice, evaporated milk versus Borden's, bottled baby foods versus homemade, enemas versus glycerine suppositories, the merits of Pablum, the new three-hour feeding schedule for hungry babies (Priss and Sloan had pioneered that!) – seemed never to have reached her ears. Ichabod, she repeated, would make his own decisions; already he had shown a taste for Italian spaghetti – she made a practice of offering him scraps of food from her plate. She did not possess a baby scales or a bathinet. He was bathed in the washbasin. She stared reflectively at Stephen. 'How old is he? Three?' 'Two and a half next Saturday.' Norine pondered. 'In his day, of course, you were still hipped on scales and clocks and thermometers. The age of measurement. God, it seems a long time ago!' She yawned and stretched her big frame. 'We had a late night last night. Some Jesuits for dinner. And somebody playing the drums. Then Ichabod burned the candle at both ends.'

Priss girded her loins for combat; it was plain to her that Norine was talking through her hat. 'The age of measurement is just beginning,' she said doughtily. 'For the first time we're establishing norms. In all fields. You ought to keep up with the latest developments. Have you heard about Gesell's studies at Yale? Finally we're going to have a scientific picture of the child. Gesell shows us what to expect in terms of achievement of a one-year-old, a two-year-old, a three-year-old. When he publishes his findings in p-p-popular form, every mother will have a y-yardstick.'

This time Norine smothered her yawn. 'I know Gesell's work. He's a fossil relic of behaviourism. His daughter was '35.' 'What does that prove?' demanded Priss. Norine declined to argue. 'You still believe in progress,' she said kindly. 'I'd forgotten there were people who did. It's your substitute for religion. Your tribal totem is the yardstick. But we've transcended all that. No first-rate mind can accept the concept of progress any more.' 'You used to be such a radical,' protested Priss. 'Don't you admire some of what Roosevelt is doing? TVA, rural electrification, the Farm Resettlement Administration, crop control, Wages and Hours. Granting that he's made some mistakes – ' 'I still am a radical,' interrupted Norine. 'But now I fathom what it means – going back to the roots. The New Deal is rootless – superficial. It doesn't even have the dynamism of fascism.'

'Does your husband agree with your ideas?' 'Does yours?' retorted Norine. 'No,' Priss had to admit. 'Not about politics. We're at daggers drawn.' Right now, they were quarrelling about Danzig; Sloan did not care if Hitler gobbled up the whole of Europe – he was for America First. 'The old Vassar story,' commented Norine. 'I leave politics to Freddy. Being a Jew and upper crust, he's profoundly torn between interventionism abroad and *laissez faire* at home. Freddy isn't an intellectual. But before we were married, we had an understanding that he should read Kafka and Joyce and Toynbee and the cultural anthropologists. Some of the basic books. So that semantically we can have the same referents.' Priss wondered that Norine should have left out Freud. 'Most of Freud's out of date,' Norine declared. 'He was too narrowly a man of his place and time. The old Austrian Empire, with its folkways, he took for a universal culture. Jung has more to say to me. And some of the younger post-Freudians. Not that I don't owe a lot to Freud.'

Priss, who had always been planning to read Freud some day when she had the time, felt relieved and disappointed to hear that it was no longer necessary. Norine, she presumed, knew about such things. She sounded almost as if Freud were dead. Priss had a flutter of anxiety that she might have missed reading his obituaries in the papers; she seemed to have missed so much. 'Of course,' Norine was saying, 'between Freddy and me there's a deep cultural conflict. Our Vassar education made it tough for me to accept my womanly role. While Freddy, as a Jew, instinctively adopts the matriarchal principle. He wants me to reign in the home while he goes to the counting-house. That's great, as far as Ichabod goes; he doesn't interfere with my programme and he keeps his mother muzzled. Freddy's philoprogenitive; he's interested in founding a dynasty. So long as I can breed, I'm a sacred cow to him. Bed's very important to Freddy; he's a sensualist, like Solomon. Collects erotica. He worships me because I'm a goy. Besides, like so many rich Jews, he's a snob. He likes to have interesting people in the house, and I can give him that.' She broke off and gave vent to a sigh. 'The trouble is – The trouble is –' She dropped her voice and looked around her. 'Christ, I can say it to you. You probably have the same problem.' Priss swallowed nervously; she feared Norine was going to talk about sex, which was still Priss's *bête noire*.

'The trouble is my brains,' said Norine. 'I was formed as an intellectual by Lockwood and those other gals. Freddy doesn't mind that I can think rings around him; he likes it. But I'm conscious of a yawning abyss. And he expects me to be a *Hausfrau* at the same time. A hostess, he calls it. I've got to dress well and set a good table. He thinks it ought to be easy because we have servants. But I can't handle servants. It's a relic, I guess, of my political period. Freddy's taken to hiring them himself, but I demoralize them, he says, as soon as they get in the house. They take a cue from my cerebralism. They start drinking and padding the bills and forgetting to polish the silver. Freddy goes all to pieces if he gets served warmed-over coffee in a tarnished pot – he's a sybarite. Or if the table linen's dirty. He made the butler change it last night just as we were sitting down to dinner. I never noticed it myself; I was too busy discussing Natural Law with those Jesuits.'

'You can go over the linen and the silver in the morning,' Priss pointed out. 'Before you have a dinner party. Take out everything you're going to use and check it.' Though a Phi Beta Kappa, she had never had any trouble with her part-time maids, who usually came to her through her mother. Brains, she thought, were supposed to help you organize your life efficiently; besides, she had never heard that Norine had shone as a student. 'I know,' answered Norine. 'I've been trying to turn over a new leaf, now that we have a new house. I start out with a woman who comes to massage me and give me exercises to relax. But before I know it, I'm discussing the Monophysites or the Athanasian Creed or Maimonides. The weirdest types come to work for me; I seem to magnetize them. The butler we have now is an Anthroposophist. Last night he started doing eurhythmics.' She laughed.

'You really feel our education was a mistake?' Priss asked anxiously. Sloan had often expressed the same view, but that was because it had given her ideas he disagreed with. 'Oh, completely,' said Norine. 'I've been crippled for life.' She stretched. Priss looked at her watch. It was time for her and Stephen to leave. Norine rose too. 'Ichabod and I'll keep you company.' She pinned a diaper on her offspring and covered him with a monogrammed blanket. '*Pour les convenances*,' she said. Together they crossed Fifth Avenue and walked along Seventy-second Street, wheeling their children. The conversation became desultory. 'When did I see you last?' Norine wondered. 'Was it at Kay's?' said Priss. 'The year after college?' 'That's right,' said Norine. There was a silence. 'Poor Kay,' said Priss, dodging a grocery cart from Gristede's.

'Do you ever hear from her?' asked Norine. 'Not for a long time,' said Priss. 'Not since she went out West. It must be over a year.' Mutely, Priss reproached herself for not having written. 'I see Harald sometimes,' Norine volunteered in her uninflected tones. 'Oh. What is he doing?' 'The same. He's back on his feet again. He took Kay's breakdown and their separation pretty hard. God, how that man suffered!'

Priss hesitated. 'But was it really a breakdown? Polly Ridgeley – Polly Andrews; you remember her – always says it wasn't. That she got worse in the hospital.' 'Did you see her there?' asked Norine sombrely. Priss had not. 'I did,' said Norine. 'The doctors sent for me right away. To get a line on her. I was supposed to be her best friend. When I went to her room, she was completely withdrawn. Told me to go away. She had persecution delusions that focused on me. The doctors felt there was some Lesbian attachment. It's a funny thing about paranoids; they always feel they're being persecuted by a member of their own sex. Who's really their love-object. When I finally got her to talk, it turned out she felt I'd betrayed her by discussing her with the psychiatrists. She didn't seem to bear any grudge against Harald, though he went there practically every day for an interview. He was lacerated with guilt because he'd treated her like hell towards the end, not understanding that her aberrations were clinical. The layman never realizes that about a person he's close to.'

'But what was really the matter?' said Priss. '*I* understood that she went there through some sort of mix-up and stayed because it was a rest home where she could work things out, away from Harald. I gathered he was pretty much at fault.' 'That was the cover story,' said Norine. 'They never settled on a final diagnosis. But a lot of basic things were the matter. Sex. Competitiveness with men. An underlying Lesbian drive that was too firmly repressed. Thwarted social strivings. She made it at Vassar with you people in the South Tower. But she never could make it again. So she transferred all her ambitions to Harald, and the insensate pressure of that was too much for him. She was killing the goose that ought to have laid the golden eggs. And all the time she was driving him to make money, she was ruthlessly undercutting him because of her penis-envy. Plus a determination to punish him for not giving her a vicarious success. Harald saw it all better himself after a couple of sessions with the doctors. I cleared up a few points for them and I got Put, my ex-husband, to go around and talk to them too. He was brilliant on the subject of Kay's spending money. He gave an unforgettable picture of her delusions of wealth. Comparing the way she lived with the way we lived, though Put was working and Harald was practically on the dole.'

'Don't you think,' said Priss, 'that the depression had something to do with it? If she'd married Harald when the economy was normal, he would have had work, and their standard of living would have corresponded with their income. Kay's false p-p-premise was assuming that Harald would have full employment. So she contracted debts. But that was a common pattern. And the theatre was slow to feel the effects of Recovery. If they'd married a little later, there would have been the Federal Theatre. But the idea of a works programme for the arts didn't come till '35, unfortunately. Roosevelt was very late recognizing the need for job security for artists and performers.'

'So you see it as an economic tragedy.' 'Yes. The high divorce rate in our class – ' 'With the New Deal as the *deus ex machina*,' interrupted Norine. 'Arriving too late to supply the happy ending.' She chuckled. 'You may have a point. As a matter of fact, Harald's working with the Federal Theatre now. If Congress doesn't kill it. Just when he's got his chance as a director.' Priss's brow wrinkled. 'I'm afraid Congress *will* kill it, Norine. Poor Harald! He does have bad luck. It's uncanny.' She shivered in her seersucker frock. Norine agreed. 'Potentially, he's a great man, Harald.' They had reached the corner of Seventy-second and Park. 'Poor Kay!' sighed Priss again, resolved to write to her this afternoon while Stephen was napping. 'It was medieval of Macy's to fire her because she'd had a breakdown. It ought to have been treated as ordinary sick leave. And then to be dispossessed from their apartment, on top of that.' 'Macy's gave her severance pay,' observed Norine. Priss shook her head sorrowfully, putting herself in Kay's place. No wonder, she thought, Kay had yielded and gone back to Utah when her father came to get her; everything in the East had failed her. 'Her whole house of cards . . .' she muttered, staring down Park Avenue.

'Why don't you come home with me?' Norine suddenly proposed. 'We'll have some coffee.' 'I have to get Stephen's lunch,' explained Priss. 'We'll feed him,' said Norine hospitably. 'We've got a lamb chop around somewhere and some lettuce. Can he eat that?' Priss was tempted. At home she too had a lamb chop and fresh spinach and his potato waiting to be cooked, and she had made him tapioca this morning with fluffy egg white. But she was flattered to discover that she had not bored Norine and a little tired of the monotony of her life. Since she had given up her job, before Stephen was born, she seldom saw anyone 'different'. 'We have three cats,' Norine said to Stephen. 'And a basket full of kittens.' This decided Priss; animals, she felt, were important to a child, and Sloan would not let them keep one in the apartment because of allergies.

Norine's house had a red door. Workmen were still finishing the wall of glass brick. Inside, a ramp, freshly painted, ran up to the upper floors. A gaunt manservant in shirt-sleeves appeared to wheel the carriage, with Ichabod in it, upstairs. This arrangement seemed to Priss very practical: bumping a carriage up and down stairs was a nuisance and to leave it blocking the entry was a nuisance too; then too when Ichabod was bigger he could not fall down a ramp. She was impressed by the house, which struck her as comfortable; it only looked strange from the street, and you could say that the other houses were out of step, not Norine's. The thing that surprised her was that Norine could have a house like this and be against progress at the same time. But Norine explained that it was 'classical modern'.

In the living-room, which was on the second floor, two walls were painted dark red; the glass bricks from the street let in a filtered light, and a short inside wall of glass bricks half shut off a bar, which was trimmed with chromium. There were round glass tables with chromium trim and big cream-coloured fleecy sofas. Great glass bowls were filled with dogwood, which proved, on closer examination, to have paper flowers stuck on the branches. In the library there was a big phonograph, a set of drums, and a white piano, like a night club. Large balloon brandy glasses, containing the dregs of brandy, still stood on the piano. The rooms were lit by indirect lighting, hidden in troughs, and the floors were covered from wall to wall with very thick cream-coloured carpeting. Everything was expensive and in what Priss recognized as 'good taste'. It was only that to Priss, who was small, all the furniture seemed very large – giants' furniture. When Norine settled her at one end of a deep sofa in the living-room, she felt like Goldilocks in the biggest of the three bears' beds.

Stephen had been led away by the manservant, to see the kittens, who lived in the laundry on the ground floor. 'Coffee will be here in a minute,' said Norine, planting herself at the opposite end of the sofa. 'Unless you can't stand it reheated.' She placed a big glass ashtray, like a tub, between them, opened a cigarette box, took off her sunglasses and shoes. 'They'll keep Stephen downstairs,' she said. 'Now we can talk.' She crossed her legs under her in the black linen slacks. 'Maybe you'll be surprised to hear that I was madly in love with Harald. For four years. I never let it interfere with my relation with Kay. I married Freddy when I saw it was hopeless. It had always been hopeless, but I kidded myself.' She spoke in a dry voice, smoking rapidly, and rocking herself back and forth on her

322

haunches; her lethargy had vanished. 'We had a few rolls in the hay years ago – nothing much. Then for him it was over: Harald is like that. But he kept coming around, as a friend; he made me his confidant, told me all about his other women. Did you know he had other women?' Priss nodded. 'Did he ever make a pass at you?' 'No. But he did at Dottie. After she was married. He tried to make an assignation with her.' 'Women were necessary to him,' Norine said. 'But I thought I was special. I figured he was laying off me because of Kay, because he respected our relationship. Every now and then, he used to undress me and study my body. Then he'd slap my flank and go home. Or off to some other woman. Afterwards, he'd tell me about it. Whenever he slept with a woman, he told me. What he didn't tell me, though, was about the women he didn't sleep with. I wasn't the only one, I found out. He went around town undressing his old flames and then leaving them. Just to know they were available. Like somebody checking stock. And all his old mistresses were in love with him. At least all the ones I knew. Harald has great charisma. He could have been a monk.'

The gaunt butler came in with a tray on which were two out-sized coffee cups, a tarnished silver pot, and a cream and sugar service. The sugar was wrapped in paper marked 'Schrafft's'. 'I can't get used to being rich,' Norine sighed. 'I always take the sugar they give you home with me when I have a cup of coffee at Schrafft's counter. But the help can't be bothered to unwrap them. Freddy is mortified.' The butler withdrew. 'Perkins!' Norine called after him. 'Empty this ashtray, will you?' He took the big tub and brought a fresh one. 'I have to keep after him about that,' Norine said. 'Freddy's hell on emptying ashtrays. It's funny, anything he's touched he wants to have taken away and washed.'

Priss had become conscious, during this conversation, that the back of her skirt was damp and getting damper. She moved from one buttock to the other, shifting her weight. Then she touched the cream-coloured cushion. It was distinctly wet. At the same moment Norine explored the seat of her linen slacks. 'Oh, God!' she said. 'They've done it again. They must have washed these cushions with soapsuds while I was out. Freddy's giving everybody here a washing complex.' She laughed. 'Freddy's father got an attack of rheumatism the other night from the damp slip cover he sat on in the dining-room.' Priss stood up; her skirt had a great wet stain.

'Perkins!' Norine went to the door and called downstairs. 'Bring up a couple of bath towels, will you?' The butler came in with two huge monogrammed towels and spread them at either end of the sofa for the two young women to sit down on. 'Thanks,' said Norine. Perkins left. 'Tell me' – she turned to Priss – 'do you say "thank you" to a servant? Freddy says you're not supposed to thank them; waiting on you is their duty.' 'You don't thank them when they serve you at table,' said Priss. 'But if they do some special errand for you, like bringing those towels, you do. And you usually say "please",' she added discreetly, 'if you ask them for something special. I mean, you might say, "Will you serve Mr Rogers the roast again?" But if you asked a maid to bring you a handkerchief or your pocketbook, you'd say "please".' 'That's what I thought,' said Norine. 'Freddy's wrong. I guess I'll have to get *Emily Post*. At my grandmother's, I remember, we always said "please" and "thank you", but they were German – my father's people. The help was like part of the family. I don't know the rules of New York society like you.'

Priss was embarrassed; she was sure that Freddy knew as much as she did. It was just that Norine had failed to understand the fine points. The butler reappeared. He murmured something in Norine's ear. 'Oh, OK,' she said, glancing in Priss's direction. 'Do something about it. Please.' 'What did he say?' asked Priss, feeling that it had to do with her. Perkins waited. 'Stephen shat,' Norine said casually. Priss leapt to her feet, turning all the colours. 'I'm coming,' she said to the butler. 'Oh, I'm so sorry!' 'Perkins can tend to it,' said Norine, firmly reseating Priss on the sofa. 'Or Ichabod's nurse'll do it. Just have his pants washed out and put a diaper on him,' she said to the man. Too willingly, Priss gave in. Stephen's disgrace and the strange past tense of that word, which she had never heard used before in regular conversation, even in the present (let alone by a woman and before a servant!), had left her giddy. Could that be the right form, she asked herself curiously. It sounded like 'begat' in the Bible – archaic. Her mind, blushing for itself, tried out other possible past forms.

'Where was I?' said Norine. 'Oh, Harald. Well, I was mad about him. But he was fixated on Kay. I never could grasp that, exactly. All the psychiatrists at the hospital would say was that there was a "certain bond". "Mutual dependency." Harald always talked about her vitality. He thought her aggressive drives were connected with the Life Force – he's never outgrown Shaw. Do you think she's more vital than I am?' Priss did not want to answer this question. 'Kay has a great deal of energy,' she said. 'And she had a great belief in Harald. Don't you think that was the principal thing? And then – I don't want to be unkind, but Kay was the family bread-winner.' 'Harald could have had a dozen rich women,' declared Norine. 'And I would have scrubbed floors for him myself. Or worked as a waitress or a taxi-dance girl. It was no sacrifice for Kay to punch the time clock at Macy's. She liked it. While I was ready to sacrifice everything.'

Tears came into her tawny eyes. 'Oh, don't say that, Norine!' begged Priss, touched by these tears almost to the point of confidence herself. She did not recommend sacrifice, having meekly given up her job and her social ideals for Sloan's sake. It was now too late, because of Stephen, but she was convinced she had made a mistake. Sloan would be far happier himself if she were where she longed to be – in Washington, as a humble cog in the New Deal, which he hated – and he could boast of 'my Bolshevik wife'. He had been proud of her when she was with the N.R.A. because she had had gumption, and now even that was gone.

'Yes!' said Norine, with conviction. 'And I'd still sacrifice everything. All Freddy's shekels.' She looked bleakly around at her possessions. 'You don't mean everything,' said Priss firmly. 'What about Ichabod?' Norine lit a cigarette. 'Christ, I'd forgotten Ichabod. No. You're right. I've given hostages to fortune. *A* hostage. Harald would never take on another man's kid.' She gave a hoarse cough. 'And he's not partial to the Chosen People. To him, Ichabod is a little Yid.' Priss was shocked by Norine's language; perhaps it was different when you were married to a Jew; perhaps that gave you a sort of licence, the way Negroes could call each other 'nigger'. But it made Priss highly uncomfortable. She set her coffee cup down. Norine smoked in silence, evidently despondent. Priss regretted having come home with her; the invitation, she now recognized, had just been a pretext to talk about Harald. Like all acts of self-indulgence, it had left Norine now, probably, wishing she hadn't. Responsively, Priss's own conscience stirred; she felt she ought not to have brought Stephen to this strange house. Sloan would disapprove. The Lord knew what they would be giving

Stephen to eat downstairs – something bad for him, no doubt. And he would be late getting home for his rest.

'I wonder,' she said politely, 'if we could take a peek at Stephen. He's not used to strangers.' Her conscience smote her again for having let these people clean him up. What if they had told him 'Bad boy!' as so many ignorant servants did with children? Yet a few minutes ago she had been almost hoping they had. Norine got up promptly. 'Sure,' she said. 'Tell me one thing first, though.' Her cigarette cough rattled. Priss could not imagine what was coming. Norine stared down into her eyes. 'Do you think Ichabod looks Jewish?'

Again Priss did not know how to answer. Ichabod was too young to have a hooked nose; his eyes were still the colour of all babies' eyes – a dark slate blue; his skin was dark, but that might be from his sun baths. It was true that he seemed somehow different from other babies. He was unusually long, Priss had observed, and this gave him a look of melancholy, like an exhausted reed. There were circles under his eyes, and his little features were slightly drawn. There was no doubt that he appeared to be a child marked for a special destiny, as they said of the Jewish people. His nakedness also gave him a kind of pathos, as though he were not just a baby but a small forked zoo specimen of the human race. But the fact that he bore no resemblance to Stephen at his age did not supply an answer to Norine's question, even had Priss been willing to give it. The real thing was, she was not sure what Norine wanted to hear.

'He doesn't look like you,' she said truthfully. 'Perhaps he's like his father.' Norine produced a large framed photograph of a dark, curly-haired, rather handsome, slightly plump man. Ichabod did not look like Freddy. 'He looks like himself, I guess,' Norine summed up. They went down the ramp. In the kitchen, they found Stephen, wearing a diaper, the butler, a cook, three big Angora cats and a basket of kittens. Stephen had finished his lunch, except for a slab of chocolate cake, which he had left on his plate. 'He doesn't seem to want it, ma'am,' the cook said to Norine. They were all gazing at Stephen in astonishment. Priss apologized. 'He doesn't know what it is. He only knows graham crackers and animal crackers and arrowroot cookies.' 'Cookie,' said Stephen. 'Animal cacka.' Just then, in the doorway appeared a very pretty blonde young woman in a low-cut thin blouse that showed her breasts; she wore a pleated pastel skirt and high-heeled shoes. 'Hi, Cecilia,' said Norine. She turned to Priss. 'This is Ichabod's nurse.' The girl was carrying Stephen's underpants and yellow sunsuit. 'The pants are still damp,' she said. 'But I've ironed the sunsuit dry, Norine. Do you want me to put it on him?' 'I'll do it,' said Priss hastily. When the girl had bent down to help him, Stephen had put a hand out to touch her breast. He still eyed her as his mother dressed him. 'Wass sat?' he said, pointing. Everyone but the butler and Priss laughed. 'He's precocious,' said the girl, hugging him, which gave Stephen the chance he wanted. He plunged his hand into the neck of her dress. 'Watch out,' chuckled Norine. 'Cecilia's a virgin and a Papist.' Priss removed his hand. She looked around for something to give him, lest he start to cry. There was nothing but the slab of cake; the stroller was upstairs. She broke off a piece of cake and divided it in two. One piece she put in her mouth. 'Look! It's good,' she said, chewing. Reluctantly, he drew his eyes from the bold nursemaid and imitated his mother. Soon he was greedily eating chocolate cake, from a Jewish bakery, with fudge frosting.

Chapter 15

After that, Priss chose a new location in the Park. Though she sometimes passed the house with the red door, she took the other side of the street and she did not see Norine again till Kay's funeral. Then more than a year had passed, a terrible year, and everything had changed. The war had broken out. Lakey had come back from Europe. France had fallen; the Luftwaffe was bombing England, and Kay was dead, at twenty-nine. It was a beautiful July day, like the June day of Kay's wedding, and once again the scene was St George's Church, and Stuyvesant Square. This time the service was being held in the church itself; there were too many mourners to fit in the chapel. The organ was playing 'And all our flesh is as the grass' from the Brahms Requiem Mass, and the undertakers had carried in Kay's casket, a very simple one. It stood at the altar covered with white baby's breath and white zinnias. The rector himself was officiating.

Kay would have been happy about that, her friends knew. They had worked with might and main to get her buried as an Episcopalian. Mrs Hartshorn had finally arranged it by speaking to Dr Reiland, an old family friend. She pointed out that Kay had been married in his church, which ought to entitle him to give her the last rites. Before that, Polly's Aunt Julia had talked to *her* rector at St Bartholomew's, and Pokey, from the country, had telephoned St James's; Helena had got a friend who was married to the son of the rector of St Thomas's to intercede. It was amazing how sticky these ministers could be about burying a person who was not a church member.

Kay's father and mother would arrive too late for the ceremony; in this warm weather you could not wait too long. On the long-distance, they had told Helena to have their daughter cremated, and they would take her ashes home – they were very bitter. But Helena was certain that Kay would have hated that, and she had telephoned back to say that her friends would like to arrange a church ceremony for her, if her parents would agree. Whatever Kay would have wanted, her father said; probably her friends knew best. That was bitter too. Yet the group were sure they were doing the right thing. Kay had grown away from her parents; they had not seen eye to eye at all while she was out West, and it had hurt them when she had insisted on coming back to New York after the divorce though she had a home with them. But they had staked her, which was sweet, just as now they had wired the funeral parlour with an authority for Helena to act. How sad that Kay had not found time – that was what her father said – to write them a single letter in the month before she 'went'. Naturally, if she had known, she would have.

At college the group had had long discussions of how you would like to be buried. Pokey had voted for cremation with no service at all, and Libby had wanted her ashes scattered over New York Harbour. But Kay, like the rest, had been for regular burial in the ground, with a minister reading the funeral service over her – she loved the 'I am the Resurrection and the Life' part (actually that came in the church service, not at the open grave), which she used to recite, having played Sidney Carton in a school dramatization of *A Tale of Two Cities*. And she hated embalming; she did not want to be pumped full of fluid. In Salt Lake City she used to go out with a boy whose father was an undertaker, she had once confided, blushing for it, to Lakey, and he had showed her all the grisly paraphernalia. How like Kay it was to have such violent preferences, her friends agreed. After all these years – seven, since graduation – the group could still remember exactly what she liked and what she despised. And she had never grown older and wiser.

This had made it easy for them – sad to say – to get her ready for the funeral. It was the first time they had ever done anything like that. When somebody close to them had died, it had been an elderly person, and they had had nothing to do with the arrangements. They did not know the first thing about laying out the dead. But since Kay was divorced from Harald and her family was not here, they had pitched in. To begin with, they had had a frightful struggle with the undertaker, who had wanted to embalm her when he had got her body from the police, and Helena had had to telephone a lawyer to make sure they were within their rights. To fly in the face of convention turned out to be so much trouble that in the end it seemed hardly worthwhile. But Mrs Hartshorn had helped and Ross and Mrs Davison, who had been in the Vassar Club lounge when it happened and Kay went hurtling down from the twentieth floor. Luckily her fall had been broken by a ledge on the thirteenth and she had landed in an awning, so that she was not smashed to bits; only her poor neck had been snapped. And luckily too Mrs Davison had been there – she had come down from Watch Hill for a meeting of the board of the English-Speaking Union – to claim the body and have Helena get in touch with Kay's parents.

They had laid her out in Helena's studio apartment on West Eleventh Street, which seemed the most suitable place, since Helena was still single and besides they had been room-mates. The undertaker had disguised her bruises, but they would not let him make her up to 'look natural'. Kay had never used rouge. They had gone through the closet of her room at the Vassar Club, looking for the right dress – there could be no question of her wedding dress, and in any case she had thrown it away long ago; she had never liked that dress with the white fichu. Holding up her clothes (many of which could have stood a stitch or two) on their hangers, they could not make up their minds. Lakey, with her clear intellect, cut through their indecision. Kay would like to be buried in a new dress, of course. The others could not imagine shopping for a dead person, but Lakey took one of Kay's dresses for a sample and went straight off to Fortuny's and bought her an off-white silk pleated gown – the kind the Duchess of Guermantes used to receive in. Then the others remembered that Kay had always longed for a Fortuny gown, which she never in her wildest moments could have afforded. Kay would have loved the dress and loved having Lakey buy it for her. They put her old gold bracelet on her bare arm; she had never had any other jewellery but her wedding ring – she hated costume stuff. Helena looked for lilies of the valley for her – they used to pick them together in the woods by the Pine Walk – but of course their season was over. Mrs Davison had a very nice thought; she closed Kay's eyes with two early Christian silver coins, which she sent Helena out to find at a collector's.

There had been a great deal to do and in such a short time. They had had no idea how complicated the last arrangements were, particularly when the defunct had been, like Kay, a stranger and a sojourner. Finding a funeral plot. Pokey, very generously, had donated a grave in her family's plot, which would have pleased Kay too, to lie among all those Livingstons and Schuylers. Notifying everyone who had known Kay. Putting an item in the newspapers. Choosing the psalms and the lesson and the prayers with the minister; Helena and Mrs Davison had taken care of that. Choosing the hymn. There were so many decisions to make. The flowers; they had determined to have only natural flowers of the season, nothing floristy. But that was easier said than done; the florists were bent on selling you wreaths and acted as if you were trying to economize when you said no, like the undertaker when you refused embalming and held out for a simple coffin. Kay would have liked a plain pine box, but that was absolutely unthinkable, apparently. Then making up your minds whether to have the casket open or closed in the church. They finally agreed to have it closed, but that those who had known Kay best and wanted to see her could come to Helena's place before the undertaker's people arrived. Helena served sherry and biscuits to those who came. Again that had involved decisions: sherry or Madeira, biscuits or sandwiches. The girls were reluctant even to think about such things as sandwiches (open or closed?), but the older women were firm that Helena had to offer what Mrs Davison called funeral meats.

You found that you got obsessed with these petty details. They were supposed to distract you from your grief. In fact, that was just what they did. You caught yourself forgetting the reason you were doing all this: because Kay had died. And the relief of finally arriving at a decision or having it taken out of your hands, as when Lakey got the dress, made you feel positively gay, till you remembered.

It was curious, too, the differences in people that came out in the face of death. You hated yourself for observing them, at such a time, but you could not help yourself. For instance, Mrs Hartshorn and Ross were wonderful about dressing Kay, even the most awful part – putting on her underwear; she had been delivered 'prepared for burial' (which they supposed must mean eviscerated), wrapped in a sort of shroud. And Polly calmly helped them, which was understandable, probably, because she had worked in a hospital. But the others could not even stay in the room while it was happening. When Ross came into the living-room to ask a question

– should they put a brassière on Miss Kay? – they felt sick. It was a hard question to decide too. It seemed against nature, somehow, to bury someone in a brassière (fortunately, Kay had never worn a girdle), and yet, as Ross pointed out, the Fortuny gown was clinging. In the end, they told Ross to put her brassière on.

The girls were interested to see that Mrs Davison, who was a wonder in a supervisory capacity and never flinched mentally from the fact of death, felt just as they did about handling a dead body. She stayed in the living-room with them, leading the conversation, while Ross and Mrs Hartshorn and Polly 'did the necessary'. 'I wonder, Helena,' she said, 'that you did not have the undertaker's people dress her. That's what they are paid for. "From each according to his capacities."' Frankly, the others wondered too, now that they grasped what it entailed, but they had taken a dislike to the undertaker with his clammy voice and his rouge pots. Yet undertakers were necessary members of society – how necessary, the girls saw only now.

Even with Kay in the next room (that was another thing), the group could not help being covertly amused by Mrs Davison, who was a card and knew she was a card, they suspected. Clad in her billowy black dress, with an onyx brooch, she chatted sociably of cerements and winding-sheets, now and then drawing an apt quotation from her reticule or loosing a dark shaft of humour. 'If only Kay could have been here,' she declared, shaking her head, 'she could have run the whole show for us, dontcha know.'

As long as there was anything to do, Libby did not appear. Nor did she offer to help with the expenses, which the others had divvied up. She had been married, last summer in Pittsfield, to a best-selling author of historical novels whose books she had been handling; only Polly had gone to her wedding, which took place in the family garden, with an Elizabethan pageant and Purcell played on recorders in the gazebo. On the morning of the funeral, she came breathlessly for sherry and biscuits, wearing a black toque and a long chain she described as a chatelaine. She did not think the Fortuny dress was Kay's colour and was full of curiosity to learn what Lakey had paid for it. And as if sensing the group's disapproval she proceeded to put her foot in it still more. 'Now, girls,' she said, hitching forward in her chair and examining a biscuit, 'tell me. I won't tell a soul. Did she jump or fall?'

Mrs Davison laid a restraining plump hand on Polly's arm. 'You may tell everyone you wish, Elizabeth. Indeed, I hope you will. She fell.' 'Oh. I know that was the police verdict,' said Libby. Helena started to speak. 'I have the floor, Helena,' said Mrs Davison. 'After all, I was the last to see her alive. Not an hour before. I invited her to have coffee with me in the lounge after dinner. I was always partial to Kay. And as I told the police, she was in excellent spirits. Her mind was perfectly clear. We discussed Mr Churchill and the air raids and the necessity of a draft in this country. She spoke of a interview she expected to have for a position with Saks Fifth Avenue. Kay had no intention of taking her own life. If she had not "done time" in a mental institution, the question would never have been raised.'

The young women nodded. That was what was so unfair about the whole thing. And if Kay had not been cleared by the police, she could not have had Christian burial. She would have had to lie in unhallowed ground.

'You might say, Elizabeth,' Mrs Davison continued gravely, 'that Kay was the first American war casualty.' 'Oh, Mother!' protested Helena. 'That's a ridiculous way of putting it.' But in a ridiculous way it was true. Kay had been aeroplane-spotting, it seemed, from her window at the Vassar Club when somehow she lost her balance and fell. She had had two cocktails before dinner, which might have slightly affected her motor reactions. To those who had been seeing her regularly since she had come back this spring, the manner of her death was a shock but not a complete surprise. She had become very war-conscious, like many single women. As her friends could testify, she talked a great deal about air-raids and preparedness. Ever since the invasion of the Lowlands, she had been saying that it was just a matter of days before America would be in the war. She was convinced it would begin with a surprise enemy air attack; Hitler would not wait for Roosevelt to arm and declare war on him. He would send the Luftwaffe over one night to wipe out New York or Washington. If she were in Hitler's place, that was exactly what she would do. It was the whole principle of the blitzkrieg. She knew an Air Force officer who said that the Nazis had long-range bombers – Hitler's secret weapon – that were capable of making the flight. They would probably concert it with a submarine attack on the coast.

The fact that America was neutral did not mean anything. Norway and Denmark and the Lowlands had been neutral too. She was keen on the idea that Mayor La Guardia should start air-raid drills in New York and impose a blackout. She wanted to be an air-raid warden, like the ones they had in England, and she was urging the Vassar Club to get pails of sand and shovels and start a civilian defence unit. She bought a radio for her room, and someone had given her a deck of Air Force silhouette cards, which she was studying to familiarize herself with the various plane shapes. When she was not listening to the radio or arguing with isolationists, she was scanning the skies.

This new craze of Kay's had amused her friends when it had not saddened them. Even Priss, who was active in several committees to get America into the war on the Allied side, did not believe Hitler would attack America. She almost wished he would, to goad the American people into action. Her fear was that the war would end this summer – how much longer could the English people hold out alone? – with Europe enslaved, while America sat back and did nothing. Or sent too little and too late, as it had done with France. Priss had nearly lost her mind while France was falling; she too had been glued to the radio. She had made Sloan get a portable to take to the beach at Oyster Bay. And now every hour on the hour in the city she turned on the news, expecting to hear that Churchill had capitulated or fled with the government to Canada. This dread, in fact, was in everyone's mind. All the while they were getting ready for the funeral, Helena had the radio turned on low, for fear they would miss a bulletin. For the rest of their lives, they thought, whenever they remembered Kay, they would remember the voice of the announcer recounting the night's casualties. Only Mrs Davison had hope. 'Mark my words, the English people will never surrender. As I say to Davy Davison, it will be another Spanish Armada.' But Kay, with her positive character, had already left England behind and was planning the defence of America. What had saddened her friends was that her interest in what she called Hitler's timetable was so obviously a rounding on Harald, who had become a fanatical America Firster and was getting quite a name for himself speaking at their rallies. If only Kay could have forgotten him, instead of enlisting in a rival campaign. Still, her zeal of preparedness had given her something to live for. What a cruel irony that it should have caused her death!

The maid who did her room at the Vassar Club told the police that she had often seen Kay craning out the window and warned her against doing it. 'Yes, Elizabeth,' said Mrs Davison. 'I questioned the maid myself. And I measured the window. A girl of Kay's height could easily have lost her balance and gone out. As I pointed out to the police, her radio was on, and she had left a cigarette burning in the ashtray by her bedside. A very dangerous habit. But no young woman who was going to kill herself would do it in the middle of a cigarette. Evidently, while she was smoking, she heard a plane's motor or several motors and got up to lean out the window. I believe I heard the motors myself as I was glancing through a magazine in the lounge. But everything was driven from my mind by the sound of that crash. I can hear it now.' She took out a handkerchief and wiped her eyes.

As the group took their seats in the church, they looked around in surprise at the number of people who were already there. It was almost a crowd and more were still arriving. There was Kay's former supervisor at Macy's and a whole delegation of her fellow-workers. Mrs Renfrew had come from Gloucester, to represent Dottie. Mr Andrews was there, with his sister, the famous Aunt Julia, and Ross. Libby and her husband. Lakey and the titled friend who had come back with her from Europe – the Baroness d'Estienne. Pokey and her husband were there, and in the pew just ahead, Polly and Helena were astonished to see Hatton, the Prothero butler. 'Hello, Hatton,' whispered Polly. 'Good afternoon, madam. Good afternoon, miss. I'm here to represent the family. The Madam sends her condolences. And Forbes begs to be remembered.' It was quite a society funeral, which would have delighted Kay.

Connie Storey ambled down the aisle and took a seat next to Putnam Blake and his third wife. 'Quite a turnout, Mother,' said Mr Davison approvingly. 'Kind of a vote of confidence.' Polly picked out Dick Brown, that old friend of Harald's, whom time had not been kind to. Jim Ridgeley slipped into the pew beside Polly. 'Do you know all these people?' he asked Polly. 'No,' she whispered back. 'I'll be damned!' he said and pointed out the psychiatrist who had treated Kay at Payne Whitney. 'Those look to me like some of the old patients,' he said, indicating three women together. Mrs Davison nodded to the secretary of the Vassar Club. Priss recognized Mrs Sisson, whom she had sat next to at Kay's wedding. Other classmates appeared. An army officer with wings over his pocket took his seat. 'I believe Kay was quite thick with him,' Mrs Davison confided to her husband. Helena nudged Polly. There came Norine, dressed in complete black with a veil; she appeared to be pregnant, and in a sort of sling that was suspended from her shoulder to her hip and joggled as she walked, there hung a small child; his bare legs and feet protruded from this species of pouch or pocket as if from a pair of rompers. 'My smelling-salts!' exclaimed Pokey in audible tones. 'What is that, a kangaroo?' said Mr Davison coarsely. 'Hush, Father,' reproved Mrs Davison. 'It's Ic-chabod,' said Priss. 'But what in the world – ?' whispered Polly. 'It's the latest thing,' muttered Priss. 'I read about them in a government pamphlet. They're meant for busy mothers who've nobody to leave their babies with. And the child's supposed to get reassurance from the warmth of the mother's b-body.' Norine took a seat next to Dick Brown. She placed Ichabod on her lap by shifting the sling. 'What's the idea of the papoose?' he said. 'You squaw woman?' Norine nodded. 'I want to give him the experience of death.' 'I see,' he said gravely. 'Early. Like mumps.'

The ripple of astonishment that had gone through the church at the apparition of Ichabod subsided as new arrivals came in. Polly recognized Kay's former maid, old Clara, who ran a funeral parlour in Harlem. Mrs Flanagan, Kay's pet teacher, who had been head of the Federal Theatre, came in with her former assistant. 'I never thought she'd come!' exclaimed Helena. The altar was completely banked with flowers.

The organ stopped. The rector came in and took his place behind the casket. The congregation stood up. 'I am the Resurrection and the Life, saith the Lord: he that believeth in me, though he were dead, yet shall he live, and whosoever liveth and believeth in me shall never die.' Lakey felt a tear fall. She was surprised by her grief. The sole emotion she had willed herself to feel was the cold fierce passion that this funeral should be perfect, a flawless mirror of what Kay would find admirable. For herself, she hoped that when she died some stranger would tie a stone around her neck and throw her in the sea. She loathed insincere mourning and, rather than mourn insincerely, she would have preferred to have her eyes put out. Another weak tear dropped. Then she noticed that heads were turning. Furious with the others, she quickly looked too. Harald, wearing a dark suit, had entered and taken a seat at the back of the church. How like him, she said to herself icily, to make us turn around to see him. Polly and Helena peeked too. They had feared he would come. And of course he had a right to be here, though they had not invited him, just as he had a right to kneel down, while the rest of the congregation was standing, and bury his skull-like head in his hand, seeming to pray. Yet they too were incensed.

In the slight pause that preceded the reading of the first psalm, everyone in the church, even those who did not know him, became aware of the presence of Harald. It was as if a biased shadow had fallen on the assembly. If you could have an evil sprite at a funeral, reflected Helena, like a bad fairy at a christening, that was Mr Harald Handfast. She set her small jaw. She did not understand why his sour mana made her milk of human kindness curdle. There was no further harm he could do Kay. A strange phrase crossed her drawling mind. Harald was 'taking the joy out of Kay's funeral'.

With a slight uneasy appraisal of the congregation, as though his practised eye had taken cognizance of Ichabod and Harald as possible centres of disturbance, the rector started the first psalm. 'Lord, let me know mine end, and the number of my days. . . .' There was a rustle and creaking. Some of the mourners remained standing; others sat down; others knelt; still others compromised between sitting and kneeling, crouching forward on the pews. Polly decided to follow Hatton, who had seated himself. He was one of the few persons in the church, she mused, who would know how to comport himself at a funeral. She thought of Kay's wedding and how young and superstitious they had all been that day and how little they had changed. She herself again had the crazy fear that some hitch might develop in the proceedings, which now would cause the rector to decide that he could not bury Kay after all. But there *had* been some peculiar features about the wedding, and there was nothing peculiar about the funeral, or was there? The peculiarity was only Harald's presence. He ought not to have come. But by coming he had made everything they had arranged – Kay's dress, the old Roman coins, the music and flowers, the liturgy itself – seem silly and girlish. 'He is Death at her funeral,' she said to herself.

The second psalm began. Polly bent her head and concentrated on Kay. The fondness and pity that had flooded her while dressing her inert body came welling back. She considered Kay's life, which had not been a life but only a sort of greeting, a Hello There. The girl who lay in the casket was finally the heroine of the hour. The rest had been nothing, a vain presumptuous shadow. 'In the morning it is green and groweth up; but in the evening it is cut down, dried up, and withered,' intoned the rector. *That* was appropriate and not just to her poor, shattered end. Polly was certain that Kay had not killed herself, though she had been very unhappy in the hospital when the psychiatrists had made her face the advisability of a separation from Harald. She had all but had a real nervous breakdown at the thought of having to be 'nobody' instead of the wife of a genius. But if, like a suicide, she had imagined everybody grieving over her, she would be satisfied now. 'I love you, Kay,' Polly whispered contritely.

When the rector launched into the *De Profundis*, Priss felt Helena and Mrs Davison had overdone it; three psalms were too many. And they had chosen the longest epistle for the lesson: St Paul to the Corinthians, I: 15. The words were beautiful, but she was worried for Ichabod. Knowing what she did about Norine's views of toilet training, she feared he would have an accident. With all the flowers the church was very close; it was surely her imagination, but she would have sworn that either he *had* or else Kay – It was useless to look at Pokey; she had no sense of smell. The congregation was getting restless, nodding and whispering to each other as they recognized familiar quotations in the lesson. 'Thou foolish one, that which thou sowest is not quickened, except it die.' '*Si le grain ne meurt*,' Priss heard Lakey murmur to her companion. '. . . For the trumpet shall sound, and the dead shall be raised incorruptible, and we shall be changed.' 'Handel,' Mrs Davison reminded her husband. '*The Messiah*.' Priss noticed that Polly was crying hard, and Jim was squeezing her hand. Lakey was crying too – tears, Priss thought, like crystal drops, ran down her rigid face; her teeth were set. Priss wished the lesson would stop talking about 'corruptible'. 'O Death, where is thy sting?' Pokey gave her husband a big nudge. 'I never knew that was where that came from!' Suddenly Priss found herself thinking of the worms in the graveyard; a sob shook her.

It was embarrassment to Helena when the hymn came, one of her mother's favourites, Number 245: 'He leadeth me.' She herself had wanted to have Bach's hymn, from the Passion Chorale: 'O Sacred Head surrounded by crown of piercing thorn.' But her mother said the other was more inspiring, which meant that it sounded like a revival meeting under canvas. She knew all the words by heart and did not even feign, as Helena did, to make use of the hymnal. Her big breathy voice, off key, competed with the organ. With the last lines, Mrs Davison let all the stops out. 'E'en death's cold wave I will not flee/Since God through Jordan leadeth me.' Helena dryly pictured God assisting her mother by the hand to cross the River Jordan, and she feared that everyone in the church had been furnished with the same tableau. Yet her mother was a complete agnostic, like the majority of the mourners. She did not believe in a future life for Kay, so what was there to be inspired about? Nothing. Helena's realism forbade her to cry. Who was there to cry for? Kay? But there was no Kay any more. That left no one to be sorry for that Helena could see.

They knelt down to pray. Suddenly it was over. The congregation found itself on the sidewalk, disbanded, and the undertaker's men went in to get the coffin. Libby wondered why they had not had pallbearers; it would have been much more impressive. And she thought the casket should have been left open. Spying Connie Storey, she rushed off to greet her. She was not going to the cemetery, and Connie, who was a working woman too, might like to share a taxi with her. Tonight, before she and her husband went out, she meant to write down her impressions of the ceremony. It had been almost unbearably moving.

Cars had been ordered to take everyone to the cemetery who wished to go and did not have a car of his own. They were lined up outside the church behind the hearse. Helena had the list and was checking it off. No provision had been made for Harald. He could have gone with Norine, except that Norine was not going, thank heaven; it was a miracle, everyone agreed, that that youngster had not acted up during the service – he had nodded wearily on his mother's lap. Harald stood on the sidewalk, alone and enigmatically smiling. 'Jim and I can take him in our car,' volunteered Polly. 'One of us *has* to speak to him.' Helena was less Christian. 'My mother will invite him. She has "an open mind". Let her do it.'

But Harald had approached Lakey. 'May I ride with you?' they heard him ask. Lakey had a smart bottle-green European two-seater waiting at the curb. 'I'm sorry,' she said. 'I have no room for you.' But the Baroness excused herself. 'If you do not mind, Elinor, I will not go to the interment.' 'Very well,' said Lakey to Harald, 'Get in. Can you drive?' Harald took the wheel. As the cortège began to move, the mourners saw the green two-seater dart out ahead of the hearse. 'What do you bet he makes advances to her?' said Polly tearfully. She and Jim and Helena and Mr Andrews were in the Ridgeley Ford. 'Let us hope he does,' said Mr Andrews mildly. 'I understand the Baroness packs a pair of brass knuckles.'

The return of Lakey on the *Rex* had been a thrilling event for the group. They had gathered at the dock one April morning to meet her, seven strong. Kay had been alive then of course, just back from Utah, and Dottie had fitted it in with a vacation trip to Bermuda. The idea of surprising Lakey by meeting her in a body had been Pokey's; Pokey was unconscious of the passage of time and scoffed at the thought that Lakey might be different. Some of the others had misgivings, though, as they watched the gangplank being lowered. They were afraid Lakey might have outgrown them. She was almost bound to find them provincial after the professors, art historians, and collectors she had been living among in Europe. The return addresses on some of her letters and postcards suggested, as Helena said, that Lakey had been 'broadened' – she always seemed to be staying with important people in villas, *palazzi*, and châteaux. The last time she wrote, to say she was coming home because she thought Italy would be in the war soon, was from the house of Bernard Berenson, the famous art critic, in Settignano. Lined up on the dock, straining their eyes for a glimpse of her, preparing their hands to wave, the more sensitive girls were conscious of being a staid settled group with husbands and children at home, for the most part; Pokey now had three, and Polly had a little girl.

When they saw her come down the gangplank, with her swift, sure step, her chin raised, in a dark violet suit and hat and carrying a green leather toilet case and a slim furled green silk umbrella, they were amazed at how young she looked still. They had all cut their hair and had permanents, but Lakey still wore hers in a black knot at the nape of her neck, which gave her a girlish air, and she had kept her marvellous figure. She saw them; her green eyes widened with pleasure; she waved. After the embraces (she kissed them all on both cheeks and held them off to look at them), she introduced the short, stocky foreign woman who was with her – someone, the girls took it, she had met on the crossing.

On the pier, there was a long wait for Lakey's luggage. She had dozens of suitcases, thirty-two wardrobe trunks, beautifully wrapped parcels tied with bright coloured ribbon, and innumerable packing-cases containing paintings, books, and china. On her customs declaration, she was a 'returning foreign resident', which meant she did not have to pay duty on her personal and household belongings. But she had masses of presents, which, being Lakey, she had declared, and she was an interminable time with the customs man and the lists she had made out in her large, clear, oblong writing. There was nothing the group could do to help, once her luggage was assembled, and they did not like to stare at the contents of the trunks and suitcases the man directed her to open, yet even Pokey's eyes bugged at the quantities of underwear, handkerchiefs, nightgowns, peignoirs, shoes, gloves, all wrapped in snowy tissue paper – not to mention dresses, hats, scarves, woollen coats, silk coats, beautifully folded and in tissue paper too. This impressive array – yet she did not have a single fur coat, Libby reported – made the girls think awkwardly of schedules, formula, laundry, diapers. They could not spend all morning on the pier. As they waited, restlessly tapping their feet (you could not smoke), they realized that the Baroness, who had finished with customs, was waiting too. She seemed to be with Lakey and was not very friendly to the girls, who tried politely to make conversation with her about conditions in Europe. She was a German, it transpired, who had been married to a French baron; she had had to leave France in September when the war broke out. Like Lakey, she had been staying in Florence, but she did not know Libby's aunt in Fiesole. Every now and then she would go over and say something to Lakey; they heard her call her 'Darling' with a trilled *r*. It was Kay who caught on first. Lakey had become a Lesbian. This woman was her man.

Slowly the group understood. This was why Lakey had stayed abroad so long. Abroad people were more tolerant of Lesbians, and Lakey's family in Lake Forest did not have to know. It was a terrible moment. Each girl recognized that she was, they were *de trop*. They had made a fearful *gaffe* in coming to welcome Lakey with open arms, as if she belonged to them, when plainly she belonged exclusively to the Baroness. They could not help gleaning that the two of them would be staying together at the Elysée Hotel. Lakey, the Baroness said, in reply to Kay's blunt question, was going to Chicago for a brief visit to her family. After that, she would look for a place in the country, outside New York. 'Something very qu-i-et,' said the Baroness. The girls got the point. Lakey wanted to be alone with the Baroness, undisturbed by neighbours and old friends. Or at least that was what the Baroness wanted.

The girls eyed each other. They had had the day planned. Pokey's family's chauffeur was waiting outside to drive Lakey to her hotel and install her. Then later they would all meet for an elegant lunch. Afterwards, each girl wanted to be the first to show Lakey her apartment, her husband, her child or children. Except Kay, who had nothing to show her but who therefore felt she had the best claim on her. Now they did not know whether to jettison these plans completely or to proceed with them and include the Baroness. They did not know whether to be discreet about this relationship or open. What did Lakey want? Would she like them to go away? Perhaps she would never forgive them for surprising her like this at the dock. By instinct, the group turned to Kay, who, with her experience in the theatre, ought to be able to tell them what to do. But Kay was nonplussed. Her open face clearly showed her disappointment, chagrin, and irresolution. It occurred to them all that Lakey, who had always been frightening and superior, would now look down on them for not being Lesbians. On the other hand, she had seemed truly glad to see them.

Studying Lakey with the customs man, they asked themselves, in silence, how long Lakey had been a Lesbian, whether the Baroness had made her one or she had started on her own. This led them to wonder whether she could possibly have been one at college – suppressed, of course. In the light of this terrible discovery, they examined her clothes for tell-tale signs. It was a Schiaparelli suit she was wearing; Kay had asked that straight out – she had guessed it was a Schiaparelli. 'Schiap makes all Elinor's clothes,' the Baroness had remarked, and they had watched that nickname, casually pronounced, take the wind out of Kay's sails. Lakey had on silk stockings, quite sheer, high-heeled calf shoes, a green silk blouse with a ruffle. If anything, she looked more feminine than before. With the Baroness you could tell, though she did not have a boyish haircut or a man's tie; she wore a heavy tweed suit, service sheer stockings, and pumps with Cuban heels. Yet it was odd to think that the Baroness had been married and Lakey had not.

As soon as Lakey was through with the customs man, she had solved their difficulties with the utmost naturalness. She accepted the offer of Pokey's chauffeur to take her and the Baroness to the hotel. And for lunch, she sent the Baroness off to the Metropolitan Museum, telling her to eat in the cafeteria: it would introduce her to America. 'Maria is a bear,' she said, laughing. 'She growls at strangers.' She had lunch with the group herself and that evening she invited those of them who were free and their husbands to have cocktails with her and the Baroness in the Monkey Bar of the hotel. That, the girls found, was the pattern. If it was an occasion when husbands would be present, the Baroness came; otherwise Lakey was on her own.

Once the group understood the convention by which the Baroness was 'my friend' like a self-evident axiom, their stiffness relaxed. Gradually, in the weeks that followed, the Baroness unbent too. Far from snubbing the group because they were not Lesbians, she seemed to find it a point in their favour. It was only of Kay, living alone at the Vassar Club and divorced, that she appeared to be suspicious. The group was surprised to find that both Lakey and Maria were strong anti-fascists. They would not have expected Lakey to be so human as to have common garden political sympathies. But she was more human in many ways than they remembered. The other surprise was that she liked children. The very thing the girls would have thought a Lesbian would be contemptuous of – their maternity – was a source of attraction to Lakey. Having brought a lovely set of Italian embroidered bibs for Polly's baby, she would put one on her and feed her in her lap whenever she came to the apartment. To Priss's Stephen, she had brought a prism and a set of antique toy soldiers; she liked to tell him stories and finger-paint with him. And when she went down one week-end to stay with Pokey at Princeton, she visited the stables and played hide-and-seek with the twins. She loved to do cutouts and make jumping mice out of her huge linen handkerchiefs.

343

Both she and Maria were very practical. They knew a great deal about food and dressmaking and were interested, for instance, in designing a new kind of maternity dress for Polly, who was pregnant. Maria had studied nursing, which, it seemed, was quite common among the European aristocracy, going back to the days when the lady of a castle had to prescribe for the peasants and take care of the wounded in war. The fact that none of the group, except Polly, could cut out a dress or make a bandage shocked Maria, as if they were barbarians.

It was astonishing, but within a month some of the girls found themselves talking of 'having Lakey and Maria to dinner', just as they might speak of a normal couple. When she and Maria finally took a big house outside Greenwich, Polly and Jim and Kay and Helena all went out to stay with them.

Yet side by side with this the group felt, with one accord, that what had happened to Lakey was a tragedy. They tried not to think of what she and Maria did in bed together. Only Kay claimed to be able to picture their 'embraces' with equanimity. They liked Maria as a person; if only she could have finished in a tail, like a mermaid! The same with Lakey, who in fact resembled a mermaid, with her large green eyes and white skin. Polly and Helena, who had become close friends now that Helena lived in New York, had tried to discuss the question as dispassionately as they could. They could not escape the gentle sense that the relationship these two had was perverted. One sign of this was the Baroness's jealousy. Maria was very jealous of both men and women – indeed, of all strangers. She carried a revolver her husband had given her and had made Lakey buy two ferocious watchdogs. And now there were these brass knuckles that Mr Andrews had somehow learned about! It was too easy to picture Maria using them on any man who would try to save Lakey. And the word, save, was indicative. On the one hand, there were Lakey-and-Maria, as you might say Polly-and-Jim, a contented married pair; on the other, there was an exquisite captive of a fierce robber woman, locked up in a Castle Perilous, and woe to the knight who came to release her from the enchantment. But it was possible to see it the other way around. Supposing it were Lakey, the inscrutable, intelligent Lakey, who had made poor Maria, who was not very bright, her prisoner and slave? The fact that it was possible to reverse the relation like an hourglass was what the girls found so troubling. In the same way, it troubled them to wonder which one of the pair was the man and which the woman. Obviously Maria, in her pyjamas and bathrobe, was the man, and Lakey, in her silk-and-lace peignoirs and batiste-and-lace nightgowns, with her hair down her back, was the woman, and yet these could be disguises — masquerade costumes. It bothered Polly and Helena to think that what was presented to their eyes was mere appearance, and that behind that, underneath it, was something *of which they would not approve*.

Harald and Lakey were driving very fast across the Queensborough Bridge. He wanted to go to a bar before putting in an appearance at the cemetery, and Lakey had agreed. 'Who arranged that comedy?' he asked, turning to glance at Lakey's profile. 'You mean the funeral,' said Lakey. 'What would you have done?' Harald did not answer. 'You have to bury a body,' said Lakey. 'Or cremate it. You can't simply put it down the incinerator or out with the trash.' He meditated. 'If there's difficulty in disposing of a body,' he observed, 'that suggests there's been foul play. I was given the impression back there in the church that the belief was that *I* had done away with her.' Lakey patted the knot at the back of her neck. 'She killed herself of course,' stated Harald. 'Why?' said Lakey calmly. 'Sheer competitiveness,' he answered. 'For years I've been trying to kill myself, ever since I've known her.' Lakey looked at him for a minute steadily; his face was quite haggard. 'She decided to show me how to do it. *She* could do it better. On the first try.' He waited. 'You don't believe me, do you, you inscrutable idol? You're right. I've never seriously tried to kill myself. It's always been a fake. Fake suicide attempts have been the Petersen speciality. And yet I honestly wish to die. I swear that to you. If we could just go off the road.' He pulled the wheel sharply to the right. 'Stop that,' said Lakey. He righted the car. 'And she,' he said, '*she* had the gall to kill herself and fake a death-by-accident.' 'How do you mean?' 'That aeroplane-spotting. The silhouette cards. Having the maid see her at the window and warn her. Those were clumsy plants. A crude alibi. So that we'd believe she'd lost her balance.' 'How do you know all the details?' 'From Mama Davison. We had a nice little chat on the phone.' 'But why would she want to fool us?' Harald shrugged. 'Her parents, I suppose. That senile "Dads"

345

she talks about. Or maybe she was ashamed to confess so ostentatiously that her life was a failure. "Everyone would know."'

Lakey studied this man, whom she had never liked, and said nothing. Her intention was limited to getting to the cemetery without having him kill them both in a dramatic effort to show her that he had the courage to commit suicide. He was a good driver; she had let him drive deliberately to test him. She had a certain curiosity about him, which she would like to satisfy, and she was aware that he had a curiosity about her.

'"The Madonna of the Smoking Room",' he said. 'It's funny, but I never picked you for a sapphic. And yet I have a good eye. When did you start? Or were you always that way?' 'Always,' said Lakey. His imprudent questions shaped a plan in her mind. 'The "group",' said Harald, 'must have been in quite a "tizzy" when you finally showed your colours. God's bowels, how tired I was of the "group" before I was through!' 'They're dears,' said Lakey. Harald turned his head and lifted an eyebrow. 'Did you say they were dears?' 'Yes,' said Lakey. 'All but one. Libby is a *mauvaise fille.*' 'A woman's taste,' said Harald. Lakey smiled. 'My friend, the Baroness d'Estienne, is enchanted with them. She loves American women.' 'Christ's body!' said Harald. 'Yes,' said Lakey. 'She says American women are a fourth sex.'

Harald glanced at her again. '"Always", you said. That means when you were in college.' His eyes narrowed. 'I suppose you were in love with the "group". All seven of them, excluding yourself. Collectively and singly. That explains it. I never understood what you – a girl with a mind – were doing in that *galère.*' He nodded. 'So you were in love with them. They were pretty to look at when nubile, I grant you. Why, you had a regular seraglio in that tower of yours. Kay always said that you turned hot and cold, picked them up, dropped them – they never knew why. But they were *fascinated.*' He imitated their collective voice. Lakey smiled. 'It's true, I had favourites.'

Harald stopped the car in front of a bar. They went in, and he ordered a double whisky for himself and a single for Lakey. They sat in a booth. 'Five minutes,' said Lakey. 'You don't have to worry,' he said. 'We can see the cortège pass.' He downed half his whisky. 'Who were your favourites?' he said. 'No, don't tell me. I'll guess. Dottie. Pokey. Kay. Helena.' 'Not Helena,' said Lakey.

'I like her now, but I didn't care for her in college. She was like a homely little boy.' 'Polly?' said Harald. 'I was a snob,' said Lakey. 'Polly was on a scholarship and doing self-help. One felt she was going to seed.' Her delicate dark eyebrows winced. 'One was so callow then. I don't like to think about it. Girls are brutal.' Harald finished his whisky. 'Were you in love with Kay?' Lakey cupped her chin in her hand. 'She was lovely in her sophomore year. You hadn't met her then. On the Daisy Chain. Like a wild flower herself. It's a kind of country beauty I'm particularly fond of. Very paintable. Who might have done her? Caravaggio? Some of the Spaniards? Anyone who painted gipsies. Or mountain people. She had a beautiful neck, like a stem. And such a strong back and tapering waist.' Harald ordered another whisky. His face had darkened.

'She was thick-skinned,' he said. 'It amused me to hurt her. To get some kind of response out of her. And after I'd hurt her I felt tenderness for her. Then she'd ruin that by trying to drag some concession out of me. She was literal, always wanting me to be sorry in words. I don't know, Lakey; I've never loved a woman. I've loved some men – great directors, political leaders. As a kid, I loved my father. But living with a woman is like living with an echo, a loud echo in Kay's case. That voice of hers got on my nerves. Meaninglessly repeating what it'd heard. Generally from me, I admit.' He laughed. 'I felt like some lonely captain with a parrot. But at least she had a kind of integrity. Physically she was straight. She was a virgin when I took her and she never wanted anybody else. Or anybody else's ideas.' His voice grew husky. 'That meant something. A chronically unfaithful man has to have a faithful wife; otherwise it's no marriage. And Kay never found out I was unfaithful to her. I can boast of that, Lakey. She occasionally suspected, but I always lied to her. Faithfully.' He laughed again. 'But her jealousy wrecked everything in the end. It was unreasonable.' 'What do you mean?' 'I never gave her anything to be jealous of. I protected her. Whenever I slept with a woman, I made sure Kay could never find out. That meant I could never break clean with them. No matter how fed up I was. Like that wench, Norine; you saw her in the church. A real blackmailer. She had the goods on me; in an idle moment I played the beast with two backs with her. For years I had to keep her hoping, so that she wouldn't be moved to tell Kay. That was weary work. For which Kay repaid me with hysterical accusations. Christ, I was only seeing her for Kay's sake.' Lakey gave him a level look of scorn and disbelief. 'Christ, don't be conventional.' he said. 'I don't expect that from you. You and I understand each other. I might have loved you, Lakey, if you weren't a lover of women. You might have saved me; I might have saved you. You can't love men; I can't love women. We might have loved each other – who knows? We're the two superior people in a cast of fools and supernumeraries. At last we meet to match swords. Let's duel in her grave, shall we?'

Just then out the window they saw the hearse go by. Harald tossed off a drink at the bar. They got into the car. This time Lakey drove. Listening to Harald's wild talk had disgusted her; she concluded that he was utterly specious. She was ashamed of the curiosity she had felt about him. To be curious about someone opened you to contamination from them. But she was still determined to play him a trick, to take a revenge for Kay, for women, and most of all for the impudence of his associating himself with her. She had no pity for Harald. Swinging the car into line behind the funeral procession, she waited for the question he would ask. 'To be superior,' he said, 'of course, is not only a pre-requisite for tragedy; it *is* tragedy. Hamlet's tragedy. We are forced to lower ourselves in our commerce with dolts, which sometimes gives us a feeling of hollowness, as if it were we who were hollow, not they. Could Hamlet love the daughter of Polonius? Could you or I "love" Kay? Of course there was her body.' He nodded at the hearse. 'To think that I've known it!' He gave a quick glance at Lakey. 'Your "love" for her, I assume, was purely platonic.' Lakey looked straight ahead. 'And yet,' said Harald, 'that's hard to believe, considering her mind. You must have wanted her, didn't you? Did she reject you? Is that why you "dropped" her?' 'I was tired of her,' said Lakey truthfully. 'I used to tire very easily of people.' 'You haven't answered my question,' said Harald. 'I don't propose to,' said Lakey. 'You're impertinent.' '*Did you sleep with her?*' said Harald violently. Lakey smiled, like a lizard. 'You ought to have asked Kay,' she said. 'She would have told you. She was such an honest girl at the end. Very American, Maria thought.' 'You're rotten,' he said. 'Completely rotten.

348

Vicious. Did you corrupt the whole group? What a pretty picture!'
Lakey was content; she had forced this dreadful man at last to be
truthful; the fact that he revealed a hatred of 'abnormality' was
only to be expected. 'What a filthy Lesbian trick,' he said. 'Not to
fight openly but to poison the rapiers.' Lakey did not point out to
him that he had poisoned them himself. Her conscience was clear.
She had made a little pact with herself to speak only the exact
truth and insinuate nothing. Moreover, from her point of view,
which he did not consider, poor normal Kay would not have
sinned by being her prey instead of his. Far better for her, in fact,
for Lakey, she hoped, would have been kind to her. 'You're a
coward,' Harald said, 'to spread your slime on a dead girl. No
wonder you hid yourself abroad all those years. You ought to have
stayed in Europe, where the lights are going out. You belong there;
you're dead. You've never used your mind except to acquire sterile
knowledge. You're a museum parasite. You have no part of
America! Let me out!' 'You want to get out of the car?' said
Lakey. 'Yes,' said Harald. 'You bury her. You and the "group".'
Lakey stopped the car. He got out. She drove on following the
cortège, watching him in the rear-view mirror as he crossed the
road and stood, thumbing a ride, while cars full of returning
mourners glided past him, back to New York.

More About Penguins
and Pelicans

For further information about books available from
Penguins please write to Dept EP, Penguin Books Ltd,
Harmondsworth, Middlesex UB7 ODA.

In the U.S.A.: For a complete list of books available
from Penguins in the United States write to Dept CS,
Penguin Books, 625 Madison Avenue, New York,
New York 10022.

In Canada: For a complete list of books available from
Penguins in Canada write to Penguin Books
Canada Ltd, 2801 John Street, Markham, Ontario
L3R 1B4.

In Australia: For a complete list of books available
from Penguins in Australia write to the Marketing
Department, Penguin Books Australia Ltd, P.O. Box
257, Ringwood, Victoria 3134.

Look out for these from Penguins!

A Woman's Age
Rachel Billington

Stepping into the world of country houses and nannies at the turn of the century, we follow the life of Violet Hesketh, from childhood, through two world wars, the roaring twenties, the depression, through years of social and political upheaval, to the fulfilment of her ambitions, as a leading public figure and politician in the seventies.

'A remarkable history of women over three-quarters of a century' – *Financial Times*

Woolworth Madonna
Elizabeth Troop

'She was very ordinary, a sort of Woolworth madonna, there must be millions like her.' Elizabeth Troop's heroine is more than that though. Faced with the demolition of her house, the slow sliding of hopes and dreams into middle age, the onset of high-rise living and flabby flesh, she still remains a force to be reckoned with – a force that is truly and unbeatably feminine and unforgettable.
'A rare discovery' – *New Statesman*

The Bloody Chamber and Other Stories
Angela Carter

From the lairs of the fantastical and fabular and from the domains of the unconscious's mysteries . . .
Lie the brides in the Bloody Chamber . . . Hunts unwillingly the Queen of the Vampires . . . Slips Red Riding Hood into the arms of the Wolf . . . Pimps our Puss-in-Boots for his lustful master . . .
In tales that glitter and haunt – strange nuggets from a writer whose wayward pen spills forth stylish, erotic, nightmarish jewels of prose – the old fairy stories live and breathe again, subtly altered, subtly changed.